THE JUDGMENT

Dina felt her face flame. They knew everything, everything! Even that! All this time! She covered her face and sat absolutely still.

"Don't cover your eyes, it won't help you. Open them for a change! 'Her faithlessness was in her skirts; she was not mindful of the end; and the land became full of lewdness,' " Kruzman shouted at her with stunning cruelty. He handed her the photographs. She didn't cry. She didn't say anything.

Dina felt hypnotized with horror as she thought of these photographs in Judah's familiar hands, his unruly head humbled over, studying them. She wanted to die. She covered her face with a pillow and wept until she thought her heart must stop or else beat in separate pieces.

"A strong story of a strong young woman caught in a conflict between her own willing obedience to ancient laws and her longings for the gold of love freely chosen . . . Naomi Ragen has told it vividly."

—Belva Plain, author of *Treasures*

SOTAH

NAOMI RAGEN

HarperPaperbacks
A Division of HarperCollins*Publishers*

This is a work of fiction. The characters, incidents, and dialogues are products of the author's imagination and are not to be construed as real. Any resemblance to actual events or persons, living or dead, is entirely coincidental.

HarperPaperbacks *A Division of* HarperCollins*Publishers*
10 East 53rd Street, New York, N.Y. 10022

A hardcover edition of this book was published in 1992 by Crown Publishers, Inc.

Cover illustration by Kam Mak

First HarperPaperbacks printing: December 1993

Printed in the United States of America

10 9 8 7 6 5 4 3 2 1

For
Bracha, Asher, Rachel, and Akiva,
with all my love and hope.

The *sotah*, or wife suspected of infidelity, was given a trial by ordeal whose purpose was to uphold marital faithfulness and also to protect the guiltless wife from unjustified and irrational enmity and jealousy.

Introduction, *Tractate Sotah*, Mishnayot Nashim
Edited by Phillip Blackman

If any man's wife . . . acts unfaithfully against him . . . and it be hid from the eyes of her husband . . . [or] if the spirit of jealousy comes upon [the husband] . . . then shall the man bring his wife unto the priest. . . . And the priest shall take an earthen vessel and the dust that is on the floor of the tabernacle . . . and put it into water. The priest shall disarrange her hair and say to her: "If no man have lain with thee and if thou has not gone aside to uncleanness . . . be thou free from this water of bitterness that causeth the curse. But . . . if some man have lain with thee besides thy husband . . . the L-rd make thee a curse and an oath among thy people." . . . And he shall make the woman drink the water of bitterness. . . . And it shall come to pass that if she has acted unfaithfully her belly shall swell and her thigh shall fall away; and the woman shall be a curse among her people. And if the woman not be defiled, but be clean, then she shall be cleared. . . .

Numbers 5, 11–28

PART ONE

CHAPTER 1

''YES, I UNDERSTAND ALL THAT!'' CHAYA LEAH INSISTED, BITing the pillow pressed to her chest to keep from screaming in frustration. "But what I can't understand is how you just agree to it all! How can you just marry him!?"

Dvorah looked at her youngest sister and smiled serenely, indulgently, feeling a strange mixture of compassion and contempt. Poor Chaya Leah with her red, puffy cheeks, her red, impossible hair! I would die if I had hair like that, Dvorah mused, putting down her knitting for a moment and smoothing back her own dark, smooth, docile locks. If you tried to braid it, the hairs kept pulling out and curling up, going their own way. If you combed it back and pinned it, it bunched together and rose up like yeast. If she would only lose a little weight, though, she might be made to look presentable, or something close to. "Child," Dvorah said imperturbably. "You don't understand. I'm very lucky. Yaakov Klein studies in the best yeshiva. His father owns an appliance store. They're willing to pay for half an apartment, to support us for two years while Yaakov goes on with his studies . . ."

"And on and on and on! . . ." Chaya Leah shouted, flinging aside the pillow. "While you get big blue veins on your legs and wrinkled, hard hands! Working day and night like our *ima* and his *ima*, earning a living, taking care of the house, the babies, one after the other!"

The knitting fell from the older girl's hands and she looked up, shocked. "G-d forgive me, you sound like one of *them*, the *chilonim*," she said with rare yet deliberate cruelty.

This comparison to the secular Jews who mocked them, who kept no Sabbath or holiday, who ate pig and shellfish, who never said a prayer or visited a synagogue, and who had probably forfeited all share in the World to Come was a sickening and shocking blow to the younger girl, as indeed it would have been to any member of Jerusalem's *haredi* community, of which the girls and their family were respected and longstanding members.

Actually the term *haredi*—literally "those who shook from fear of G-d"—was a catchall phrase used by secularists that ignorantly lumped together many diverse and warring religious groups. It encompassed the many separate Hasidic clans, each united under their own charismatic leader and each cordially despising the other as well as their age-old opponents, the study-conscious Misnagdim. The latter heartily returned the contempt, viewing their Hasidic brethren as pathetically misguided in their blind belief in a leader and for putting prayer above study, emotion above intellect. However, there were two things that united all the groups, giving some credence to their collective title: their sincere, uncompromising adherence to the tiniest dictate of law and custom and their boundless contempt for and rejection of the secularists.

Dvorah knew she could have said nothing more damning. Yet she felt no guilt in having flung the epithet. (The child deserved it. Richly. The nerve!) Still, as a daughter of Rebbetzin Faigie and Rabbi Alter Reich, *haredi* Misnagdim, brought up to suppress not only every bad word, but every unkind thought, her hands shook as she took up her knitting. "Where were you brought up that you talk to me this way? May G-d forgive you!"

"Please, please. Don't fight. I can't stand it," Dina interrupted softly, placing herself between her two sisters, her delicate white hands reaching out to connect the three of them. "Dvorah, how can you be so unkind? Chaya Leah, our Dvorah is almost engaged! She's happy, *baruch Hashem*, G-d be blessed! Why are you doing this? Acting this way?"

Chaya Leah's eyes brimmed hotly, but her mouth was defiant. "He is short and overweight and slurps his soup. I heard him. He is . . . fat!"

"Those are all petty, physical things. If you were on a higher spiritual level, a different *madrega*, if you'd learned more Torah instead of wasting time sneaking off to goodness knows where . . ." Dvorah said loftily, her head lifted, her back stiff with insult.

"She's so young. She'll understand when she gets older," Dina tried.

"And more mature," Dvorah interrupted with growing malice, her black eyes snapping with disgust. "You'll both understand what a bridegroom is. You'll understand what we are," she added darkly, her ominous glance reducing the others to an uncomfortable silence.

It was a tiny room in which the three sisters sat, crowded with two bunk beds, an old hanging wardrobe of peeling light wood, and one small desk piled with books. Yet they felt themselves almost privileged. In contrast to the rest of the family, they had the roomiest bedroom in the house. Their parents shared a tiny alcove created by covering a back porch with sliding aluminum windows, and their five little brothers slept two and three in a bed in the third bedroom. The apartment was in a new building in one of those huge apartment blocks that had sprung up like mushrooms on the acres and acres of no-man's-land incorporated into Jerusalem right after the Six Day War, buildings ten stories high with twenty-five or thirty tiny two- and three-bedroom apartments. True, the ten of them shared one bathroom, but at least it was new and indoors. Besides, they had not one but two porches overlooking Judea's lovely rolling hills, its undulating, dark green forests. On clear days they could even see King Hussein's unfinished summer palace, like the skeleton of a dinosaur caught in a cataclysmic change of ages.

Indeed, by the standards of Jerusalem's *haredim*, it was a most roomy and enviably comfortable home. In fact, considering their former residence in Meah Shearim—a crumbling, one-bedroom walk-up built during the Ottoman Empire, a place with rusty outdoor plumbing and a roof that wept like a mourner during the short winter rains—Rabbi Reich often viewed his new place as almost sinfully luxurious. Often he asked G-d to forgive him for his delight in it and prayed that no disaster should befall the family because of their new material luxury. Leaky roofs, broken pipes, exploding boilers, were viewed as G-d's mercy, his way of exacting payment for sins from metal and stone rather than human flesh. Secretly he worried that the reward he had so painfully and diligently accumulated for himself in the World to Come might be badly depleted as a result, like an overdrawn bank account.

There was silence in the room. "What's wrong with us?" Chaya Leah asked slowly, accusingly.

"You're fourteen years old. You know nothing."

"And you're twenty and beautiful and intelligent and a *tzdakis*, a saint! You can find someone better!" Chaya

Leah ran over and held her sister's languid, smooth hands, caressing them. Dvorah shrugged her off impatiently.

It was ice cold in the room, as the heating system was run collectively and the majority of their neighbors had voted for only four hours of heat during the coldest winter months, all most could afford. All the sisters wore flannel pajamas and robes and slippers, each set handed down to them through a dizzying network of relatives and connections. The great-aunt in Milwaukee bought the clothes for her granddaughters, who in turn gave them to poorer cousins in New York, who in turn shipped them to Israel.

Until recently Dvorah had always gotten first pick. But now America's return to short skirts and her own gain of several inches in height had resulted in most of the skirts and dresses falling shamefully shorter than midcalf, making them immodest and unwearable. But when they'd been younger, the clothes had been routed routinely from her to Dina to Chaya Leah.

They had all learned to be careful with clothes, except Chaya Leah, who knew she was the end of the line. She always looked untidy. A blouse that looked crisp and demure and sweet on Dvorah, soft and romantic on Dina, always looked unironed and loose-buttoned and messy on Chaya Leah. She was a big, strong girl who would have looked right in overalls with a hoe; the kind of woman who had drained the swamps in the Hula Valley and outlived malaria, typhoid, and Arab snipers to bear nine or ten children. The genteel pleated skirts and tucked-in blouses of Beit Yaakov Seminary for Young Women looked flimsy and painfully strained over her big bones.

Dina was her exact opposite. Petite and fragile, slim and porcelain fine, she seemed almost too delicate to be real. Everything about her seemed softly molded, like a piece of blown glass coaxed to an evanescent bubble shimmering with light, too beautiful to last. Her face was like a blooming, watered garden: a rosy, blossoming complexion, eyes of sun-reflecting, blue-green water, brows a shining arc of sun-kissed blond. It made a person smile and feel somehow lighter, warmer, just to look at her. She made people forget themselves, ordinary, busy people. Strangers would just stop and stare at her the way people sometimes do at a lovely sunset. And if modesty allowed her to look back at them, she did so with eyes that were like a newborn's—so clear and clean somehow, without depth, but not smug or shallow. Just uncomplicated, direct and fine. Her hands and feet were tiny, almost childlike, so that it seemed almost cruel to her mother to send her on chores like carrying the heavy bags of bread and milk from the grocery. Only her hair kept her from being a raving beauty. The light blond of her childhood had darkened with adolescence into a dull, indistinct color, neither blond nor quite brown. Had she been an American girl, she would have used one of those blond highlight rinses and given herself a rich, genteel ash-blond look. But such things were unheard of among Jerusalem's young *haredi* women. That and heavy makeup of any kind was considered cheap and bold. Mrs. Reich often thanked G-d for Dina's mousy hair. Too great beauty was almost a defect in the *haredi* world. People were suspicious of it, feeling a really beautiful girl was a danger, a pitfall, too difficult for average men to overcome. A really stunning girl had trouble finding a husband.

She was sixteen, the middle sister. The peacemaker. The peace seeker. The passions of jealousy and anger that rocked Dvorah and Chaya Leah passed over her most of the time. She had a naturally even temper and could remember only two times when she had been torn with uncontrollable passion. Once, when she was eight years old, an old man had stopped her on her way home from school to ask the way to the central bus station. He seemed as bent and fragile as the old piece of wood he leaned on as a cane. It hurt her almost physically to imagine the long walk ahead of him. She explained the road very carefully, then anxiously watched his slow progress. But a few minutes later she saw him stop and ask again, this time a group of older boys who pointed him in the opposite direction. She watched him turn and to her horror walk in the wrong direction. The boys were laughing. She stood paralyzed, unable to scream at the laughing boys, unable to protest her innocence to the old man when he passed her and sighed accusingly. She'd wanted so much to do something, to say something, to put it right, but her body wouldn't move. She stood like that until both the boys and the old man had disappeared. Only then, in the dark, did she run crying all the way home, her fists beating her thighs in frustrated fury.

The other time was when a small clique of classmates had sent their teacher an anonymous picture of a woman with a mustache. The teacher's face had boiled red, and she'd sat down and covered her eyes and her mouth and her mustache with her hands. Dina had cried so hard and so long that the teacher was convinced she'd sent it. The principal finally sent her to the nurse, and the nurse sent her home.

"What's wrong with us?" Chaya Leah repeated belligerently, her face getting that bullish menace that meant more loud noises and probably *Ima* rushing in shocked and hurt and blaming herself for her failures in child rearing.

"Please, Dvorah, you might as well finish," Dina begged her, prompted equally by expediency and curiosity.

Dvorah lifted her slim legs off the floor and slid them under the covers. "I might as well tell you both, even though Chaya Leah has no business thinking about these things yet. But you, Dina. You'll be next, so you might as well know. It isn't easy for girls like us to get married at all."

"What! Why not?!" Chaya Leah bellowed.

"Sshhhh!" Dvorah and Dina said fiercely. "Do you want *Ima* in here? Do you want *Aba* asking us what we're talking about?"

The very idea of their father asking them to explain themselves made their hearts freeze. You could never lie to

Aba. It was like lying to G-d himself. And you could never tell him any truth that would hurt him, either. The very idea of doing the slightest thing that might fill their father's kind blue eyes with disappointment or pain was unthinkable to the sisters.

Chaya Leah whispered: "I'm sorry. I'll be quiet. But tell me already. I have a right to know!"

"When each of us was born, Chaim Garfinkel wrote our names down in his book, along with the names of every other boy and girl born at the same time. Now, he looks into his book and sees when one of us turns sixteen and begins to look for a match. First he looks at the boy and the boy's family. He asks questions at the yeshiva, in the neighborhood. If the boy has a reputation as a serious student, a *talmid chachem*, and the family has *yichoos*, ancestors who were scholars, then he goes looking for the top, *aleph*, *aleph* kind of girl."

"What kind is that?" Chaya Leah demanded.

"The kind that is first of all from a family descended from *talmidei chachamim*, Torah scholars. A family with a good reputation that hasn't had any physical or mental defects anyone knows about. Then he sees the girl herself. Is she slim and pretty? Did she go to Beit Yaakov and have a good reputation there?"

"We come from a good family. On Mother's side there was Rabbi Eliezer from Minsk, on Father's, Rabbi Reich from Munkatsch . . ."

"Rabbi Eliezer from Minsk! Rabbi Reich from Munkatsch!" Dvorah mocked. "No one has ever heard of them! They didn't write any books, they didn't found any yeshivas."

"They were pious people, ancestors to be proud of. You know that not everyone who earned the title of rabbi in Europe had a congregation or a yeshiva! Look at the great *tzadik* Chafetz Chaim. He ran a grocery store! So Rabbi Eliezer was a shoemaker, but everyone in town knew that he studied day and night. His scholarship was respected," Chaya Leah insisted.

"I've heard these stories. I believed them. But there is something you don't know. There was a woman. A great-great-great-aunt . . ." The eyes of the other two sisters widened. "I don't know when she lived exactly, fifty or seventy-five years ago. It was in Poland. Her name was Sruyele. And she ran away from her fiancé."

Chaya Leah looked blank. "Where did she go?"

Dvorah looked at Dina as if to say "I told you so. Too young!" "She ran away with another man!"

"Was it on Mother's side or Father's?"

Dvorah exploded, "What difference does it make! She was like a *sotah!* She ran off with another man! She ran away and left her fiancé, her parents, behind."

The sisters held their breath in hearing the horrible term. The *sotah*, a married woman suspected of adultery, was held up to public ridicule whether or not she was guilty. Her hair was uncovered, her dress ripped by the priest at the very gates of the temple. And then, if she continued to insist on her innocence, she was made to drink a potion of water and dust. If she was guilty, her stomach swelled and burst; she died in agony. If she was innocent, well, nothing happened to her. But still, the disgrace of the ordeal . . . !

"But how could she be like a *sotah* if she wasn't even married yet?" Chaya Leah asked thoughtfully.

"It was after the *tena'im*, the formal engagement, had been signed."

"What happened to her? Who did she run away with?" Dina asked, sick with apprehension. She couldn't stand stories of people going wrong. She couldn't bear the idea of G-d's anger and punishment and the yawning pit of sin that lay in wait around every corner. Yet she was overwhelmed with a horrible fascination—almost ecstatic with it—so that it was strangely akin to joy.

"He was a goy, or married? Something horrible? . . ."

Chaya Leah asked hopefully, wanting the story to reach its full potential.

"No, thank *Hashem*. As if it weren't bad enough! Simply a poor local boy from the yeshiva. The boy she'd wanted to marry ever since she was a little girl. But her parents didn't think he was right for her. He didn't seem bright enough, ambitious enough."

"Did she marry him, the one she loved?"

"She did, in a town where no one knew her. She even had a child. But then they all found out about the *tena'im* with the other and made them get a divorce."

"How can you make people get a divorce? Who made them? Was it the Morals Patrol?" Chaya Leah continued, referring to the *haredi* community's well-known vigilante group whose effective, if brutal, tactics discouraged *haredim* —married and unmarried, male and female, young and old —from straying down sinful paths, which included everything from adultery and child molestation to attending movies or reading secular newspapers. It was the most extreme of several such quasi police forces operating in the *haredi* world, and by far the most feared. However, like most police forces, average, law-abiding citizens like the Reich girls knew about them only by reputation.

"I don't think they had such a thing back then. It was the rabbis, her father, his father. She was practically married to another. She had no right to marry until the *tena'im* were annulled. She would have been better off marrying and then getting a divorce. *Tena'im* are almost impossible to get out of."

"Well, at least she wasn't married. If she'd been married and run off . . ." The three sisters looked at each other with horror. Adultery. It was a sin too unbearable to contemplate. A sin for which there was only one appropriate punishment: death. No one questioned that.

"What happened to her?"

"They made her marry the first man, the one she was engaged to. She died young." Dvorah returned her sisters' incredulous stares with defiance. "I heard *Ima* and Aunt Simcha talking about it in whispers on Yom Kippur. It's all true."

"She had a child," Dina whispered. "An innocent child left with no mother." She was like her father. Every whiff of human misery, present or past, filled her lungs with despair. "A little boy?"

"A boy," Dvorah confirmed. "So now you understand about us!"

The younger sisters, lost in thought, took a moment to refocus. They understood nothing. Dvorah saw it.

"This is known about our family," she said in exasperation, defeated in her attempt at subtlety. She didn't bother to elaborate. The girls knew what that phrase meant. It was one of those stories that had been handed down ear to ear, generation to generation, and had reached Israel. Now it was common knowledge among their very tight-knit compatriots.

"I can't think! Let me think!" Chaya Leah pleaded. "This thing that happened—fifty, seventy-five years ago, you say?—this Surele, Sruyele—what?—is held against us?"

Dvorah nodded. "It's part of it. It's a taint, a black mark that spreads over our genes. No one ever forgets or forgives anything. Just as we wouldn't if someone wanted to introduce us to a boy whose mother or grandmother had gone off and done . . ." She stopped, seeing Dina's soft, pained face, and feeling a twinge of pity. "But that's only one reason that it's hard for us to find husbands . . . maybe not even the most important one. The worst part is the money. There is no money. No money at all for dowries. For any of us."

There was a terrible moment of pained recognition. They all knew this, had known it, but had never said it out loud before.

"But money is not important. Everyone knows that! G-d doesn't measure your worth by how much money you have!" cried Chaya Leah.

"But the family of a future husband does," Dvorah answered with quiet bitterness. "They want brides whose fathers own businesses. Brides who have apartments already bought and paid for; apartments with three bedrooms and a refrigerator, a stove, and a washing machine. They want cars. Why do you think I'm still not married when practically every other girl in my class at Beit Yaakov already has a child or two?" Her words hung in the air like a poisonous mushroom cloud after the dropping of an atom bomb. There was devastation in the room and complete, stunned silence. "So don't you dare say anything about fat Yaakov Klein!" She wiped her eyes with the back of her hand and pulled the covers over her head.

Dina put out the lights. She could hear Chaya Leah tossing defiantly in her bed, Dvorah's soft sobbing ebb and flow and disappear into the soft breathing of sleep. But she herself could not sleep. She tried to imagine the face of her sister and Yaakov Klein's side by side on a pillow; then she tried to envision a small child, bereft, the child of Sruyele. She tried to feel appropriately shocked and sad, yet all she could think of was Sruyele running away, her small feet tapping the icy cobblestones in the Polish village, while in the distance the pale, long face of her beloved hovered like a ghostly apparition, lighting her way down the dark, cold street. Over and over again she felt the leap from the cold pavement into the warm arms. Sruyele's leap. It made her shiver and feel short of breath, like someone who has been crying for a long time. She took short, deep breaths which she was afraid to release. Her temples throbbed, her mind full of contradictions and a fearsome kind of pleasure. Hours into the night, she could still hear the frightened beating of the strange heart, unseen and unknown, hiding deep within her.

CHAPTER 2

FAIGIE REICH OPENED THE DOOR TO HER DAUGHTERS' ROOM carefully. This was odd for her. She was a big, almost overpowering-looking woman, given to large, decisive gestures: pot lids were lifted and lowered with a clang; rugs were beaten with whomping vengeance; and erring young bottoms received righteous whacks that boded no room for shilly-shallying or idle dreams of reprieve.

Yet without her being aware of it, a new softness born of doubt had crept into Mrs. Reich's disciplined, staunch, and unflinching vision of life ever since Dvorah's wedding six months before. Perhaps it was the devastating vision of every mother of the bride: the tiny creature suddenly heartbreakingly beautiful and pure under the wedding canopy encircling a strange man who would now be her whole life.

You lost a daughter, whatever they said about gaining sons. Dvorah's husband would be her life now. And you hoped—you so hoped and prayed!—that she would be happy with that life.

So many things could go wrong.

That was why she and other *haredi* mothers raised their daughters with such discipline—harshly, many would say. There was school eight to ten hours a day, then homework, and household chores that lasted several more hours. They had to be steel once they reached that canopy, tempered steel beams that could uphold the whole Jewish people. Let's face it. The men did all the learning, all the praying. They could tell you if a chicken's lungs were kosher or the exact moment to light candles on Friday night or how to search for crumbs before Passover. But who made it all happen? Who turned an ordinary day into a holy day, where the house shone from cleanliness and the boys and men wore spotless white shirts and prayer shawls? Where the Sabbath and holiday table groaned from the heavy platters of steaming meats and succulent chickens and kugels and a hundred delicacies fit for a king? And who made it possible to buy the food and clothes, when the husband and father spent all day learning, as was his rightful role? As much respect as Rebbetzin Reich felt for her husband, and all scholars like him, she admitted to herself that the men were all theory. Their learning, their piety, could only exist because of the protective cocoon their women wove around them, allowing them some distance from the harsh realities of buying, earning, saving, cooking, cleaning, and giving birth. As high as the men floated near the heavens, so must the women plant their feet firmly on the earth. And in her heart of hearts she faced the truth that as weak as the men were, so must the women be strong.

In this matter she had taken her cue directly from G-d. After all, how many concessions did the Torah make to man's weak nature? In war, for example, if an Israelite man captured a beautiful woman, it was expected that he wouldn't be able to resist her. Even the best men (those who left the desert and came into the land of Israel with Joshua were considered extremely pious, *tzadikim*, men who had passed the terrible trials of wanderings, the loss of faith that had their parents building golden calves: a perfect generation) weren't expected to have an ounce of willpower, hence all the laws concerning the captive woman. Oh, you could take her home, the Torah conceded (you probably will, won't you, even though she's a pagan and will bring her idols with her and probably drag you down). But once there, she had to take off her finery and put on mourning; she had to cut her long nails and be allowed to weep for her dead family a month. Only then could the man "go in unto her" and take her for a wife. The Torah in its wisdom was so wonderful, so wise, Rebbetzin Reich thought. For after she took off the finery, cut off the long, painted nails, and cried for a month, let's face it, how good was she going to look? And thus the Torah goes on to say that if the man changes his mind, he can't keep her but must send her off free, because "you have humbled her." That was man's nature.

Faigie Reich had raised her daughters as she had been raised: to accept this world as it was and to enter it on its own terms. And she had been rewarded. Dvorah had married well. Indeed, thrillingly well. Thank G-d! She had prayed so hard and so long ever since the girl was seventeen that G-d find a good *chassen* for her. It had taken a long time, but G-d had his ways. Yaakov Klein! Such a fine boy from such a wonderful family! Now, only two more girls to go.

She padded softly into the room, which seemed almost empty now. How fast they grew up and left. She sat a moment on Dvorah's empty bed and watched her two daughters.

Chaya Leah was sleeping deeply. She couldn't help smiling in triumph at the child's bigness. The only one who took after her. A pleasure to have such a daughter and a joy to have such a wife. Big strong hands, wide hips, firm, strong thighs and calves. Some man would be blessed. She would make his life a paradise. His home would be scrubbed, filled with healthy children. There would always be an income. She expected to bring Chaya Leah into the business full-time in a year or two. The little store selling balls of yarn and crocheting thread that had put food on the table and paid the mortgage and helped marry off one daughter would just have to provide enough for two. She could already imagine the girl behind the counter, carrying in the big boxes of yarn from the delivery trucks, arranging the storeroom into neat piles, balancing the books.

Then her gaze shifted to Dina and her smile turned sad. She could never envision Dina in the knitting goods store. She was such a flower, she would fade in the shadows of the boxes, the sunless cold storerooms. Her hands were so small, childishly tender. She was a lovely piece of china, the kind you received as a wedding gift and never used except once, for once-in-a-lifetime events: engagement dinners, fiftieth wedding anniversaries.

She was bright. She could always finish the seminary and teach. Rebbetzin Reich twisted her simple gold wedding band around her large, gnarled finger as an uncomfortable, almost sacrilegious thought came to her, a thought she would never even be able to share with anyone, least of all her husband: Dina must marry well. Someone who could support her. Someone who could take care of her. She was not cut out to be a *kollel* wife, supporting her husband through years of study. There was sadness as Rebbetzin Reich admitted this to herself, frustration, and a sense of failure, too. After all, being married to a boy who would rise in the yeshiva rung by rung was what every *haredi* mother hoped for her daughter. As the Talmud teaches: Marry your daughter to a scholar. It meant fulfilling the highest vision of womanhood. But who knew better than the rebbetzin that it also meant endless years of sacrifice. It meant there would never be any money. It meant scrimping on food, on clothes. It meant walking instead of taking a bus; buying tomatoes going soft and watermelons ready to rot. It meant one chicken for the Sabbath and perhaps another during the week. And it meant no help, ever, with the children, the housework. Chaya Leah was built for that. But Dina, beautiful little Dina. Faigie Reich's heart ached.

Already Chaim Garfinkel had been to see her. He had been to Dvorah's wedding, of course. The *shadchen* was always invited to the wedding and at the end was given his fee. It was considered very bad luck for the young couple to underpay or (G-d forbid!) withhold payment from a *shadchen*. As Reb Garfinkel had taken the money-filled envelope, he had stroked his long, thin beard and returned Rabbi Reich's enthusiastic handshake. "I have someone in mind for Dina," he'd whispered. "A fine boy. A scholar."

Rebbetzin Reich had found herself lying awake nights hearing those words. She'd resisted her husband's suggestions that they begin the long, involved process of finding Dina a husband, and Rabbi Reich had put off talking about the subject for a month or two after Dvorah's wedding, indulging what he believed was his wife's reluctance to contemplate the loss of yet another daughter's willing hands around the house so soon. Yet as time went by, the pressure was mounting. The *shadchen* was calling more often, hinting that there were opportunities that shouldn't be casually lost; hinting that "we wouldn't want Dina to wait as long as her sister did, would we? It would be a bad precedent. Bad for the family name. It would only make things more difficult for Dina. For Chaya Leah."

The rebbetzin sighed. She was going to have to deal with it. Time was racing. Dina was almost seventeen. Her friends were getting engaged. She leaned over Dina and hesitated. It actually hurt her to shake Dina awake. She—mother of eight, who mercilessly routed five reluctant boys out of bed with cuffs and harsh words, who pitilessly berated her daughters for everything from not saying the morning prayers on time to wearing stockings without seams—actually hesitated to touch Dina, to shake her from her sweet sleep. But it was Dina's turn to do the morning shopping, to bring back the three loaves of bread, four milk, and two margarine needed for breakfast. She thought of the heavy plastic baskets that would cut into the tender flesh of those childish palms and hesitated, tempted to ask Chaya Leah instead. But she stopped herself. In her life Dina would carry many heavy baskets. To spare her now would mean to leave the flesh tender when she as her mother should be helping to provide those calluses that would eventually protect her from more pain.

It was getting late. If she didn't hurry, the boys would miss their bus to the yeshiva or go without breakfast. She thought of her five little sons with something like awe. After three girls, after almost giving up hope, and then five circumcision ceremonies!

Ezra, the oldest, was going to be Bar Mitzvah in two months and had already memorized an hour-long Talmudical discussion as well as the entire Torah reading. He was a quiet boy, refined, an excellent student. Asher, eleven, was the opposite. Loud, rambunctious, with no *zitzfleisch* to sit in one place and memorize. Still, she shook her head indulgently, he had a good head, quick and sharp. She had faith that the yeshiva would whip him into shape eventually.

Though infinitely more difficult, this same faith held for eight-year-old Shimon Levi, his sisters' scourge, his teacher's bane. She couldn't help smiling. What a healthy rascal he was, G-d bless him! Always full of high jinks, always full of scrapes and cuts and bruises. . . . But underneath the bravado, she knew, there was this sweet little boy who secretly allowed his mother to kiss him good night, hugging her around the neck.

Six-year-old Benyamin was next. She had a soft little spot for Benyamin, the only one of her children who had been born with a physical disability, a small heart murmur that had been corrected by an operation at age two. He was a pale, delicate child whom the other children instinctively protected. He had a soft heart like his father and couldn't stand to see any of his brothers punished. He had gotten into the habit of taking responsibility for all their wrongdoings, knowing that the blows that would fall on him would be easy ones.

Then there was the baby, not a baby anymore: Duvid. Her last child, born right before menopause. He had turned three last year and they had cut his hair for the first time, as custom stipulated. Something had cried inside her as his blond curls fell to the ground with heartbreaking finality. Her last baby.

She looked up with guilty haste. It wasn't like her to brood. There was no time. Reb Reich was long gone; having prayed with an early *minyan* at the synagogue at four A.M., he was already at the yeshiva studying his daily Talmud portion before his tiny students began arriving at *heder*. He instructed three- and four-year-olds and had great satisfaction in teaching them their first words of Torah. It was a responsibility that often made him tremble. After all, their whole attitude, their whole lives, might be based on the feelings he instilled in them when their minds were clean slates and their hearts pure soft clay that would hold forever the imprints of these early experiences. He loved these little boys like a father and worried over them more than their own parents.

More than he did over his own children, Rebbetzin Reich sometimes perceived resentfully, a feeling that sent her praying for forgiveness every Yom Kippur. She wouldn't see her husband until the evening, until after he'd eaten dinner at the yeshiva, said his evening prayers, and then learned his daily portion of the *Mishnah*. But how could she dare complain? His day was full earning merit for them both in the World to Come. And hers was dedicated to getting them through the mundane paces of the lowly, material world that was.

She had gotten up at four-thirty, said a shortened version of the prayers her husband said, put up a load of laundry and hung it out to dry, prepared a kugel for Shabbat (four days away) that she would freeze, and put up a whole chicken in broth that would be their afternoon meal. When the boys were dressed and fed, she would finally dress herself and hurry to Mahane Yehuda to open the store.

She had no pity on herself. I'll rest when I'm in the grave, she told herself whenever exhaustion made her doubt her blessings. There will be more than enough time then. And I'll be sorry for every mitzvah I didn't do when I had the chance. So in between her housework and her work at the store, she managed to cook meals for neighbors who were in mourning and couldn't cook for themselves; prepare Sabbath meals for women just after childbirth; visit the sick in hospitals. And in those rare moments in the store when no customers demanded her attention, she managed to knit sweaters for the pious elderly, whose thin cracked walls—and even thinner flesh—did little to keep out the penetrating cold of Jerusalem's winters.

She leaned over and turned down the covers. Dina's nightgown, a too big hand-me-down, had slipped off her shoulder. Her mother touched the naked skin, and the contrast between its lovely, fragrant youthfulness and her own harsh, onion-smelling wrinkles awoke a strange compassion in her heart that almost frightened her. She felt a wave of pleasure and a sharp stab of foreboding.

"Dina," she whispered, shaking her gently. "Dina, *maideleh*. It's time to get up."

Dina opened her eyes willingly. As she did most mornings, she woke refreshed and full of calm, sweet energy. Her life was a clear, clean, simple puzzle, large pieces that fit together instantly. Her obligations to her family, friends, and neighbors were mapped out definitively and stemmed ultimately from her obligation to G-d—His Law, His Will.

She didn't mind hard work. It had a purpose, a reward, a blessing. Honor thy father and mother. Learn Torah. Help the poor. Keep the Sabbath. There were almost no situations in life in which her love of G-d, the example of her parents, the teachings of her rabbis and rebbetzins in school did not provide her with a consistent and satisfying course of action. Most of the time the path of life rose up before her, a clear, obstacle-free highway, scented like spring roses beneath a cloudless, benevolent heaven.

She was young and healthy, without regrets about the past or worries of the future. Her life, which an average American girl would have found suffocating and narrow and full of endless hardship, seemed to her not only happy, but bursting with the best possible happiness. She was not imprisoned, but wrapped in a cocoon, a womb of endless love, approval, and safety. Her faith, like those of saints and of the very young, turned hardship into a joyous challenge and cast a redeeming, friendly light on want, transforming it into wholesomeness, the simplicity of a good life, preferable to any other. All her dreams were rosy and calm, a little too blissful, perhaps. And even those doubts that fell over the landscape of her mind and heart came like gentle summer showers, not even darkening the sky. They were simply a refreshing interlude amid the endless sunshine of cloudless summer days.

"What time is it, *Ima?*"

"Five-thirty already. Why, when I was your age . . ." Her voice was loud, blustering.

"I know, I know. You could have knit a whole stocking by now."

Her mother smiled. "So you've heard that story already?"

She smiled back and kissed her mother's clean, soap-smelling cheek. "Once or twice!"

"Never mind." She swatted her daughter's bottom in a friendly way. "The boys will be up any minute, so hurry. If they miss the bus to the yeshiva again, Ezra and Asher and Shimon Levi will need extra carfare and Benyamin and Duvid will have to walk all the way!"

Dina moved more quickly. It had happened once, last month, when it was her turn to buy breakfast. It hadn't even been her fault. The bread delivery truck that deposited the still-warm loaves from the main bakery had been late, and she'd waited for it. Still, the onus of her responsibility weighed upon her. She felt so protective of delicate Benyamin and baby Duvid, and their yeshiva was almost a mile away. Anyway, her mother had only to look at her reproachfully and all her resistance melted. All the children felt that way. *Ima* worked so hard, so endlessly. None of the older children especially could bear the idea of adding another wrinkle to her collection. They tried to handle their problems by themselves, and each one took responsibility for the younger ones. Soon Chaya Leah would be up and dressed and in the boys' room, helping them to get dressed, preparing their books and lunch bags.

So Dina began the long string of ritual that carried her through the day. She said her first prayer of the day even before getting out of bed: "I give thanks before thee, King that lives and endures, for returning my soul to me in your great compassion and faith." Then she reached beneath the bed for the pitcher, basin, and cup she had prepared the night before in order to wash her fingertips and rid her body of the unclean, harmful spirit, the residue left behind when her soul had left her body in sleep. It was believed that even to walk several steps without doing this put one's body in physical danger, for anything the unclean fingertips touched would become impure and diseased. She cupped her hands and poured the water over them three times each, then dried them. There was a prayer to be said over washing the hands, even one to be said after relieving herself in the bathroom: "Blessed be Thou, O G-d, King of the Universe, Who has formed man in wisdom and created in him manifold orifices and cavities. It is known before Your throne of Glory that if one of them be opened or one of them be closed, it would be impossible to keep alive and to stand before You. Blessed be You, G-d, Healer of all flesh and Doer of wonders."

She hurried and opened the closet, looking with satisfaction at the immaculate piles of clean folded underwear, the carefully ironed and crisply folded blue blouses, the dark, gleaming row of wide navy blue wool and polyester skirts. It was the school uniform the girls were all forced to wear to Beit Yaakov. There were mornings she longed for color: a red cotton blouse and a plaid skirt, or a turquoise sweater dress—anything but that light and dark blue! Yet she was able to concentrate her individuality and pride in the condition of her clothes. All her clothes had gone through many owners. Yet that did not lessen their value in her eyes. Once she received them, they became hers. She was meticulous. She examined everything she wore for the tiniest tear or grease spot and refused to wear it if all her concentrated efforts could not remove the blemish. She dressed quickly, gave herself a hurried look in the full-length mirror, then grabbed the basket and ran out the door.

Her forehead and underarms were beaded with sweat by the time she'd run down the four flights of stairs to the street. The spring warmth that hit her the moment she left the building dried her body like soothing talcum. The sky was a silvery net of interweaving clouds that blurred the distant hills, giving magical shapes to the trees and houses that touched the horizon. There was the caravan, Dina thought, playing her old childish game. The dromedaries, laden with gifts for Laban and his family. And there was old Eliezer, Abraham's servant, leading the caravan of precious jewels and fine silks to be bartered as wedding gifts for Rivkah, the lovely bride he would bring back for Isaac. Her steps slowed as the image of the far hills took on a fairy-tale beauty. Everything seemed silver-dripped, transformed, and turned into mere line drawings, lighter grays and darker grays. Even the dark pine forests were covered with a magic silver sheen that made them indistinguishable from the hills and the white stone houses. Whenever she found herself face to face with an image too beautiful to assimilate, she felt almost paralyzed. Was it real? And what did one do with the realness of windows that blazed like white-blue diamonds, slick roads of liquid mercury, a sky of gleaming, beaten silver plate? How could you just leave it and walk on, eyes on the ground? It was so good, so wonderful, to be alive! She felt the sky, the earth itself, had been formed in beauty just for her and that whatever else happened in all her life, this one moment, rich in unforgettable loveliness, made it all a blessing, a gift. She stopped and waited, just waited for something to happen.

"Forget something, Dina?" Baila Fruma, a neighbor, called out as she hurried past. Dina shook her head, ashamed of her idleness, and rushed forward. And although she had been taught to look at all people with a kind and forgiving eye, she couldn't help feeling profound distaste as she glanced at the hurrying Baila. Fifteen years old and already she went into the street in a long messy bathrobe, dark stockings, and slippers! The only difference between her and an old married woman was that her hair was still uncovered. Many of the married women never bothered getting dressed at all, spending all day in bathrobes. It was considered perfectly modest and acceptable to walk out into the street like that. Still, Dina always found herself torn by guilt and antagonism at the sight of them. She appreciated that these were women with three, four, or even five children under the age of five who often didn't have time to get dressed. Also, there didn't seem any point in putting on real clothes—such an expensive item in their ridiculously small budget—which would just be ruined: slobbered over, spit up on, and splattered with cooking spills. There were no casual clothes in a *haredi* wardrobe. No denim and sweatshirts. *Haredi* women dressed formally, with dignity, in clothes that were of fine materials. When they did get dressed, for the Sabbath and holidays, they shone immaculately.

Still they were only a few years older than she, and look how they had already let themselves go! She would never let her husband see her in those shapeless *shmattes*. She would always look exquisite to him, no matter how hard it was.

The grocery was crowded. The fragrant, still-hot loaves of crusty white and rye, unwrapped and unsliced, disappeared into baskets two or three at a time. For a large religious family with little money, the inexpensive, filling loaves (whose price was lowered by a government subsidy) were a main staple of the diet. Bread with margarine for breakfast. Bread with jelly for dinner, with perhaps a small chicken schnitzel or fish and vegetables for lunch. Most of the men and boys ate their main meal in the yeshiva, where they spent their day. But the girls and women, coming home at noon or later, ate their main meal at home.

By the time Dina added the milk, which was sold in plastic bags, the margarine, and the bread, the baskets pulled her arms painfully. She wrapped a plastic bag around the handle to keep it from tearing or blistering her palm and hurried home. The number of stairs seemed to have multiplied magically as she struggled back up the four flights she had so casually skipped down.

There was a lot of activity during breakfast with eight of them to feed and get off. Yet there was no shouting, no pushing. A cordial yet clearly disciplined atmosphere of subdued cheer reigned, presided over by the imposing presence of Rebbetzin Reich. The boys were typical boys. But just the fact that there were so many of them in one crowded living/dining room somehow dissipated the rivalry between them. There was a lot more noise, fighting, and temper in a house with two children than with ten, *haredi* women who had experienced both often testified. Perhaps because in big families, expectations were less. There was none of the fanatic "This is *my* chair!" or "I want *this* bowl!" that children in smaller families were led to expect would be tolerated. Most of all, the unquestioned respect—and no small touch of fear—for their mother made the children lower the flame beneath whatever unacceptable rages they felt boiling within them.

Most of the time they were perfectly good-natured, perfectly happy. They were loved. They were fed. They knew what was expected of them every minute of the day. And it was relatively easy to earn approval and understanding from parents and teachers. As long as they didn't question. As long as they went along. As long as they learned, learned, learned.

Also, there was an unwritten concession to boys' high spirits: they knew that they could have the screaming, spitballing, wrestling, ball-throwing time of their lives during recess and on the bus to and from school. Yeshiva kids, when left to their own devices, outran, out-high-jinked, outscreamed, and outpushed anyone in their peer group. Not because they were wilder. They just had less time and opportunity to express themselves as boys, so they concentrated it all in the hour or two given to them within their daily schedule.

When the boys were gone, Rebbetzin Reich sat down with her daughters for a quiet few minutes.

"I hope your grades are improving in prophets this term, Chaya Leah."

"*Ima*, I'm trying. I just can't stand reading Job. It's so depressing."

"I never understood Job," Rebbetzin Reich had to agree, a rare thing. She felt her role was to push her daughters to be what was expected of them and to leave her own feelings out. "But, of course, you have to try. You have to work hard, and I'm sure your teacher will help you."

"Mrs. Morganbesser hates me. She always thinks I'm dreaming. She's constantly giving me moral lectures, *Mussar!*"

Dina nudged Chaya Leah under the table, raising her brows. But it was too late.

"About what?" Rebbetzin Reich said suspiciously.

Chaya Leah groaned inwardly at yet one more example of where talkativeness got one. "Oh, you know, *Ima*, everything!"

The rebbetzin's hands left the warmth of her hot coffee cup and rested, folded tightly, in the chilling damp of her apron. "No, Chaya Leah. I don't know. Why don't you tell me?" she said with deceptive pleasantness.

"Well, maybe tomorrow. It's getting so late now." The girl got up abruptly.

Her mother caught her arm. "Oh"—she smiled—"this will only take a minute, I'm sure."

"Oh, *Ima*. You'll think goodness knows what!" Dina broke in. She nudged her sister with exasperation.

"It's just . . ." Chaya Leah began reluctantly.

Her mother's face was still, calmly, chillingly expectant. Her hands twitched in her lap.

"She just doesn't like how I dress!"

"You wear the uniform, don't you? So how can she not like . . . ?"

"She just doesn't like the way it looks on me! She's constantly complaining I'm not neat enough. I try, *Ima*. But what can I do? Clothes just ride up on me. They get loose and go their own way. It's not my fault everything's always untucked and twisted around."

The rebbetzin relaxed, suppressing a small smile of relief. "Maybe you just need a bigger size, *maideleh*."

"But our cousins in America don't," Chaya Leah said morosely. "They never seem to gain any weight, and they're all so small!"

"We'll see. Maybe in next month's budget there will be enough for a new outfit."

"Really! Brand new!"

"And if there isn't, I'm sure Dina could always try to let out what you've got?"

"I could try. But you know American clothes never have any decent seams or hems."

The girls began hurrying and kissed their mother good-bye. "Don't work too hard," they called out to her, their familiar parting.

"Don't work too easy," she answered them with a laugh, her familiar rejoinder.

CHAPTER 3

"I CAN'T BELIEVE YOU BROUGHT THAT UP, CHAYA LEAH." Dina shook her head. "You like to live dangerously." "I just forgot. Anyway, the truth is not so terrible."

"Have you gotten rid of them?"

"What for? I don't see any reason to get rid of them. They're perfectly beautiful."

"Mrs. Morganbesser will call *Ima!* Did you ever think of that?"

"*Ima* is never home. Did you ever think of that?" she said carelessly. "Anyway, what's it her business what I put in my ears?" She bent her head, slipping off her plain gold loops. Out of her pocket came a long, tinkling pair of silver earrings, made the Yemenite way, all filigree with little blue turquoise stones. She quickly slipped them into her lobes.

"How do I look?"

Dina widened her eyes and tried to keep her lips firm. But it was too much. "You look like one of those girls they brought to King Ahasuerus's harem." She grinned. "And not the one he picked to replace his dearly beheaded Queen Vashti. The other ones. The ones he tried once and then kept locked up in the women's house the rest of their lives."

Chaya Leah tossed her head and stopped to check her reflection in a store window.

She had as many layers around her feelings as she did around her bones, her sister thought, wondering once again at Chaya Leah's amazing ability to slough off criticism that would have left anyone else devastated. She didn't defend herself. She didn't even consider taking off the earrings. Instead she inclined her head and gave one of the earrings a little tap that made it sway and tinkle.

Dina looked at her, appalled and yet transfixed with a strange admiration.

Chaya Leah laughed, delighted. "Morganbesser is just jealous! I don't care. There's no *halacha* which says you can't wear earrings. So I wish everyone would just leave me be!"

"Be careful, Chaya Leah." Dina shrugged, giving her sister's ample upper arm an affectionate squeeze as the two girls parted for their separate classrooms.

A woman's body, like an official map used during a border dispute, was clearly marked off by rabbinic authorities into two kinds of territories: those parts lawfully open to men's wandering eyes and *ervah*, an erotic stimulus, absolutely closed to trespass. The border lines were these: the neck (above, all was permissible, below, all was forbidden); the elbow (above, all was forbidden, below, all was permissible); and the knees. The knees were a problem. All authorities agreed everything above the knees was *ervah,* but some felt that everything below should also be included. The disputed area—the calves—were a bone of contention. Thus, some rabbis insisted women wear dresses to their ankles, while the liberals felt stockings and a skirt that covered the knees were enough. Those who agreed that stockings were enough disagreed about what kinds of stockings. Some insisted they be opaque or black or seamed.

Mrs. Morganbesser, short, plump, determined, wore blouses that buttoned at the wrist and just below the chin; skirts that fell midcalf season in, season out; and heavy, seamed stockings. In this war to keep the female form properly draped, she felt herself in the position of a vigilant general holding strict orders from the chief of staff to "hold the line." In order to do this, however, she felt the accepted territorial map was not enough. She needed a buffer zone, a no-man's-land, in which to ward off any enemy invasion. Thus the girls who came in round collars, just a brush above the collarbone, were sent home to get a shirt that buttoned below the chin. Girls who wore thin, pointy, cutout shoes were sent home for sensible, laced-up, rubber-soled oxfords. Girls who wore midcalf skirts with stylish open pleats to the knee were sent home to sew the pleats closed.

But Mrs. Morganbesser's biggest problem was not keeping girls within the letter of the law, but imbuing them with its spirit. Every year she girded her ample, well-covered loins for the latest onslaught from the fashion world.

This year it was leg warmers.

Technically she couldn't find anything wrong with them. They were another layer of clothing. They covered the calves. Yet she looked at them and all the sirens in her finely wired, highly sensitive early-warning system went off screaming like the electrified fence system that kept murdering terrorists from infiltrating from Lebanon to Israel.

Anything that did that, which did not have a specific place on "the map," she told the girls had "the smell of the street" and was thus to be excluded not only from the classroom, but from their lives until further notice. This included leg warmers; belts that hugged and defined the hips or waist; eyeshadow; high-heeled shoes or boots; long, glamorous hairstyles or too short punky ones. And, of course, eye-catching jewelry.

Mrs. Morganbesser had very definite ideas about all these matters. That generations of *halachic* scholars and rabbis had overlooked such things she viewed as both a vexing and dangerous lapse, one which created an untenable vacuum she felt personally responsible to fill. Any girl walking into her class knew that she would be scrutinized and—despite all the wonderful rabbinic ordinances against embarrassing someone in public—publicly ridiculed and humiliated for any perceived digression.

Although she would never have admitted it to herself, Mrs. Morganbesser's main guideline in these matters was not the heavy volumes of the *Jewish Code of Law*, the Mishnah, or the Talmud, but simply her own, highly individual, carefully developed, and unbending image of what a religious Jewish girl should look like. She pushed and ridiculed, lectured and lambasted, pleaded and warned, until every single girl under her tutelage was patted, squeezed, or shoved into an acceptable approximation of that image.

And this was her vision: hair very long and braided or just below the ears and held back by barrettes. A light blue or white high-collared, long-sleeved, buttoned-down shirt of loose cotton or polyester, well ironed. A dark blue or black skirt that hung wide from the hips until four inches below the knees. Dark or white opaque stockings and sensible low-heeled or laced shoes. Small delicate gold earrings, a barely visible necklace, and a good strong watch.

As for makeup—young faces needed no other decoration than the beauty of their characters as displayed in their eyes, their well-washed cheeks, and pure, unsullied, prayer-filled lips. As for attracting men, the kind of men these girls and their parents should and must want would only be those who thought the same way she did.

Chaya Leah walked into the room quickly, but not quickly enough.

Mrs. Morganbesser adjusted her wig, pulling it forward until the bangs practically hid her eyebrows, a nervous habit the girls had come to recognize as all the sirens going off.

Dina took the dutiful three steps forward and three steps backward, bending her knees in the prayer which began each day's studies in Beit Yaakov Seminary for Young Women. She tried to keep her concentration pinned on the words. Mouthing them did nothing, she felt. "G-d of Abraham, Isaac, and Jacob," she prayed, beginning the prayer of Eighteen Benedictions, the holiest and most important prayer in the Jewish religion, the culmination of all the lesser prayers that preceded it. It was a prayer said at least once a day by women and thrice a day by men. It was a prayer that was said silently, standing at attention, feet together in one place. It was a prayer that could not be interrupted or spoken during except if death threatened. It was a prayer that expressed the desire of the human soul to rise above its fleshly desires in total devotion to G-d's will and service. It was a prayer of thanks for the joy, the gifts, the sustenance, daily granted to us by G-d. And it was a human promise to ensure all physical achievements, all worldly possessions, served and pleased Him.

Although the words of the prayers never varied, the experience of saying them each morning always did. Sometimes Dina found herself thinking so deeply about every word, every sentence she uttered that it brought tears to her eyes. Often she achieved a level of concentration so strong that the room disappeared, her body vaporized, and there was nothing left but her soul, naked and vulnerable, crying to an invisible yet intimate, infinitely understanding and compassionate Father. She found herself trembling, bursting with a secret joy, a connection that banished all loneliness, all doubt.

Yet there were also times when the prayers were strange in her mouth, unknown words in a superannuated language that brushed the surface of her lips, never penetrating any deeper. They were a bore and a nuisance to be gotten through. She never knew when she began to pray just which experience awaited her.

Today she felt her mind wandering. The words flew past her like birds, too high and too swift for her to glimpse more than just a flash of color, a vague outline of form. She looked up listlessly, gazing through the dusty, closed classroom window towards the campus of the nearby secular state high school. The students wore jeans, multicolored sweaters, and sweatshirts with sneakers. They sat on the ground in small groups, their legs spread open carelessly and lazily. They were seniors like herself, yet they were already making their mandatory visits to army recruiting stations, taking exams and physicals that would decide if they would be tank drivers, pilots, or foot soldiers for the next three years of their lives. They were working hard to pass exams which would earn them their *bagrut*—national matriculation certificates—their passport into local colleges and universities once their army service was completed.

She had absolutely nothing in common with them. Even though she had received a draft notice like everyone else, there was no question of her being drafted or serving. Religious girls who wanted it were automatically exempt from army service. All she had needed to do was go to the rabbinate and declare herself too religious to serve. She was then given an official letter, which her parents mailed to the army. As far as the army was concerned, she no longer existed.

She never understood exactly why it had to be this way. The Torah stated specifically that during a war of defense even the bride under the canopy was not exempt from participating in the battle, although she was forbidden to carry arms. She never did understand how the rabbis got around that. It was stated so clearly. And yet not only didn't *haredi* girls participate in the country's defense during war or any other time, but neither did *haredi* men, all those learning in the yeshivot, something for which there was no basis at all in Jewish law.

She had no idea that it stemmed from Ben Gurion's 1948 concession to rabbis who demanded that their few hundred yeshiva students be draft exempt in light of all the thousands of yeshiva students killed during the Holocaust. Now the number of draft exemptions had risen into the thousands and was a constant source of antagonism between *haredim* and secular as well as modern Orthodox Israelis, whose own yeshiva students combined Talmud study with army service.

She understood more about the girls not serving. After all, how could she, or any of the girls around her, be expected to wear pants! Or be in a unit where men and women were together all the time! She had heard many stories about officers and the girls they commanded sleeping together. Going to the army was unthinkable for girls, she often thought wistfully.

Still she often found herself examining the young girl soldiers she came across in the street or on buses. Their khaki skirts and shirts seemed so tight and revealing to her, yet also wonderful. Adventurous. She wondered what it would be like to board a bus at an army recruiting station with a hundred girls she had never met; to ride off to a training camp and learn to live in a tent and crawl through the mud and shoot a gun. Or perhaps to fix a tank or work in an office surrounded by handsome young officers.

There was also no question of her, or anyone else she knew, going to the university, either. Beit Yaakov did not allow the girls to take their *bagrut* exams, much less follow a curriculum that prepared the girls to pass them. There was no reason to. Colleges, as everyone knew, were simply hothouses for the corruption of pure Jewish men and women. Not only did the sexes mix indiscriminately, but they also learned indiscriminately: alien philosophies, the lies of Darwin, the nonsense and filth of novels . . . How often had it been hammered into her since childhood how weak she was and how strong temptation; how she must constantly guard her eyes, her mouth, her heart, from seeing, tasting, feeling, all things that could lead to sin and G-d's displeasure.

The reality of the army or the university was beyond frightening. Nothing in her upbringing or experience had brought her close enough to even create an unfulfilled longing for such things.

Yet she had no control over her dreams. She dreamed not of being allowed to go to the army and university, but of *being* there and how it would feel. She dreamed of it the way, long ago, she had dreamed of being a bird, or a cloud, or a lion in the jungle; or the way now she sometimes dreamed of being a bodiless soul soaring to G-d's heavenly throne after death.

She was not hungry for the reality of new experiences, she often convinced herself, experiences that required decisions, produced complications, and bandied about temptations that led so effortlessly and horrendously into the dark abyss of sin. She felt safe in her reality. Her home, her school, the people around her, the clear lines of duty and faith, provided the strong footbridge over the turbulent, threatening world of choice, doubt, and dangers that crashed constantly below her. She walked securely, holding on to the narrow sides that encompassed and supported her. Seldom did she peek over the side. Her reality was safety. It was the promise of a good, pure life.

The need for adventure she sublimated rose up in dreams. In her imaginings she was constantly unfulfilled and constantly searching. Nothing was too dangerous, too wicked. She allowed herself complete freedom of thought, entering the churning chaos below like a ghost through the soft mist of dreams. Like a glass blower, she breathed her own living breath into her fantasies, giving them unique shapes and lovely iridescent colors. She had both worlds, she told herself. She was utterly safe, utterly protected. And wasn't it delicious, to explore new worlds without actually being strapped in on top of that exploding rocket launcher; without feeling your body vibrate, your ears deafen, your stomach lurch. In dreams you could edit all that out, leaving only the unearthly calm of floating in space, the glorious adventure of painless, dangerless discovery.

She finished her prayers, bowing with deep reverence and an even greater sense of guilt than usual. She knew G-d had read her mind. The sense of nothing being hidden was part of her faith. And yet she had somehow constructed a small, private trunk that could be firmly locked where she hid all she was ashamed of feeling and imagining. She did this even though she felt G-d was kinder than her teachers, more open than her parents. If someone had to read her thoughts, she would prefer it was He rather than anyone else she could think of. He would realize that it was just dreams that brought her inside the hot, heavy metal of tanks in a green khaki uniform; just dreams that put her in tight jeans inside the campus of the university. Reality was *Ima* and *Aba*. And being inside this classroom. And Dvorah's being married to fat Yaakov Klein. She looked around the classroom.

Of the thirty-five young women in Dina's senior class, two were married and eight already engaged. It was only October. By June another ten would also have announced dates for weddings. In this they bore no resemblance to any other group of girls their age in the entire city or country.

Except for other branches of Beit Yaakov, and schools run by Hasidic groups like Lubavitch, Belz, or Satmar, there were no other high school classes in the city or country where this was considered normal, or even acceptable.

When she stopped dreaming and looked at reality, she saw that this too was what she wanted, longed for. To be one of the first to be married. It was prestigious. To come to the graduation ceremony with a married woman's wig in maternity clothes was like being valedictorian elsewhere. It meant that you came from a fine family, that you were pretty and good and most desirable. It was like winning a beauty pageant or being chosen Miss Universe.

Dvorah's words often came back to her as a small, tingling chill that rose up her spine. It had taken Dvorah so long to be chosen! There was no money. There was a taint on the family name.

The modesty of her outlook, the high ridicule in which vanity was held, the near contempt in which the physical, material world was viewed, kept her from gaining any comfort from her lovely face, her exquisite body. Had she been a girl in jeans and a sweatshirt across the street, the knowledge of being a beautiful, desirable woman would have come to her as a fact, like the inevitable rise of the moon in the starry sky. It would have filled her with subtle female understanding and that deep confidence that makes a beautiful woman carefree and careless and happy.

She did not know that she was beautiful. So she worried and ached and despaired about who would ever be willing to marry her. She thought of the years passing, of having to go out to work as a teacher of small children and everyone looking at her, as they had begun to look at Dvorah, with that sly, pitying curiosity. *Im yirtza Hashem by dir*, "G-d willing, it will happen to you"—hated phrase! —would rain down upon her head like little pelting stones every time she went to a wedding or engagement party or circumcision ceremony.

Yet, marriage! She felt it was so big, so important! It

was for grown-ups, like *Ima* and *Aba*, or those women in the grocery with their long, unkempt bathrobes and tightly wound head scarves. She was still a girl, a young, innocent girl, her conscious mind reiterated countless times. You want to go on the way you are, being home with your family, that same sane, calm voice told her. You want to keep on learning, it insisted. To keep on blowing and blowing into the dreams and watching how they grow and shape themselves into new patterns not yet tried or conceived.

But there was another voice, hoarse, rude, and dangerous. A voice like the earth—soiling, yet rich and basic and shamelessly fertile. It was like having your period or going to the bathroom or watching your naked body in a mirror. Shameful and yet with the undeniable excitement of dangerous realities coming too close to ignore. She tried desperately to keep it away from her. She pressed it down in her trunk, which she bolted with a heavy steel lock. On the trunk she piled the soft cushions of her proper ideas, her parents' and teachers' clear, untainted vision of Dina Reich, soft, pious daughter and dutiful little student. The higher the cushions were piled, the more distant and muffled the voice became, so that she could often convince herself it had gone away for good or had never existed at all.

And then something totally unexpected would happen, scattering the cushions wildly, springing open the lock, and flinging the trunk lid open with a crash. And then the voice would thrust itself in her face like an angry, violent escapee from prison, a mocking cruel stranger.

The first time it had happened, she'd been fourteen years old.

There was a new boy in the grocery. She noticed him immediately. He was crouching on the floor, piling cans on the shelves. She stood just above him, reaching up for the warm, fragrant loaves. And as she stretched, she felt her whole body arch in a graceful taut curve that somehow pleased her, and she knew, just knew, his eyes had also seen it, and the voice all at once shouted at her that it had pleased him, too.

Instinctively she looked at him and found him looking back, boldly and questioningly. Then he relaxed, his eyes calming into a smile that crinkled the corners of his eyelids and the sides of his nose. A smile not involving his mouth at all. He was very dark, with gleaming coal black hair cut like a good child's, very short and neat with a well-loved child's delicate, even part. His eyes were small and slanted, almost hidden under dark, overhanging brows; his skin was olive dark and stretched smooth over high cheekbones and a square, cleft chin. There was a handsome delicacy about his face that made her heart leap. His eyes caught hers and held them.

She fumbled with the loaves, almost dropping them. The dark, shameful voice shouted all manner of terrible things in her ears with the roar of a wild, dangerous beast got loose.

From then on her heart always tripped a little before entering the store. Sometimes she saw him right away and jerked her eyes down, but never soon enough to avoid his ironic, cool, bold eyes, which were at once insolent and yet flattering. And sometimes he would not be immediately apparent, and she would find herself lingering by the loaves, her head turning furtively in all directions, searching, until very soon she glimpsed the soft, burnished gleam of dark hair behind the shelves, and she felt her stomach ache with excitement and strange foreboding.

He never spoke to her, nor she to him. Nor did she ever hear him speak. It was as if he had no voice, no actual presence, except in her secretive, fertile imaginings where her own loud voice roared and crashed all around her like high, threatening waves.

She tried to think of him as a husband. To imagine him sitting down at the table to eat, next to her father and mother. But he wore no skullcap. He had no beard. He did not fit, even in her wildest dreams. And, interestingly and frighteningly, this made him even more attractive and exciting. She dreamed of teaching him the Torah, of buying him his first *kipah* and *tsitzis*, the four-cornered, fringed undergarment needed for prayer. She could almost feel her palm lifting back with the springy resilience of his thick dark hair as she pressed a skullcap to his head, affixing it with bobby pins.

Then one day she went to the store and saw him standing outside by a delivery truck. He stood sideways in clean, slim jeans and scuffed shoes and a short-sleeved cotton shirt. His arms were slim and long and corded with muscles. His white teeth shone. He was helping unload a delivery of flour, and as she neared she heard his voice. "*Inshalah*," he said in Arabic. "If Allah is willing."

She remembered that moment, like the moment of a bomb hitting and mushrooming with poisonous accuracy over a self-made cataclysm. An Arab! A goy! She had not known. She had thought him merely a secular Jew, which was bad enough. But an Arab! She remembered the horror and the shame and the birth of a deep self-distrust that never left her.

She never went back to the store.

The sane voice spoke to her now. The other one was gone, she told herself. The trunk was deep, the lock strong. The cushions as insulating, as suffocating and vast, as the clouds in heaven itself. She could not hear it anymore, she told herself, no matter how loud its siren's call, how frightening its blood-stopping roar. She was safe from it. She missed it.

CHAPTER 4

"YAAKOV," DVORAH SAID SOFTLY WITH GUILT. HE WAS SITTING at the dining room table with an open book. She hated to interrupt his learning. But he was hardly ever home. They both left early every morning, he to the *kollel* and she to her job teaching third-graders in a Hasidic girls' school. They spent time together each evening from eight until they retired at ten. Twice a week he had a study group in Mishna that lasted until nine-thirty; and once a week he tutored students to bring in a little extra money.

Only on Friday evenings and Shabbat did time stretch before them with luxurious slowness, allowing them to talk and get to know each other. Despite their physical intimacy, in many ways they were still strangers. They had spent only five or six evenings together before meeting under the wedding canopy and had been married only about six months.

Yaakov looked up immediately, putting aside the sefer. He smiled at her and reached out for her hand. She smiled back, reaching out timidly toward him, trying not to notice that his hand was soft and heavy, the knuckles white and fleshy. But he was a kind man, she thought again, moving closer to him. She didn't love him. Not yet. But that would come. He was so warm and affectionate. It was clear that he loved her.

"Yaakov, I hate to bother you, but I want to talk to you about something serious. Maybe it could wait for Shabbat, I don't know"—she hesitated—"but I can't. I keep thinking about it."

He patted her hand and pulled out a chair for her, making that mock severe face he used when he was joking, the eyebrows lifting, the mouth turning down in a clown's frown. "Do you have to apologize to talk to me? I should beg *your* forgiveness for never giving you enough time. After all, a man is supposed to spend the whole first year of his marriage making his bride happy. The Torah even gives you a draft deferment to do that."

She wasn't quite comfortable with him, not yet. He still seemed like a stranger, a visitor she had to be nice to in the courteous way of good hostesses. Yet now, encouraged, she took the plunge. "It's my sister Dina."

He couldn't imagine what was coming next but waited patiently. Yeshiva boys, *kollel* men, had so little experience with women. Every day he was married was a new experience for him, a new world. The ideas women had, the way they looked at everything, was so far removed from the familiar men's world he had moved in exclusively since beginning heder at age three. Her heart was soft. She was constantly telling him of tragedies and celebrations of people he did not know. She seemed connected to everyone. Their lives touched hers. She was always baking cakes or making chickens for neighbors who were ill or after childbirth. Or baby-sitting. Women were so full of *chesed*, kindness, he thought. Through her, his sterile world of learning about goodness was connected to the world of doing, of actually reaching out to help other people.

He looked at her face, her pretty dress with the frivolous bows, and touched her shoulder. Every time he did it, he felt a little guilty. Being permitted to touch a woman, after all those years of not being allowed to even look at one, still made him flinch with pleasure, like a little boy finally given permission to cross the street himself who crosses up and back simply for the sheer pleasure of doing it.

"I think it's time we found Dina a *shiddach*." She looked at him expectantly. He looked back in utter confusion.

"Well, yes. As it is written: 'Eighteen to the marriage canopy.' "

She looked at him, nodding, clearly waiting for something more.

"I could show you some very interesting discussions of matchmaking in the Talmud. Perfectly fascinating *sugiot!* . . ."

She cleared her throat, puzzled. "Well, sometime, it would be interesting, I suppose, but first we have to settle this." She smiled brightly.

He stared at her, his smile fading a little, his mind wandering back from the section on matchmaking in the Talmud he had been reviewing mentally. Only slowly did it begin to dawn on him that something more was expected of him. "My dear wife"—he finally gave up—"could you be a little more specific?"

She flushed. Wasn't it self-explanatory? "Well, Yaakov. You must know some fine young men in the *kollel*. Or perhaps your family might."

"What about the *shadchen*, Reb Garfinkel? Wouldn't it be better—"

"*Shadchens* cost money. They get so much for the initial meeting and three times that if there's a wedding. And if you don't pay, they come to the wedding and curse the couple!"

"Not Reb Garfinkel!"

"I'm not talking specifically of him," she hedged, although she *had* heard certain stories. "I'm sure he would never do such a thing. But my parents have taken out so many loans just to help with our wedding and to furnish this house. I would like to save them something if I could. Also, the professional *shadchens* are never as good as friends and relatives who really know the couple. It would be a mitzvah, and I'd be so grateful."

He patted her hand, thinking. Almost all the men in the *kollel* were married. Almost all the men he knew were married. "Eighteen to the marriage canopy," was an edict yeshiva boys tended to obey. After all, how long could normal human feelings be suppressed? They married them off quickly, so that frustration and weakness wouldn't lead them down the back streets of Tel Aviv.

He looked at his wife's expectant face and hated to disappoint her. He racked his brain again.

Abraham Breitman. He wasn't married. He was a sharp fellow, a good learner, he thought hopefully. What kind of family? He had no idea. Such things didn't interest him. He took a man as he was. His performance in the study hall was all that mattered. A little surge of panic went through him. He didn't even know Abraham's mother's name! What if it was Dina? Then they couldn't get married. A man wasn't allowed to marry a woman with the same first name as his mother. You haven't promised anything yet, he calmed himself. Of course you will investigate.

"I can think of one fellow, a good learner."

She pressed his hand eagerly. "Tell me all about him!"

He shifted uncomfortably, opening the vest on his suit. His stomach protruded with an involuntary sigh of relief. Dvorah watched him, her eyes blinking with distaste.

"I don't know very much, Dvorahle. You know how men are."

"But just something. How does he look?"

Oh, now I am in for it, he thought with alarm. Was this *loshen hara*, slander, or wasn't it? He thought of the Talmudic teaching that said that at the throne of Judgment a man will be held accountable even for the casual conversations he has with his wife. Yet, she looked at him. It was for a pure motive, a good cause. He tried to think of Abraham Breitman. What does one yeshiva *bocher* really notice about another?

"His clothes are always clean. And he wears glasses," he offered.

She smiled charmingly. "What else, Yankele?"

He felt his neck begin to sweat and chafe under the tight collar of his shirt. He opened another button. "Well, honestly, my dearest, I can't think of anything else. He is bright, argumentative."

"Is he tall or short?"

He tried to pull up a mental picture of Abraham, but it was always one of him sitting behind the *shtender*, the study desk, in the *kollel*. He had no idea how long his legs were.

"Well then, what color are his eyes?"

He shrugged.

"Well, is he good-looking or not? You must know that," she persisted, her voice becoming an iota less friendly.

He was beginning to feel peevish and wronged. "Dvorahle. *Neshama sheli*, my soul. Be reasonable. What reason would I have to notice something like that?"

She saw his mood change and cautiously shifted tactics. She didn't know all that much about him and had no idea how fast he would go from annoyance to fury. Besides, this was a favor she was asking.

"Well, do you think he'd be suitable? If you do, could you speak to him, or his parents? I'd be so grateful."

He let out a sigh of relief and kissed her hand. "I'd do anything for you, Dvorah. Of course. I'll speak to him tomorrow first thing."

She got up and moved toward him. Tentatively she leaned over and brushed his cheek with her lips.

He felt a tremor of excitement roll through his body. It was a small step forward. The first time out of the bedroom—which was all holiness and duty bound up with the mitzvah of procreation—that she had showed him any spontaneous affection. He tingled and flushed. She felt her power.

"You will find out tomorrow, won't you, Yaakov?"

He nodded, holding his breath.

Everything was happening so fast, Dina thought. Her first *shiddach* date. Her first new dress.

"How does it look?" Dvorah called from outside the dressing room door. Dina thought it an odd question. There never was any mirror inside of dressing rooms in these shops, forcing you out into the store to see what you looked like and giving the shop owner/saleswoman the opportunity to talk you into buying a dress no matter what it looked like.

"I'll be out in a minute." Most *haredi* girls had developed an instinct about new clothes, perfecting a method of feeling its fit before seeing it so that they took off anything that was too embarrassing to be seen in public. But Dina, who had never shopped before, had no idea. She sweated a little at the idea of leaving the dressing room, as someone might who has been forced to put on makeup without a mirror.

Cautiously she opened the door. "Well, what do you think, Dvorah?"

"I don't know. . . ."

"Come out, come out. What are you hiding, a beautiful *maideleh* like you. What are you ashamed? Come out into the light so we can take a look," boomed the shop owner's strident, almost frightening voice. She took Dina by the shoulders and steered her into the middle of the shop toward the only full-length mirror, in front of which three other women were also jockeying for position. "This fits you perfectly, a *kapparah*," the woman said, making the O mouth of delighted surprise.

"It's big," Dvorah said, eyeing it critically, "too long. Too wide at the hips. The shoulders just fall off you."

"Well, well, little problems, easily fixed," the woman placated anxiously, filling her mouth with pins, which she hurriedly started sticking into the dress, hemming it, picking up the shoulders.

"It looks like you're dressing up in *Ima*'s old clothes."

Dina looked at herself in the mirror. The dress was definitely, embarrassingly awful. It didn't even approximately fit. In Israel there were only a few sizes, going from size eight to fourteen. There was no such thing as clothes for misses, or petites, or women. Each dress had the same size no matter what its dimensions, and you had no choice but to try it on and hope for a lucky fit. All stores had seamstresses who did the alterations that were almost always necessary to make a dress fit the buyer.

Dina looked at herself in dismay, then began to giggle.

Dvorah made a face at her, but then was hopelessly caught up as well. They laughed in loud, hiccuping sobs of laughter.

"Well, if I knew you weren't serious," the store owner said, deeply offended. "We aren't used to such behavior from religious girls. To waste a person's time," she went on, getting angrier and angrier.

The sisters caught themselves. "We *are* serious," Dvorah managed with some degree of dignity. "But it's just as big a sin to try to sell someone goods that aren't appropriate."

"Are you saying there is something wrong with my merchandise? That I am, G-d forbid, not being a thousand percent honest?"

Dina dove out of the dress and into her old one, grabbing Dvorah by the arm and heading out the door. "We're so sorry. It was just too . . ." She felt the giggle rise up inside her again, irresistible. "Too . . . big," she managed to say just before the laughter exploded once again inside her, making her helpless with weakness.

The owner stood at the door, glaring, as the two girls hurried down the street.

"So, you see. It was a blessing all these years, not having to buy new clothes. Remember how much we wanted them, how angry we were that our clothes always came in boxes, washed and starched, smelling of other people's closets!" Dina mused, her heart still beating rapidly from the whole experience. "Let's go home. I'm sure I can find something in the last batch. . . ."

Dvorah grabbed her arm. "It's out of the question. You must have a new dress. You're a *kallah moid*, not a little girl anymore. You must have your own dress. A few dresses!"

"A few?" The thought had never even occurred to her. More than one new dress! "Dvorah, who will pay?"

"Never mind. It's all taken care of."

"It's a *gemach*, isn't it?"

A *gemach*, or a free loan fund, was the unofficial bank of the *haredi* world. It was a religious obligation to give ten percent of one's income to charity every year. Part of that could, if desired, be distributed in the form of interest-free loans to any comer. Thus there were *gemachs* that made housing loans, that loaned medical equipment like wheelchairs and breast pumps, that lent wedding clothes for brides and grooms or gave out used refrigerators and stoves. There were *gemachs* housed in people's homes that provided medicines on Friday night and holidays when the pharmacies were closed. There was even a *gemach* that specialized in returning lost pencils and pens.

"I hate to take charity," Dina said.

"It's not charity. It's a loan that has to be repaid."

"And who will repay it? *Aba* and *Ima?* You know how much they're still paying off for your wedding." She stopped. "Oh, I didn't mean—"

"I know what you meant. But, believe me, *Ima* and *Aba* got off cheap with me. Yaakov's parents paid for almost everything else. Anyway, this is the way things are done. I'm not happy that *Aba* has all these extra debts because of me. But what would be better, for me not to get married at all? This is the way our world works. The parents break their backs their whole lives supporting their children. We will do the same for our children."

"But, it doesn't seem fair! I don't need more than one dress."

"Do you want your *shiddach* to think you aren't respectable? That your family doesn't care enough about you to get you decent clothes?"

"But how will he know if I've got more than one dress?"

Dvorah patted her younger sister's head as she would a small child's. "You hope there will be more than one time you will meet, don't you?"

You couldn't argue with that. You couldn't argue at all, Dina thought, confused and resentful. She didn't understand the way these things worked. Never had, never would. She was the dutiful daughter. She was used to doing things the way she was told to do them. It was so much easier that way. So if Dvorah insisted she needed more than one dress, she realized that she would no doubt buy more than one dress.

"But at least can we go to a store where there is a mirror in the dressing room?"

"I don't know any stores like that. Anyhow, it's hopeless for us to go to stores. You're much too little. Nothing will ever fit."

They walked along silently. "So, we're going home?" Dina asked hopefully.

Dvorah raised her eyebrows and batted her lashes. "Of course not! We'll go to a seamstress and pick out the patterns and she'll measure you and then everything will fit. Then we'll go to a store and buy the material."

"But how will I know what it looks like?"

"It will look beautiful. It will fit," Dvorah said with finality.

The patterns, taken from new German, French, and American fashion magazines, were stunning. There were four altogether, three dresses and a lovely, softly skirted suit. The dresses were all modest, sleeves to the wrist, high above the collarbone. Yet they were also chic and delicately form-fitting.

The material store was not one of those that lined downtown Jerusalem with windows filled with patterned flannel and garish polished cotton prints.

"Are you sure you're not lost?" Dina asked Dvorah as they wandered through twisting alleyways and up unmarked streets.

Finally Dvorah went through the door of an old apartment building and walked down two flights of dark stairs. Dina followed behind skeptically. But then all at once they opened a door and found themselves in the middle of a store the size of a soccer field. Great bolts of fabric lined the walls, piled up ten or twelve feet in the air. There were velvets and soft satins that gleamed sumptuously, like an evening at a rich man's house; there were modest little cottons and flannels with cheerful childish prints. There were yards and yards and yards of every conceivable color and texture and pattern. Hundreds of *haredi* women, old, young, some in various stages of pregnancy or toting tiny crying babies, milled about as harried, bewigged saleswomen pulled and measured and cut fabrics, creating a strange chorus of little rips and tears.

"Look at this green watered silk!" Dvorah exclaimed, her hand closing over it. "Come here, quick!"

Dvorah pulled the bolt of fabric, draping it over her sister's shoulder. It did amazing things to Dina's eyes, deepening the color and making them somehow shine like little jewels. She was like a summer day, Dvorah thought. A summer day early in the morning when the light is pale and golden, not yet harsh enough to fade all the colors in the hills, allowing the dark green pine forests and the lighter green apple orchards to stand out against each other distinctly, like acrylic paint squeezed full strength from the tube.

She placed a small, sad kiss on her sister's young cheek. "Marry a man you want," she told her, and then felt with horrified certainty her eyes sting with tears. A summer day in a lovely watered garden, Dvorah repeated to herself, making herself look at her sister as if she were a stranger.

"Dvorah, be happy! You are, aren't you? I will be, won't I?"

"Yes," the older girl said, nodding, her face bright with misery, with the secret knowledge of things women do that cannot be undone.

A watered garden. A blooming watered garden, the older girl thought, still nodding.

CHAPTER 5

She stood in the middle of her bedroom like a statue.

"Dina, turn around!" Chaya Leah demanded.

"Again?" Dina said, affecting exasperation but feeling none. She was too happy, too overwhelmed.

"The jacket is not too tight?" her mother said, cocking her head doubtfully.

"*Ima*, you don't want her to walk around like some old *bubee* with no shape!" Dvorah retorted, feeling the implied criticism. After all, she had been the mentor for the whole enterprise.

"Well, I suppose you're right, Dvorahle. I don't know about such things. Just . . . I don't know." She moved her head up and back slowly, filled with the doubt, the fear, and the pride of a mother seeing her daughter for the first time as a woman. It was almost terrifying.

Dina glanced at her mother's troubled face and felt a shiver of doubt crawl up her spine. She looked hard and long at the mirror, much longer than necessary to just ascertain her simple blooming beauty. She wanted to see what her mother saw, the problem that made the wrinkles on her face quiver and tremble.

She wore a two-piece suit. It was a square, lightly quilted jacket and a flouncy skirt. The colors were brilliant —lavender-and-green paisley with soft gold highlights. It had little gold buttons and a braided trim of twisted gold and black. Even to someone like Rebbetzin Reich, who had never in her life seen a fashion magazine or been to a fashionable clothes store, it was absolutely clear that the seamstress had done a magnificent job. Dina looked like a model on a magazine cover.

"She looks gorgeous!" Chaya Leah practically shouted.

"We want to see, too!" cried Benyamin and Duvid, pushing their way into the room.

"Don't. It's not right," Ezra said severely, trying to stop them.

"Fancy-shmancy. We're going to a wedding!" said Shimon Levi, his nose in the air, his behind swinging, while Asher started doing a spirited wedding dance, pretending he was balancing a bottle on his head.

They were smothered by a chorus of horrified shushes from their mother, Dvorah, and Dina.

"He'll be here any minute! Do you want him to hear you halfway down the block?" Dvorah said severely. Then she relented. "You do, you know, look beautiful."

"Phtu, phtu, phtu," Rebbetzin Reich said warningly, herding the boys out of the room. It was an amused but not wholly unserious imitation of the traditional three-spit formula for warding off the evil eye. "You should just have a beautiful *mazel*," she added, coming back in and closing the door behind her.

This was not good wishes, her daughters knew, but a rebuke that they accepted. Looks had no way of influencing G-d's will. An ugly girl's piety could earn her a fine husband and a wonderful, happy life. A beautiful girl's sins, the opposite. Looks had nothing at all to do with it in the long run. It was G-d's compassion, his *hashgacha pratis*, private care for each individual, which led a man or woman to find their perfect mate. This was all decided long ago, even before conception, in heaven itself. However, although each man and woman had their perfect counterpart, there was no assurance they would necessarily ever find each other. It was something to be prayed for with great humility. It was a gift, a boon, a reward dependent on one's worthiness.

"Put on a little lipstick." Chaya Leah, ever practical, broke the mood.

"Do you think I should? *Ima*, Dvorah?"

Her mother and sister considered. "Well, maybe just a touch of pink," Dvorah said.

"Yes . . ." Mrs. Reich considered, her doubt fading as she got used to her daughter in the new dress, the new role. *Kallah moid*, bride girl, a girl ready, willing, and able to have a husband. "A little lipstick. And maybe some perfume!" After all, a person wasn't supposed to rely on miracles. There was no harm in helping *hashgacha pratis* along a little.

"Will *Aba* be home in time?" Dina asked anxiously.

"Your *aba* promised, so he will be home," Rebbetzin Reich said with a conviction she didn't feel. Who knew? Of course he would start home on time as promised. But maybe he would find an old man lugging a heavy basket from the *shuk* and have no choice but to help him home with it. Or perhaps there might be a hungry vagrant whom he would have no choice but to take to dinner. Rebbetzin Reich knew her husband. He was the kindest, gentlest, most wonderful person in the world. Everyone protected him from the slightest distress because he felt it so deeply. If he heard that the Jews in Russia were frightened of pogroms, or the Jews in Ethiopia were hungry, he would weep for half an hour, wondering perhaps if he had done some transgression that had weighted the scales of justice in the heavenly court toward punishment for the Jewish people. He didn't consider himself a separate human being, but a part of a great whole. The Jewish people were a body. When some part of that body ached, Rabbi Reich moaned.

And so his wife couldn't bear to bother him with unpaid bills, with clogged drains, with broken beds and the need for warm sweaters; with mortgage payments due and water bills overdue. The girls were her allies, keeping their small woes to themselves or sharing them with her.

"Of course he will be here soon." There was a short silence in the room. "And if he is a little late," Rebbetzin Reich allowed, "well, we all know that what he does will earn us all extra merit. And Mr. Breitman will understand."

"*Aba* can always meet him when he brings you home," Dvorah soothed. She had been through this more times than she wanted to remember. Sometimes her father's absence when her dates came to pick her up made an odd impression, but most of the time it didn't really matter. The boy just assumed he was off somewhere studying. Sometimes they were even relieved to be spared, if only temporarily, the traditional paternal grilling, which took place long before they knew if they wanted to pass.

"Besides, Yaakov is coming with Abraham. It'll be fine."

Dina nodded, then suddenly sat down on the bed, the skin of her legs bitten by nervous cramps. The excitement was almost unbearable. She wanted to cry. She wanted to be alone. She never wanted to be alone. With him.

The doorbell rang. Mrs. Reich jumped up to answer it. Chaya Leah charged into the boys' bedroom, her job to keep them from stampeding over the young man and scaring him away. Dvorah took her sister's warm, nervous hand and the two girls sat on the bed, shoulders and heads touching lightly as they listened for sounds in the next room. They heard Yaakov's voice, pleasant and friendly, and then a deeper tone, very masculine but not overbearing. Dina squeezed her sister's hand. Dvorah patted her helplessly. "It's time now," Dvorah said.

"Just a few minutes more! What if I have to go to the bathroom! I'll just die."

"No, you will not. He will probably take you to the lobby of the Plaza Hotel. That's where they all go, all the *shiddach* dates. You will simply excuse yourself. There is a bathroom downstairs on your right," she said with calm authority, hoping it wouldn't happen. It wouldn't be right to leave him sitting in the lobby by himself. "Now, let's go."

She saw his back, straight and slim, and the deep, dark velvet of the skullcap that sat on thick auburn hair. Her mother's face seemed to lift in pride as she pressed her lips together in a little encouraging smile. Yaakov jumped up and made the introductions. Dina saw Chaya Leah standing behind the slightly opened door to the boys' room, staring. She flushed, reminding herself to murder Chaya Leah.

But maybe not. The blush just made her that much prettier, she saw as she looked at Abraham Breitman's shy, appreciative eyes. He stood up when he saw her. He was taller than her brother-in-law, she noticed, and slim. He had a young beard in the first stages of thick, full growth. Most of it was beneath his chin toward his neck. There was an elegance about it that was distinguishing. The mustache too was neatly defined, with no stray hairs cascading over his mouth—a look she hated (how did such men ever eat, ever kiss?). Behind the familiar black framed glasses, she could see his eyes were dark and receptive. His smile was genuine—a little shy and awkward, perhaps, but she perceived a gleam of hidden mischief in the corners, a vitality. He was a very good-looking young man, she thought growing shier and happier by the minute.

They sat down again around the table, making small talk. Rebbetzin Reich had set the table with elegant Sabbath china. Little silver platters overflowed with nuts, dried fruits, and home-baked delicacies. Abraham drank the tea that was offered him, took a polite sampling of the cakes, then stood up and looked at Dina expectantly. She got to her feet, feeling more comfortable now, and wished her family good night. And then they were out in the fragrant Jerusalem night, alone at last.

"I thought we could go to one of the hotels," he said. "Is there any place you'd like to go?"

"Well, the Plaza, perhaps?" She kicked herself. Now he'll think I am spoiled! He'll think I wanted him to spend a lot of money on me! Why, why did I say it? "I mean, we don't have to go anywhere special. Why don't we just take a walk."

"Perhaps. Perhaps afterward. When we've been to the Plaza. I've always wanted to go myself." He grinned. "Let's face it. We two won't get much opportunity for such things the rest of our lives. We might as well go, no? To everything, there is a season," he said kindly.

She smiled back gratefully.

She had never been to a hotel before in her life. She fought the temptation to take the revolving door full circle and escape straight back out into the night. She gaped at the marble columns that rose to twenty feet, framing dark silver mirrors. Abraham looked with her and nodded with slow pleasure, like a child entering an amusement park with a pocket full of change and a spring afternoon stretching delightfully ahead. They wandered to the back and found an empty alcove in the lobby. There was a couch, a love seat, and a chair surrounding a low table. She waited for him to sit down. He chose the love seat, she then decided on the chair, separating herself by the entire length of the coffee table. No point in becoming too familiar. He took off his hat and laid it carefully on the seat beside him. She took her arms out of her coat sleeves and clasped her hands in her lap, the knuckles going white. He leaned a little toward her. His hands were very mobile and expressive. His voice was gentle and clear.

"What are you studying in school?" he asked her.

"The book of Joshua, and Exodus."

"Does it interest you?"

"Very much."

"What part interests you?"

She felt a little awkward, as if she were being examined by an indulgent teacher. She thought a moment. Exodus—the whole beginning of the exile of the Jews from home, their enslavement in Egypt, their suffering and redemption. "Well, I understand why the Jews had to be enslaved. Why they had to suffer. It was a punishment, but one meant to refine and correct, not destroy." She looked up at him for approval. This was what she had been taught. He seemed troubled. "That's right, isn't it?"

"Oh, yes. Of course. Just. I myself have always had so many mixed feelings about what exactly the Jewish people were being punished for. I remember reading the commentary *Emek Davar*, the work of the Netziv, the great rabbi of the Volozhin Yeshiva. He discusses the verse that refers to the Jews in Egypt which states: 'The land filled with them.' He says this means that not only the land of Goshen which was especially assigned to the Jews by Pharaoh was filled with Jews, but the whole land of Egypt as well. Wherever it was possible to purchase a dwelling, there the Israelites went. The fact that the Angel of Death passed over the doorposts of the Israelites when all the firstborn of Egypt died shows they lived side by side. The Israelites were punished, the Netziv says, because they violated Jacob's wish that they all remain together in Goshen, one family, living apart from the Egyptians."

"Because they wanted to assimilate, to be like the Egyptians?"

"They didn't want to be different. And this is the reason why we suffer persecution in every age, because we don't want to keep apart, to be different."

She shook her head, so interested in the conversation, she forgot all about her shyness in expressing her disagreement. "But we learned that the Exile was ordained even before they got to Egypt, so how could anything they did there have made a difference?"

He looked up, startled, with a new respect. "That's true. It makes the whole thing rather complicated, doesn't it?"

"But that's what's so beautiful about learning Torah. It is so rich, so varied. There are a million questions on every verse, a million answers. You can learn and learn and learn the same phrases all your life and never be bored. For example, this suffering as slaves in Egypt, we learned it was to teach us never to be unkind to or despise a stranger. To make us feel firsthand the sufferings of being a stranger in a strange land."

"It's the image of the furnace, melting down all the impurities in the precious metal, refining it until only pure gold remains: 'Behold, I have refined thee . . . I have chosen thee out of the furnace of affliction.' "

"Do you think it's true?"

"What?"

She took a deep breath, shocked at her forwardness at questioning so obvious a truth, something they both had learned was beyond question. "Does suffering really refine? Or does it just destroy?"

"Ah, it does both. Only G-d knows how much suffering a person can bear without being destroyed, and the measure is different for every man. We believe that G-d in his infinite mercy never gives one more suffering than one can bear. His purpose is to correct, to chastise, not to kill."

"I believe that. But people do die, don't they? Their hearts break?"

He gave her a long, slow glance, a kind, slightly ironic smile. She looked so delicate and fragile. "You needn't worry. Women are naturally pious and good. G-d has so little need to punish them."

"But, sometimes, in my thoughts . . ." She stopped, appalled at the sudden, intimate turn the conversation was taking. Would he think less of her? Would he be shocked and take her home immediately in disgrace?

"One is not punished for thoughts. Only those that result in acts. Wait . . . that isn't strictly true. There is one case where the thoughts themselves are a punishable sin. It's when a man specifically thinks of another's wife with impure thoughts."

She caught her breath, shocked, blushing furiously. But, looking at him, she saw he was very comfortable. To him it was words of Torah, she realized, which elevated any topic to holiness. She let out her breath and her hands untwined, resting more easily in her lap, the good, pink color returning to her fingers.

"I was learning something so interesting this week," he began, not having noticed either her distress or her recovery. He was in his element and found her interest, her questions, charming. "I learned that when G-d created Man, the whole universe participated, each part of the Creation making some contribution. There is even a story that Adam was created so tall, he reached from heaven to earth and that G-d put his hand on him and squashed him to a certain size. I like that idea. A man being multistoried, one above the other. At the highest level, man is just like G-d. On the lowest, just a physical being, close to the earth."

She looked at him shyly. "I always used to think there were so many different worlds all going on at the same time. When I was a little girl, I would imagine that just at the moment I was sitting down to breakfast, there was another child somewhere who was hungry and in her world there was no food. Or if I would fall down, I would imagine that in another world at the same time there was no pain, no blood."

"I'm not talking about different worlds coexisting so much, but of each human being having different floors, different places in themselves where they get off and live."

"Like an apartment building!"

He flushed. "It does begin to sound silly."

"No, no. Not at all. It just means there is no real, one, true you, but many yous, all depending on which floor you choose to live at any given time." He was so interesting, she thought, forgetting he was a man with broad shoulders and a slim, young man's body. It was so easy to talk to him, as if they had known each other forever. "How do you move from the basement to the roof, though? Can you do it yourself, or do you need a teacher, a guide?"

"Theoretically, and I'm quoting my own teacher here, you can do it independently. But practically, it's almost impossible without some help. But that teacher can be alive or can have died two hundred years ago. After all, even something as simple as reading, you have to be taught."

"I don't think I have the right teacher," she said, surprising and almost mortifying herself. How could she have said such a thing? But he didn't look shocked. He looked interested. He waited patiently for her to continue. "I mean, I don't ever feel challenged, or even elevated. So many times I just do what I'm told. Yet I so much want to feel some movement upward."

He nodded, his eyes meeting hers. "It's a yearning every one of us feels. But we men are fighting our way upward through the Talmud. It's like a war, a battle. Sometimes I grapple with a text and feel it is winning and I am being pushed farther and farther into darkness, into ignorance. Women are more fortunate. You were born closer to the truth. You can feel it instinctively, isn't that true?"

Was it true or simply a tired cliché? A way of discouraging women from venturing out onto the battlefield? Not that she had any desire to do that. Talmud study was like the Torah itself: enclosed in a velvet robe and silver chalice, hidden behind the closed doors of the Ark in the synagogue. No woman could ever hope to approach it. But sometimes she wondered about all the things she was taught about the reason for women not learning. "Women's minds are weak," the Talmud stated. Women don't have the ability to learn. And then, in the next breath, they told you women didn't have the time to learn, that they had another role in life that was equally important but different. But if women didn't have the ability, why did they need to say the other things? Anyhow, she had heard of a religious group of modern women who had opened their own *kollel* and were studying Talmud full-time. She looked up at Abraham, wondering if she should bring any of this up, deciding not to. After all, what would he think? He might think she was one of those American women who kept insisting women were the same as men. A "libber," she thought they were called. And if he did, he would never go out with her again.

"I don't always feel that I know what I ought to be doing."

He'd been sitting with his head bent, his ear inclined toward her, looking down at his feet with utter concentration. But at these words he lifted his head and looked at her, his eyes intimate and knowing, his mouth sly with mischief. "That is why you need a husband," he said, sliding a fraction of an inch toward her. It was a movement that seemed to her as bold and intimate as an embrace.

The waitress brought some tea and cake. This was unusual, though she wasn't experienced enough to know it. Until the situation was more serious between a couple, they avoided the intimacy of watching each other actually eat. It was a delightful treat, the rich cake on china plates, the little china teapot, which she handled delicately, pouring the water into her cup. She gave a moment's thought to filling his cup as well but dismissed it in horror. It would have been too domestic and unacceptably romantic to be pouring a handsome young man, a stranger, tea. He poured his own, waiting until her hands were safely far from the area so that no accidental physical contact could take place, unthinkable for both of them.

They ate and drank, almost in silence, her eyes wandering over the luxurious surroundings that made her feel delightfully spoiled and catered to in a way she had never experienced before and left her with a slight uncomfortable feeling of sin. It wasn't right. But it was lovely, she told herself. Surprising how many things were.

They walked out into the cold Jerusalem night, and she shivered deliciously. The wind was mild, and the dark trees swayed with the gentle tinkle of wind chimes. They walked toward Yemin Moshe and its windmill. Once a dilapidated slum on the Jordanian border, a place only the poorest lived, it had been transformed by changes in the territorial map into one of the most desirable areas in Jerusalem. The windmill was real, built by a European philanthropist in the 1890s to encourage Jews to leave the safe—if suffocatingly crowded—Jewish quarter within the walls of the Old City in order to pioneer new settlements. The settlement had failed, and the windmill had never had much practical use other than simply as a quaint historical landmark. In fact, the area had never seen more success than it enjoyed now. The poor had been transferred to small apartments on the outskirts of town while rich foreigners and well-connected local artists had been allowed to restore and lavishly expand the run-down stone dwellings.

It was strange, she thought as she walked along the long narrow cobblestone streets. The houses were so close together, the streets so narrow, it reminded her of her old poor neighborhood in Meah Shearim. And yet, how beautiful it all was! Artistic grillwork had replaced rusting metal. Fine polished wood framed the windows. The houses had been enlarged, while somehow retaining the original architectural detail. And gardens, trees, hanging vines, and potted plants were everywhere. She felt a sudden, untoward respect toward wealth, the kind of wealth that made such things possible. To turn the familiar, the ordinary, into something so amazingly beautiful and charming. To create such loveliness out of the dull, practical ugliness of everyday life. It was a kind of blessed magic, wasn't it?

Or perhaps, she thought, it is simply the dark beauty of the night that I am feeling, that is speeding through me like a drug. My first night with a handsome, intelligent young man so close beside me, attentive and solicitous in the faint moonlight. The magic hour had touched her with its potent charm. She too was transformed from her everydayness into a creature of infinite loveliness, desirable and gifted.

Their footsteps echoed in the dark as they wandered together down the steps toward the little park below. There the white, illuminated walls of the ancient Old City rose before them like smoky incense out of the darkness, almost a dream. The fresh, raw scent of wet leaves rose from the Aleppo pines, the early blooming almond, and the olive and carob trees. The spicy aroma of bridal veil, cattail, winter jasmine, and lavender combined and wafted around them, filmy and tenacious as a spider's web. They did not stand very close to each other, so that even a casual brush of arm against coat was not possible. Yet they were breathing the same scent, drinking in the same ancient ghostly beauty of the city, their faces touched by the same gentle wind. They were together.

He was a complete stranger, she told herself, trying to make some sense of it. To be sensible. It was just the thrill of being out with a young man that made her heart beat so fast. It was only because it was her first time. The thick dark color of his hair, the dark, beautiful curve that hollowed his cheeks, the muscles she sensed beneath the good black Sabbath coat, had nothing to do with it. Nothing, she told herself severely, close to tears of frightened joy, nothing at all.

They walked, sharing a short sentence, a word, but mostly in silence. It had begun to drizzle lightly. She watched the drops mist his black felt hat, making it sparkle under the lamplight as if touched by fairy dust.

"Your hat," she finally said, reluctant to acknowledge the impediment to the evening lasting forever.

"What?" He looked up at her, puzzled.

"Do you like the rain?" she said with a little smile.

"Is it raining?" he asked her.

CHAPTER 6

"How can I explain it? It just feels like I've known him such a long time. Did you feel that way with Yaakov?" Dina asked Dvorah.

The two sisters were walking through the crowded *shuk* in Meah Shearim, buying baked goods for the Sabbath. It was a crisp, cold Friday morning with a sky like blue glass. All along the cobblestoned streets Dina could see the puddles of water being swept out front doors as the tired old houses were scrubbed and polished to a high gloss in final ablutions before the day of rest. The spicy smell of cholent, a heavy stew of beans, barley, potatoes, and meat, wafted into the street. The old stones glistened pink and beige from the morning dew, their dark crevices bleached by the warm winter sun.

Did she really feel that way, after only four meetings? Dvorah thought with a touch of envy. How odd. She still didn't feel comfortable with Yaakov, even now when their bodies were finally joined together in the most extreme manner possible. She had just found out she was carrying his child.

She hadn't told anyone yet. First, because it was considered an invitation to the Evil Eye to talk of it until the fetus was three months old; and second, because she hadn't sorted out her own emotions yet. She knew when she presented this news to the world, she would have to develop the proper face to go with it. The face that revealed the correct feelings of gratefulness to G-d, recognition of blessing, anxious maternal yearnings, undiluted joy. But first, first, she told herself, I must find out how I really feel, and then it will be all right. I can go through anything if I know how I really feel, she told herself. Right now was too soon. There was only shock now, and a secret, shameful dismay. Nothing there she could admit or reveal.

It would take time. She looked at Dina, blossoming and full of calm happiness. "Don't compare your experience with mine. Remember, Yaakov wasn't my first *shiddach*."

"But does that matter? Isn't it just the way you feel? Does it matter when the person comes along? If he's your first or your hundredth . . ."

"Hundredth!"

"Well, you know what I mean."

"I suppose I do," Dvorah said uncomfortably. She had no answer. "I'm very happy for you, Dina. Just . . ."

Dina looked up suspiciously. This was happening a lot lately. Dvorah seemed to be backing off, to be hedging.

"I care for him. He is a good man. He is right for me. I feel this."

"You're so incredibly young, how can you know?"

"I know," Dina repeated with uncharacteristic stubbornness.

"Just don't get too attached yet. There is a long way to go," Dvorah warned. She was sorry the moment she'd said it, seeing Dina's face burn into a flame of unhappiness.

Dvorah felt the complex emotions of unworthy envy and unselfish concern coalesce with uncomfortable results. She was really happy for Dina. After all, hadn't she engineered it all? Yet she couldn't help contrasting her sister's uncomplicated excitement and joy with her own misery and uncertainty. And then there was something else, a conversation with Yaakov that weighed on her like a sack of ice on a winter's day.

"But what's wrong?" Dina asked. "Abraham's already spoken to *Aba* and *Ima*."

"I know. And *Aba* thinks the world of him. But it isn't over yet. There's still, you know, his parents have to meet ours."

"*Aba* said next week, Thursday. That isn't so long." A young man passed her, and she saw the furtive interest in his quickly averted glance. It was something she wouldn't have noticed just a little while before. But now she'd become highly sensitive, like a quivering bud unfolding in its first bloom. She was aware of every inch of her body, her eyes, her hair, her tiny waist and slender, perfect legs.

The world seemed so different. This connection between men and women was so strong, a current that flowed with the dangerous high voltage of electric power, invisible until you felt the powerful shock in all its numbing reality.

She was not the same person she had been two weeks before. She didn't even recognize that little, ignorant girl, that sheltered child, satisfied with childish things. The person she was now was frighteningly willful. Something long slumbering had been shaken into life and had sprung up and grabbed her in an intractable embrace, molding her will to its.

Was it Abraham? Or was it simply the sweet, dangerous knowledge that he had brought her?

A person was not supposed to learn Kabala, the mystic

secrets at the heart of the Creation, until one was forty, because before then one didn't have the maturity to survive being swept away by it. Only four had learned this knowledge: one had died, the other gone insane, and the third had lost his faith completely. Only Rabbi Akiva had ascended into the stratosphere of forbidden knowledge and returned unharmed.

But what knowledge was there, she wondered, more perilous than what she had just discovered? The knowledge that the body yearns for connection, for hands and lips and the press of one heart against another? And that these things had nothing to do with her soul? What could be more perilous, more startling, than that? she wondered. And now, traveling so fast into her own stratosphere, which of the four things would happen to her? she wondered. Death, insanity, apostasy, or survival?

She was a little angry, too. Why hadn't anyone thought to tell her? All the teachers in Beit Yaakov with their mealymouthed hints and pious platitudes. Even her mother and Dvorah, married women! Why hadn't they prepared her for what her body was going to do, how it would rise up and assert itself and block out all reason? They must have known, she thought.

"Dvorah, Dina!" A familiar voice broke her reverie.

It was Mrs. Schwarzberg, a neighbor. "I understand a mazel tov should be coming soon!" Both sisters looked up, appalled.

"Oh, I shouldn't have said anything?" She gave herself a mock slap on the mouth. "But a few times I have seen him come to get you. Such a fine young man! It should be in a good hour! Such lovely girls, all of you. And your parents, the most wonderful people, they deserve only the best. . . ." She went on and on.

Dvorah exhaled a small sigh of relief. Of course, Dina's going out was the only thing anyone could know about, she thought, her hand going instinctively to her stomach. But her relief was short-lived. How many people knew about Dina and Abraham? she calculated with sudden panic. The neighbors, Dina's friends, relatives? The conversation with Yaakov flashed through her mind like a steel blade:

"Of course, he'll be going on to *kollel*, so there's the matter of support. There has to be an income," Yaakov had said offhandedly.

"Dina will work. She'll teach, as I do," she'd answered comfortably.

"It won't be enough. For a scholar like Abraham, the parents have been led to believe they can demand and get the four keys from any prospective bride."

"The four keys?"

"House keys, car keys, safe keys, and office keys!"

"Oh, so why didn't you get this settled before they met! What can be done now?"

"I am not a *shadchen!* What did I know?" he'd replied with what was lately becoming a very familiar look: abused, peevish.

"But surely the Breitmans are good people. If the match is *beshert*, ordained from heaven, then certainly they will make some compromises. Leave that to *Aba* and *Ima*," she'd placated.

His only reply before returning to his reading had been a helpless shrug.

Dvorah looked at her sister smiling shyly at Mrs. Schwarzberg. She was blushing at the woman's compliments, feeling herself just a fraction away from being able to lift her face to the sun and accept the mazel tovs and good wishes that would sprinkle magic over her life like a delightful summer shower.

Dvorah felt her face grow hot, then ice cold as she considered the other possibilities.

CHAPTER 7

THE DOOR OPENED SLOWLY. "COME IN, PLEASE, A GREAT honor!" Abraham Breitman's father told the Reichs. Rabbi Reich extended his hand, and the two heavily bearded men shook with real warmth. The women were more formal.

"Rebbetzin Reich." Rebbetzin Brindel Breitman nodded correctly.

"Rebbetzin Breitman," came Faigie Reich's mild reply.

Dina and Abraham were not present. Rebbetzin Breitman especially had thought this wise.

The house smelled of furniture polish and cookies baking in the oven. The living room was dominated by a twelve-foot-long bookcase that held hundreds of volumes of *sifrey kodesh*, holy books, and silver ritual objects: heavy silver candlesticks, spice boxes for *havdalah*, wine cups, heavily inlaid silver ethrog holders, Chanukah menorahs, silver knives to cut the challah bread, and even a little silver box to hold matches just for lighting the Sabbath candles.

The table, however, held only a few ordinary glasses and a plain pitcher of juice. It was a boardroom table, set for serious business negotiations. They had hardly been seated when Brindel Breitman, her hand at her throat, said plaintively: "I must say this is all most irregular. Most disturbing. That the children have met and, as I understand from Abraham, formed some kind of connection, before any of the *siddurim*, the arrangements, have been discussed between us . . ."

Rabbi Breitman held up his hand, silencing his wife. "We have heard only wonderful things about Dina. We know she would make a fine, G-d-fearing *baleboosteh* for any Torah scholar. We know the Reich family, and it would be an honor to join our two families together."

The Reichs relaxed a little, Rebbetzin Reich adjusting her wig, which suddenly felt like a tourniquet around her sweating brow, Rabbi Reich smoothing his fingers nervously through his beard.

"But my wife is right. Yaakov, your son-in-law, is a wonderful *talmid*. But a *shadchen* he's not. This discussion between us was delayed too long. We should have settled all this long before the children even met."

"To settle, to settle," Rabbi Reich said cheerfully. "Is it not all in G-d's hands? Is it not a *chesed*, an act of divine compassion, that two wonderful people, my daughter and your blessed son—may he grow great in Torah!—have met and decided to marry!"

Rebbetzin Breitman stood up abruptly from the table, almost knocking over her chair. "To marry! We are very far from any such talk! Why, nothing has been settled! Who will provide the wedding? And the apartment? Who will furnish it? And who will provide a monthly income so that

Abraham can go on learning? Weddings! Weddings we talk about at the end, not at the beginning. It's . . . it's . . . too much!" She sank back onto her seat.

"I know that everything that is said here, in the home of such wonderful, G-d-fearing people, about which it is written, 'Blessed are you, O tents of my people Israel,' comes from goodness, from fear of heaven." Rabbi Reich spoke softly, addressing his remarks directly to Rabbi Breitman, not even allowing his eyes to stray in the direction of Rebbetzin Breitman. Anything else would have been an unforgivable breach of modesty. He stroked his beard meditatively. "It is so wonderful how you tremble for Abraham's welfare, wanting to make sure he continues to learn Torah. May all the fathers and mothers of Israel be blessed with sons like yours, and may they all be comforted by seeing the days of the Messiah speedily upon us."

This calmed everyone down slightly.

"Now," Rabbi Reich continued in his same kind, gentle, unworldly tone, "of course plans must be discussed, decisions made on how our children can be joined into a life of Torah and mitzvahs. You know, it's written that forty days before conception a *bas kol* goes out from heaven and says, 'This man for this woman.' But not only that is written and ordained. It is also ordained on what day and hour the wedding will take place. Who the wedding guests will be, and who will play the music. Where the bread, fish, meat, and wine will come from. If we have the *zchus*, the merit, then G-d will help us to see our children completed in life."

"Of course, Rabbi Reich." Rabbi Breitman nodded approvingly. Then he slapped his hand on the table. "But now, *tachlis*, to the purpose."

"Why, weren't we talking *tachlis* all along?" Rabbi Reich said, puzzled. "What could be more to the purpose than what I've said?"

Rebbetzin Reich looked at her husband with pity and undiluted love.

"Let's begin at the beginning. The wedding," Rebbetzin Breitman said firmly.

"It is customary nowadays for both families to share the costs," Rebbetzin Reich said. "This is what we did for my first daughter."

"This isn't the way it's done among our people. We intend to pay for our daughters' entire wedding and to ask nothing from the groom's family," Rebbetzin Breitman said haughtily.

"We'll pay for the wedding. This is not important," Rabbi Reich said with a dismissive wave that made his wife go pale. "For a few shekels, let there be peace between us." In response to his wife's sharp intake of breath, he merely closed his eyes in her direction and nodded.

"Would you like a cup of tea, perhaps, Rabbi Reich, Rebbetzin?" Rebbetzin Breitman offered suddenly.

"Very kind of you," Rebbetzin Reich muttered in a strangled voice.

"*Eshet chayil mi yimtzah!* A woman of valor, who will find!" Rabbi Reich said to Rabbi Breitman, who accepted the compliment on his wife's behalf.

Brindel Breitman's long, cold face seemed to defrost slightly, the mouth melting into a tentative smile as she excused herself and went into the kitchen.

An elaborate silver tea service on a silver tray was brought in along with a plate of cakes.

"Now, I think we should go on. It would be so wonderful if we could settle everything tonight and have the *tena'im* by the end of the month," Rabbi Breitman urged.

"Once the decision is made, the best thing is speed," Rabbi Reich agreed.

Rebbetzin Breitman smiled at Rebbetzin Reich. "Now, the question of the apartment . . . ? Do you have one purchased for your daughter, set aside?"

"Rebbetzin Breitman," Rebbetzin Reich began earnestly.

"Brindel. Please."

"Brindel, let us be honest right from the start. My husband and I are not rich people. I have a little wool store in Meah Shearim, my husband is a teacher. We have eight children, including another daughter who will soon be of marriageable age. Our resources are limited."

"What did you have planned, then, for your daughter?"

"Well, our eldest married a boy whose parents bought half an apartment. The couple took out a mortgage for the second half, which we are helping them to pay."

"So you expect us to give half an apartment?" It was not a question. It was a cry of outrage.

"Rabbi Reich," Rabbi Breitman began in his long, slow, yet oddly determined way. "Thank you for being honest with us. So that there shouldn't, G-d forbid, be any bad feeling between us, let us be honest with you. Our son, Abraham, as you must know, or have probably learned, is a very promising scholar. He is also quite young yet."

"Twenty-two is he, Brindel?" Rebbetzin Reich interjected with eyebrows raised. "Eighteen is still young. Not twenty-two."

"Among very promising scholars, age is not important," Rebbetzin Breitman said with a dismissive wave of the hand.

"Still, as it is written, 'Eighteen to the marriage canopy,' " Rabbi Reich pointed out, his back turned away from the women, addressing his remarks to Rabbi Breitman.

"Yes, well . . . truthfully, we have had many other offers for Abraham. A girl whose father owns a plastic bag factory who has an apartment already furnished," Rabbi Breitman admitted a bit reluctantly.

"An apartment facing south, so sunny you don't need heat in the winter, where diapers would dry on the porch in ten minutes!" Rebbetzin Breitman interrupted her husband.

Rabbi Breitman pointedly ignored his wife's shocking lack of etiquette. "This girl's father, a G-d-fearing man, wants to support them for seven years, and then bring Abraham into the business."

"With a turnover of thousands and thousands a year!" Rebbetzin Breitman interjected excitedly.

"Not to mention all the plastic bags you can use," Faigie Reich muttered under her breath.

"What was that?" Brindel Breitman inquired.

"Nothing important." Faigie Reich smiled wanly.

"Does Abraham want to marry this girl?" Rabbi Reich asked.

"Well, actually, he hasn't actually, gone . . . that is . . . he hasn't met her yet. He refuses, until we can settle this, of course," Rabbi Breitman went on, his discomfort growing.

"One way or the other," Brindel Breitman concluded ominously.

"One way or the other," Faigie Reich repeated painfully.

"One way or the other?" Rabbi Reich questioned. "My dear, wonderful righteous Jews! The children are happy together. We are both G-d-fearing, *bnai Torah.* How could it end other than in marriage? How could we mar this G-d-given happiness that is such a precious gift? And for what, for a few shekels here, a few there? My wife, a true *tzdakis*, a rare pearl, may she live until a hundred and twenty, had no dowry at all when we married. Times were hard in Jerusalem. There was all the destruction from the wars. There were our brethren pouring in from Yemen and Morocco. We lived off the stipend from the yeshiva. My wife knitted sweaters and sold them. She began to sell wool on the street, and then the city let her set up a little wooden shack which finally became a little store. We lived in one rented room. We had four children before we took out loans and bought a place of our own. Two and a half rooms. We asked for nothing from anyone. We put not our faith in the generosity of anyone. He"—Rabbi Reich pointed heavenward—"fed us from His kind, broad, generous hand. We didn't live a good life? G-d didn't bless us? Our children will have a good life together. *No one has the right to destroy that.*"

The delicate porcelain teacups rattled in their saucers.

Brindel Breitman's hand fluttered protectively at her throat. "Things are different now, Rebbetzin. We don't want our son to suffer the way we did, or you did."

"Suffer? To marry a wonderful girl whose parents will make the whole wedding? Whose parents will pay off half a mortgage for their apartment?!" Rabbi Reich told Rabbi Breitman.

Rabbi Breitman felt sharp tears of shame sting his eyes. "All right, all right, then, Rabbi Reich. But what about *parnosa?* Who will support them? How will they live?"

"We could help them a little," Rebbetzin Reich said, feeling renewed hope. "But as I said, we are already paying off our own mortgage, half our married daughter's mortgage, and when"—not if . . . when, she insisted to herself —"Dina marries, half of her mortgage."

Rabbi Breitman shook his head mournfully. "You have to understand. We are not asking for luxury. We just want to make it possible for our son to go on learning as long as he can."

"Dina will work. She will teach," Faigie Reich said eagerly. "She's a bright girl, a hardworking girl. All of my daughters have been brought up to give much and take little. Another kind of wife, used to luxury, might be more of a burden in the long run to an ambitious, pious scholar like your son," she pointed out shrewdly.

"A teacher's salary," Brindel Breitman scoffed, ignoring her. "A chicken a month and watered-down soup!"

"This is not it, not it at all," Rabbi Breitman said, staring coldly at his wife. "We are not talking about luxury. Dina will work. But then comes, G-d willing, the children. Then what?"

There was silence. Brindel Brietman got up and

cleared away the dishes. Faigie Reich pulled down the corners of her wig, feeling the blood pounding in her temples. Rabbi Reich ran his delicate, gentle fingers through his beard.

"Well, sometimes the boy's parents are also willing to help," Rebbetzin Reich said finally.

"Yes, yes," Rabbi Reich exulted. "This is the answer. We must both help when the children come. I will get another job. I could work evenings, late, as a mashgiach." His eyes lit up.

"Rabbi Reich, my dear friend . . ." Rabbi Breitman laid a heavy hand over the other man's. "We are also not wealthy people. Abraham is our eldest. We have five other children. All girls, all in their teens. We must provide for them. We were counting on Abraham marrying a girl with means. If he doesn't, it will make it difficult, if not impossible, for us to provide for our girls when the time comes."

"Let me understand this, Rebbetzin—"

"Brindel, please," the other woman corrected her.

"Yes, well. Brindel. I want to be very clear. So you are not willing to help with their *parnosa* at all?"

"It's not that we are not willing," she answered uncomfortably. "Everyone who knows me knows the kind of person I am. I live for my children. I think only of their welfare. And not only my own children, but all our children. All the children of Israel are precious to me," she said piously. "But think about it. What a burden for you! And for us, of course, this other offer, it would make a difference. He could have a real *parnosa*, not just handouts from his family. He would be able to help his sisters, too. . . ."

"I understand," Faigie Reich said, the pounding in her head growing worse, her heart feeling a sudden sharp, debilitating stab of pain. She grew pale and poured herself a drink from the pitcher of juice.

"And your daughter is so young yet. I am sure she will have many offers. Such a lovely girl, such a wonderful family," Brindel Breitman said expansively, wallowing in generosity now that she saw it wouldn't cost her anything. "It will be better for you also, if the boy's family is more able to help."

"I don't understand. I don't understand why it has to be this way." Rabbi Reich shook his head in sorrowful confusion. "But perhaps in this case, it is not meant to be after all."

"This is what seems to be the case. G-d works in his own ways," Brindel Breitman said almost joyfully, pouncing on the opportunity to align herself with G-d in this delicate case.

The two men shook hands sorrowfully, Rabbi Breitman avoiding Rabbi Reich's eyes. "I wish Abraham and the whole family a long, good, healthy life. May we see peace in our land, and Jerusalem rebuilt speedily in our days," Rabbi Reich said. His eyes watered with pain.

"May your daughter find her *beshert* soon and get married in a good hour." Brindel Breitman smiled, the warmest smile of the evening, the polar cap melting and little laugh and pleasure lines running like swollen streams down from her twinkling eyes to her broad, happy lips.

"And may your son enjoy the sunshine on the porch." Faigie Reich nodded pleasantly. "Boys get a little too old," she whispered to the other woman, so that the men wouldn't hear, "and people begin to wonder what's wrong. I'm telling you this for your own good. My Dina is only seventeen. She is beautiful and intelligent. She will soon get over her disappointment. But at twenty-two, disappointment hits harder. A boy lives with a woman, Rebbetzin Breitman, not only with plastic bags. May he marry in a good hour!" She walked out quickly and did not turn around, although she would have given a not inconsiderable part of her share in heaven just to have glimpsed for a second the reaction on Brindel Breitman's face.

CHAPTER 8

REB CHAIM GARFINKEL HATED AMATEURS. MEDDLING AUNTS, foolish fathers, pushy mothers, misguided *chumash* teachers, even an occasional *rosh yeshiva*. All those busybodies who dove headfirst into the swampy quagmire of matchmaking, dragging poor, sweet young girls and innocent boys down with them.

He stroked his long, scraggly reddish beard, picking out the crumbs left over from breakfast. He stirred his tea, then took tiny burning sips through a cube of sugar that rested on his tongue. Would these same people presume to write out prescriptions with no medical training? Would they dare to drill teeth without having been to dental school, or prepare tax returns or build houses, or even unclog drains! . . . He felt the burning liquid course down his throat like a hot stream of indigestion. Yet putting two people together, joining two families whose genes would determine the looks, the intelligence, of countless human beings still unborn, that they felt was easy. *That* they presumed.

If Reb Garfinkel had been artistically or literarily inclined, he would have likened his predicament to that of the skilled, talented writer or artist. Just because everyone knew how to put words down on blank paper, or brush colors on a blank canvas, people thought nothing of trying, of calling themselves writers or artists, of producing countless unreadable pages and unbearably bad pictures. And each time someone with no experience or talent or skill sat down and wrote or painted, what he produced was an affront, a virtual slap in the face, to all those who spent years slaving to earn the right to produce just one sentence or a paragraph worth its name, one simple line drawing worth looking it.

In very much the same way, Reb Garfinkel was insulted and angered by all those who had the offensive indecency, the sheer, stupid gall, to horn in on his exclusive territory: matches among the Misnagdim, *haredi* families whose near ancestors came from Poland, Russia, or Hungary. That was his stake. His homestead. He guarded it with the same rabid jealousy, the almost insane covetousness, of an 1890s prospector in Alaska who has just struck gold.

Sometimes people came to him (mostly ignorant Americans or out-of-touch Europeans) asking his help with a match for a Hasidic family. Depending on his mood, he would either curse them and slam the door or offer them a seat by his rickety table and begin the long, involved explanation of why such a thing was out of the question.

He would sit with these ignorant fools, these outsiders, who looked at the black hats, the long *payess*, the beards, the black coats, and saw the same homogeneous world, the way some Caucasians looked at Orientals and thought they all had the same face. To explain the profound and manifold differences in the *haredi* world, he began with history, with the bitter differences between Hasidim and their fierce opponents, the Misnagdim.

Being in the Misnagid camp himself, his description was hardly objective. He tended to show the beginning of the Hasidic movement in Poland-Lithuania in the late eighteenth century as the banding together of Jews too ignorant to study themselves, who put all their faith in a charismatic leader, a rebbe, whom they would follow blindly. He left out the sincerity of these followers and the many scholars who were among them. Perhaps these things were not truly relevant, or perhaps he was just doing what any good businessman does—simply making his goods more attractive than the competition's. He would emphasize how the great tzadik and leader of the Misnagdim, the Vilna Goan, had outlawed and excommunicated the Hasidim—the whole bunch of them—and with good reason.

The idea that "all is in G-d" promoted by Hasidim was sheer blasphemy, leading to thinking of the Torah in unclean places, erasing the distinction between clean and unclean, licit and illicit. The claims made for the rebbe, tales of supernatural powers, healing, direct mystical communion with G-d, were also sheer arrogance. And the elevation of prayer above study, or emotion over intellect, was tantamount to *bitul Torah*, the denigration and neglect of Torah study. Besides, the Hasidim did ludicrous things. The Bratslav howled at the new moon in prayerful ecstasy. And (so Reb Garfinkel claimed with a straight face) some turned somersaults in the synagogue. Besides, they drank and smoked, all part of feeling "joy," Garfinkel related with derision, and back in Europe they encouraged their young men to leave home early and spend long years at the court of the rebbe. An anathema.

Then, if the audience seemed receptive, and the day before had seen a few matches progressing well, he might launch into a few jokes about the Hasidim. How they recited the morning prayers at noon because their rebbe did and how it turned out the rebbe had stomach problems that kept him in the bathroom until noon. Or the one that went this way:

There were two Hasidim discussing which one of their rebbes was greater. "My rebbe," said the first one, "is the greatest. He was on the road from Minsk to Pinsk when suddenly a great downpour of rain began. Being without his boots and raincoat, a long way from home, the rebbe looked up into the sky. First he pointed to the right and said: 'Here's rain.' Then he pointed to the left and said: 'Here's rain.' Then he pointed to just above his head and said: 'Here's no rain.' The rain immediately poured all around him, leaving him dry."

"That's nothing," said the second Hasid, waving his hand deprecatingly. "My rebbe was riding a horse on Friday from Minsk to Pinsk when suddenly the sun disappeared and the Sabbath came in. Now, everyone knows that you are not allowed to ride a horse on the Sabbath. He pointed to the left and said: 'Here's the Sabbath.' Then he pointed to the right and said: 'Here's the Sabbath.' Then, raising his hand just above his head, he said: "Here's no Sabbath.' And lo and behold, he continued to ride his horse."

They were jokes his audience seldom laughed at, although Reb Garfinkel did, every time. Time after time.

Although the bitter wars between the Hasidim and the Misnagdim had ended over two hundred years ago, and each group had grudgingly accepted the other as faithful soldiers in G-d's increasingly beleaguered army against such real enemies as Conservative and especially the unconscionable and objectionable Reform Jews, no love was lost between them.

To tourists, secular Israelis, and even the uninformed among the moderately religious who walked through the streets of Bnai Brak or Meah Shearim, the two groups looked indistinguishable. Both wore the black hats, the black coats, the long beards. Both studied Talmud in large, imposing yeshiva halls that rang with the voices of hundreds of fervent students. Both kept the laws of the Torah, the *halacha*, with the fearsome, trembling dedication of those to whom G-d is a constant companion.

Among those who lived in the *haredi* world, however, there was never any doubt to just which camp someone belonged. It was written all over them. All you had to do was learn to read.

For example, you could tell a Belz Hasid from a Vishnitz Hasid by which side the bow on their hatband rested: A Belzer wore it on the left, while a Vishnitzer wore it on the right. Every Polish Hasid wore a *spodik*—a high, narrow fur hat—on the Sabbath, and a Hasid of Gur wore the biggest one of all. When a boy married, he traded in his *felush* (a flat, low hat with a wide brim known among the boys as a "flying saucer") for a *shtreimel*, a hat consisting of a skullcap surrounded by a thick animal pelt—fox, mink, or even sable—that could cost up to $1,500 and was considered an appropriate gift from a bride to a groom.

The gold-striped kaftan and fur *shtreimel* on holidays meant you were a Belzer Hasid. The mink-trimmed *spodiks* on your head and tailored black silk kapote as an overcoat showed you were a follower of the rebbe of Gur. And if you were one of those Bratslav Hasidim, mostly born-again Jews, you took pride in mixing everything up and wore the special shoes of Vishnitz, the overcoat of Gur, and the hat of Belz. They were the "hippies" of the *haredi* world.

Misnagdim, of course, didn't have special clothes or hats. But if you were a respectable *ben Torah*, a sincere follower of the law, you tended to look exactly the same as every other Misnagid *ben Torah*. Your hat was large and black, but stylish, the kind a conservative American businessman might wear to church. Your clothes were, of course, mostly black, although dark navy was sometimes acceptable. Sometimes you might even have a dark gray or blue pinstripe suit. Years ago this was more likely to have been true if you were a Misnagid from America and your parents had taken you to Barney's to outfit you for your year's study in a Jerusalem yeshiva. But nowadays everyone was into pinstripes, even on overcoats. But to Reb Garfinkel's taste and opinion, a Misnagid worth his salt wore a conservative black suit and a hat or a black velvet skullcap. He deplored some of the more stylish yeshiva boys who wore colorful ties, knotted with a rakishly loose knot, fancy white-on-white print shirts and fedora hats tilted back forty-five degrees (he didn't understand how they stayed on their heads at all).

Among *haredi* women, the differences were much less noticeable, with one exception. The Hasidic girls of Toledot Aharon wore black stockings and long braids until they married, when they shaved their heads and wore a black scarf. It was getting harder and harder for Toledot Aharon boys to find girls willing to do this outside their own circles. Almost to a woman, *haredi* women were insistent on wearing expensive, stylish wigs and fashionable although extremely modest clothes.

Being lumped together in the eyes of the ignorant, however, had not brought the *haredim* and Misnagdim any closer. While marriages occasionally did take place between Hasidim and Misnagdim, they were considered intermarriages and usually mourned by both groups. They were accidents, the result of a girl and boy somehow, against the odds, meeting and falling in love without their parents' knowledge. Or they were, very rarely, the result of a family of Misnagdim losing its mind and consciously deciding to join some Hasidic sect or other. Rarely, however, did it happen that a Hasid became a Misnagid. In Reb Garfinkel's experience, once a Hasid lost faith in his rebbe, he usually lost faith in G-d too and went over to the secularists altogether.

There were only about twenty professional matchmakers in the *haredi* world. There used to be many more, Reb Garfinkel would hasten to tell all prospective customers. But it was such a hard business, it drove people out! As it is said: Two things are harder than parting the Red Sea—finding a mate and earning a living. So being a matchmaker, which involved both, was a few hundred times more difficult. Most matchmakers had a second job that didn't take up all of their time. They worked either as a mashgiach—a supervisor of kashruth, ensuring that meat and milk were kept separate in the kitchens of kosher restaurants—or they taught.

Like doctors, every *shadchen* had a specialty. One took widows and divorcées. Another catered to the poor. The most prestigious ones (among whom he counted himself) even operated internationally, maintaining subagents and a stock of brides and grooms in America, Australia, Europe, and Canada.

Each Hasidic group had its own designated matchmaker. A Hasid of Gur would never bother to ask for a match from the matchmaker of Belz, who considered a Gur Hasid as desirable a match as an Eskimo, a Zulu, or a kibbutz farmer. This rule, however, was suspended among royalty. It was considered perfectly politic for the daughter of the rebbe of Gur to marry the son of the rebbe of Belz, in the same way that the warring kings of France and England often mated their offspring.

Garfinkel had great respect for his fellow matchmakers in the Hasidic world. What a degree of control they had! How they divided up the territory so that no one would dare poke a tiny finger into another's pie! But then they had the advantage of having the rebbe's blessing for their work, whereas he, he thought glumly, had to rest on reputation, on results. But on the other hand, the rebbe himself was involved in the matches, which could not go forward without his blessing. Imagine! The second-guessing, the wrench thrown into the works at the last minute!

Fortunately he didn't have that problem with the Misnagdim, who usually made up their minds themselves and no nonsense about it, either. Or there had better not be.

They had better not start up with Reb Chaim Garfinkel or they would find (and had found) their precious merchandise piling up on the shelves going stale. Parents of rosy young girls of seventeen who had been too choosy, too greedy and unrealistic, often came crawling back to him when the girls were twenty-two and using rouge. Families with boys studying in the yeshiva who demanded not only an apartment and a car, but a duplex, three-bedroom palace, and a new Volvo could be persuaded when the boy was a nervous, frustrated, unmarried wreck at twenty-three that soon no girl would have him. Then they'd settle pretty quick for half the rent money on a one-bedroom place out in Judea or Samaria, and a motorbike.

Reb Garfinkel looked at Rabbi Reich sorrowfully as he listened with one ear of absolute glee. This is what happened! Amateurs. The girl was growing paler every month. She didn't feel like going out anymore, not even to family celebrations, because she was heartbroken and embarrassed. Seventeen years old and she was heartbroken! Feeling on the shelf, like used, unwanted merchandise! And the boy? He'd also refused to consider another. He'd spent months defying his parents until his *rosh yeshiva* had to get involved and pressure him. His studies had suffered. He'd lost weight. In short, a real *tsimmes*, a boiling pot from which no one would eat.

Only recently had the young man begun to see reason. A plastic bag factory. Was that something to defy? The girl's face he would soon get used to. Anyhow, he'd be in yeshiva, in *kollel*, learning all day. It would be dark when he came home.

He raised his sad eyes to Rabbi Reich's even sadder ones.

"*Nu*. So you come to see me now? Why not before?"

Reb Reich wiped his brow. "Reb Garfinkel, it was the children—Dvorah and Yaakov—may they live and be well. They meant well."

"Children," Reb Garfinkel muttered knowingly, then

softened his tone as he remembered that he'd been the matchmaker between Dvorah and Yaakov, as he remembered all the wonderful things he had said in the too recent past to extol Yaakov Klein to his father-in-law. "Well, a good-hearted boy, that Yaakov. Surely he only meant well," he agreed, his joy fading as he realized his limitations in milking the subject. He gave up. "So, now we start."

He took out a pencil and licked the tip, rummaging through his pockets and withdrawing a ragged-edged notebook full of coffee stains and mathematical calculations. He flipped it open.

"Name: Dina Reich. Age: Seventeen. School: Beit Yaakov.

"Now, what does she want in a boy?"

Rabbi Reich looked blank.

"Well, then what do *you* want in a boy? Better yet, what happened with Abraham Breitman? What wasn't good?"

"Everything was good," Rabbi Reich mourned. "She was so happy. But his parents wanted more keys than I have on my ring."

Reb Garfinkel shook his head. They'd gone out before this was discussed! Imagine! Before the parents had met and thrashed it all out, they'd let the young people meet and form an attachment! Amateurs! *Amateurs!*

He cleared his throat and closed his eyes, rocking back on his chair. He remembered the Reich girl from the wedding. A little one, skinny. With big green eyes and childish hands. Like a little doll. Some men liked that, he thought, shrugging. His own wife was five feet eleven and weighed two hundred pounds. She had borne him eleven children.

And the finances. He remembered that, too. The little store, Rabbi Reich's job. The mortgages they were paying. His memory was faultless. Being a Talmud scholar sharpened the mind. He had put his to good use. To marry off his daughter, Reb Reich would have to add still another job to his list. He would work around the clock if he had to, with complete selflessness. Most *haredi* fathers were like that. They never complained. Their joy was to see their children married to worthy partners. To see new, precious families begin to blossom. New grandchildren. What else was there?

Skinny and little, he remembered. She (and her parents) needed someone with a job, an apartment. Someone very pious and learned, of course, but a worker, not a full-time learner. Perhaps someone a little older who had set himself up with an apartment, a business. Not a widower, G-d forbid, or a divorced man. That was for a different *shadchen*. But still, someone who'd provide a gentler, easier life for her.

Of course the parents wouldn't like the idea. At first. They all wanted men who would learn full-time for their daughters, even the ones who couldn't afford it. It took a little more talking. And the Reichs were ready to talk. He had sensed that. They just wanted it settled. They wanted the girl in a white dress under the canopy, beaming and young again, with color in her cheeks. They wanted a wedding, and fast.

He began to feel that old pump of adrenaline that meant all his experience, his unique powers, were beginning to take up the challenge. A good match was in the air. Just the thing!

He nodded. "Rabbi Reich, I think, G-d willing, I have just the one. Let me call you."

Rabbi Reich clapped the other man on the shoulder. "It's a mitzvah, Reb Yid," he said affectionately.

"They're all mitzvahs," Garfinkel said slowly. "Every last one."

Alone in his living room that afternoon, Garfinkel made the necessary calculations. This one's parents were anxious for a marriage. The boy was twenty-six already, his business was booming. He had no time. But they were suspicious people, from his experience. The type that hired private detectives to check on family trees ten generations back. The kind that wanted medical reports and would ask for the maximum financially. There was something in the Reich family tree, he'd heard rumored. Fifty years ago, something, a woman . . . And also, why get the Reichs involved with another set of hard bargainers? He crossed the boy off his list. The next one was better. Also older, twenty-four. An accountant. But not very good-looking. Actually, not at all. Short, fat. So soon after Abraham Breitman, it would never work. She'd never go for it. Sure, if a year or two had gone by. If she was desperate. She'd had a hard time, through no fault of her own (amateurs!). With a flourish of compassion that he tried to keep to a minimum, he crossed that one off the list, too.

Then behind his tired, wrinkled lids a vision began to form. A store with wood shavings all over the floor. A broad young man with a black skullcap, beardless, strong hands, and discolored nails, wearing work clothes. He flipped open his book, looking through the others who were available under his private coding system. But somehow . . . He couldn't even say why. Yes, that one, he thought, reaching for the telephone.

CHAPTER 9

THE STORE WAS CROWDED WITH HOUSEWIVES PRESSING UP TO the counter in the Thursday afternoon madness that always prevailed in Minskoff's Fish and Poultry store in Geulah. This was the last possible time to buy the obligatory carp and have it ground in order to prepare gefilte fish in honor of the Sabbath. The carps, swimming joyously, oblivious of their fate, were netted, whacked, cleaned, ground, and handed to the customer in wet plastic bags rolled in newspaper. It was the freshest fish imaginable.

The little signs calling for modesty, indicating which side of the counter was for men and which for women, were roundly ignored as skinny, newly married yeshiva boys, under orders from their harried new wives, jockeyed with experienced 200-pound matrons for a closer place by the counter.

"Who's next?" the owner said with good humor, wiping his fish-bloodied hands on his apron. Frantic hands went up, indignant shouts of "Excuse me, but I was here first! . . ." All of which Mr. Minskoff ignored unless blows seemed imminent. Usually he searched the crowd for regular customers and took their orders, no matter their place in line, a strategy that ensured the maximum amount of churning turmoil and indignation.

Chaya Leah stood in the back patiently, making no move forward, letting the front door admit new customers who surged heedlessly ahead of her. She let them push her back in line without a murmur of protest. She was in no rush.

He was in the back room, but he'd be out soon, she knew. She wasn't disappointed. He was tall and solidly built, with dark brown hair and a smooth, creamy complexion. His payess, like those of his peers, other Belz Hasidim, were long and extravagantly curled, bouncing on his shoulders. His eyes were a deep, rich blue and his lips generous and amused. Chaya Leah watched him as he worked, his white hands quick and somehow gay as he tossed the fish onto the counter and expertly split and descaled them. When voices in the store began to rise dangerously, he'd begin to hum a Hasidic tune, swaying, his eyes closing mischievously in mock ecstasy. He had a good voice, Chaya Leah thought. Better than most of those yeshiva boys who made the tapes of Hasidic songs that were hawked all over the streets of Meah Shearim; the ones who sold tickets and appeared at *haredi* concerts in real concert halls—the men downstairs, the women upstairs.

His name was Moishe. He was the owner's seventeen-year-old son. She'd heard about him through a classmate, Fruma Rabinowitz, who lived near here. And while this store took Chaya Leah two buses and quite a bit of walking to reach, she had begun making the trek weekly a few months before, telling her mother the neighborhood carp were pale imitations in comparison. While Rebbetzin Reich had had her suspicions, the truth was that the gefilte fish had never tasted so good. So she decided to let it go. Anyhow, her mind was busy with other things.

Chaya Leah inched toward the counter. Already outside the store she'd switched earrings, slipping on the Yemenite ones and pocketing the little gold hoops. Mrs. Morganbesser had finally given back the dangling Yemenites, but only after humiliating her and causing her endless problems and near total disgrace in a parent-teacher conference, which both her mother and father had been forced to attend, taking precious time off work.

If Dina hadn't been sick, and Dvorah pregnant, she'd probably still be confined to the house like a prisoner, *mussar* lectures pounding in her ears from all sides. She tossed her head and inched closer to the counter. He was as handsome as a movie star, she thought, comparing him to the pictures she'd seen on bus stop posters and outside movie marquees. She'd never actually been to a movie and had only seen TV shows in store windows selling TVs or at the new shopping mall near the central bus station, which had TVs mounted on the walls. At home there were no magazines, but sometimes she'd go to the center of the city and sneak into used-book stores, where she'd flip through old copies of *Teen Movie Magic* or *Redbook*. Her grades in English had improved considerably since discovering *Teen Movie Magic*.

She tried to compare Moishe to the slick images from the magazines. He looked like . . . Matt Dillon, she thought. Or a dark Jimmy Dean. He looked better than any of the singing yeshiva boys. Definitely. Or any of the local boys whose faces she'd studied from behind the high, curtained partition in the women's section in the synagogue. Even better than Abraham Breitman.

She felt little shivers of anger down her back as she

remembered Breitman. May he rot in hell! Him and his parents both! He'd hurt her sister so! They said it was his parents doing, but then he'd started going out again, hadn't he? No one could force you to do that. You could just pine away, grow pale, refuse to eat, refuse to get out of bed. Then your parents wouldn't have any choice, would they? If he'd been any kind of *mensh*, instead of a wet *lukshen*, he'd have made it all right somehow.

Look at Jacob, the patriarch. Seven years he worked for Rachel his beloved, only to have her father, that rat, that *menuval*, switch brides on him and give him Leah, the homely older sister, instead at the last minute. Had Jacob given up? Did he say, "Okay, I guess you know best"? Not in a hundred years! He'd waited a week and then got Laban to give him Rachel also. So he had to work another seven years. So he had one more wife than he really wanted. But he hadn't given up!

She tried to think of some other stories in the Bible where love had conquered all, but couldn't come up with any. David and Bathsheba, but that was a sin. She'd been a married woman. Shocking, the whole thing. Good thing she hadn't had to learn about it with Rebbetzin Morganbesser, who'd probably have edited the whole thing out. Come to think of it, the Bible according to Morganbesser would be very short. You'd have to take out Adam and Eve, Lot's daughters seducing him in the cave, Dina getting raped by the Prince of Shechem, Judah mistaking his daughter-in-law Tamar for a harlot and "going in unto her." It would be a very, very short story. Maybe not even one volume, let alone five. She suppressed a giggle and smoothed back her hair neatly into the approximation of a ponytail. It was hopeless, she knew, but she didn't let it bother her.

The store was emptying out and she had no choice but to take her turn or look conspicuous.

"Next," called Minskoff the elder. "What can I do for you, young lady?"

"Two big ones. Cleaned and ground, please."

She watched him fish them out of the dark tub and gave them the obligatory poke of approval, touching the damp, satiny surface with repugnance. She winced as the dark, silver-yellow fish wiggled in his hands until receiving the firm blow that put them beyond their misery and one step closer to the Sabbath table.

She moved along the counter, her insides tingling as Moishe slapped the fish onto the counter. His hands and mine have now touched the same spot, she rejoiced inwardly, hardly able to stand straight. She kept her eyes down modestly, caressing his back in furtive little glances.

"Don't throw out the livers!" she suddenly spoke up.

"Don't worry," came the reply.

"And don't throw away the heads, either."

"Don't worry, I never do."

She paused. "And make sure you cut out the big bones before you grind it. And save the skin. And . . ."

He put down his knife and turned around slowly, looking at her with his amused blue eyes. "Would you like to come back here, maybe, and show me how it's done?"

"Why would I want to do that?" She tossed her head, making the Yemenites tinkle. She saw his eyes move slightly toward her ears, then back again to her face.

"Now I recognize you. You're a regular customer, aren't you?"

"So far," she said with a great show of indifference.

"Well, at Minskoff's you know how we treat regular customers." He gave her a mock bow. "Now, what else, please give me the list!"

"Oh, you seem to know what you're doing. The fish looks like it's in competent hands."

"Oh, very. Experienced and competent." He held up his hands to show her.

She examined them, blushing. The flat, broad palm crisscrossed with fishy remains, the strong knuckles and quick, agile wrist. "Perfect," she said with a bold smile. "That is, for this purpose."

It was his turn to blush. He gave her an odd look, half-appreciative and half-shocked. Then he turned around and finished the job quickly.

When she got home, she found an extra liver and an extra head in the bag.

CHAPTER 10

DATE: 10 ADAR (FEBRUARY)

I have never written in a diary before. It feels silly in a way, as if I'm talking to myself, yet also to another, a stranger. I can't talk to anyone real, and so I will try words on paper, instead of going mad! They won't leave me alone. Any of them. And I feel so alone anyway, despite all Ima's forced talks, all Aba's kind little gifts. He thinks I don't know the effort it costs him to just think of things I might like—hair barrettes and pretty handkerchiefs. He goes to little stores and ponders. I can just see his face, all bewildered and full of pained concentration in front of the little bows, the little linen squares, deciding which one will please me. Dear Aba.

I wish I could snap out of it. I feel overly dramatic and

slightly ridiculous. After all, as they keep telling me, he was just the first boy I ever went out with. And I am only seventeen. And I do believe that it is all in G-d's hands, as they never fail to remind me, convincing the convinced.

Despite what they think, it's not my pride, nor am I angry or embarrassed. I don't even feel personally rejected. I wish I did. I have such little pride that the damaged part would heal like a little scratch. And if I cared much about being embarrassed, I'd have the sense to stop embarrassing myself now. After all, isn't this wretched mooning and childishness much worse?

I don't know myself why I'm taking it so hard, except that simply, very simply, I miss him. Or perhaps the idea of him. I don't even remember very vividly what he looks like anymore. It's more like the outline of the sun. You can only just see the very edges. The rest you just imagine, filling in the blanks.

I'm not embarrassed. But I am ashamed of myself.

And yet, I feel I've lost a whole world, completely furnished, with little curtained windows and couches, with little babies and dinnertime conversation. It's all gone up in smoke, like Hiroshima.

DATE: 15 NISSAN (MARCH)

I wonder sometimes, what she looks like, the other girl. I want her to be beautiful and charming and intelligent. I want him to feel happy. Why should he suffer, too? I don't blame him. Honor your parents. Honor your teachers. They were all on top of him and he couldn't push them off without sinning. Without giving up a fraction of his share in Heaven. I know I will see him in Heaven one day. Many years from now. And I will ask him how his life went. And he will turn to me and sigh and search my face and be afraid to answer.

I must work on myself. I've lost too much weight and now all the new, lovely clothes drop from my shoulders as if I were a clothes hanger. I don't get out much. I don't like running into people on the street. Their eyes seem to know so much. They either pity or they laugh. Or maybe it is just all in my head. I don't know anymore.

School is fine. At least I think so. My teacher, Mrs. Heiman, makes me come to her office sometimes to talk. We have long, aimless discussions on faith and on marriage and on motherhood. I like her. She is still young and looks so happy all the time. Her husband learns full-time and everyone says he is an illui who will become a great rosh yeshiva *one day. I wonder what he does to make her so happy? All the things, the kindnesses. It is not so hard to imagine.*

DATE: 21 NISSAN

Sometimes I find myself thinking about the gardens in Yemin Moshe. I must go there soon. All the spring flowers are blooming now: roses and daffodils, tulips and pansies. I should like to walk up and down the steps one evening and just breathe the air and watch the shadows on the stones.

I cannot go myself, though. It wouldn't be right. It would look as if I were searching for someone, waiting for someone to find me. It would look cheap and obvious. My presence would be misunderstood and condemned. So I sit in my room. I read psalms and books of mussar. *I am still a good person. I accept all my trials as G-d's will, his way of making me reach within myself for new resources, for new heights. I must overcome these obstacles to be a better person, to win His love. I think I am making some progress. Day by day, the prayers seem to flow with greater force and sincerity. I seem to be able to envision a future now, without him.*

DATE: 29 NISSAN

I am not going to lie anymore.

I reread all the pious drivel I've written, all the adolescent mush and feel physically nauseous. Oh, the piety of Dina Reich! Oh, her large-heartedness, her saintliness!

She is ridiculous. She is a little child weeping in the dark waiting for a pat on the head that will not come. Did you think if you were good, if you were kind, if you were full of compassion anything would change? Would it make your father a rich man, your mother an heiress? This is all that matters. Money and more money.

All these months, I've lied. Even to you, a lifeless piece of paper with no eyes or ears, no mouth to repeat, I lied.

Do I even know the truth?

Yes, it's shouting to me from beneath all the pillows. It's banging like a drunken drummer, demanding some attention.

I am furious.

If I knew anything about the world, I would run away and find him and make him go with me. I would slap him once, very hard, and force him to explain to me why he has broken faith and started to go out again!!

I went to his yeshiva the other day and stood across the street in the alleyway just as the boys were coming in for morning prayers. I wore my mother's dark wig and dark glasses. I watched for him. But I did not see him. At least, I do not think I did. I saw someone who looked vaguely like him, though. But thin and pale and very tired in a rumpled black suit. This could not have been Abraham. Perhaps he has changed yeshivot. Dvorah will not tell me anything. She says all this has given her enough trouble. She tells me to forget it. To begin again.

I probably hate her, too. She will not tell me where he is, and so how can I know?

That boy, the one that looked like him . . . It could not have been, could it? My heart is cold and closed, like an old water cistern rusted shut by bad winters and neglect.

I mouth the prayers.

DATE: 1 IYAR (APRIL)

Ima and Aba and Dvorah are pressuring me to go out with someone new. Rabbi Garfinkel even spoke to me. He came by the house and sat by the dining room table and ate some cookies and drank some tea. He told me that he had made inquiries and had a few possible shidduchim *for me. They are all tradesmen. Businessmen. All have money. And I shall go to the highest bidder, I suppose.*

That is all I think about lately. Money. Wondering why some people have so much and others so little, and why we are taught that it is not important when it seems that it is the only thing that is.

Yet, Abraham and I would have had enough to eat. We would have had a roof over our heads. We would have had the richness of Torah and mitzvahs. Why wasn't that enough? If what they have been telling me my whole life is actually true, it should have been, as it was for my aba and ima.

Why is it that nothing I learn at home or in school ever matches the reality of my life? Perhaps it is my life that is all wrong. It doesn't seem to fit into the world as it is supposed to be. Why must I learn all the truths myself with no help from anyone?

They talk to me, and I seem to listen, but I don't know anymore if I can believe what they say. Can people be partly right? Or, when they tell one small untruth is it just the tip of the iceberg? Underneath, is it all a huge, crumbling facade of lies and half-truths or simple foolishnesses?

I've lost faith in what I hear, in what I learn. And even what I see. The only thing I believe in now is what I feel.

And what I feel frightens me.

Rabbi Garfinkel sat by the dining room table and looked at his little book. It seemed soiled and worn. Can anything new and fresh and joyful come from such a book?

There are two fine young men he has in mind. The owner of a fine bakery inherited from his father and grandfather. A hard worker. A pious Jew. And an accountant who learns in the evenings. Who already has an apartment. Furnished tip-top.

He spoke these strangers' names to me. He brushed the crumbs from his beard.

And there is a third, he said doubtfully. A carpenter. A pious Jew, but rather old for me. Nearly 26. He makes "trees of life," the wooden staves around which the sacred parchment scrolls of Torah are wound.

Garfinkel, of course, prefers the baker. "Trees of life" are not loaves of bread, he warns me. People don't commission new Torah scrolls every day.

What is his name? I asked him. You haven't told me his name yet.

He sighed, flipping through his book. "Judah," he said. "Judah Gutman."

Gutman, I thought. Good man.

"Well, it doesn't fit you the way it should. Maybe we could tuck it in a little," Rebbetzin Reich said doubtfully, the lines around her eyes deepening, her mouth taking on the tragic slackness that had lately replaced the solid, confident strength of her youth. She lifted the material off Dina's shoulders, pushing it in slightly towards her neck to make it fit better. Then she released it hopelessly.

"Here, *Ima,* you hold the baby. I'll do it."

Dvorah handed the active infant carefully to her mother, who looked down with a bright flash of forgetful joy that made all her features suddenly relax and breathe with new life.

"Look what a fist he makes." She took the tiny fingers into her mouth. Was there anything more delicious, more blessed, and more redeeming than a first grandchild? It filled her with so much love that it physically hurt, like some ballooning inward pressure pushing out against her bones and muscles. A little treasure. "*Neshamalah,*" she called him. My soul. Nothing else even came close. G-d, in His infinite mercy, always provided the healing salve for any wound inflicted on the faithful. Little Shlomie (short for Shalom, meaning peace) had been her medicine during these awful days since the breakup of the *shiddach.* The quick, easy birth, the perfect, beautiful little boy, the joyous circumcision ceremony, had kept her too busy to brood over what was happening to Dina.

She was not allowed to brood. This the doctor told her when she came to him with the pains in her chest. Lose weight and don't brood. Rest, he said. She smiled at the baby. Rest was out of the question. Doctors! But she tried to cut down on the slices of potato kugel and helpings of cholent on the Sabbath, the pieces of cake and cookies at kiddush, the herring in sour cream at Saturday night's Melave Malka feast. She tried, but it was not easy, and the weight was not impressed. It stayed put.

But little Shlomie—she rocked the cheerful, squealing little darling—he was the best medicine. Just feeling him in her arms, so healthy and new and full of careless happiness, oblivious of any taint or care or sin or trial, made her burdens disappear for a time. She straightened up and cuddled him, he who was so warm and wriggling with the force of irrepressible new life! He seemed to imbue her with new joy and strength simply by osmosis.

It was so easy when they were babies. So easy to give them everything they needed or to convince them the things they wanted they didn't need. You could distract babies, change their minds. Oh, the rattle is gone, take a teething ring. Or a lollipop. They forgot. They accepted.

She looked at her middle daughter, her precious, doll-like Dina, feeling again the ache of regret, the pang of failure. She couldn't be distracted. Yet the dress was so pretty still. Green silk, like a still lake in the mountains shaded by tall trees. It flowed down her lovely young body fluidly, modestly. If only her eyes would smile again! Who would ever have thought? Dvorah had gone out with at least a dozen young men, maybe more. She had accepted her fate. And Dvorah was . . . Mrs. Reich hesitated. She was not a fool, but a very sensitive, perceptive observer of the people she loved. Whatever affected their well-being beat inside her like a second heart. And so she hesitated to tell herself Dvorah was happy. It was too simple, and she had seen Dvorah's face at rest, the small disappointed corners of her mouth, the tired eyes.

She remembered her own days as a young bride: the intimacy with the unfamiliar male body, the hesitant, short conversations with the stranger whose life you now shared, the duties piling up with heavy, suffocating weight on young, inexperienced shoulders. Yet there was no other life. If the man was kind, as she knew her son-in-law was, her daughter would eventually find a deep satisfaction and a deeper happiness. Of this, she was confident. Dvorah's life was rich with all the most important elements: she had a pious, learned man who loved her and who spent his time learning Torah, earning them both a fine place in the World to Come; an earthly home that met all her basic material needs; and a healthy child to love, a son to say kaddish for her when she died, a boy who would learn more Torah and add further to her merits. She would have other children, as many as G-d in His compassion granted her.

As a *kollel* wife she also had status, no small thing. She was an accepted and treasured member of the community, with many friends whom she helped and from whom she received help. Why, when she'd given birth, women in the neighborhood had filled her freezer with enough cooked meals to last three weeks! And they'd taken turns watching the baby weekday afternoons so that she could rest and regain her strength. This was the way in the *haredi* world. You did not live alone. Your neighbors were your friends, and your friends were part of your extended family. Nothing could happen to you—no happiness or unhappiness—in which that extended family was not involved.

Of course, this had its price. She looked at Dina. Everyone had known about the botched match. About the reasons for its failure and about Dina's difficult recovery period. After all, they saw she came home and did not go out. They saw her face. There was no such thing as a private grief. Everything was shared with the community.

This was the way things were. Rebbetzin Reich could not imagine any other kind of life. The concept of "minding your own business" was a hostile, foreign one. For if you did not know what went on in your neighbor's home, or in your neighbor's heart, how could you help him? Guide him? Give him material and spiritual sustenance? Life was one big ship where everyone was rowing toward the days of the Messiah. One who let down his oars because of sickness or heartbreak or sin had to be healed, shored up, because he endangered the whole crew and all its passengers. He slowed down the journey and left the ship open to typhoons and battering winds and the destruction of lethal, mountainous waves that would drown them all.

Dvorah was fiddling with the material on Dina's dress, pinning it here and there. Dina's face was listless, frozen.

"There. I'll sew it up for you now, before I leave, so you'll have it for tonight." She felt Dina tremble and laid her palm over her shoulder. She could feel the shoulder blades, fragile and sharp, through the thin material and drew back her hand. She was filled with a spasm of guilt, followed by the familiar brief flicker of anger at her husband. Unfairly, she still had not forgiven him for botching the *shiddach* so badly.

The baby had done nothing to repair their relationship. It was her baby. What had it to do with him, really? She had given him this wonderful gift, and he had failed her. They had not had any more arguments about it, because he refused to argue. He was saintly in his pleasantness, saintly in his calm, affectionate good humor, no matter how she twitted and provoked him. He was kind, gentle, forgiving, understanding, helpful. He did everything she requested: he got up in the middle of the night and at the break of dawn to diaper and rock the child. He brought home mountains of paper diapers so she should never dream of washing a cloth one, as most of her thrifty friends did. He took the baby for walks in the carriage on Sabbath afternoons, giving up his precious hour of afternoon sleep, the only opportunity he got all week. He did it all cheerfully, graciously.

And the more he did, the more cheerful he was, the more she raged inside herself with uncontrollable, unreasonable dislike.

"You will have a lovely time tonight. He is sure to be very amusing," Dvorah said.

Dina looked up suddenly with interest. "How do you know? Amusing? Why, what a strange thing to say!"

It was. Dvorah couldn't explain it herself. Why not "learned" or "interesting"—the usual words? Or even "a good personality" or "fine-looking," the familiar terms in which men were praised?

"Because, *tuchteral*, my dear daughter, you look like you need to be amused," Rebbetzin Reich interrupted. "I hope he tells you a few good jokes and then you can repeat them to me!"

The girls looked at their mother with amazement. She, who never joked! She, for whom the world was a flinty, duty-filled obstacle course! But their mother's face was averted, looking down at the baby. The sisters exchanged guilty glances, Dvorah's a bit sanctimonious (really, how you have been carrying on, Dina, just look how you've worried *Ima* to death so that she's speaking in such a strange way. Jokes, for heaven's sake! So cheer up now!), Dina's accepting the criticism, but with hostility (after all, Dvorah, you were the one who started it all, who didn't know what you were doing!).

Dina forced a smile, taking the baby from her mother. She held his heavy, insistent little head and felt the tickle of silky hair inside her forearm. She ran her thumb over his satin-smooth, powdery knuckles.

What difference did it make whom you married? This was all that really mattered in the end. And wouldn't the rest all be the same, no matter who the man? The home you scrubbed and swept and shined? The home smelling of fresh clean linens, hot cookies, and brown, crispy chickens? The prayers in the synagogue would sound the same, the cantor's voice would rise and cry and carry you off with it every Yom Kippur. The smell of the citron and the fresh lulab branches would fill your nostrils every Succoth. Life would go on, one slow, circular motion, like a sluggish merry-go-round, and you would find yourself rising up and down, up and down, against your will, with no place to get off, no reason to get off. The important thing was to hop on before it was too late. To get your ride, along with all the others.

She looked at the baby. A new person, with no past, she suddenly realized. The infant giggled. The sun came pouring through the windows. In the next room her brothers were already clattering in, home from yeshiva, hungry and tired. The smell of warm cooked potatoes and boiling chicken soup filled the spotlessly clean home. She felt inexplicably happy as she thought of the evening ahead.

Later that night, alone in the bathroom, she took out the diary and read it through from beginning to end, a certain sick pain of recognition making her blush. Then she tore the pages into tiny, tiny pieces and flushed them away.

A future. It almost seemed possible.

CHAPTER 11

THE NOISE OF THE LATHES, THE SAWING AND HAMMERING, filled the street known in Meah Shearim as the "Street of Carpenters." The small, matronly woman strode heavily but surprisingly briskly on swollen, ankleless legs, her arthritis-deformed and twisted fingers holding a heavy tray with clumsy care. She nodded curtly to passersby, barely acknowledging the respectful greetings of the workingmen who called out to her at every turn. Her eyes trained low, her head butting forward like an angry bull, she rushed on with frustrating slowness, intent on her errand and filled with anxiety.

"Judah," she called into the shop, forced to scream with unladylike loudness above the screech and scrape of the turning lathe. A cloud of sparks and dust boiled up out of the shop front. "Judah," she repeated, exhausted and nearing the extreme limits of frustration bordering on despair. She balanced the tray precariously on one arm and used the back of her hand to create a tiny clean circle in the dirty window, opaque with dust. She peered through and saw her son standing by the machine. Blind and deaf, she thought. Oblivious. Time was passing, it was getting late, and still he worked on! And what would he have from all this? A good living, it was true. But a home with his mother. It wasn't right! He was already twenty-six years old.

Oh, she knew what the neighbors thought. She a widow and he her only child, and on top of that a *ben zikkunim*, a child born late in life. They all thought she wanted him home with her. That she liked his company. That he helped her.

That was all very well and good. It might even be true. But she could never understand what relation or relevance any of that had to the difficult and nearly tragic fact that he was twenty-six years old and still not married. A man needed a wife. This was the rightful scheme of things. A wife. A home. Children. It was a disgrace to her that he was still at home. She hadn't done her job right.

She caught a vague glimpse of him within the storm of flying wooden chips and golden sparks and the cloudy screen of sawdust. His eyes were squinting in concentration, carelessly unprotected by goggles; his forehead, intent, in pleats. His whole body was bent toward the wood, which he grasped expertly, in powerful yet oddly delicate hands.

Everything about him was large and handsome: his hands, his feet, his shoulders, his chest. Had there been any arrogance in him, the swagger of a less sensitive, commoner man, his imposing height and broadness would have seemed kingly, even a bit dangerous. But the unruliness of his curly brown hair, the boyish gentleness in his dark, intelligent eyes, drained the threat out of his largeness, leaving behind a presence that was wholly friendly and without demands.

The sight of her son's absolute absorption only increased Mrs. Gutman's fury, if that was possible. She knocked on the glass and screamed his name through the door. She saw him suddenly rear his head, bewildered, and heard the low moaning protest of the lathe closing down, the slow scraping movement of his footsteps through the wood shavings.

"Momma!" His tone was cheerful, surprised.

She shoved the tray at his chest like a lance. "Don't say one word! Not another word. Look at the clock, my fine son!"

"The clock?" His tone was vaguely uneasy.

"The clock, of course the clock! The time, dummkopf!" She was in a near panic.

"Momma! Why did you walk so far, and with this heavy tray," he protested, pained.

"What else can I do if my son is a dummkopf and forgets to come home to eat! Forgets that tonight he has to meet, G-d willing, a bride?"

He hung his head, running nervous fingers through his untamed crop of heavy curls. He towered over his mother, yet his body seemed bent in utter submission, like a bear beside its trainer.

"Is it so late already? I must have forgotten. . . ."

"Four o'clock and you haven't eaten lunch yet! You'd forget to live, if I let you! Eat, then remember, home by six," she ordered him. "And don't forget the haircut!"

"Yes, Momma," he said dutifully.

"And don't forget not to lacquer anything today. You know the smell of that stuff is impossible to wash out of your hands."

"I'll remember, Momma."

"And remember, pretty young girls like Dina Reich don't grow on trees! Although why she's agreed to go out with you is beyond me. Even Garfinkel doesn't understand it. So be on your best behavior. And none of that turpentine, either. It never gets out of your hair. You'll smell like a new table instead of a prospective new husband."

"Of course, you're right, Momma."

The tone was just a bit too respectful, she thought, looking up and scanning his face. He coughed, covering his lips with his paint-stained hands. But she could see the laughter in his eyes. She gave him a shrewd smile, reaching up to slap his shoulder. "So laugh at a mother. What do I care? Just get married already!" She turned to go, lifting her cheek up to him, still aggrieved. He bent down and planted a gentle, dutiful kiss. "And don't 'Yes, Momma' me anymore. Just eat, drink, live, and get married. Do I ask more from life? No. Is that too much to ask? No." She shuffled off, muttering softly to herself.

He watched her painful progress with guilty relief until she finally disappeared around the corner.

He balanced the tray on a sawhorse, then with a wide energetic sweep of arm cleared a cluttered tabletop, sending wood chips and used sandpaper and old newspapers flying into the air. He washed his hands carefully under a rusty faucet, soaping them with vigor. He dried them carefully on a surprisingly clean towel. He examined his nails under the light to make sure no particles still stuck beneath them, to double-check the absolute cleanliness of the hands from wrist to nails' ends. Satisfied, he took a large two-handled cup and carefully filled it to the brim, then he poured it first twice over his right hand and then, switching hands, twice over his left. He rubbed his hands together, squeezing out the excess drops, dried them, then closed his eyes and said with devotion: "Blessed are You, O G-d, King of the Universe, Who has sanctified us with His commandments and commanded us on the washing of hands." He then took a piece of bread and salted it: "Blessed are You, O L-rd, King of the Universe, Who brings bread from the earth." Only then did he sit down [illegible] eat. He dipped the fresh warm rolls into the thick hot soup and ate like a machine, not tasting anything. His mind was elsewhere, still behind the lathe with the exquisite, emerging stave. He had been working on it for two days, and only now was it approaching the proper smoothness, the correct, perfect swell, the gradual narrowing. He thought about the design of the disks that would hold the holy Torah scroll. Usually he tried to pattern it after the design of the holy Ark in the Tabernacle in the Temple of Solomon. Not that he knew, exactly, what that had looked like, either. But the common imagination ran to a fleur-de-lis pattern, flowers and buttons, intertwined. Sometimes, however, some new idea came to him, filling him with rare excitement. Scenes from the Bible or combinations of letters entwined like branches of a mystic tree. He envisioned the complicated, three-dimensional relief. Just a bit too much gouging and the ends would break off altogether and the disk would be ruined. There was always that constant tension. The more beautiful the design was, the greater the chance of total failure. He didn't often push himself to the edge, being too practical a man. Certainly not as often as he dreamed of it. The designs were frequently burned into the wood with a soldering iron, and the smell of burned wood, lacquer, and dust filled the air.

For him, it never became just a job. The magic transformation of a piece of plain beechwood into a sacred part of the Torah scroll was always pure magic, turning the ordinary into the sacred. If he had been an articulate man, he might have said it was the best job in the world for a believing Jew, whose entire life was dedicated to just such an alchemy—turning the ordinary into the sacred. Even something as commonplace as washing your hands and eating lunch.

He had never said this to anyone. Never even expressed it to himself. Yet what he felt, he felt deeply, with the wordless depth of a small child or a great visionary.

The other carpenters, rough men who spent their days making Formica kitchen cabinets and bedroom closets for tight-fisted housewives and their debt-laden husbands, often came to visit him just to see his handiwork. Many times, too, they came for small loans to tide them over until customers paid, or to borrow tools. He was known as a great pushover. He was also universally respected and held with the deepest affection and a bit of contempt as well. A great baby, many of the younger men thought. Living with his mother, going home for lunch. Never seen with a woman (they would have known). And what woman would have him, the great lummox! Never a word to say for himself.

But the older, wiser men regretted they had no unmarried daughters.

It was in Judah's shop that all the religious carpenters gathered three times a day to create a minyan, the required quorum of ten men needed for prayer services. From behind the power saw, wooden lecterns were pulled out and dusted off, a shoe box filled with prayer books was taken out, and even a small, precious Torah scroll made its appearance, completing the unlikely transformation of the dusty shop into that of a small synagogue. Often, one or another of these men would ask him to carve them little wooden menorahs or mezuzah boxes to hold the sacred scrolls put up on doorposts to guard against evil spirits and to remind them of their religious duties. It wasn't just the beauty of his work. Sacred objects imbued a special merit on their owners, which increased when the hands that made them were particularly worthy ones. They could think of no hands more worthy to make these holy objects for them than Judah Gutman's.

He brought the great meat sandwich to his lips and ate dutifully. Already he could see the mystic tree rising from the wood. Of course, it would be pushing it, putting stress on the grain in sensitive places. But the result, if it could be achieved! He got up, forgetting all about the sandwich, which dropped to the floor. He looked down h regret and lifted it up, shaking off the wood shavings and carefully removing the meat. The bread he would give to the birds on his way home. It would be their gain. He hurried to the back of the store and found the disk. With a sharpened pencil he sketched the preliminary design, his heart floating a little as he imagined the intricacies and the difficulties of the execution. He was elated.

He was also totally unaware of time passing until he felt a hand on his shoulder.

"Reb Yid, *maariv*," Lazarovich, the bedroom closet maker, said with amusement. Always someone else had to remind Judah that night had fallen and it was time for the evening prayers. Judah was the one who rounded up everyone else for the morning and afternoon prayers, dragging them to the minyan so they wouldn't miss the time deadline. But with *maariv*, which could be said all night, he needed reminding.

"Maariv already?" He was absolutely stricken. "What time is it?"

"Six-thirty!"

How could it be? He had just sat down for a few moments! The girl! he thought with sudden alarm and shy pleasure. His mother! he groaned.

Still, he joined the quorum of men and prayed with his usual, unhurried devotion. But when he'd finished, he ran to lock the store. Then he remembered the bread for the birds. He unlocked the door, found it, and pushed it into his pocket.

"Good night, Judah. Good luck tonight!" the men's hearty voices rang out.

Everybody knew everything, he thought. But how? He felt the blush rise up his cheeks, and he waved to them with good-natured acceptance. Then he flew home, his dusty, paint-flecked shoes pounding the pavement like a guilty little boy's.

His mother opened the door, and he avoided her wide and stricken eyes, rushing past her into his bedroom.

"Special order," he called out. "I'll be ready, you'll

see." He began stripping off his clothes and rushed into the shower before her voice caught up with him.

The hot sharp needles of water pounded relentlessly on his skin as he soaped himself with energy. Beneath the merciless beating, he turned his thoughts to the terrifying topic he had so successfully avoided all week: Dina Reich. Rabbi Garfinkel had described her wonderful family, their willingness to help with the wedding and living expenses, and last (although it was the only part that interested him) the girl herself.

He already had an apartment, thanks to his mother's thrift and her foresight. For years she had taken the monthly profits of the store he handed her—he wasn't even sure how much it came to—and invested it in linked bonds, stocks, and mutual funds. And then, about a year ago, she'd told him about the three-bedroom apartment she'd purchased, along with the appliances and even a living room set.

He didn't need or want a penny from the girl's parents, even though everyone insisted that was the way things were done. He remembered the things Garfinkel had told them about Dina and tried to envision the girl.

It almost seemed like a dream. *Shadchens* always exaggerated, everyone knew. But a fellow at work had told him he knew the Reich family and that Dina Reich was a "little beauty." And smart. And sweet.

He loved delicate, small things the way only a big, awkward man can. Tiny flowers etched into wood. Tiny birds pecking away at little crumbs. Small, opening buds. There was such a thrill for him in the charm of small things, their grace and loveliness contained in such a limited space. He worked in small spaces, little corners of wood. Or perhaps it was just his heightened sensitivity to anything beautiful, and small things seemed to carry more beauty about them per square inch.

A little beauty. He shut off the water, feeling guilty about how much he had used. Usually he bathed the Jerusalem way, wetting himself just slightly, turning off the water, soaping himself down, then turning the water back on for a quick rinse. It was a method born of the city's chronic water shortage, which had only recently been alleviated by modern water systems. Still, every drop of water was precious. Water left on for the whole shower was a luxury.

He scrubbed his body harder, as if trying to scrape away some of its bulk. What would she think of him? he thought without much hope. Women never liked him. They liked lanky, elegant yeshiva boys with white hands and spotlessly clean nails, hands that touched nothing but the outside corners of Talmud pages and prayer books all day. They liked men who knew how to joke or tell inspiring stories. And he never knew what to say. Oh, he knew jokes and stories. But just being with a young woman tied his tongue into so many knots that he wound up acting like an idiot. It had happened with every girl he'd ever gone out with. He wanted to be friendly and warm, yet they made him feel so stupid and clumsy that he felt himself acting that way, fulfilling their expectations.

He took shampoo and poured it into his hair, then reached up to massage his scalp. Only then did he remember. A haircut! That was why his mother had looked daggers at his head when he'd come in.

What was to be done about it now? All the barbers were long closed. A slow panic began to eat at his bowels, and he felt the sharp, knifing contraction of his intestines. "Dummkopf!" He slapped himself sharply across the forehead. He shouldn't have started with the new design. That had been his downfall, where he'd gone wrong! He was always going wrong and not even feeling it until it was too late, he berated himself.

He shut off the water and took the big, rough towel and rubbed himself raw with it. He used a corner of it to wipe off the steam from the bathroom mirror and then looked at himself. The steam still rising around him gave his complexion a ghostlike pallor. But what was very, very vivid, what filled the entire mirror, was his long, thick, unruly crop of hair. He flattened it down with both palms, but it was hopelessly long, hopelessly thick, hopelessly curly.

He combed his thick mustache, then took out an electric shaver and cleaned the day-old stubble from his cheeks and chin, mourning as usual that long beards and carpentry did not go together. Most *haredi* men wore beards because of the biblical edict not to follow the custom of the gentiles of putting a knife to one's face. Modern technology, however, had invented the shaver, which worked like a scissors, not a knife, making it *halachically* acceptable to shave without really changing the custom. With few exceptions, *haredi* men still wore beards.

He put on his bathrobe and went out into the hall.

"Sit," his mother commanded.

He sat. A few minutes later she was back. Greenberg was with her, from downstairs. He took out his scissors and a clipper.

"In Budapest, Mr. Greenberg was known as the barber of the aristocracy. Isn't that right, Mr. Greenberg?"

Greenberg nodded phlegmatically, clipping away. Judah felt his head growing lighter. "Momma, I'm sorry."

"I know. I know. You forgot," she said with rare resignation. "Listen, my son, I'm not yelling. Don't be depressed. Be cheerful. Be happy. Smile a lot. Talk about the rebbe's speech in shul. About the nice apartment with the new appliances. About how good the business is going." She wrung her hands in anxiety, hovering around him, taking long, critical looks at the work in progress.

When Greenberg finally wrapped up his scissors, his mother was smiling. "Beautiful. For this no money can pay, but take it anyway." She pressed a generous amount into the barber's hands. He opened his palms in alarm.

"G-d forbid! I should give up my merit for a mitzvah like this for a few shekels! Please, Mrs. Gutman. Invite me to the wedding. That's all I want." He hurried to leave as she chased after him with the money.

"He was faster than me, what can I do?" She sighed, pocketing it. "You'll make his wife a beautiful mezuzah box. Don't forget." A small glimmer of humor flashed in her eyes. "Never mind. I'll remind you. Go eat now, and then get dressed."

Although he had no appetite whatsoever, he felt the spoon and fork and knife in his hands, the food going into his mouth. The plate was clean, and he felt neither more nor less hungry than when he had started.

The clothes were laid out on his bed, all spotlessly clean and spanking new. A suit he had been forced to buy custom made, given the paucity of selection of clothing in his size. It wasn't so much his height as the broadness of his shoulders. He could never fit his physique into the flimsy little proportions of the average suit.

He dressed quickly and searched for a full-length mirror. He didn't exactly remember where in the house it was, so seldom had he had occasion to use it. His mother's look was one of startled pleasure.

"Now, just a run with the comb through the hair," she said. He bent down, and she combed and patted the hair into place. He looked into the mirror and couldn't believe his eyes, nor could he decide, exactly, if he was appalled or delighted. He certainly looked different. The dark suit, so beautifully fitted, actually gave his body a fine definition. He looked wonderfully manly, even distinguished. Only the paint stains on his fingers and clean-shaven face belied the picture of a *kollel* man. He could have been an elegant businessman on his way to an important meeting.

When his mother's back was turned, he remembered the bread and stuffed it into his pocket. He had rushed home, forgetting to scatter it along the way.

His mother brought out a tie.

"Do I really need one?"

"You won't choke. And if I know you, you'll need all the help you can get."

CHAPTER 12

"You look so pretty. If only you would smile," Rebbetzin Reich beseeched. She was standing next to Dina in the living room, giving her lovely dress a few appreciative pats.

Dina gave her best imitation of a smile, a little too gay to be real. Her mother shook her head and took her daughter's cold little hands in hers. "The dress is so *shayn*, so beautiful. Turn around again, let me look."

She turned around. She let her mother look.

A small pain, like a sudden needle prick, pierced the elder woman's heart. She sat down. "Try to have a pleasant time, won't you?"

"Is this the shopman, the carpenter one?" Chaya Leah

came bounding in from the bedroom. "Is he a big man? With a mustache and great, big hands?"

"Have you done all your homework, Chaya Leah?" Rebbetzin Reich asked her wearily.

"Of course, *Ima.*"

"Well, have you straightened out your room, then?"

"Why, yes. It's perfectly clean."

"Well then, why don't you help the boys with their homework?"

Chaya Leah looked around the room with resentment. "I don't see why I always have to be shunted off in these situations. Really, I don't see why I'm not wanted. I wouldn't disgrace anyone, or ask embarrassing questions. . . ."

"Please, Chaya Leah! Just . . . go!" her mother pleaded.

"How am I ever going to learn anything if I keep getting shoved out of the way whenever anything interesting happens? You're all so mean to me!"

Her tone, bordering on defiance and disrespect, left a shocked trough of silence in its wake. Ezra hurried into the room, his serious face shocked; gentle Benyamin and little Duvid looked close to tears. Even wild Asher and Shimon Levi the troublemaker seemed overwhelmed.

Then the uproar began.

"How dare you speak to *Ima* like that!" Dina shouted, her nerves already stretched to the breaking point.

"And to upset Dina just now, why, it's just typical," Dvorah lambasted her.

But most devastating of all was the mild rebuke of Rabbi Reich: "Can this be my dear Chaya Leah speaking?" he asked in his soft, patient way. "It can't be, it must be someone else. A mistake. My dear good child would never speak in such a way to her parents. Would never upset her sister a few moments before a fine young man was to come to meet her. . . ."

Chaya Leah burst into loud sobs.

Just then the doorbell rang.

Everyone froze. Chaya Leah's sobs were still filling the living room. Dvorah took her youngest sister firmly by the hand, leading her into the bedroom, while Ezra rounded up the boys into their own room. Chaya Leah's sobs suddenly got softer, then were replaced by an odd, muffled silence.

Judah Gutman stood at the threshold, his silent presence filling the small room.

Dina looked at him with a tinge of despair and yet an odd sensation of excitement. He had no beard, and he was so big! Yet handsome, too, and manly.

The conversation with Rabbi Reich went swiftly and easily, the two men finding much to discuss. It would have gone on all evening if not interrupted by a softly murmured suggestion by the rebbetzin that she was sure he didn't want to stay out too late with Dina because she had school the next day.

Judah had caught only a glimpse of her when he came in, just enough to make his heart pound and the beads of perspiration dot his forehead as he realized that not only had Garfinkel been telling the absolute truth, but he had positively understated it: Dina Reich was the most beautiful girl he had ever seen in his entire life.

Numb, he followed her out of the apartment and into the fragrant, cool April evening.

"Where would you like to go?" she asked him as the silence grew between them.

"Why, wherever you would like to go," he said, hoping that was acceptable.

"Well, why don't we just take a walk, then? It's so lovely out."

"Yes, all right. Only . . ."

She looked at him expectantly.

He blushed and stammered, "Only . . . well, perhaps. Could we walk someplace else? I mean, not here."

People were staring at them left and right, nodding to Dina, examining him curiously.

She recognized the agony of his self-consciousness and felt a stab of pity. Physically they were an odd match. But, strangely, this didn't bother her at all. It was almost a comforting feeling to be walking beside such a man if you were a small, fragile woman. She felt enveloped, totally secure. "I didn't mean here."

"We could go to town, perhaps. Yemin Moshe?"

She looked up at him, flashing a real smile that lit up her serious features with the first real warmth he had seen in her since the evening began. "I'd like that."

The bus took forever to come. They stood apart, almost offensively distant. He put his hands behind his back, gripping his fingers painfully. He racked his brain for something to say.

"How do you like school?" he asked her.

"Fine," she answered, looking at her shoes.

Again a long, awkward silence. He glimpsed the bus in the distance and said a short, heartfelt prayer of thanks. But getting on the bus was even worse. He had to bend down to get in, and the little seats were not meant for his knees. If he shared the two-seater benches with her, he would leave her no room at all. She'd be crushed into a corner. So instead of sitting down next to her, he stood up in the aisle. He could see the questioning surprise in her eyes.

Why haven't I written him off yet? she asked herself. They were a ridiculous couple, weren't they? Look at people's secret smiles! Yet his silence intrigued her, and she felt rather grateful to have been spared the usual cross-examination. Perhaps he isn't all that interested in knowing about me, it suddenly occurred to her, a thought like a slap. Perhaps he's already decided.

The scent of the blooming spring flowers hit them immediately, even from across the street. They crossed the wide boulevard, he taking careful, measured steps to match hers, to keep from reaching the other side long before she did. Perhaps it was the darkness, or the vivid riot of flowers, or just being alone, but a wave of relaxation coursed through both of them.

"I love this place," she told him.

He nodded, engrossed in the silver sheen of moonlight on her hair, her shapely, delicate hands and feet. She seemed to belong in this setting, a rare species blooming with heart-stopping loveliness. You are so beautiful, so very rare and lovely. It hurts me to look at you, he thought.

"Do you like it, too?"

"Yes, I like it, too," he answered, almost not fully conscious of what he was saying. The white stones, bathed in silver, seemed like ancient obelisks in the courtyard of the holy Temple, sacred and full of hidden meaning. Then, with stunning suddenness, her exquisite, womanly body in the soft, silky dress was all he saw. Her face, like an angel's, unreal and smoothly sculpted by the moonlight, blotted out the universe.

They walked down the steps in silence.

She felt close to tears. He had hardly opened his mouth. Had she become that undesirable, that unattractive to be with, that a man didn't even want to talk to her anymore? She sat down on a stone bench in the park near the windmill, her feet suddenly weary. Carefully he placed himself next to her, making sure not to touch her in any way.

She felt exhaustion overcome her, rising up from her soul. She didn't care anymore what happened. It was just as she had thought. After Abraham, there would never be anyone else. "The first time I came here, it was raining. The stones were all shiny, almost polished. I'd never been here before, even though I grew up in Jerusalem. Do you think that's odd?"

He shook his head no.

Wasn't he ever going to say anything? "I think it is. After all, Jerusalem is such a small place, and to have lived here all your life and never to have seen anything as beautiful as this! It makes you sad, doesn't it? To think that there was this lovely place, so close to you, and which could have made you so happy, and to realize that you just hadn't known about it. It makes you wonder what else is out there, just around the corner, that can make you happy, that you're missing." She looked up at him. Again he nodded, wordlessly.

She found his silence terrible, bordering on offensive. And yet, oddly, instead of it evincing a similar silence from her, it had the opposite effect. She found herself pouring out intimacies and confidences she would never have dreamed of sharing with a more talkative stranger; it panicked her into an untoward articulateness born of desperation, the need to say almost anything to fill the terrible void. She just couldn't stop herself.

"The first time I came here was with my first *shiddach*. He was in *kollel*. But it didn't work out. My parents didn't have enough money. He's going out with someone else." She was appalled at herself! Yet she had kept all these feelings bottled up for so long that now, once she began, she was like a train on a track rushing down a mountainside with no place to detour. Anyhow, except for a slight alertness in the way his eyes looked at her, he didn't even react. Was he even listening? she wondered. She kept on talking. "I was very hurt, because I wanted him. I felt it was right. But G-d didn't let it work out. And G-d always knows best."

His heart contracted, feeling her pain, the pain of a helpless small creature caught in a trap. There wasn't a trace of bitterness in her words, he noted. How good she was! He felt angry at the unknown suitor. Jealous. All emotions he was unfamiliar with.

"Girls never like me," he suddenly blurted out. "They think I'm stupid and clumsy. That I don't understand anything because I don't speak very well. I never really cared too much about it before. But I wouldn't want you to think I was. I don't think I could stand that." He slapped the stone bench in frustration. "I feel things, but I somehow

. . . I can't . . . say them." But I could draw them for you. Or make them out of wood, he thought. If you would only come to my shop once, I think I could show you what I mean. But of course Dina Reich would never come to his shop. Why should she? He was a great big silent lump. Yet he wanted so much to comfort her. "I wish I could tell you stories and make you laugh. It would be good for you to laugh."

Her eyes raised themselves slowly to his face. It was shining with a strange light that comforted and mystified her. She studied the dark, sensitive, kindly eyes, lowered with shy awkwardness, the cleanly shaven, strong jaw whose muscles strained with strange emotion, the tender lips like a young boy's.

And still how strange and stilted were his words. And she felt she needed words. They were important to her. With horror, she felt the tears well up in her eyes and drop slowly down her cheeks.

His heart melted in compassion, and he reached into his pocket for a tissue, but all he felt was the bread. It took almost every ounce of willpower he possessed to keep himself from reaching out to her. He almost felt the satin smoothness of her wet cheek on his rough palm, almost felt the slow, infinitely patient draw of his large thumb wiping away the wetness, first from one cheek and then the other. He got up, turning his back to her, shoving his hands forcefully back into his pockets. "Don't cry," he said, turning around slowly. "I'm not worth very much, but all I can say is if you had wanted me, I would have let them bury me before I would have given you up."

The unexpected, surprisingly tender words felt like fingers on her skin. They injected a shock into her system like electrodes used in therapy. So unfamiliar, so wrongly, sinfully intimate! And yet it felt so natural, so right.

He took out the bread and flung some crumbs to the ground. First one bird came, a tiny sparrow, and then another. Pigeons and tiny blue-gray *nachnialis*, all shy, tiny. They surrounded him, eating out of his hands.

She watched them, her tears drying in the soft, spring breeze.

CHAPTER 13

DVORAH LAY IN BED, LISTENING TO THE BABY'S INSISTENT CRIES, unable to move. Her whole body felt like lead. She was so tired, so incredibly, achingly tired. A heaviness that started at the top of her head pressed down, compressing her sinuses and making her temples pound. Her arms felt weighted, her thighs and calves ached.

The baby's cries became more insistent. With tremendous effort she raised her head. A strong wave of nausea enveloped her. She groped to the bathroom, heaving miserably. Nothing came out. Nothing could come out. She had been too nauseated to eat for days now.

A virus, she told herself, giving herself hope. Mrs. Kornbluth upstairs had it. The grocery lady had it. It was going around. She groped for a bathrobe. As she put it on, her breasts ached. They felt swollen, tender. Many women didn't get their periods so regularly so soon after giving birth, she told herself. She hurried to the baby, lifting him. His diaper was wet and dirty, wetting her clothes. She put him down, and he screamed in protest. "Leave me alone," she shouted at him, furious. "I'm doing the best that I can!" His face screwed up with wretchedness, red and angry. She changed him. She took off the diaper, and the sight of the disgusting mess made her grip the table as she fought down a new wave of nausea. "Shut up! Shut up, shut *up!*" she screamed, something suddenly snapping.

The baby's face looked startled. He was strangely silent for a few moments, and then his heartbreaking, terrified screams began.

"Oh, G-d forgive me! Oh, baby. I'm sorry. . . ." She felt the tears running down her face, blinding her. She washed him off quickly and changed all his clothes, then wrapped him in a warm, soft blanket and rocked him.

"I can't be pregnant. I just can't," she told herself. You couldn't get pregnant while you were nursing! It was a virus, that's all. In a few days she would feel better. She would start eating again. She would call her mother and get into bed and rest. *Ima,* she thought. She would come and hold the baby and keep him quiet. She'll cook me soup and press her cool hand over my forehead. And I will sleep. She put the baby in her lap and dialed her mother's number, then, as it began to ring, she slowly put the phone down.

Ima had the store. She had the little boys. She had Dina on her hands, going in and out with new men. A baker, an accountant. And Dina looking more depressed than ever. And there was Chaya Leah, who was driving everyone crazy as usual. She had gone out and gotten her hair cut short. Curls, curls everywhere! And she was suddenly on a diet and starving herself and demanding a whole new wardrobe. *Ima* hadn't been well, either. More chest pains.

She rocked the baby back and forth helplessly. Then, taking a deep, courageous breath, she picked up the phone and dialed the clinic. She would go in and take a pregnancy test at nine. She would have the results by the afternoon.

The baby tugged at her robe. She lifted out her breast and took a sharp intake of breath as the baby's healthy, greedy mouth pressed over her nipple. She closed her eyes and tried not to think. She'd taken a year off from teaching to be with the baby. A year she'd looked forward to at the beginning. Yet now it was starting to grate on her, being home all the time. She missed the little students and getting dressed up every morning and talking to the other young teachers. She was bored to tears. Her life felt empty.

G-d will punish me! She quickly wiped the thoughts away. She was thinking all wrong. She had everything a woman could want, hadn't she? How she'd prayed for a husband, prayed for children! And now G-d was probably looking down on her and thinking: Ungrateful wretch! How you spit on your gifts.

She was filled with guilt and remorse. Anyhow, it was probably just a cold. A stomach virus. Please, G-d, just a stomach virus!

Yaakov got home at eight-thirty in the evening. The house was dark. He walked into the kitchen and put on the light. Dishes were piled high in both the meat and dairy sinks. The usually spotless counter was awash in little crumb-filled puddles of dark brown and white. He opened the oven, examined the stove, sniffed the air. There didn't seem to be any supper in the works, either.

He felt his annoyance grow.

"Dvorahle, my dear," he called out softly. He opened the bedroom door, and she was lying there, her head resting on the pillow, her eyes shut. He felt alarm replace his vague resentment. He touched her shoulder, shaking her gently.

"Are you all right?"

Slowly she opened her eyes. He saw the pupils dilate and the look of grim distaste and resentment flash with unguarded swiftness across her features. He was familiar with the look, but usually it was replaced quickly by a pleasant smile. Now it just stayed there, frozen.

He was immediately defensive. "I got home as soon as I could. The others are still there. The *rav's shiur* went on longer than we expected. It was, as usual, wonderful. But I left early, seeing as you haven't been feeling well." He looked at her expectantly for some sign that this was appreciated. Seeing none, he went on the offensive: "I see there is no dinner."

She stared at him, the grim distaste deepening.

"Well, at least can I know what's wrong? Is it the baby?" He began to grow alarmed.

She shook her head, and the slight movement made it explode with pain. "I went to the clinic today. . . ." She lay back, closing her eyes. "I took a pregnancy test."

He sat down beside her heavily, his hands reaching out for hers. But she kept them clasped together, tight under the pillow. "I called them in the afternoon for the results." She paused.

"Well?"

"It was *shlili.*"

"*Shlili?*" he said almost stupidly.

"Negative. That is, I'm not."

He felt a twinge of faint disappointment coupled with relief. "My dear, it's so soon after the first one. We'll have others. There's no need to be so disappointed."

She opened one eye and looked at him in contempt. "I'm not disappointed, Yaakov."

"You're not?" He felt himself slipping down that slippery slope into dangerous waters that he always felt now with his wife. Try as he did to find something to latch on to that would hold his head above water, he seldom did. Now was no exception. "I don't understand."

"As usual," she whispered. "What do you understand

about me, Yaakov? Do you understand anything? Do you know who I am, how I live, what I feel? Or am I just a strange woman to you, living under your roof? I didn't want another baby, Yaakov. I hate being home with this one! I'm bored, I'm tired." She caught herself. There was a limit to just how honest she could be with him. She could never go the limit, the distance she had to in order for them to be really close, because it would mean describing the biggest obstacle of all to her happiness. Him.

"So you're not pregnant! So what's the problem?"

Were all men like this? she wondered. Were all of them so thick that you needed an industrial-strength drill to bore a few ideas into their heads, to let some light and air shine through? How much did she have to spell it out for him? All day he learned. All day. And yet what did he know?

She tried to imagine her mother and father having this conversation and felt her cheeks burn with shame. Her mother would never speak to her father this way! She'd be mortified if she knew any daughter of hers had such feelings, or expressed them. Why couldn't she be like her mother? Why couldn't she look forward to the idea of ten or eleven children, one after the other, with faith and joy and submission to G-d's infinite wisdom?

She began to weep uncontrollably. Yaakov reached out and held her in his arms. "Sha, my darling wife. I know it's so hard for you, for all women. And I don't do enough to help you. I'll try harder." He stroked her hair gently, soothingly.

She buried her face in his shoulder. "I didn't want another baby. I was so frightened, Yaakov. I'm not such a good mother. I get angry and I yell at the baby. My own little baby! I love him so much, and yet today I yelled so loud, I frightened him! How could I do that? And I was so angry and resentful when I thought I was pregnant again. I'm so afraid G-d will punish me. I lose my temper all the time."

"All the time?" he whispered gently, stroking her head, her cheek. "Is that your nature?"

"I don't know. I don't remember ever feeling this way for such a long period of time. If it is, won't I be able to change?"

"Can a fish become a lion?" He smiled sadly. "You'll have this nature until you die."

"It can't be true! People change, they improve."

"G-d gave you this nature so that you should constantly work to overcome it. If you were always perfect, always feeling correctly, acting piously, you might feel like the creator of yourself, your own boss. It's weakness that reminds us of G-d, that makes us cry out to him in need. Listen, when you bump into the wall, are you angry at the wall?"

She smiled faintly shaking her head no.

"No, you can't get angry at the wall. Or the baby. Or me. We're just the messengers. G-d's sending you the message, reminding you of your weakness and also comforting you, telling you that you have the strength to overcome it, to go beyond your nature."

"Doesn't G-d have more important things on his mind than me and my temper?"

"Do you get *naches* from the baby? From every tiny little flicker of his eye, every tiny step forward he makes—holding his head up, grasping a spoon? Do you have more important things to think about? G-d is also a father and mother. He's our creator. He takes pleasure in us, in every tiny step we make to transcend what is base and shameful in our natures."

"I don't know if I can please G-d. I'm so tired, so very tired. I can't even imagine having another baby!"

"He won't give you one until you're ready."

She lifted her head from his shoulder. "Does that mean that we . . . can . . . prevent it?"

He held her at arm's length and looked into her eyes,

shocked. "You can't mean it? My dear wife, to prevent G-d's will from happening? To defy him?"

"It's not like that. It's just, taking a break, a breather. You know, the *halacha* allows it."

"Only under very strict circumstances, if the mother's life, her health, are in danger."

"Yaakov, can't you see I'm not up to it? Not yet."

"We'll talk about it, my dear. You're feeling tired, weak. You're not yourself. I'll help you more. Have you eaten? Wait, I'll make you something." He tucked her back in with motherly care and then went into the kitchen. He leaned heavily against the sink, anger, frustration, and sorrow mixing together; resentment, compassion, and love fighting each other off, making him feel weak. He took off his good suit jacket, rolled up his sleeves, and began to wash the dishes.

He searched his mind for appropriate knowledge to help him. Of course, there was the passage in the Talmudic tractate *Yevamot* of a contraceptive tampon used by lactating women to prevent any harm to her or the baby. This extended to women only. Men were forbidden to use any device. The L-rd punished Onan by death because "he had spilled his seed unto the ground." Modern views, in light of the Holocaust and the need to replenish the Jewish people, were stricter. Each case had to be decided individually by a rabbi. Some considered the mother's mental state, and others required there to be a purely medical reason for the request.

He finished the meat dishes, then started on the milk ones. He felt an irrational mourning fill him, as if he had lost something. They only had one child! They had not even yet fulfilled the mitzvah of "be fruitful and multiply," which required at least two children, a boy and a girl. He had always expected to be the father of many children. And now, so soon, she was talking about birth control!

Then a thought came to him that literally knocked

him over. He sat down heavily on a chair. Perhaps it was just *his* children she didn't want! Perhaps it was him? His stomach turned over with hurt pride and a sense of failure. Perhaps she didn't, and would never, love him.

He had been so patient. So kind. So considerate. He had tried in every way to be good to her. But it hadn't helped. Yet he took small comfort from their recent talk, her pretty, soft head leaning on his shoulder. She was a good girl, Dvorah. He loved her.

But did she love him? And if she didn't, what would happen?

He felt an emptiness gnaw him, taking large, painful bites from his lungs and chest so that he could hardly breathe. She was his wife. She was supposed to learn to love him. He would make her love him. He would try harder to reach that pure, good part of her nature. He would try to encourage it, to nurture it.

He went to the refrigerator and took out eggs and milk. He found a frying pan and poured in the scrambled eggs. He put it on a newly washed and dried plate, made a salad, toast, and orange juice, and placed it all on a tray. Ignoring with fortitude the rumblings of his own empty stomach at the sight of it, he took it into the bedroom.

"Dvorah, eat something!"

She sat up and smiled at him and at the tray, a smile that warmed him and took away some of the emptiness.

"This is so nice, thank you!"

He sat on the bed just watching her eat, hoping his stomach wouldn't grumble too loudly.

She took his hand in hers and kissed the knuckles, for the first time not noticing how heavy they were, noticing only the smell of dishwashing liquid, and that they were kind. An unfamiliar jolt of desire went through her as her lips touched his soft fingertips.

"Thank you for being so good to me. For being so patient."

"I love you," he said with simple, helpless honesty.

She searched his dark eyes and, satisfied, relaxed. Her husband was a good man. He loved her. And she wasn't pregnant. She ate with appetite. It tasted wonderful.

CHAPTER 14

The baker had had a red beard and flaming red hair, both of which seemed dusted with flour—or perhaps it was just her imagination, she thought. He had taken her to a coffeehouse on Ben Yehudah Street and insisted on ordering her two kinds of cake, a roll, and a croissant, all of which he had proceeded to taste and analyze. She had spent two hours listening to a blow-by-blow comparison of yeasts, mixing machines, oven temperatures, and cookie cutters. In a corner of her mind she could see him grown ten years older, the mild midriff bulge now visible through his good dark suit inflating to truck tire proportions. She could almost feel the heavy, dead weight pressing into the mattress beside her; see him shuffling through the house at daybreak to get to work, coming home early. He'd be there, bothering her, talking shop, just when the children needed to be tended to, and she'd have to pretend to listen and be interested. Worst of all, she'd caught him looking with deep concentration at her breasts and legs, a look of hunger. After that vision, she hardly heard a word he said and was too alarmed to eat anything.

The accountant was, if possible, even more talkative. And he played the game of Jewish geography—favorite pastime of the *haredi* world—with more interest, forcefulness, and persistence than she had ever believed possible. All evening it had gone something like this: "Are you any relation to Morris Reich, from the Munkatsch Yeshiva in Poland? No? Your family is from what town in Czechoslovakia? Teich? My father had a very close friend in Teich, Gluckstern. Mr. Gluckstern was a banker. Very well known. Did your father ever mention a Gluckstern? No? Well, what about the Reich family that lives in Kiryat Arbah? Any relation?"

After about an hour of this, her nerves felt raw. He was the first real male *yenta* she had ever encountered. He didn't say one word that could be mistaken for an idea.

Garfinkel couldn't believe she wouldn't go out with either of them again. "So the baker talks about baking, is that something to hold against a man? You know how much he takes in clear every week? Two thousand shekel. And that's only what's on the books! And the accountant, so he's interested in families and he talks a little too much. He'll soon learn all about your family and stop asking questions. Anyway, he won't be home most of the day, and Shabbat he'll go to shul. Listen, you know what happens to girls who are too particular?"

She knew. Garfinkel was pressuring her mother and father in his not-so-subtle way. He came to Mrs. Reich's wool store and sat down and gave her a long speech about young girls making up their minds while there were still lots of offers coming in. The baker was desperate to go out with her again and wanted to settle everything quickly and have the engagement party at the end of the month. The accountant too was in a hurry. He had even offered to forget about a dowry altogether and to pay for the wedding himself. He too wanted the *tena'im* held as soon as possible.

What about the carpenter? Mrs. Reich suddenly asked. Is he also interested?

Garfinkel didn't like the question. Judah Gutman was not for Dina Reich. The *shadchen* was a bit embarrassed by the strange impulse that had prompted him to bring the two together in the first place. Judah was too big, too quiet. And although it was true he had a good business, he was not in the baker's league, nor could he hope to build up the accountant's steady income. Aside from that, he was the only one of the three who was not breaking down Garfinkel's door. He hadn't heard anything from Judah after the date, and finally, although it was bad business practice to be the first one to call, he had had no choice but to contact Judah's mother. She had sounded close to hysteria.

"What have you done to him?" she'd accused. "He eats nothing! He walks around like a mourner during *shiva!*"

"So he liked her? So he wants to see her again?"

Her voice had taken on a pitch that made the phone wires tremble: "He won't tell me anything!"

"So he wants to go out with her or not?"

"What've I just said? He tells me nothing. Nothing."

In every business there were certain customers who were simply not worth the trouble. Judah Gutman and his mother were a case in point. But now, faced with Mrs. Reich's reasonable interest, he felt that in this case he had not acquitted himself with his usual thoroughness and style, a fact that, gone unattended, could have serious repercussions. A man's wealth, after all, was his good name.

So Garfinkel created a plan of action that was two-pronged. First, to keep up the pressure on the Reichs with broad hints about time being ripe and dire predictions about missed opportunities, elaborate compliments, and descriptions of pious, wealthy men pining away for love of Dina. The second, a less interesting and fruitful pursuit, yet one absolutely required in the name of good business practice, was to get the Judah Gutman loose end tied up once and for all.

So early one hot summer day, he went down to the Street of Carpenters. It was very hot, the kind of day that *haredi* men dreaded. For, unlike most people, their wardrobe made no concession to changes in weather. The dress code, established in European villages two hundred years ago, had been transplanted with almost ludicrous accuracy, ignoring geographic and climatic realities. They wore the same heavy hat, the same shirt, the same sun-absorbing dark suit and overcoat, in the sweltering Mideastern summer as they did during the freezing days of winter.

Garfinkel sweated beneath the brim of his large black hat. He sweated under the black suit and overcoat and heavy laced leather shoes. Once, he felt so hot he thought he might faint. He took a detour into a bank and waited on line in air-conditioned comfort until he felt ready to continue his journey. Although *haredi* families often banked with private individuals who kept accounts, gave loans, and generally managed money on their kitchen tables and on the backs of envelopes, *haredi* men nevertheless found reason to stop into real banks often during the hottest days of summer. They read advertisements on the walls, collected deposit slips, and even discussed opening new accounts until the heat beneath the heavy black fabric began to chill sufficiently for them to face the sun again. During the hottest days—the dry, dust-filled scourge known as a *hamsin*—they stopped into every bank on the block.

By the time he got to Judah Gutman's store, he felt his knees buckling and his throat contracting with the desperate thirst of a desert castaway.

Nevertheless he put on a cheerful smile. "Shalom aleichem, Reb Gutman," he said weakly.

Judah looked up from the wood beneath his hands, putting down the soldering iron. His face changed colors.

Garfinkel pulled up a chair and sat down. It was boiling in the carpenter's shop. "Please, Reb Yid, a drink."

"Of course, of course!" Judah hurried and took a cold bottle of water from his little rusting refrigerator (it had come with the shop; he would never have thought to equip his shop with a refrigerator just for the luxury of cold water in the summer), then took a clean glass and handed it to the older man.

"*Vus machst du?* How goes it?" Garfinkel said, handing him back the swiftly drained cup with a shake of the head and the closing of one eye, which said: Fill her up again, please! Judah filled the cup again, then stood awkwardly against the wall, waiting. Garfinkel sighed. "Mr. Gutman, a month ago you went out with a lovely young lady with my help. While I know that people such as yourself are extremely occupied with G-d's work, still, we expect a little crumb of information now and again. So I'll ask you again, Reb Yid, *vus machst du?*"

Judah suddenly fell onto a seat, his long legs stretched out in front of him, his head hanging down, supported by two fists on either side of his temples. "Rabbi Garfinkel, forgive me, and please don't hold this against me when Yom Kippur comes. But what can I do? What's the point of continuing? She doesn't . . . can't . . . want me." Then he looked up desperately. "Can she?"

Garfinkel looked him over. This was a different story! He found new energy going through his tired, iron-deficient blood. This was something a professional understood. Not indifference. Not reluctance. Simply romantic desperation masquerading as indifference and reluctance. Judah Gutman was terrified. Judah Gutman was hooked. It was written all over him.

This was worse than anything he could have imagined. What a terrible situation! A real work accident.

No one was supposed to fall in love. Certainly not

under his aegis and certainly not until they were safely married and preferably the parents of a few children. That was his whole role, to be the lightning rod in the *haredi* world, deflecting the wanton, dangerous, destructiveness of passion among unmarried men and women, serving as a roadblock to romance, a concrete lead wall sheltering young men and women from foolish attachments based on notions of love and desire. He was a professional. Just his presence, even his voice on the phone, was usually enough to cool down any feelings of warmth between a young man and woman. He was there to remind them that it was a mitzvah and also a business decision they were dealing with, and he did so with remarkable success. Romance had never gotten past Chaim Garfinkel.

Until now.

What was to be done? He looked at the miserable, lovesick carpenter and sighed. What decision was there to make? He'd started all this, and he would have to bring it to a respectable conclusion. That or have Judah Gutman's mother bad-mouth him all over Meah Shearim. Not to mention watch this poor fellow wallow in misery indefinitely. Who needed that in his book of deeds written in red next Yom Kippur?

"Well, a question," Garfinkel stalled. "This, I have to investigate. But while I'm here, let me understand your side. You're willing?"

"Willing?"

This fellow was a real talker, Garfinkel thought, sighing. Well, Dina Reich didn't like talkers, did she? A small triumph of irony overcame his reluctance. "My dear fellow, do you want to marry Dina Reich?"

"Yes!" the answer exploded.

"And do you have an indication from her of any kind that she might consider this to be a good idea?"

"No," he whispered miserably.

"Do you have any idea if she would consider going out with you again?"

"I don't see why she should. I made a total fool of myself. Why, I hardly said two words to her!" He was up and pacing, his big shoes mucking up clouds of sawdust from the floor.

"Well, I happen to know—and this is a fact—that Dina Reich doesn't like men who talk too much."

"Really?"

The hope in his voice was so pathetic, even Garfinkel felt moved. "Really. Of course, I have to look into this further. I cannot promise anything. I must speak to her, her parents. We must figure out who pays for what. . . ."

"I don't want anything. I will pay for everything. I want to give her everything. . . ."

"Wait, not so fast." Garfinkel held up his hands. "I represent you too in all this. It has to be a good deal for you both, a fair arrangement. After all, she would not like to come into a home as a pauper, an orphan."

"I only meant . . . I only thought. It's her I want. I don't need anything else. But why would she consider someone like me?"

"And why not?" Wasn't there even a fan in this place? Garfinkel fanned himself. He was literally melting. "Another drink, please."

As Garfinkel drank down the cold liquid, Judah watched his Adam's apple bob. Each swallow seemed to take an eternity. He was burning with impatience. His whole life depended on the next sentence.

Finally, satisfied, Garfinkel continued. "You're nice looking—when you get dressed up. You have a good store, a good income. A good reputation . . ."

"Then you don't know anything at all, do you? You haven't really spoken to her about me." It was a statement, a cry of infinite disappointment and sadness.

Chaim Garfinkel hated emotional messes. Scenes. Disappointments. Cries for help. It wasn't good for his delicate stomach. It wasn't good for his business. "Calm down, my friend. I'll talk to her today. I'll give you an answer today. But I have to tell you, she didn't like anybody else she went out with better. Complaints she had plenty. She wasn't shy. But she didn't say a bad word about you."

Judah laughed and grabbed the *shadchen* by the shoulders. "Really? Not a bad word? And about the others she did? She didn't like them at all?"

"And they talked and talked and talked. . . ." Garfinkel allowed himself one small, dry cough of amusement.

Judah laughed again and spun around the room, knocking wood pieces, nails, bottles of glue, and drill bits to the floor.

Garfinkel got up in a hurry, backing out toward the door. He was in the room with a man in love. He was safer in a lion's cage. "I'll call you tonight, when I hear."

Judah nodded wordlessly.

It was noon. The sun was low enough to scorch your forehead, to liquefy the leather of your shoes, to heat the paving stones to the temperature needed to bake a pita bread. Garfinkel hurried. The banks would be closed soon. Then, just as he turned the corner, he heard the pounding of a herd of bulls behind him. Arab terrorists, he thought. Or fanatic hooligans from the Morals Patrol. Garfinkel covered his head for protection and put his back against the wall.

"Reb Chaim, it's just me! . . ."

Judah Gutman's voice reached him. He looked up. The carpenter was covered with a fine sheen of moisture, his eyes were bright. He shoved a package into the *shadchen's* trembling hands:

"It's for her. Give it to her."

"This is not the way it's done," Garfinkel protested. "No gifts until everything is settled."

"Please, just give it to her. Today, before you ask her. And I want her to have it. No matter what she says." And then he was gone.

CHAPTER 15

"OH, PLEASE, *IMA!* NOT GARFINKEL! NOT AGAIN. I'VE ALready told you and him that I won't consider the baker or the accountant. I don't care how much money the baker makes, on or off the books! Or how much time I'll save not having to bake challah or cakes for the Sabbath or holidays. I like baking cakes! And challahs are cheap enough to buy. As for the accountant, I detest him. It won't do Garfinkel a bit of good to come here and pressure me!" She was feeling out of breath, as if she were running very fast, yet not fast enough.

"Dinaleh. He's not coming about either of them. He wants to bring you a present, he says."

"A present. I know. A cake. Or an account ledger. *It won't help.*" Just the thought of those two buffoons made her want to scream. I'd rather die an old maid. I can teach in Beit Yaakov and be the good aunt, her mind improvised rapidly. I'll bring expensive presents to my married sisters and brothers and their children. I'll be the most welcome invited guest every holiday.

"The gift, as I understand it—not that I approve, mind you—is from Judah Gutman."

She felt herself flush. The carpenter.

She had thought about Judah Gutman a great deal in the last few weeks, her thoughts growing strangely dreamlike and not at all to the point. The awkwardness, the almost insulting silence of their time together, had not completely faded yet just enough to make his oddly intimate and passionate words stand out in fine relief: "I would have let them bury me before I would have given you up." They were words that frightened her and set off a thrill, like the jangling of tiny bells, through her whole body. In her memory he didn't seem quite so big nor quite so clumsy as she had found him in reality. Her mind had insisted on focusing on his handsome, kind face, his alert, sensitive eyes. Remembered, his silence gained a fine, rich patina of sensitivity, hinting of spiritual depths and special intelligence.

Yet for all that she could not tell herself that she had enjoyed the time she'd spent with him. But she also could not ignore the fact that she had found it strangely moving. All this had been true before she'd gone out with the baker and the accountant. Afterwards, in comparison, her mind had treated the carpenter even more kindly. Yet when she compared him with Abraham, she felt the emptiness, the futility, gnaw at her once again.

Also, she had too little an idea of what he thought of her, despite his oddly passionate words, which she had finally discounted as mere style, a manner of speaking. Politeness, even. And Garfinkel had never even mentioned him again. She had just assumed the worst. What would she say if he wanted to see her again? She didn't know.

"When is Garfinkel coming?"

"Another hour or so. The boys will be in bed, and Chaya Leah is sleeping over at a friend's house. She's certainly become very close friends with Fruma Rabinowitz lately. But it couldn't be bad. Look at the weight she's lost, how she dresses now, and her hair. G-d be thanked!"

"You'll get rid of all of your daughters, *Ima*. Don't worry."

"Get rid of you? Why, what a thing to say. . . ."

Dina laughed happily. It was not the baker or the accountant. She would never have to see either of them again. And Judah Gutman, the tall, the handsome, the sensitive, had liked her. Liked her enough to send her a gift. She loved gifts.

Garfinkel's knock came exactly on time. The thin, tired *shadchen* was breathing heavily from the climb up the stairs. Fourth floor, with no elevator!

"Come in, sit down, Reb Chaim," Rabbi Reich said, ushering him in.

The table was set with cookies and little candies and tea cups. Garfinkel felt slightly mollified as he sat down and helped himself to tea with three lumps of sugar and two or three pieces of cake. Then he licked his fingertips, shook out his beard, and wiped his lips on the back of his hand. He looked at them expectantly. They looked back at him expectantly. He sighed.

"So where is the *kallah moid*, the bride-to-be?" He thought fast. What was this one's name? Chana . . . no, that was the butcher's daughter. Malka? No, that was the one with the slight limp. This was the little one. The pretty one, he jogged his reluctant memory. Dina. "Dina," he said casually, feeling the beads of sweat under his hat. He took off the hat.

"Do you want us to tell her to come out? But maybe you wanted to talk to us first? We don't want her hurt again."

Garfinkel's eyes widened. "My dear rebbetzin, I would

like to point out to you a very small thing. . . ." His voice grew in indignation. "The first time she got hurt was because things were handled by someone else. Well-meaning, good-hearted, but a schlemiel. For this, I do not deserve suspicion. For this, I do not deserve warnings and reprimands. Your Dina is like my own child. Believe me, I have spent sleepless nights wondering what is going to happen with her. When I pray, I pray for her happiness, and yours." So he was overdoing it a bit, but it was not a lie. You prayed for the welfare of the Jewish people, didn't you? And who was the Jewish people if not himself, the Reichs, the Gutmans, and all the Dinas and Malkas and Chanas? . . .

"Reb Chaim, don't get excited. Here, some more tea?"

He allowed himself to be served, maintaining his dignity.

"All I meant was that I was surprised you suddenly want to talk about Judah Gutman. After all, weren't you the one who said how much better the baker or the accountant would be for our Dina? So I can't help but wonder what happened exactly to change your mind."

Garfinkel coughed and took a long sip of the tea. "A question!" he said.

"And the answer?" Rebbetzin Reich persisted.

"The answer is, my dear rebbetzin, that I am just a messenger. G-d's errand boy. I think this, and then I think that. But what does it matter what the messenger thinks? What's important is what the boss thinks. And the boss"—his long finger jabbed upward meaningfully—"thinks that Judah Gutman and Dina Reich would be happy and blessed if they married."

"With all due respect, Reb Chaim," Mrs. Reich said mildly, "we know that the age of prophecy ended with the prophet Habakuk."

Garfinkel looked her over more carefully. She and Gutman's mother, now that was a *shiddach*, he thought painfully. What had he done to deserve this? Charity, he hadn't given enough lately, he thought, vowing to correct the error of his ways. G-d's punishments were fearsome and manifold. "My dear rebbetzin. The young man is good, pious, kind. He has a thriving business. And he has fallen in love with your daughter."

"Love!" Rebbetzin Reich said in a shocked tone of mild outrage. "They went out once!"

"Who are we to question G-d's ways?" he said piously, kicking himself. Of course, it was unacceptable. It was shocking. Why had he even brought it up? A vacation, he thought. A few days' overeating in Safad, that's what he needed. But there was no backtracking. The word had been spoken. It had to be defended.

"Love comes in many varieties. Just as the world is full of His manifold creatures, the thousands of species of birds and fish and animals. . . ." He felt himself waxing poetic. He was charmed. "All living things, and different trees and vegetables and all the kinds of spices and fruits—" Rebbetzin Reich coughed, cutting him short, making him lose his concentration. "So I call Judah Gutman's feeling for your daughter love. You might call it admiration for her good family, her fine reputation, her piety. You might say he can divine her good qualities as a housekeeper and a mother. Her thriftiness and her talent with a needle. So call it what you like. The man is interested in your daughter. Seriously interested."

"And financially? We don't want any more disappointments. We've told you what we can afford."

"This is all negotiable, of course. But there won't be a problem. They are reasonable. You are realistic and respectable. I give my personal word, no matter what the financial problems, I guarantee to work it out." He patted his chest importantly, as if undertaking a dangerous and complicated mission. The fact that the Gutmans wanted nothing, not even that which was due them, was nobody's business, certainly not the Reichs'.

"Well, then, perhaps . . . it's entirely up to Dina. But we have no objection if you talk to her."

Garfinkel nodded, noblesse oblige. "And when will I have the pleasure of seeing the young lady again?"

"I'm here." Dina came in. She had been listening the whole time, and her face was bright pink, like spring roses. Love, she thought. The magic word had been spoken, touching her life with the powerful, transforming tap of a fairy's wand in a children's story. And then Garfinkel had ruined it all, explaining it away. She sat down at the table opposite the *shadchen*, noticing the pile of crumbs, the bad teeth, the tired, sagging eyes. He was never going to sprout wings and grow cherubic. What else could you expect from him?

"My dear child," Garfinkel said heartily, happy to see her mother voluntarily withdraw. Charming, articulate little Dina Reich, he thought. And big, silent Judah Gutman! He shook his head, thinking the unthinkable. Perhaps, after all, he was just a messenger. For how else could one possibly explain how he had been responsible for getting two such opposites together! It went against all his instincts, it cried out in protest against all his long experience and talent and intuition. But on the opposite scale was Judah's mother. The idea of having to see her again. Judah's mother won.

"First, I have to ask you if you know why I'm here."

"It's about Mr. Gutman," she said.

He nodded. "He wants to continue. He asked me if you're willing. I didn't know what to tell him."

She looked down at her hands, deciding.

"Ah, wait, before you answer, I forgot. This is for you. He said to give it to you no matter what you said. A gift."

She looked at the clumsily wrapped package with a stab of disappointment. Reluctantly she peeled off the creased paper.

It was a little windmill carved in wood, a replica of the one in Yemin Moshe. She held it in her hand, feeling the polished, warm surface of the wood, examining the exquisite carving. There were tiny birds in it, and delicate flowers blossoming. And it had a fragrance, like lilacs or honeysuckle. Strong, real. Where was it coming from? she wondered. Then she found a tiny golden clasp and opened it. The top part fell back, and inside she saw the aromatic dried petals. The lovely smell swelled up against her, enveloping her with its potency. She felt transported.

"A spice box. Very practical. He has good hands, Judah. This is a good design. He could branch out. Spice boxes, dreidels, doorknobs . . ." Garfinkel's mind was filled with infinite possibilities.

Would he never shut up? "Tell him yes, Reb Chaim. Tell Judah Gutman that Dina Reich would be happy to see him again."

This caught the *shadchen* off guard. He had at least another half hour to an hour's worth planned before they got to that point. He had the whole list of the usual things: "You're not getting any younger," "You'll get a bad reputation for being too particular," etc. etc., as well as a list tailor-made to this case: "Think of your parents' financial situation." He had even been prepared to bring up Sruyele, the wanton ancestor. But that he'd planned only as a last resort. Sruyele was best forgotten.

He'd only found out about it because of Dvorah. The parents of one of the boys had hired a private investigator before agreeing to the *shiddach*, and the man had done his job a little too thoroughly. The *shiddach* had been called off. Luckily Sruyele could now rest in peace. Still, like a ballet dancer who has been primed for a great performance only to be rained out, Garfinkel felt cheated somehow.

"It's not good to be too hasty," he cautioned her. "To make up your mind too quickly, even though, honestly, you have made the absolutely, one-hundred-percent right decision. Judah is a fine man. Why, you know how good he is to his widowed mother? Well, you can tell a lot about a man from how he treats his mother. He treats her like Esther the queen—"

"Someone who is too attached to his mother is not a good thing," Rebbetzin Reich said, coming back into the room and sitting down.

"Of course. Not too attached. . . ." The *shadchen* rose hastily. "But why should I waste your time? I asked a question, I got an answer. Now I have also a home to go to, a wife, thank G-d. I have my nightly Talmud *shiur*, a few more pages to learn . . ." He hurried to the door. "I'll give Judah your answer. It should be with *mazel*." And then he practically ran down the steps before anything else could happen.

CHAPTER 16

THE NEXT TIME JUDAH GUTMAN SAW DINA REICH, NEITHER was fully prepared for the experience. For Judah, despite all the first impressions he had kept and embellished in his mind, was still overwhelmed by the reality of the lovely girl who stood before him, as fresh and blooming as a verdant spring morning. The moment he set eyes on her, he knew he was lost. All the self-control he needed to keep his big, clumsy movements in check and to untie his stricken tongue evaporated in the searing heat of his emotions.

For Dina, the meeting was no less difficult. In her imagination, she had succeeded brilliantly in editing out all the disturbing, painful realities of Judah Gutman. But now, faced with the real man, she felt her heart sink. He was very awkward. He was very quiet. Only the tangible evidence of the beautiful turn of his mind and heart of the spice box kept her from turning around and fleeing. She came home awash in disappointment. Yet she picked up the windmill. The polished wood was as smooth and warm as flesh. The engraved flowers that trellised up the sides were brilliantly rendered, so dazzlingly beautiful it made tears come to her eyes. She tried hard to reconcile the man's work with the man. She found it almost impossible. His big hands, his heavy footsteps, his deep silences and awkward attempts at conversation, all defeated her attempts to form a picture consistent with the intelligence and sensitivity revealed in the little work of art.

What was to be done? She could give him up. She considered that. Seriously. But aside from all the problems it would bring down on her head—Garfinkel's rage, her parents' disappointment, and Judah's distress—she wasn't ready to give him up just yet. That little windmill revealed a man so sensitive, so loving, so full of rich, hidden possibilities, that she felt it would be like throwing away an unlocked treasure box. If she could only find some way to pry it open, to see clearly all she was convinced it contained. If she could only do that, she might find a man in a million, someone she could love and respect with all of her heart.

"*Ima*, what should I do?" She had poured out her heart to her mother, telling her everything. Rebbetzin Reich had sat thoughtfully on her daughter's bedside, listening wordlessly. She reached out and took Dina in her large, warm arms, pressing her to her soft, motherly breasts as she would a small child in need of comfort for a painful, small wound. She rocked her up and back. Then she put her at arm's length and smiled into her face.

"You are much wiser than I thought, Dinaleh. Would it help you if some people you respected got to know Judah and told you their opinion? Perhaps he would be less awkward with another man."

"Like who?"

"Well, *Aba*, of course. And then Yaakov Klein, and perhaps one or two rabbis you respect."

Dina thought about it. It might just be the answer. Perhaps one of them held the secret key. Garfinkel, of course, had only good things to say, but that was to be expected. She just didn't trust her own judgment. She was confused. She agreed with alacrity to her mother's suggestion.

For the next two weeks Judah Gutman met the male relatives and respected acquaintances of Dina's family. The conversations, which took place mostly in his shop, went easily, comfortably. Judah had no problem opening up to other men. They had so much in common: their love for Talmud, their exercise of the commandments, their discussions of Torah law. And those who spoke to his fellow carpenters got a very clear picture of the nature of the man who wanted to marry Dina. He was a pearl, a rare jewel of a fellow.

"Dina," her father told her, his face alight with unrestrained joy, "this fellow is a tzadik. No one can say a bad word about him. He's generous, compassionate, giving, kind. And he loves you. I think he'd make you very happy."

"Dina," Yaakov Klein told his sister-in-law, "Gutman has a beautiful nature and skillful hands. You'll never want for anything. He's special."

"Dina," Rabbi Krantz, the rabbi of their neighborhood, told her, "I have spoken to your young man, and I think he is not only a good lamden, very expert in the law, but also a very talented and pious *baal melacha*, a skilled craftsman. You have my blessing. I am very happy for you."

She listened, almost trembling, to all of them. Yet it was just words. Nothing seemed to change. The secret key needed to turn the lock still eluded her. She lay awake all night, the words going through her head. And in the morning she got up, exhausted and depressed with indecision. Yet sometime during the course of the week, a decision began to take form. What do I know? she told herself. What am I looking for? Another Abraham Breitman? My parents can't afford an Abraham Breitman. And remembering him was getting harder and harder. After all, she had only gone out with him a few times, months before. Even his image was no longer clear to her, nor was the feeling she had once possessed with such stunning clarity. Everything was faded, muddled. The only reality was Judah.

What bothered her about him? His awkwardness, his silences. Yet none of the men she respected had found that in him. With them he had been articulate, friendly, impressive. Of course, he was big, and people tended to smile when they were together. But his physical features didn't bother her. Nor did they particularly attract her. She liked his face, the shape of his large, beautiful head. He was very manly, very strong. Only his extreme shyness had kept that powerful maleness from frightening her. Yet, truthfully, she had to tell herself, she did not love him.

"But that doesn't mean you might not learn to, Dina," Dvorah told her.

Dvorah was holding the baby. Already her stomach was bulging slightly beneath her cotton robe. She was three months pregnant. Her face was pale, with dark rings under her eyes. She looked tired, but not unhappy. "You can learn to love a man. Especially if you respect him and he is always good to you. Look, if you married someone you thought you loved and he never helped you and was always gone when you needed him, and he spoke to you harshly and disrespectfully, would your love continue? No. So starting out in love doesn't really ensure anything, does it? What's important is the man himself. Are you sure that he is a fine person, pious, good?"

Dina nodded.

"Are you sure he can support you and give you the material things you need?"

Dina nodded again.

"Well, then . . ." Dvorah shifted the baby on her lap, letting him suck from the other breast. "Well, you don't dislike him, do you?"

Dina shook her head no.

"Then what's holding you back? Is it still how you feel about Abraham? He's getting married, you know. Next week. A very rich girl. But ugly."

The news struck her like a blow. What was holding her back? she thought. Just foolishness and pie in the sky. Just a silly notion of what she was supposed to feel like. Perhaps she'd never feel that way. (She didn't add "again." She must exorcise Abraham Breitman. Abraham Breitman was a young girl's foolish dream. He no longer existed. He was getting married.)

"Nothing is holding me back. He is a good man, everyone says so. And I think . . . that is, I have reason to believe, he lo—that he cares for me deeply."

"Then you are the luckiest girl in the world." Dvorah leaned over and gave her sister a kiss. "Marriage isn't easy. But we have to work at it. It's our role in life. It gives G-d the greatest pleasure to see a good Jewish home filled with love and growing children."

She is lecturing, Dina thought. Giving me a speech. She doesn't look well, and yet she seems fulfilled. The house is clean and pretty with delicate little womanly touches: flowerpots hanging on the wall with little pink bows, clean curtains at the windows, fresh laundered linens in the bedrooms. How lovely it would be to have my own home! To have more than just a tiny corner and a few small shelves to call my own. She looked at the baby, her heart yearning. She lifted him from her sister and held the active little warm body in her arms. Her lips brushed the sweet, satin softness of his newly washed hair. A home. A baby. A good man. G-d was offering it to her on a silver platter. All she had to do was reach out and take it.

She thought of all the other girls at Beit Yaakov. Half were married, another quarter engaged. She had been going to weddings and engagement parties all summer. The "G-d willing by you's" had rained down on her head like a warm summer shower. If she didn't get married soon, she thought, they would grow as cold as snow and then as big and punishing as hailstones.

He is a good man, she told herself. And he can provide for me. My parents will be spared worry, expense. *Aba* won't have to work another job or pay another mortgage.

And then she thought: Perhaps Judah will open up to me when we are married. He is simply shy now. But I will show him love and care, and he will become calm and show me everything I know he has inside. That was the key to Judah Gutman, she told herself suddenly. My acceptance. Once I agree to marry him, he will change. I will see the man who made the windmill, who carved the flowers, who thought to fill it with fragrance. Everyone in the family would rejoice.

She could envision a life with him. He would always be kind and gentle. He would look well in the lamplight, steady and comfortable. There would never be any great disappointments or major unhappiness. He would work hard, pray regularly, learn diligently in his spare time. He would divide his charity among the poor and hand his salary over to his wife. There would never be reason to argue with him bitterly or difficulties in getting or giving an apology. Calm waters, she thought. A clean, straightforward, and reliable path through the straits of wanton desires and shameful surprises. It would be a good life.

The following day she called her parents together and informed them of her desire to marry Judah Gutman. Their dear kind faces shone with naked joy.

CHAPTER 17

THE FIRST NOTE CHAYA LEAH HAD HARDLY BEEN ABLE TO READ, it was so stained with fish blood. She had opened it in the bathroom, her fingertips sticky and red, tingling with the unfamiliar thrill of guilt and excitement. It read:

To the honorable Chaya Leah, may she live long,

Surprised I know your name? I have my ways. We can't go on meeting like this. I'm not at my best in a stained apron. Anyhow, I'd like to be able to talk to you about something besides fish. I will be, G-d willing, at Sanhedria Park at 5:00 p.m. on Thursday. If you should happen to be in the area next to the last exit, we might accidentally meet and have a real conversation.

Moishe

She'd carefully folded the little blood-soaked paper and hidden it in her drawer inside a package of sanitary napkins. It had taken her only about ten minutes to decide whether or not to go. Actually it had taken her ten minutes to decide how to cover herself. The idea of not going never even entered her mind. She felt a curious lack of guilt. It was like the earrings. She had her own definite set of values, which surrounded her like a fortress. The light artillery of Mrs. Morganbesser and even the heavy cannons of her parents had never really made any inroads.

Why this should have been, she never really knew. She was different and, deep in her heart, stubbornly proud of it. Oh, not different enough to defy G-d or the Torah, or the *halacha*. Just different enough to give what she learned a personal interpretation she had no trouble trusting even when her ideas clashed with those around her.

She had seen nothing wrong with the earrings. And for the past six months she had seen nothing wrong with meeting Moishe at Sanhedria Park, Zion Square, and many other places. After all, they were both unmarried. They weren't going to touch or anything like that (she blushed to her toes at the very thought of any physical contact with him). She just couldn't find a single *halacha* she was defying. Modesty? Well, what was immodest about meeting a boy in broad daylight in a public place? Respect for parents? Well, what did her parents have to do with it, anyway? They hadn't said no, had they? The fact that she hadn't told them also didn't bother her overmuch. A person was entitled to a private life. Where was it written that you had to tell your parents everything?

Besides, her intentions were strictly honorable. She had found the boy for her, and she was going to be damned if she'd let her private life fall into the hands of Reb Chaim Garfinkel. No, thank you very much. No one was going to bargain over her like a pile of old tomatoes in the *shuk*. Besides, they never fixed you up with anybody good-looking. Would Garfinkel even know a good-looking boy if he bumped into him, naked, in the mikveh? Chaya Leah seriously doubted it. Besides, being married to someone who spent the whole day learning and came home late every night to learn some more was not her idea of a good time.

She looked at her sisters with pity and a little contempt. She knew they all felt sorry for her. That they considered her the ugly duckling, the slob. But look who they wound up with! Stuck-up Dvorah got her Yaakov Klein (how could she stand having his fat little babies, one after the other?). And now Dina had given in to Garfinkel and was actually going to marry that silent giant. Sickening. She felt a small surge of victory. Her beautiful, good sisters with their neatly ironed and tucked-in blouses. With their "Chaya Leah, fix your hair!" "Chaya Leah, how can you be so rude!" "Chaya Leah, look how you're upsetting *Aba!*" Well, she wondered what they would all say if they could see Moishe, tall and slim with deep blue eyes. Sending her love notes and meeting her once or twice a week. With nobody the wiser. Her eyes narrowed into shrewd, triumphant slits.

With the plans for Dina's wedding under way, nobody had had time to check her excuses. That was the only part that bothered her. Lying to her mother about where she was going. But, she reasoned, if lies made to spare someone's feelings were commendable rather than despicable, hers fell into that category.

Since the dates had begun, she'd lost weight, inveigled some new, form-fitting clothes from her parents, and gotten her hair cut to bring out all its natural curl. She'd also used a rinse on it, lightening it so gradually that not even Mrs. Morganbesser had caught on. She liked what she saw in the mirror.

She had a waist, a full, soft bosom, slim hips. An hourglass figure had been carved out of the solid, uninteresting block of sensible female flesh that had destined her for matronliness at seventeen. Her hair framed her face with strawberry-blond wisps of fashionably frizzy curls. She looked like a girl instead of a pioneer wife or one of the formidable rebbetzins who ruled the community with an iron will. She was never going to have Dvorah's dark, lovely, feminine charm or Dina's dainty blond beauty. But she looked striking and attractive. Her eyes sparkled with lively expectation.

Now she sat waiting for him, shivering a little. He was ten minutes late. She was sitting on the *tayelet*, Jerusalem's oceanless boardwalk, a lovely promenade surrounded by gardens overlooking a spectacular view of the Old and New cities. It was where lovers came to walk.

Men were looking at her curiously. She tried to ignore them, but her curiosity got the better of her. Some of them were old and creepy, but a few were quite acceptable. One especially. He was tall and wore a black leather jacket. He looked at her with a forceful and ironic smile. Suddenly he was sitting next to her.

"Shalom." He leaned very close to her, his cheek almost touching her hair. She jumped back. He laughed. He leaned forward again. "Pretty," he said in a low, husky voice, almost a whisper.

Her knees felt like jelly, and her heart began to pound with fright, and something more. It was the something more that frightened her most of all. She liked it.

"That's a nice color dress, blue. It picks up the blue in your eyes."

She didn't know what to do. Of course, he wore no skullcap. He actually had a gold earring in one ear!

"I was waiting for someone, but she didn't show. It looks like you're in the same boat. Maybe we were both lucky." Again that half smile, half jeer. Her whole body was turning into liquid. She couldn't find her tongue. "You understand Hebrew, don't you?"

"Yes," she managed.

"So, are you coming?" He stood up and put his hands into his pockets, nodding his head in the direction of the long, dark promenade.

"I can't. I'm waiting for someone."

"Sure he'll show?"

"Yes."

"Well, maybe next time." To her utter relief he started to go. Then, all of a sudden, he circled back and handed her a bit of paper with a phone number. "Call me. We'll set something up. We'll go to Tel Aviv one night. Jerusalem has no night life."

Just then Moishe turned up. Her feelings were mixed, but the biggest component was relief as she saw the dark stranger saunter off and disappear. Nevertheless she pocketed the phone number and gave him one last, lingering glance before turning her full attention to Moishe.

He looked wonderful. As usual he had wound his long *payess* behind his ears so she could hardly see them, something he always did outside Meah Shearim. Those shoulder-length *payess*, he'd once explained to her, were like a neon sign, and he just wanted a little privacy, not to be a walking advertisement, a representative of the whole clan. They began to stroll down the long avenue, looking at the sparkling lights of downtown Jerusalem, the ghostly, milky pearl glow of the Old City walls, kissed by moonlight. All around them young couples were paused, caressing each other, lips to lips.

He looked at her shyly. She looked back curiously. The tingling feeling, the melting, was still with her. Impulsively she reached out and took his hand. He gripped hers back, a slow smile of delightful surprise spreading over his face. They walked farther down a little side path. On either side of them lovely fresh violets and petunias, roses and daffodils, perfumed the air. He looked over his shoulder then all around, twice, then three times. Satisfied, he reached up and placed his hands beneath her hair, clasping them around her smooth young neck. His palms cupped her cheeks as he drew her face toward him. Their lips touched. He froze with fear. But then he felt her arms suddenly around his waist, pressing him toward her.

"Moishe," she whispered, "is it wrong?"

"I don't know," he answered, pulling his lips away only far enough to say it. She wanted him to stop talking. He did.

They sat together in the darkness for a long time. She rested her head on his shoulder. He held her gently around the waist.

"We'll get married one day, won't we?"

He hesitated. "Your family is Misnagid and mine are Hasidim. Will they accept me?"

"Well, will yours accept me? I mean, it's not like you are a goy or anything. And you're religious. So why should anybody care?"

"You'll have to listen to the rebbe. Follow all the customs. It won't be easy for you."

"You could become a Misnagid!"

He shook his head incredulously. "We have a much better time than you Misnagdim! Your prayers have no life! We have music, song, dance."

"I don't know. My parents wouldn't like it."

"My parents would hate it. The rebbe would hate it. Unless, of course, you converted and became a Belzer, like me."

"What would I have to do?"

"Well, not much, really. Belz women don't shave their heads the way Toledot Aharon women do. And you can wear regular-colored stockings, not just black ones."

"That sounds all right," she said with relief.

"The hard part would be getting used to going to the rebbe for blessings and to ask questions, sometimes even very personal questions."

"Like what?"

"Like which doctor to go to for an illness. Or where to buy an apartment."

"Why would you bother your rebbe with questions like that? How can he know better than you?"

"We believe because of his greatness of spirit, he is on

a higher level than mere human beings. He has a mystical connection to G-d which gives him greater understanding and insight. You wouldn't want to do anything serious without getting his blessing. Also"—his face got red—"our habits in bed are different from you Misnagdim."

He gave her a swift glance, making no eye contact. "You might as well know it now. We don't believe in going to bed with no clothes on, the way you do. We keep covered up from head to toe."

"The way I do?" Her voice rose with amazement.

"I mean, the way your leaders teach. I was reading this book by this Misnagid *rav*, and he says specifically that just as there is no separation between G-d and the Jewish people, there should be no separation between a man and wife."

They were both silent. "What else does he say?" Chaya Leah asked timidly. Even for her this conversation was getting a bit much. But her curiosity took over, driving out her natural modesty.

"He says that a married couple can do anything they want, except that the man shouldn't kiss 'that place.' But otherwise, everything else is okay."

She was beginning to feel very hot. "Well, how are your rules different?"

"We're taught not to touch anything. A man should kiss his wife's face and that's it. Also, there is only one position that's acceptable, and the room has to be totally black. It's also preferable to wait until midnight, when you won't be distracted by voices in the street which might lead a man to think of other women."

"Do you always do everything your rebbe says? I mean, couldn't you adopt some of our customs, too? After all, marriage is a partnership. And as it is written, a man should make his wife happy. Actually, you'll have to do whatever pleases me." She gave him a long, languid look. "You don't need your rebbe's blessing for everything, do you?"

"But of course I do!"

"What about what we're doing now? Have you gotten his blessing for that also?" she said slyly.

He took his arm off her waist and clasped his hands together, studying them in chagrin.

Then she started to giggle.

He looked up with distress, and then his face contorted with laughter. "We'll get married one day." He pressed her against him.

"Without a *shadchen!*"

He traced his fingers down her back. "Without a *shadchen.*"

"With or without the rebbe's blessing or my parents'? And we'll do whatever we want in our own house, in our own bed?"

He hesitated. Her arms went over his shoulders, her fingertips pressed softly into the back of his neck. She brought his mouth down again over hers.

He didn't answer. He didn't have to.

She crumpled up the bit of paper in her pocket and threw it away.

It was late when Moishe finally wound his way through Meah Shearim, yet he felt exuberantly alive. A few times he grabbed on to lampposts and swung himself around them. He tiptoed across low stone fences, he leapt over fire hydrants.

Streets in Meah Shearim were almost always full, even this time of night. There were always boys coming from or going to late-night prayer gatherings or *shiurim.* So the footsteps behind him did not even entice a backward glance. Then, suddenly, the footsteps were no longer behind, but on either side of him in perfect time. Two arms linked violently through his, and he felt himself dragged to a small alley.

They were yeshiva boys a little older than he, he saw,

yet lean and muscular. Their faces were clenched in hatred.

"Brothers, what is this?" he began mildly, but his heart was already beating with an animal's fear. He knew who they were. They were the commandos of the Morals Patrol, young thugs in yeshiva boys' clothing. They came from every group in the *haredi* world, Hasidim and Misnagdim, who worked together in rare harmony united by a shared fanaticism and a need to sanctify somehow the natural violence of their natures. In the name of purifying the community's morals, they were not above putting you in the hospital. Or worse.

Haredim didn't believe in going to the Zionist police force, didn't want the secularists involved in their private lives. This estrangement from the government had begun with the very creation of the State in response to certain government-inspired outrages. It was a common practice, for example, for newly arrived, deeply religious Moroccan and Yemenite immigrant families to be broken up, the children sent to secular kibbutzim where their *payess* were shaved off and their skullcaps thrown out in an attempt to integrate them culturally into the mores of the ruling secular Zionists. In outraged response, *haredim* had washed their hands of the government, building up a wall of suspicion and resistance to any incursion into their communal life. They created their own court system and several quasi-official police forces that guarded *haredi* streets, catching thieves or child molesters, investigating rumors of adultery, and disciplining wanton yeshiva boys and girls.

The oldest and most venerable of these forces, the one officially sanctioned by most of the communities' rabbis, was a group called the *mishmeret hatzinius*, or "Modesty Protectors." They were always solid family men over forty. They never went after anyone unless the rabbinical court had accumulated tremendous evidence and no other course was possible. And even then they usually spoke to the people involved, trying to get them to cooperate voluntarily before resorting to any physical threats. Often this reasonable, responsible behavior had inflamed the impatience of younger, more zealous members of the community, who saw in it a despicable lack of zealousness and decisiveness in cleansing the community's streets from criminals. The result had been the creation of several vigilante groups, each vying to outdo the other in their activities to "sanctify" the neighborhood. The more outrageously severe and punishing their actions, the more people they found to punish, the more attention they received and the more important they felt.

The current winner was the Morals Patrol.

The group was headed by Reb Kurzman, a complex, almost contradictory personality. A Hasid, brought up by strict, pious parents, sent to the most prestigious yeshivot, he was a dazzling scholar, zealous in word and deed to keep all the laws he studied. Yet he had been known to blow up newsstands that dared to sell secular magazines and newspapers, set fire to advertising posters and billboards with pictures he deemed immodest, and put young men whose activities he found questionable into wheelchairs for a considerable length of time.

In some ways it might be said that he was a perfect product of the society that had nurtured him, a society where every feeling reached total expression without compromise, where everything was conducted at a fever pitch of intensity: praying meant involving all your senses, all your concentration, your whole heart, your whole soul. Studying Talmud meant learning all day, every day, your entire life. Being modest meant covering everything head to toe, never looking at a woman, never sitting next to one on a public bus or taxi. Admiring a leader meant total, unthinking devotion. Hating someone meant total rejection, total war, where the end justified all means.

As a young yeshiva student, Kurzman had soon tired of the careful, thoughtful work of the *mishmeret hatzinius*. He could see the evil all around him, on every street corner, and nothing, nothing was being done! His model was the biblical figure of Pinchas, who had stilled G-d's rage by publicly slaughtering an Israelite man during an act of whoredom with a Midianite woman.

And so in his early twenties Kurzman's growing reputation had attracted an ever-increasing and -changing group of yeshiva boys and men from every group in the city. They were hot-tempered, zealous activists who, like himself, were fed up with the gentlemanly pace of temperate men whom they fiercely believed were allowing immorality to flourish and contaminate the community. Kurzman's group used modern methods. They had their own spies. Walkie-talkies. Photographers. They achieved results.

Now they held Moishe firmly on either side. He struggled and then stopped. They weren't increasing the pressure or lessening it. If they were going to beat him up, they would have done it already, he reasoned. Before he could figure it out, they dropped his arms. He rubbed them, then looked up. Standing before him was a stocky man, with a short dark beard, wearing white gloves. Rabbi Kurzman.

Moishe felt the sweat break out on his forehead and under his arms.

"You know that the Torah teaches men to live in modesty, to curb their animal instincts. You are a good boy, from a religious home. This you know, yes?"

Moishe nodded, too afraid to open his mouth.

"Well, you know that the daughters of Israel must all be treated like the daughters of priests. Anyone who treats them lightly is trespassing an important commandment of the Torah that Hashem, may his name be blessed, has commanded us. Do you understand that?"

Moishe nodded.

The tone changed mildly. Moishe felt a fatherly hand on his shoulder. "The temptation is always there, my son. You must suppress it. Soon you will marry and so will the girl. You do not want any taint to come to your honorable, righteous parents because of some foolishness on your part?"

"No," Moishe said, his wits suddenly returning. "But I think what I do is my own business. The law does not prohibit an unmarried man from speaking to an unmarried woman."

"But we know that it does not end with words. 'Do not go after your own heart and your own eyes. Numbers fifteen, thirty-nine. 'The thought of the foolish is sin.' Proverbs twenty-four, nine. We know everything, my son." The tone dropped suddenly to a menacing threat. " 'Neither shalt thy eye pity him, neither shalt thou spare, neither shalt thou conceal him.' " The fatherly hand on the shoulder squeezed him. The pain was excruciating. "Our sages of blessed memory have said, 'All who become merciful to the cruel, in the end become cruel to the merciful,' as it is written in *Yalkut, Shmuel* fifteen, one twenty-one. We hope that we will not have to talk to you about this again, my son. I would be very sorry if I needed to speak to you more than once about this. Very sorry indeed, my fine *bucherel.*" The grip slackened. The three walked rapidly down the street until they disappeared.

When he was sure they had gone, Moishe wiped the sweat from his brow. And then he spit in their direction.

CHAPTER 18

It was the second week in "bride class." The wedding was three weeks away. Dina greeted the other young girls with pleasure. Some she had known before, and some she had met at the class. It was held at Rebbetzin Felder's home three times a week.

The rebbetzin, wife of a distinguished rabbi who headed a rabbinical academy, had chosen this work as her special mitzvah. She took no money from the girls or their parents. "Does it make sense for me to lessen the richness of my reward in the World to Come by accepting a few paltry shekel in this world?" she would ask with real surprise whenever the subject came up.

She was a tall, imposing woman with a chest like a ship's prow. Her face was scrubbed and shiny clean, her eyes were blue and shone with a clear, untroubled light. Her clothes were extra modest, even according to Mrs. Morganbesser's standards, and well cut. And always freshly washed and ironed. The whole house felt as if it had just been totally immersed in a tub of detergent and scrubbed to a high shine.

It was a perfect setting to talk about sex, making even that dark, mysterious, hitherto taboo subject emerge somehow into the light, all scrubbed and shiny clean. It was now acceptable to think about it, plan for it, ask questions about it. It was, after all, for the sake of heaven. It was now part of building a pure home, bringing pure, innocent new lives into being. It was now the Creator's will that they think about it, plan for it.

Rebbetzin Felder smiled at the pretty young faces that crowded around her living room, looking at her with such shy interest. "A man marries a woman. She says to him: I have seen what looks like a red rose; and he separates from her. What kind of wall is there between them? What sort of serpent has stung him? What is it that restrains him—the words of the Torah!" The rebbetzin looked at the girls. "The blood that is built up in your bodies is meant to nourish new life. When that doesn't happen, when it leaves your body, it is an impurity. This impurity, if not carefully guarded against, can contaminate your whole marriage. So you must separate from your husbands at that time and for seven days afterward, coming to him only after you have immersed in the mikveh, the ritual bath. It's not a question of being unclean, but simply impure in a spiritual sense. The immersion is a spiritual cleansing. Your husband and you are united in purity and holiness. From this purity will come pure healthy children, not cursed with the ugly stain of having been conceived in impurity."

The girls shuddered at the very thought. The rebbetzin smiled at them. She beamed. "And there is another reason, too. An added benefit to adhering strictly to all these laws of family purity. Each time you return to your husband after having separated from him completely for almost two weeks every month, a separation which means you must sleep in separate beds and not touch each other in any way; each time you return to him, you will be as beautiful and precious to him as you were on your wedding night. He will long for you and wait for you with the impatience of a new bridegroom no matter how many years you have been married. He will never tire of you, nor you of him."

Dina shifted on her chair. Two weeks every month! It was a long time. . . . Yet it depended how you felt about . . . *it*. If *it* was terrible, so you had two weeks off. If *it* was wonderful, then it would be pure torture. Yet there was no choice. The idea of being with a man when you were impure was abhorrent to her. Besides, it would mean that you would have to develop another kind of relationship, one that had nothing to do with sex. If that connection was strong enough, then perhaps it really wouldn't matter so much that you couldn't actually touch.

"And what is the reward for our conquering our basest natures, for allowing Hashem to be part of our marriages, our most intimate moments? The reward is great. It is a marriage that is full of mutual respect and long-lasting love and desire. It is clean, pure, healthy children," the rebbetzin repeated, drumming the message home. "Why, in Europe, in places where there was no mikveh, women would travel many miles to reach one. Some even put their lives in danger by immersing in a frozen lake or the ocean. And those who were prevented from going to the mikveh kept apart indefinitely, for years, making a tremendous sacrifice." The girls looked at each other, startled. Years?

"The Jewish people have been blessed by their stubbornness. We have survived because of the strength of our beautiful family lives, the traditions handed down over the centuries. Great sacrifices have been made to do this." The rebbetzin relished the words. Repetition was not a bad thing if the message was important. "It is in your hands to keep this wonderful tradition alive." Her voice was inspiring, demanding, severe. Then her face softened. After all, she was talking to Beit Yaakov girls, most of whom had no need to be convinced. They were all good girls who would be happy to do as they were taught. Who sought the very life she was advocating. There was no need to be severe. These lovely, sweet young girls. She looked them over with pleasure. Pure and good, the daughters of mothers who were pure and good. They just needed to be told what to do, to be taught. Not frightened, not reprimanded.

Her face softened with love. "My dear daughters. Your whole lovely, sacred lives are before you. You please your Creator by getting married. You will please Him by keeping your marriages full of kindness, modesty, and respect. He will watch over you and bless you."

Then she went into detail. How you must anticipate your period and separate the moment you saw blood. How you checked yourself to see if the flow had stopped and for seven days afterward by inserting a clean, white cloth into the vagina and checking it in natural sunlight for signs of red or black. A yellow stain was borderline and needed to be brought to the rabbi for a decision. White was acceptable. If in the middle you suddenly spotted, you had to start counting from scratch again. Another seven days.

The details made the girls feel queasy, just as the general information inspired them. They were all hoping for a little more detail that would be helpful concerning the wedding night. But no one had the courage to ask.

Finally a tall, dark, heavy girl in the back raised her hand. "Rebbetzin . . ." She blushed, hesitating.

"Yes?" The rebbetzin nodded encouragingly.

"I'm not sure . . . what. I don't know what to do."

She sat down, blushing heavily. The others leaned forward slightly, their eyes directed on the older woman.

"My daughters, I know this is a new experience for you all, to go from being innocent girls to being wives and mothers. But G-d will help you. Always your husband will help you. He will, if he is a *ben Torah*, a good man, as I know all your bridegrooms will be, treat you with kindness and patience. After all, he is commanded to please you, to make you happy. But it is also your responsibility to make him happy. A woman who separates from her husband for no reason is called 'rebellious.' She can be punished for her ways by the Beit Din. Just as a man who is unkind can be punished. So try to be patient and cooperative."

"But what if you're . . . tired?" a little blond girl who looked barely fourteen piped up, emboldened. Dina knew her. She was just seventeen and had been engaged a month to someone she had met only once. Her pale lashes fluttered, and her pink little face seemed to blanch.

"My child," the rebbetzin said gently. "You must not be selfish. Your husband must not be selfish. But a man's nature is more sensual than a woman's. A good wife will be understanding. And patient," she repeated.

Dina listened carefully, wonderingly. A man's nature was more sensual than a woman's. She smiled to herself with strange relief. Sometimes her feelings absolutely appalled and frightened her. She was almost petrified by the idea of going to bed with Judah Gutman. And yet a part of her longed for it. Was that wrong? she wondered. Did she have a more sensual nature than most women? And what would it mean? She was too ashamed to ask the rebbetzin. And she couldn't very well ask her mother. Even Dvorah . . . well, would Dvorah know?

She raised her hand: "Rebbetzin, are there some books you could recommend for us to read further? I have so many questions!"

"Why, of course, my dear. And you should get answers to them all."

Not to them all, Dina thought. Like everything else, the personal experience would no doubt be totally different from all she read and heard. Still, she wanted to know as much as she could. Everything else in life one prepared for by reading the proper passages in the Bible, in the Talmud.

By learning. She knew no other way to prepare for this great experience than by using the same methods she had used all her life for everything else.

Yet deep down in her heart she recognized that she was being foolish. One could not prepare for the deepest, most physical of experiences by reading or thinking. This was what frightened her more than anything else, the idea that the old methods no longer had any power or validity. She was entering totally foreign territory, with no real guidelines. After all, all the stuff the rebbetzin was telling them had to do with menstruation, abstinence. But the act itself, the supreme moment of connection with another human being in the most physical of acts, could not be prayed away. It was her body, not her soul, that would be involved. All the rest was just beating around the bush.

She was shocked at herself—she, who had been so respectful of her teachers and her rabbis. She, who had always looked at them with real humility, trying to follow in their footsteps. Yet in this new country, all the trails they pointed to seemed faded and inconsequential, dusty, winding cow paths made faint by erosion and fierce winds. She was alone in an uncharted wilderness. All the words, the pious niceties of the rebbetzin about sacrifice and the glory of the Jewish people, what, in the final analysis, did it all have to do with how his flesh would feel on hers? Perhaps they could not tell her. Perhaps, she thought with a little horror, they did not know.

The days passed so quickly that she could not keep count; so slowly that it seemed they would never end. The date of the wedding had been fixed according to her menstrual cycle to ensure that she would have time to count seven clean days and immerse in the mikveh before the ceremony. A bride who accidentally got her period too near the wedding to do so was placed in a horrible position. She would spend her wedding night in separate bedrooms, chaperoned. That was Dina's, and every *haredi* bride's, biggest nightmare: entering the marriage canopy in a state of impurity. Miscalculating, or having one's body simply go off schedule. If Dina worried about anything, she worried about that most. Many girls even went on birth control pills months before the wedding to ensure that it wouldn't happen.

But then the day neared, and like a well-wound clock her body entered its monthly cycle. For the first time she looked at the blood as a potential nourisher of new life and not simply as a messy nuisance. The time was coming when it would not have to be shed, she told herself. Counting the seven clean days was a bit disgusting at first, a bit shameful. After all, one was not used to being on such intimate terms with those parts of one's body. But then she began to feel uplifted by it, as the cloth emerged clean, pure white, day after day after day.

On the seventh day she prepared to go to the mikveh. Her mother and Dvorah accompanied her. The woman who supervised the bath, a dead ringer for Rebbetzin Felder, welcomed them with a broad smile of joy. "A *kallah!*" She beamed. "Welcome and G-d bless you!"

The mikveh was a large one, just off the main street. One entrance was used in the mornings for the men, who immersed before their morning prayers; the second was strictly for women. It was hidden from the street by a high wall, which allowed women to go and come without being observed. Inside was a waiting room with chairs and a table piled high with books outlining the laws of family purity. On crowded summer days, when women could enter the mikveh only after dusk, dozens of women waited patiently to be called to the rooms upstairs.

But a *kallah* was special. None of the women waiting objected to her being whisked ahead. Her mother kissed her, and Dvorah held her hand encouragingly. Then she went upstairs.

She was led into a large bathroom with a bathtub, mirror, and sink.

"Do you need anything? Towels, cotton, nail polish remover?"

"Nothing," Dina said. "I've brought it all with me."

The laws pertaining to cleansing the body before immersion were strict and numerous. The whole body had to be scrubbed clean with vigor. Areas like the belly button, ears, and teeth needed special care. A loose scab needed to be removed. Head and body hair combed. Nails pared. All makeup, all jewelry, removed. Nothing at all was to separate the purifying flow of water from touching every part of the body.

Dina lay in the tub of deep hot water luxuriously. At home, sharing a hot water supply and bathroom with five little brothers, a sister, and her parents, there was never time for more than a quick shower. She relished the unique luxury of all the time in the world, all the hot water in the world. She shampooed her hair and combed it. She scrubbed her toenails with a nail brush and carefully scrubbed her heels with a pumice stone until all the dead skin was removed. Then, with a little embarrassment, she combed her pubic hair.

The combing, the twice daily examinations, all seemed designed to direct her attention toward that once very taboo, very hidden and forgotten part of her anatomy. Now, suddenly, she found herself paying inordinate amounts of attention to it, but in a good way. There was something matter-of-fact and calming about the checking, the ablutions. It was now a useful, respectable part of life to be given its rightful share of her attention. There was no real shamefulness in any of it, she felt. Just a twinge of embarrassed modesty, which was not the same thing at all. Shamefulness was dark, dirty, ugly, sinister. She felt all of those things far from her. Her whole physical being was a precious holy vessel being polished until it gleamed for its holy task.

When she had finally, carefully cleansed every possible part of her, her whole body tingled with a sense of utter cleanliness and well-being. She had never in her life felt so perfectly, immaculately clean and pure. It was a feeling that radiated down like small, electric currents from her forehead and eyes to the tips of her fingers and ends of her toes. She tingled and glowed with a rare joy.

After climbing out of the tub, she pressed a small buzzer. A discreet knock was soon heard at the door. She hastily wrapped her dripping body in a towel and opened it.

"Ready?" the rebbetzin asked her.

She nodded.

"Have you remembered to cleanse your ears? Your navel? To comb all of your hair?" The woman's questions were all said with a broad smile of encouragement. Dina smiled back through her embarrassment.

"A kosher *maidel.*" She beamed. "Now let me check you." She waited. Dina looked at her, confused.

"The towel, *maideleh,*" she said gently.

With deep humiliation, Dina removed the towel and stood naked in front of the older woman, who looked her over matter-of-factly, picking off stray hairs, looking over her toes and fingernails, clipping away at any stray cuticle she'd missed. The woman's palm brushed over the soles of Dina's heels, checking for rough skin. Dina felt herself blushing deeply.

But before she had a chance to sink into an agony of discomfort, it was over. The rebbetzin nodded in approval and motioned her toward an inner door. On the other side was a deep, small pool of water. Totally private. She stepped down into the water, hurrying, acutely aware of the stranger's eyes on her naked flesh. Yet soon the water covered her nakedness. It wasn't very deep, just enough to cover her breasts. It was deliciously hot and held her like a caress.

"Dip once, just to wet yourself," the woman said, beaming.

She closed her eyes lightly and bent her knees, plunging deep into the clear water until she felt it cover her head.

"Kosher," the woman said approvingly. "Now, say the blessing: 'Blessed art Thou, O G-d, King of the Universe, Who has made us holy and sanctified us with His commandments and commanded us the ritual immersion.' Cross your hands over your breasts, and cover your head with this towel." She lowered the towel just above Dina's head and waited.

Dina did as she was told. Closing her eyes, she felt her arms touch her hot, clean breasts. Her whole body tingled, immaculately clean and pierced with a new sense of holiness. Her mind was full of pure, good thoughts. The love for G-d mingled with a new love for the physical life of her good, clean, pure body. All her sense of shame vanished. She felt a bleached newness, spotless and untainted by anything dark or corrupt. This must be the way angels feel, she thought. Utterly white and unblemished, their very existence a song of holiness, a psalm of praise.

She said the blessing, plunging once again into the hot, clean water.

She stepped out, dripping, and the joyous rebbetzin handed her the towel. She wrapped it around herself, feeling an odd lessening of the urgency to cover her body that had been with her just a little while before.

Alone in the bathroom again, she unwrapped herself, touching her body with slow pleasure. It had been cleansed and sanctified. Nothing shameful could touch it now. Everything that would happen between her and her new husband would be done openly, before the eyes of G-d, with His full approval and benediction. She felt a sharp stab of unknown pride.

She would give herself in all her purity to this kind stranger. She would make him happy, she knew. Whether or not she would be happy, she did not for the moment consider. She was still dazzled, still a little numb with joy from the searing experience of her ablutions, her plunge into new, hot, strange waters that had grabbed and uplifted her like the strong, unrestrainable currents of a vast sea. For the moment, her body and mind and spirit were all in that remarkable state of absolute communion.

She had not dreamed it possible that the small doubts, the confusions, the second thoughts, that stuck to her like unhealed scabs would suddenly, miraculously fall off, leaving behind smooth, glowing health, a wholesomeness that was indescribable. She was one with her desires and her beliefs and the thud of her racing heart. All one, all blessed. It had never happened to her before.

And, blessedly, she didn't know it might never happen to her again.

CHAPTER 19

THE *TENA'IM* CEREMONY WAS TO TAKE PLACE IN A SMALL hall behind the synagogue a week before the wedding. Although the bride's parents had politely suggested that it seemed a waste, coming as it did so near to the wedding itself, Judah and his mother had been pleasantly, though firmly, insistent. They had even agreed to pay all expenses.

"My son will feel more relaxed once it's taken care of," Mrs. Gutman explained. "With a lovely girl like Dina, you can't blame him!"

Mrs. Reich had smiled understandingly. Yet she felt slightly troubled, as if there were some lack of faith, some doubt in the air, polluting the calm, confident joy that should reign before a wedding. Nevertheless, she saw no reason to object.

A week before the engagement, Judah had shown up at the house one evening unannounced, stammering and bumping into furniture, knocking over glasses of water. Barely looking at her, he had handed Dina a velvet box. Inside, burning against the dark velvet with rich, fiery beauty, was a watch of eighteen-karat gold. The band was an exquisite hand-wrought gold filigree, such as Yemenite craftsmen are famous for. The dial was surrounded by twelve tiny, perfect diamonds, and twelve small rubies marked the hours. It was an expensive, subtle, and breathtaking creation, as unlike the clumsy, heavy gold watches that weighted down the arms of her engaged and married friends as a piece of Waterford to a jelly jar.

Dina spent many happy hours looking at it, running a finger over the beautiful handiwork, convincing herself that it was real and it was hers. Still, one thing bothered her. He hadn't consulted her. He had simply gone out and bought it. Most of her engaged friends had been taken along, or at least had gone separately to the jeweler with their mothers to discuss their preferences, letting the jeweler pass on the information to the groom and his parents. Of course, she couldn't have imagined anything more beautiful or more to her taste than the watch he had chosen, but still, not to have been consulted at all rankled her.

She had no way of knowing that Judah's reason was simply the fear she might reject it because of its cost. Often brides chose jewelry they didn't really want in order to impress their in-laws with their lack of materialism. It was considered bad form for a future daughter-in-law to set her heart on something too expensive. This was Judah's fear, that Dina might ask the price and be shocked and give up the piece he so wanted her to have. So he hadn't discussed it with her, just brought it over and almost dumped it on her with a really inappropriate lack of ceremony. His eyes kept flicking to hers, then down to the floor. When he glimpsed her reaction, her blue-green eyes turning suddenly as bright and fair as a lovely spring morning, he felt he had been amply rewarded. He'd floated home in a daze of happiness.

He had taken on a great deal of extra work in order to pay for it and all the other things he wanted her to have. Everything had to be the best. He consulted with his fellow carpenters, and his shop had become the scene of many loud debates over the relative merits of American refrigerators, German stoves, and Dutch washing machines. Judah listened carefully, remembering every word but keeping his decision close to his heart. Price did not enter. The apartment in which he would welcome his fragile, adorable new bride would be a wonder of mechanical efficiency. Everything would whir and grind and mix with delightful ease, with the touch of a button.

"A drier? What does she need a drier for?" his mother pleaded. "With all this good, hot sunshine, winter and summer? It takes a minute to hang it out! You'll spoil her!"

But he just smiled, stubbornly resolved. If there was anything that could take a minute's work away from his dear future wife, he would track it down, buy it, and plug it in. There was no reasoning with Judah on that point.

As for furniture, he had resolved to shop for it together with Dina, letting her pick out what she wanted. But he hadn't counted on the outpouring of gifts from the rough, silent men around him. There was a finely grained coffee table, a kitchen set with built-in benches, a bookcase with glass shelves . . . all handmade with care and singular affection.

The bedroom set, a collective purchase of the members of the carpenters' minyan, was the biggest surprise. Each piece of hardwood had been carefully chosen by the men from the lumberyard, and the work had been entrusted to their most respected senior member, a man everyone knew as "the Austrian," because before Hitler he had been foreman of a prestigious Viennese custom furniture workshop. Though now reduced—as were they all—to making boxy pine kitchen cabinets, the Austrian had not forgotten his old skills.

The design was a bit old-fashioned and heavy, but there was no mistaking the skilled and loving craftsmanship that had gone into its creation. All the joints were either smoothly dovetailed or were secret haunched tenons, a complicated version of the simple mortise-and-tenon joints, one that beautifully concealed all the rough edges. The carving on the headboard and the night tables, the almost mirrorlike finish that brought out the lovely, rich grain of the wood, filled the men with admiration. They couldn't wait to give it to Judah.

"Judah," Lazarovich called out one morning. "You know, we're not going to have a minyan this morning. The Austrian refuses to come. He says you've insulted him. What did you do to him, Judah? So soon before your wedding to start fights, to create such anger. Why, I've never seen the Austrian so upset!"

Slowly Judah wiped his hands and looked at the man. His face was deeply troubled. "I don't know," he mumbled. "Why, perhaps he wanted to read the Torah last Monday and I didn't let him. Perhaps that's why," he mused, full of honest distress. "I will go to him right away!"

"Good idea." The man nodded. "No use letting these things fester. Besides, how will we pray this morning without a tenth man? You wouldn't want that on your conscience, now, would you? A real *shandah* that would be! And you two weeks before the wedding canopy! Go quickly, quickly," he called after Judah's hurrying figure, almost bursting with laughter.

"Reb Nissim, it's Judah Gutman," he said, tapping on the dusty workshop window. "I want to talk to you."

"Well, I don't know if I want to talk to you," came the haughty reply.

Judah's heart sank, his chin falling to the top of his chest in dismay. "Please, Reb Nissim, just a word. I've come to apologize, to beg your forgiveness. . . . I'm not a good *gabbai*, I always make mistakes about who should be called up to the Torah. I keep telling the men to replace me, that I'm totally worthless at it. I always insult people, because I am just no good at it. . . ."

Slowly the door inched open. Judah stepped inside, still apologizing profusely, abjectly. And then the lights went on and he saw the Austrian's broad smile. His eyes darted in confusion around the room. It was filled with all his friends from the minyan and practically everyone else who worked on the Street of Carpenters.

Roars of delight greeted Judah's dumbfounded surprise. And then he saw the bedroom set.

"For you, a wedding present from the minyan," the Austrian said with deep pleasure. "And Judah, you are an excellent *gabbai*. You never make mistakes."

To their great surprise, and for the first time in their long relationship, Judah Gutman got up before them and spoke: "*Chesed*, loving-kindness, is what G-d loves most to see in human beings. G-d himself begins the Torah with an act of kindness by clothing the naked Adam and Eve, and he ends it with kindness, by himself burying Moses. There are so many good deeds one person can do for another. You can lend your possessions, give charity and free loans. You can welcome guests into your home, visit the sick, comfort mourners. But one of the biggest acts of kindness is to gladden the heart of the bride and groom." He ran his hand over the lovely dark wood. "As it is written: 'Whoever gladdens the bridegroom is privileged to acquire Torah, and is considered as if he had made an offering in the holy Temple, or rebuilt the ruins of Jerusalem.' Our father Abraham, through whose merit we continue to live, gave only goodness and kindness to all the world. And all of you are his true sons. May G-d bless you all!"

They saw he was close to tears, and they felt their own eyes welling up. Even the younger, coarser men who wore no skullcaps and had come just out of curiosity, found themselves oddly moved by the big, silent fellow's sudden articulateness. They all loved Judah Gutman, and never more than at that moment.

Afterward he had had no choice but to tell Dina that some of the furniture too had been acquired without her. She was understanding. A gift, after all, was a gift. He did not see her bite her underlip in dismay when she saw the dark, old-fashioned set she would have no choice but to live with every day for the rest of her married life.

"The house seems to be filling up," she said dryly.

He smiled at her gratefully, missing completely the pointed, critical edge of her words. The more things a woman had, the better she liked it, no? And he wanted to give her everything in the whole world. His only regret was that it wouldn't fit into a three-bedroom apartment. Thus, he was already scheming how to get another mortgage and trade the place in for a four-bedroom apartment and then maybe a duplex cottage with a garden. . . . He envisioned working his fingers to the bone, humming all the while a hymn of thanksgiving.

The day of the *tena'im* arrived. He and his mother were picked up by one of his fellow carpenters and driven to the hall. He had invited all ten men in the minyan and their wives. He would have invited the whole Street of Carpenters if his mother hadn't stopped him.

Dina was already there. He sucked in his breath. This gorgeous, wonderful girl! His bride! His whole simple, innocent soul expanded and rose with unrestrained joy. She looked heart-stoppingly fragile, almost luminous to him in her soft, high-collared pink dress that fell in soft pleats from her small, delicate waist. Too beautiful to be real. Her eyes rested on his a moment, the golden lashes dropping down in modesty, making shadows on her soft, rosy cheeks.

She was the embodiment of everything sacred and good to him. Everything worth living for. A gift, a reward from G-d himself.

He walked over to the table where the men were sitting drawing up the official engagement papers. These stated the date and place of marriage, the financial obligations of both sides, and the monetary penalty to be leveled in case of breach. The rabbis were there and the bride's male relatives. The groom initialed the agreement quickly, without reading it. Then Dina's father, reading it over carefully, did the same. When it was signed, Rebbetzin Reich and Mrs. Gutman took either end of the same plate and smashed it to the floor. Cries of "Mazel tov!" rang out. The men formed rings and took wild, leaping steps as the small band began to play. The room filled with cries of joy and the stamp of dancing feet, which grew more meaningful and more frenzied by the minute. The Austrian balanced a chair on his forehead, and a great clapping began with whoops of laughter. Then he added a bottle of wine and on top of that a plate of cakes.

Dina sat behind the partition that separated the men from the women, surrounded by her female relatives and friends.

"Now, you are almost a bride!" Dvorah hugged her. She was in her fourth month of pregnancy. Baby Shlomie was crying in a carriage, and she walked over to him tiredly, her hands massaging a sudden ache in her back.

"Come and see all the fun!" Chaya Leah urged Dina. "Why, he's now put a jug of water on top of the plate!" Her eyes blazed in excitement.

"In a minute," Dina said calmly, with an icy sense of growing panic: the *tena'im* had been signed! It was easier to marry and get a divorce than get out of it now! What have I done? she thought with a little horror, thinking of Sruyele, that pitiable, forlorn relation who had disgraced them all. She looked past the merrymakers to Judah and wondered in a paroxysm of fear: Who is this man, anyway, this stranger? She wrung her hands and felt the gold watch. As she looked at it, she felt a sudden new confidence. She had this lovely watch. And her own apartment filled with everything you could ever dream of. And then she thought of Judah, his powerful frame, his shy eyes.

He was such a good man; everyone said so. She wanted to love him, to appreciate his goodness and respond to his obvious passion for her. He wanted her, of this she had no doubt. Whether or not she really wanted him was not important. As Dvorah said, that would come. She would learn to love him, as Dvorah had learned to love her husband. She looked again at the lovely gold filigree, suffused in brilliant light. It was the beginning of a beautiful life.

She got up and wandered to where Chaya Leah stood looking through a gap in the divider. Judah was in the middle of a circle. His large frame was moving with mincing, self-mocking daintiness in a Hasidic dance to the rhythmic clapping of the delighted men who joined him. He was deliberately exaggerating his clumsiness, his bigness, his awkwardness, eagerly forgoing his dignity to increase the joy and laughter all around him, as was traditional on such occasions.

"Just look! He's wonderful!" Chaya Leah called out.

"Wonderful," Dina repeated, trying to suppress the slow burn of humiliation that crept up her cheek as she watched him.

CHAPTER 20

"I DON'T KNOW WHY YOU'VE LEFT IT FOR THE LAST THING," Dvorah complained. She, Dina, and their mother were headed for the wig store. It was three days before the wedding. "What if you choose something that needs to be styled and set? They might not be able to do it in time for the wedding!"

"Then I'll just cover my hair with a *tichel* after the ceremony," Dina replied calmly, refusing to get nervous over the million and one little details that vied for her attention each day. There never seemed to be an end to it. The gift for the groom (a beautiful tallith, prayer shawl, with a hand-embroidered tallith bag). The flowers. The menu. Choosing the blankets and sheets her parents were giving them as a wedding gift.

She had gotten over her initial confusion and now rested in some pacific sea, well behind giant breakwaters. After all, the act of choosing a partner for life, the man who would sleep and eat next to you for the next fifty years or so, dwarfed anything and everything else on the horizon.

"You can't be serious! A *tichel!* Do you want to look like some old *bubee* from Poland? No one wears head scarves anymore." Dvorah patted the elegant, stylish waves of her own chestnut-brown wig.

"You're right not to get excited about it. It is a foolish worry, my child," Rebbetzin Reich said mildly, effectively overruling and chastising her eldest daughter. "Anyhow, we are here already."

The store was not crowded since most religious women worked or cared for small children in the morning and had precious little time to spend in wig shops or beauty parlors. It looked like a cross between a hat shop and a beauty parlor. There were chairs placed in front of mirrors and brushes and combs on the counter. In the rear were dozens of Styrofoam heads bearing wigs.

Dina looked over the selection. It was enormous and intimidating, ranging from an almost punk-looking short, spiky one to a waist-long fall of human hair. The long ones were usually French-braided or ponytailed, or bunned, depending on the client's mood. A beautician who specialized in wig styling was employed full-time. She also cut the clients' real hair so that it wouldn't bunch under the wig. Religious women didn't go to regular beauty parlors to get their hair cut because of the male hairdressers who would have to not only witness their hair uncovered, but actually touch them, which was completely unacceptable.

"Dvorah, dear, how are you? Sit down, sit down," the store owner greeted them effusively. She was a tall, thin woman whose hair was beautifully done in a shoulder-length flip. It took Dina a moment to realize that it too was a wig. It was unbelievably natural. "That wig looks lovely. I knew it would. I told you, didn't I, that it would?" the saleswoman gushed at Dvorah, a steady client. "Are you ready for another one?"

"I've brought my sister. She is a bride," Dvorah said, pointing at Dina. Imagine the storekeeper thinking she had come for herself! Why, her wig was hardly three months old, and a very expensive one, more expensive than most *kollel* wives could usually afford. More expensive than she could afford! But the owner had talked her into it. Now she imagined she was already in the market for another! What must she think of her?

Yet she was admiring the owner's own hairdo, scheming on how to get one just like it. Wigs were the *haredi* woman's biggest vice. They were terribly expensive, yet one had no choice. And most of them simply wore out, especially if you wore them daily. Those who could afford it had several, allowing them to send one to the beauty parlor to be washed, set, and styled while they wore the others. In a way it was a great time-saver. They couldn't imagine the hours secular women spent waiting under hairdriers. It seemed so much easier just to send your hair in, the way they did.

"A *kallah!*" The shop owner clapped her hands. "Lovely, lovely. Don't worry, we will find you a beautiful *shaytl*. Now, did you want a long or short one, human or synthetic hair, and what color?"

"I have no idea," Dina murmured, looking beseechingly at her mother and sister.

"I think a long one would be best, something she could style different ways," Dvorah answered decisively.

"And the color?"

"My own color, I think," Dina broke in, beginning to feel a bit left out.

The shop owner lifted a lock of the mousy, light brown hair and stared at it a moment. "Of course . . . whatever you wish. But I'm not sure we have exactly that color. Maybe something a little lighter. . . ."

She went hurrying off to the back and emerged with

five or six boxes piled up in her arms, something like a shoe salesman.

"Try this," she said, whipping out a shoulder-length blond wig from the box, shaking it out and brushing it lightly. She pulled it over Dina's scalp.

It felt tight, and although it wasn't very heavy, there was a slight sense of discomfort and confinement. The store owner fussed with it.

Rebbetzin Reich stared at her daughter. The wig was a gorgeous light blond, unbelievably natural. The color, sun-kissed and glamorous, made her daughter look absolutely stunning. The hair, Dina's only plain feature, was suddenly one of her most striking. She looked like a model in a magazine.

"This," the saleswoman said with authority, "is your color."

"I don't know," Dina protested weakly, shifting on her chair with vague discomfort. She couldn't believe that the girl in the mirror who looked back at her with such striking good looks was someone she would learn to live with. She was a bold, sophisticated stranger.

"Believe me, this is a very versatile model. You have the length you need for a braid or a ponytail." The woman fussed with the hair, pinning it up and pulling it back. Dina watched herself go from cool elegance to pert young blondness. This, definitely, was her color. Yet something was bothering her.

She looked too good. Too attractive. Too . . . And while she could not even say the word, and probably did not even think it, she no doubt instinctively felt the truth: she looked too sexy.

"It's a bit too flashy, too attractive," the rebbetzin said, shaking her head.

"My dear rebbetzin, the laws of modesty that demand a religious woman cover her hair after marriage don't say she has to look unattractive! Where is it written that a head covering needs to be dull? I assure you, my clients are the biggest rebbetzins in Jerusalem. Their husbands head the most prestigious *kollelim* and *batei medrash*. They are judges and rabbis. And believe me, they wear the nicest wigs we can offer them. I know, years ago things were different. Women covered their hair with *tichels*. But nowadays no self-respecting *haredi* woman would dream of going to an affair without a beautiful wig. Don't you think the men want their wives to look attractive? And isn't it better that way, than having them look at other men's wives?"

She had gone a bit too far, and she knew it. She took a sharp intake of breath. "Forgive me. But believe me, I feel a great obligation that every woman who comes into my shop goes out with the wig that will bring the most happiness to her life and her husband's."

"No doubt, no doubt," Rebbetzin Reich said, thinking of all the posters that had gone up around the neighborhoods of Meah Shearim and Bnai Brak several years earlier when the rabbis had taken arms against the sea of long, natural-looking wigs that had suddenly flooded the *haredi* world from America and Korea. Their women had suddenly started looking so good and so natural that the men could no longer tell who was wearing a wig and who wasn't, creating a panic among *haredi* men who could no longer tell apart married from unmarried women by a simple glance.

The rabbis had issued warnings to all the wigmakers that G-d would punish them for selling such things and warned them that wigs that reached lower than the earlobe were unacceptable. Women had been warned against the long wigs and exhorted to go back to wearing short, sensible ones or scarves. The rabbis had even pointed to the death in childbirth of a young religious woman as a sign from heaven that G-d was against the long wigs.

Nothing had helped. *Haredi* women ignored all the warnings, all the exhortations. They liked the long wigs. And since the *halacha* stated only that a married woman needed to cover her natural hair, they knew that all the rest was opinion.

Rebbetzin Reich touched her daughter's head with a touch of sorrow. Dina's mousy brown hair. It had always seemed the one flaw in her looks, the one thing that kept her from dangerous, overwhelming beauty. And now, ironically, by keeping the laws of modesty and covering it, she would finally reach her full, dangerous potential. There had to be something wrong with that! The rabbis who had formulated the laws of the Talmud and Mishnah could not possibly have foreseen a day when a married woman's modestly covering her hair would make her more conspicuously attractive to men than leaving it uncovered! They could not possibly have imagined a hair covering more attractive than a young girl's own hair! Yet that was the law and the reality.

All these thoughts went rapidly and vaguely through Rebbetzin Reich's mind as she looked at her daughter. But the truth was, all the young girls got beautiful wigs when they married. Despite her misgivings, she could not have her Dina looking unattractive at all the parties that would take place after the wedding. The *sheva brachot*, the seven dinners given in honor of the young couple for seven days after the wedding, were festive occasions in which her daughter would take her place among the matrons of the community. It wouldn't do at all for her to look as if she couldn't afford a fine wig. People might begin to whisper that something was wrong with the match if poverty had set in so soon! The rebbetzin shuddered. "What do you think, Dinaleh?"

All this time Dina Reich had been staring at herself in the mirror, playing idly with the soft, shining blond curls. A gentle, satisfied smile played around her lips, and in her eyes—a little wide with surprise—there was a look of strange triumph. I look so pretty! She couldn't help admiring herself. So rarely was this kind of vanity permitted to young *haredi* girls; so often were they admonished that it was the soul, the spirit, that was the true repository of human beauty, not the flesh that aged and wrinkled and faded back into dust.

Yet, being a bride, she was caught up in her body. The immersion in the ritual bath, the careful examinations beforehand, had awakened in her a new knowledge. She was discovering her body, her flesh, as an explorer does a new, beautiful untrammeled wilderness, finding in it breathtaking vistas, unheard-of joys. She was so young, so very lovely. Judah's eyes had told her that. And another's. . . . If only certain people could see her now! If only Abraham . . . ! She stopped, horrified.

She took the wig off quickly.

"Do you want to see another?"

"Yes, something shorter and my own color."

"What! But it looks so pretty on you," Dvorah protested.

"Really, Dina. It was very lovely."

Dina looked at her mother. What would she say if she knew?

I am a horrible person. Wicked, simply wicked. She pressed the terrifying thoughts down, down, slamming the trunk lid on top of them, locking the trunk.

"All right. I'll get it."

"And now, one for every day. . . ." The saleswoman went off to wrap the purchase, smiling broadly. She loved brides. She felt a real sense of mission in making them look good in the wigs, thereby getting them to accept the *halacha* about covering their hair after the wedding without too much protest. The better she made them look, the less they seemed to mind. This alone, she felt, would earn her a respectable place in the World to Come.

CHAPTER 21

THE WEDDING WAS OVER. JUST LIKE THAT, DINA THOUGHT, astonished, as she watched her friends and relatives pick up the flower arrangements from the white-clothed tables and head for the doors. She had not really been awake for it, she thought. Just snatches had come through to her: the trembling flicker of the candle flames held by her mother and mother-in-law as they linked their arms through hers and urged her down the aisle; the solid white blank of Judah in his kittel—the groom's traditional white robe—waiting for her underneath the wedding canopy; the slow burn of the wine down her throat as she broke her bride's fast; the thunderous clap of men's shoes against the dance floor. And, of course, all the delighted, warm, pitying faces staring into hers; all the smiling, peering, searching, joyous faces inspecting hers. Her mouth was weary from smiling, her throat dry from responding.

And now, suddenly, she was a married woman. Her father's face, bright with indescribable joy and touched with sadness, seemed white and disembodied as he took his leave, pressing his daughter's hands gently into his. Dvorah, visibly pregnant, sat on a chair, her little Shlomie resting his sleeping head against her swelling stomach. She looked exhausted, yet her parting smile was full of encouragement.

Only Chaya Leah seemed genuinely untouched, unfazed, and full of unspent energy. She had organized all the women's dances, leading the hora rounds with vigor and skill. She seemed chagrined it ever had to end and reluctant to leave, her energetic feet tapping the floor with impatience. Her good-bye kiss was gay and—so Dina thought with annoyance—callous.

Dina rested her head on her mother's shoulder and felt her big, comforting arms meet at the small of her back, supportive and protective. She closed her eyes, and for one moment everything that had just taken place—the prayers: "You are hereby sanctified to me according to the law of Moses and Israel," the groom's intense, moist forehead, the touch of his tentative fingers slipping the cool gold on her finger, the glass smashing against the floor, the cries of "Mazel tov!"—dissolved into a dream. She was safe. She was home.

But then the arms were gone, and a slight chill began to climb up slowly from the base of her spine, spreading out to her shoulders and chest, making her lips tremble with cold. She grabbed her mother's hand and kissed it just before it slipped away.

She was alone with the man she had married. She looked at his powerful male body, his kind, gentle face, and felt, perhaps, that it might be possible, feasible, after all. Nevertheless she felt somehow heartbroken.

They took a taxi. She walked behind him up the narrow stairs to her new home. There was a strangeness in the aromas of the building, the echo of her footsteps on the stairs, the soft scraping of Judah's shoes, the metallic scratch of the key turning in the lock. She was almost afraid to look at him.

"Tired?" he asked her.

"Not really. Are you?" She felt her teeth begin to chatter, and a momentary panic gripped her. She fought against it, fought against the slow, unraveling motion that was taking place in her mind and heart. She could almost hear the words that made up the shout that was deafening her ears and pushing her heart to the limit. "I am only seventeen years old! I don't know you! I want to go home to my dear narrow bed in my sister's room, in the bedroom next to my *ima* and *aba*. *Ima!*"

He made no move to touch her.

"Would you like a drink, something to eat?" His voice was gentle, solicitous.

She thought about it a moment. It wasn't possible, was it, after all that food that she could be starving? And yet she was. Absolutely ravenous.

"I myself am just about ready to faint from hunger!" he admitted.

She looked up at him gratefully and laughed.

"All that money! All that food! The stuffed chickens and the beef in mushrooms! The borekas and the slices of kugel! And here we are, both starving. What would you like to do? I don't think there is much in the house," he said apologetically.

"Why don't I just go and see?" she offered, trying to sound wifely. She was relieved to have something as ordinary as getting a meal together to focus on; grateful for anything that would postpone the inevitable strangeness of their first night together.

She wasn't afraid of him, she told herself. But the whole idea, the whole scenario, just seemed so utterly preposterous! That she, Dina Reich, who had her whole life been taught to cover her body, to lower her eyes, to stand in separate lines in the bakery, to stand hidden behind partitions in the synagogue, should now be expected to enter a room with a man and take off her clothes and climb into bed with him! The thought went beyond absurd. It was simply terrifying and irreconcilable.

Someone had stocked the large, clean, hummingly new refrigerator generously and carefully. How pretty the kitchen was! How much expense and care had been given to make it a pleasant place to be and work, she thought with covetous pleasure. "Would you like some eggs? Coffee?"

"Fine," he said. "Don't go to any trouble. You must be very tired, no?"

He had walked in and stood very close to her as she puttered around the sink and stove. He leaned back against the cabinets, watching everything she did with the utmost concentration. She could almost feel his eyes as a physical touch, a soft caress running up and down her body and face. Trembling, she placed two new, clean plates on the table, filled two shiny blue earthenware cups with coffee, and went to get the milk and sugar.

"I can't believe we are both still milchig!" He shook his head. One had to wait six hours between eating milk and meat, and the milk on the table was a sign that neither of them had even so much as nibbled at the wedding food.

She sat opposite him, cradling the coffee mug comfortingly between her cool palms. Slowly she began to feel a cleansing warmth spreading out concentrically from her chest, traveling slowly up her arms and neck. Shyly she studied the strange man she had just married.

He did look well in the soft, domestic light of the kitchen. Very safe and predictable, surrounded as he was by the scrambled eggs and salad, the plates and forks and place mats. The food slid down her throat, easing the terrible protests of her rumbling stomach, so long denied sustenance.

"I thought that the rabbi's words were very good. Did you think so, too, Judah?"

"Yes." He looked up at her, and his passionate, longing eyes startled her, piercing through her calm like a bullet. Not predictable at all! A flash of danger tore through her stomach. She felt his hand, large, gentle, yet increasingly possessive, squeeze her arm.

She got up abruptly. "I'll just do these dishes. . . ." She hurried to clear off the table. But his arm was insistent on hers.

"Leave them!" It wasn't harsh or commanding, simply compelling, and she felt helpless against it. Slowly she felt the plates slip into the hot dishwater with a soft, faraway tinkle that didn't even seem to be in the same room.

"Then I think I will get dressed for bed," she tried to say casually. But there was a choked, quivering acquiescence to her tone that made him sad.

"Yes. And I, too," he agreed, beginning to feel a little doubtful—the same sad, remorseful feeling he had when he accidentally frightened the little sparrows he came to feed. But you couldn't very well leave your bride untouched, could you? It was their wedding night. This was her right, as his bride, not something due him. If he didn't measure up, she could get rid of him. The thought almost paralyzed him.

They stood together, not moving. The idea of changing in and out of clothes in front of each other kept both of them rooted to the floor.

"I'll go in and use the bathroom," Judah said solicitously.

"Thank you," she answered politely, her heart beginning to pound.

She went into their bedroom, turning on the light. It reflected harshly off the magnificently polished surface of the bedroom set. Again it struck her how very dark and old-fashioned it was, how much she disliked it. A hard knot of pique formed in her chest. She undressed quickly, not bothering to fold her clothes but hurrying to quickly cover herself. She was terrified he might come out of the bathroom before she finished. She felt her fingers fumble with the zipper on her silky skirt, then slip nervously around the smooth buttons of her blouse.

A hesitant knock on the door.

"May I come in?"

"Please!"

He was too large for the room, she thought. His pajamas, old-fashioned and dark brown, made him seem almost bearlike. He took a few hesitant steps toward her. Yet his face was very handsome, his shoulders broad. Quickly she backed away, climbing abruptly and instinctively into the twin bed nearest the door.

She pulled the covers over her high-necked, long-sleeved nightgown, then reached into her night table for her prayer book.

She took it out and found the prayer for intercourse:

. . . purify my body, sanctify my soul and thoughts and intelligence and feelings. Strengthen me and dress me in Your good and generous spirit, that I might build up my household in truth and righteousness. . . . Give this new life that may be conceived completeness in charity and mercy. Have compassion on all its doings, its health and creativity. Let nothing in its body be defective or wanting all the days of its life. Let it never feel pain, or sorrow, illness or disease. Bless me and my household and my offspring with wholeness, completing our ideas and intelligence and feelings, so that everything we do will be according to Thy will. Bless us with heavenly blessings from the world above, and the worlds that lie beneath. And from Your blessings will Your servant's house be blessed all the days of our lives.

It was a long prayer that filled her heart with a feeling of calm and decency. It was startling and uplifting to be reminded of children at such a time. But just that reminder, and the constant idea of G-d being with them in the room, she found infinitely comforting. Nothing could happen that was shameful or wrong in this room into which she had just invited G-d's presence. She thought of Rebbetzin Felder's words and the feeling of intense purity that had enveloped her in the mikveh. Her mind, her feelings, were ready. But was her body?

She felt Judah move in slowly beside her. His fingers were long and sensitive, surprisingly smooth as they explored her in the darkness, the way a sensitive blind man might explore a rare and beautiful sculpture, trying to understand and appreciate it fully. Slowly she took off her nightgown and inched toward him, reaching out timidly for his chest. It was big and strongly muscled, covered with downy hair. She pressed her neck into the crook of his arm. It was not so different, she thought, from the loving warmth of a parent's caress. She snuggled closer, gaining confidence and boldness.

And then she felt him move toward her, and things began to move out of control with frightening rapidity. There were no longer any clear expectations. Everything was unbearably new and surprising, and exquisite, with a terrible, unbearable strangeness.

"Shall I stop?" he whispered to her anxiously, full of concern.

"No." She felt the corner of her mouth catch a large and salty drop as she felt the painful tear that cut her off irrevocably from her past. She closed her eyes and thought: What do I know about life? Reward and punishment. Love as a sacred duty. Kindness and charity and obligation. If you did everything you were supposed to, it didn't make you good. But if you didn't, it made you bad. Even going out of your way, doing something extra—carrying the packages of a stranger—was nothing special, just the ordinary threads of life's fabric. Not silk or velvet, just simple cotton and wool. Natural and ordinary.

It had been bred into her and into her parents before her and their parents before them. Life was always on a higher level. You always prayed. You always set aside ten percent of your earnings for the poor, invited strangers for meals, cared for aging, often ungrateful relatives. All your goodness, your sacrifices, flowed together, an ordinary stream of life. It never added up into any great achievement. There was always something missing. Always one could have prayed with a little more devotion, invited a few more guests, given a little more time and effort to visiting the sick and comforting the bereaved, fed a few more odd and distasteful strangers, learned a few more pages of Torah.

What act would be truly whole, truly great? she wondered. She could think of nothing, for even giving up one's life was within the ordinary limits of the law, prescribed and delineated with clear certainty. Many had done so rather than deny the one true G-d, rather than rape or murder or commit adultery. It was expected.

Was there anything one could do, any gesture or act so unusual or magnificent in its piety and sacrifice that it would rise above the stream, creating its own separate flow? This idea had often troubled her.

She felt the great weight of the strange man above her bear down on her in the holy act that would bring the joy of new life into being. She felt wholly consumed, utterly sacrificed. Perhaps, she thought, perhaps this. She moved upward towards him and toward the future, giving herself wholly to the moment, and felt a great wash of understanding and comfort and joy sweep through her. She heard his sharp intake of breath in surprise and happiness as she gave herself to him, clutching him close to her.

He seemed no longer a great, strange weight above her, weighing her down, but simply part of her, like her arms or legs. No one had ever touched her so deeply, so thoroughly. It was almost inhuman, unthinkable. Yet the prayer, the darkness, kept out all shame, all humiliation.

And then, beyond imagining, she felt the surge of pleasure that had been wholly left out of everything she had been taught. Her whole body arched toward it, laughing in wondrous eagerness. More and more and more. It was . . . She could not think anymore. This, too, then, they had kept from her. Not sacrifice at all! Not painful or burdensome. This surge of pure, incredibly intense beauty. It had been there all the time, but she had not known it.

She felt herself reach out to him once more, beyond all shyness, all restraint. Gratefully.

CHAPTER 22

"I PLAN TO GO INTO THE ARMY."

Chaya Leah's mouth gaped. "Moishe, what are you talking about? Your parents would kill you!"

He shrugged. "I'm not learning in yeshiva full-time, so I don't have an automatic deferment."

"Lots of boys who work part-time still get out of the army. They get notes from rebbes or psychiatrists. They pretend that they're learning or crazy—"

"It's disgusting!" His tone was contemptuous.

She let go of his arm, aware of their passing from the darkened park toward the illuminated center of Jerusalem's cafes, restaurants, and movie theaters. "Why is it disgusting?" She was amazed at his heretical attitude. Everyone in the *haredi* world felt it was a G-d-given duty to get out of doing any army service. Military food wasn't kosher enough. There was guard duty on the Sabbath and holidays. The army was full of secular, rabidly antireligious elements. Most of all, army service would cut them off from their main task in life: learning Torah full-time. *Haredim* viewed with the greatest alarm and suspicion any move by the government to change or limit draft exemptions for yeshiva students.

"But if it wasn't for the yeshiva students who learn Torah and pray, we would never have won any of the wars. Our learning and praying is equal in value to all the bombs and planes and foot soldiers in the army!" she exclaimed, repeating the oft-expressed rationale that even the smallest child in the *haredi* world knew.

"All very well and convenient. But where is it written that studying or praying exempts one from military service? When Joshua led the children of Israel into Canaan, did Hashem say, 'Draft everyone from age twenty and above who isn't learning or praying'?" he scoffed. "Every Jew has to learn and pray."

"That's not the same thing! Joshua was leading the Jews to a religious war, a war to take over the land and build the holy Temple. But the Zionists aren't building a Jewish country. They eat pig and desecrate the Sabbath. So all their wars to protect their secular state are not holy wars like Joshua's. . . ."

"But what about saving Jewish lives? Isn't that important? Isn't that holy?"

"G-d will help us if we keep His commandments, if we learn Torah and pray. . . ."

"You're just spewing out all that junk they've been feeding you since you were little! I'm surprised at you, Chaya Leah! I thought you had a mind of your own. You're not supposed to depend on miracles. Remember Jacob? When he came back home after twenty years of fleeing his brother Esau, he didn't just sit back and wait for G-d to provide a miracle. He sent ambassadors with presents to soften Esau up. And then when that didn't seem to work, he divided his wives and children into three camps so that if one was attacked, the others could flee and be saved."

"I don't understand you! Why would you want to risk your life if you don't have to? If you can get out of it?"

"It's called being a coward."

She turned bright red with anger. "So, are you calling my father, and Yaakov, and my brothers—"

"I'm not calling anybody anything," he continued stubbornly despite her obvious anger. "I'm just saying that I personally am not going to be studying full-time. I don't see any reason why I shouldn't learn how to shoot in case we're attacked."

"But G-d will help us!" she repeated helplessly, beginning to feel out of her depth.

"But how do you know *how* G-d will help us? Maybe His help will come in the form of letting the bullets we fire land where they're supposed to, or having our grenades fall and explode on target! It's not all having enemy bombs fall harmlessly into the sea, you know. I'll give you an example. Did you ever hear of the story from the Yom Kippur war about the tank driver, Zvika?

"Well, you know the whole Golan Heights was overrun by the Syrians. Syrian troops were advancing from the north and south. Only a thin line divided them, keeping their forces from combining and taking over not only the whole Golan Heights, but Tiberias and the Galilee as well. Our side was completely unprepared and outnumbered. In fact, the Syrian commander was so shocked at how easily he had been able to get his tanks in that he thought it was some kind of trap, that our army was simply waiting for his forces to advance in order to surround and destroy them.

"This, of course, wasn't true at all. There was no plan, no tanks, and no tricks. All there was was this one lone tank commandeered by a soldier called Zvika. Now Zvika had no idea what was going on. He was totally alone. He'd gotten up to the Heights on his own initiative, gotten two or three tanks to go with him, and they were riding up and down the thin dividing line that separated the two Syrian divisions. He kept shooting at everything in sight, until he was the only Israeli tank left. But he kept calling over his radio, identifying himself as part of "the Zvika Brigade," making it sound like he was leading thousands of tanks. The Syrian commander, of course, intercepted this and was convinced his ambush theory was correct. So instead of giving orders to steamroll down the mountain and capture Tiberias, he ordered his troops to retreat to Damascus and lost the war. He was later hung as a traitor."

"So what's the point?"

"The point is that we were saved by a miracle. And that miracle was Zvika. He was G-d's instrument. But if he hadn't been in that tank, how could G-d have used him? If he had been sitting in some yeshiva somewhere praying, it wouldn't have done much good."

"Well, some people are meant to fight and some are meant to pray. Anyway, there are enough soldiers. And you'll serve eventually."

"Right." He nodded sarcastically. "When I'm forty and have six children and they can only take me in for three months instead of three years, and I'll be checking pocketbooks at the movie theater. . . . Anyhow, who decides who fights and who learns and prays?"

She took his arm, which had stiffened in offense. "Let's not fight, Moishe. You'll do what you want. Only, I don't want you to leave me. . . ."

"I'll be here for the next six months at least, and then there will be home leaves. . . ."

He held her tight around the waist, forgetting himself.

And just then, as the hand of G-d had no doubt arranged it, standing on the corner in profound shock and watchfulness, stood the living incarnation of Judgment Day, as seen in the worst nightmares of Chaya Leah Reich.

"Chaya Leah!" said Mrs. Morganbesser, the steam (or was it simply a low evening fog?) boiling around her head.

There isn't even time to throw myself in front of a truck, Chaya Leah thought. Or to take Moishe's hand off my waist.

Her parents' voices, low, then suddenly, sharply, higher, seeped in under the bedroom door of the room she now had entirely to herself. It had been two hours since Morganbesser left. And still, her parents had not called her in. She went to her knitting, dropping more stitches than she made. She looked over the sweater sleeve she was knitting. Would it all unravel, all the careful work, all the planning and care? Would it all go to waste in the end? Would she have to tear it all out completely and start over from nothing? All the good, careful stitches . . . would they be undone, erased, as if they had never happened at all? She threw the needles down on the bed. It was intolerable! Why didn't they ask to speak to her at least?

Just then her mother came in, shutting the door behind her. Her face was a mask of pain. Chaya Leah looked at her in shock and dismay, the defiance draining from her tight, closed mouth. "*Ima!*"

"It's a little late for your concern now, isn't it, Chaya Leah?" Rebbetzin Reich sat down heavily on Dina's empty bed. She picked up the little bow-tied pillows and fluffed them, then arranged them neatly against the wall. She folded her strong, work-roughened hands in her lap. "Is it true? Have you been seeing this boy, this Moishe, in the city at night without our knowledge?"

Chaya Leah nodded wordlessly.

Rebbetzin Reich felt the sharp stab that went through her left shoulder down her arm. "What were your intentions, Chaya Leah?" Her voice was soft, almost painfully intimate, as if she were telling her daughter a secret.

"My intentions are to be his wife," she said, her courage returning for a moment.

"So, we will not discuss that you have lied to me and

your father, that you could have brought our entire family into disgrace and made us the topic of *loshen hara* of every busybody in Meah Shearim. I say 'could have' because Mrs. Morganbesser has promised not to breathe a word, and I trust her. G-d has taken pity on your father and me by having someone as piously concerned with spreading slander as Mrs. Morganbesser discover you and not some hypocrite who would have made it the talk of the town. Do you know what would happen if it became the talk of the town?"

Chaya Leah tossed her head. "It's nobody's business, anyway. . . ."

"I see that you don't," her mother continued, undeflected. "Well, let me paint a picture for you. First, you would have been thrown out of Beit Yaakov and not allowed to graduate."

Chaya Leah's mouth dropped open.

"Then, your father would probably have been asked to leave his job as mashgiach at the yeshiva. After all, a man who can't control his own daughter can't be entrusted with the spiritual control of young students. The parents would have insisted on it. And then there is the store. Do you know who buys my wool? Respectable women. True, they come to me because they trust me to give them the best quality at the lowest prices. But they also come to me because they like to talk to me, to be with me. They are my friends, neighbors, and acquaintances. If they hear embarrassing things about us, do you think they will want to come to my store and look me in the face?"

Chaya Leah looked stricken.

"Oh, so finally the defiant one begins to understand! But only begins! Have you given a thought to what will happen to your brothers? The best yeshivot will not accept them if there is a taint on the family, nor will they be able to find brides. You will utterly destroy this family with your foolishness!" The strength that had rested for the most part on anger suddenly drained from Faigie Reich's determined face as her own words began to become more real to her. Chaya Leah! Her own child. How had she failed so utterly and completely? Her shoulders shook in painfully controlled sobs.

Chaya Leah had never in her life seen her mother cry. It was like having a bomb explode and shatter the whole known world. She started to think about all the things she had done in the last few months in her mother's terms and began to tremble. She forgot that she had ever had a point of view, a perfectly justified rationale, for acting the way she had. She forgot that she thought it was perfectly fine to choose your own husband and date him without your parents and the community interfering. She forgot that she thought it was perfectly all right for you to kiss and hug him. She had no point of view any longer, but simply a white-hot blazing fear that rampaged through her mind and took the form of her strong, demanding mother crumpled before her in tears.

The only thing she remembered was that she was a fifteen-year-old Beit Yaakov girl who had been caught redhanded in an embrace with a boy by Mrs. Morganbesser; that she had almost totally destroyed her family's income, reputation, and probably their hearts. She felt herself shrinking with each new revelation of sin like a storybook character drinking some magic potion until she was reduced to nothing but dust on the floor. She felt she had never been so frightened in her life until her mother looked up and told her something that sent her beyond her wildest nightmares. It was something so simple, so self-evident, and yet something that she had never thought about at all when enjoying her plans, whether because it just hadn't occurred to her or because it was too unthinkable to deal with:

"Now, go in. Your father wants to speak to you. You have hurt him deeply."

• • •

The next morning, in the dark of daybreak, on his way home from his daily immersion in the mikveh before his morning prayers, Moishe walked home listlessly. He was feeling a little depressed over having put Chaya Leah in such a compromising position, and he wondered how she was doing. There was no way he could get in touch with her without causing her more problems. He was trying to think of a respectable way out. So immersed was he in these thoughts that he didn't even hear the white Volvo that pulled up alongside him. By the time he looked around and saw the lean bodies, the *spodiks*, the white gloves, it was too late. He felt himself dragged into the back of the car. A rag was wrapped around his mouth so tightly that he felt the blood trickle down from the corners of his lips.

They drove about fifteen minutes. He felt his arms pulled harshly, his legs lifted. He was in the middle of a forest. Dark pine trees scented the cold morning air. He felt his hands tied roughly behind his back.

"You have been warned, my son. You did not listen. It is out of my hands." The low, menacing, pious tones sent an icy chill of hopelessness down his spine. Then the blows began with merciless, methodical cruelty. Two to the stomach, two to the kidneys, two to either side of his head. On and on they went, like a machine, until his eyes were so blackened that he couldn't see. He felt his head scrape along the hard, stony ground, pressed against gravel and pinecones. He felt the scream rising in his throat but could hear nothing. Again he felt his legs, his buttocks, battered. The pain was excruciating. He was suddenly choking, the blood filling his mouth.

And then, just as suddenly, the blows stopped. He felt himself lifted carefully. He felt his matted hair stroked with fatherly concern. "He who hates his son does not chastise him," a low voice whispered. He could feel the white-gloved hand as it brushed against his cheek, dabbing water over his bleeding face with incongruous gentleness.

"You should have listened; you were warned. I mourn for you, my son. Turn now and take the right path, the path that leads away from destruction. And remember, if you call the Zionist police with accusations, your parents will have to find out why you were targeted. The girl's parents, too. It will accomplish nothing. The Zionists don't like to get involved in our wars. They let us run things here our own way. So take your punishment and change your ways." He felt himself dragged into the car again and then lifted out carefully to the sidewalk in front of his home.

When his mother stopped screaming, he told her he'd been hit by a car.

CHAPTER 23

It was a very pleasant—no, more than that—a very luxurious life, Dina thought those first few months of their marriage.

"Don't get up," Judah pleaded with her the morning of his first day back to work.

"But your lunch, your breakfast!" she insisted, scandalized by the very thought of sleeping on into the morning.

"I don't eat before morning prayers, my dove. As for lunch, I've already taken care of it. I prepared it myself the night before." His voice was gay with triumph. "Why should you get up? Sleep, my sweet one, my little one." His voice caressed her.

It was a new world, wasn't it? She had no idea of the

ground rules yet, the boundaries. She had no memory even of a weekday morning untouched by the cold, merciless nudge of duty: the heavy shopping baskets, the washing and dressing of small children, preparing countless lunch sandwiches, taking in the morning's icy laundry from wind-chilled lines . . . To be treated so tenderly, so indulgently, was beyond her experience. She simply didn't know what to do with her sense of propriety and obligation, her well-honed work ethic.

After all, it was just the two of them. He had already prepared his lunch and wasn't eating breakfast. There were no little brothers around with countless needs. . . . She smiled at Judah and pulled the warm covers over her head. "Well, perhaps, just this once," she murmured.

It is absolutely amazing how quickly human beings not only get used to luxury, but begin to take it for granted. Two weeks later she lay restfully in bed, listening to his quick, quiet morning movements—his slipping into clothes and running the bathroom water, the opening and closing of the refrigerator, and the gentle click of the front door—without so much as a dim memory of her earlier guilt.

With the end of the summer, she'd begun her first classes in the Hebrew Teachers' Seminary, a two-year course that would give her certification to teach early-childhood classes. She didn't really want to teach. The idea of standing before a classroom made her forehead prickle as if her circulation had stopped. But she couldn't think of what else to do with herself.

About three months into the school year, she heard herself being called.

"Dina!" a familiar voice rang out in the hallway crowded with female students hurrying to classes. Most of them, despite their extreme youth, wore the elaborately styled salon wigs that distinguished them as married women.

It was Malka Rachel, a former classmate. They hugged each other.

"Your wig is such a beautiful color. It looks wonderful on you!" Malka Rachel gushed.

"Thank you very much," Dina said seriously, patting her head with an exaggerated motion that mimicked that of a vain woman primping.

The other girl giggled. "What are you doing here?"

"The same as you, learning."

"Oh, I'm not one of the students. I work in the office," the girl said, a little haughtiness sneaking into her tone. Are you a student here? *Baruch Hashem!* Thank G-d! What *mazel* you have that you can keep on studying," she finally said after her narrowed eyes had enviously taken in Dina's lovely dress, her gorgeous watch, the rested bloom of her cheeks, her neat school bag. After all, they were both still teenagers. "My husband is in *kollel*, and I'm supporting him. Your husband is learning only part-time, then? Or perhaps his family is well-to-do?"

She didn't ask if Dina's family was supporting them, because, like everyone else in the *haredi* circle she was part of, she knew everything there was to know about the Reichs' finances and every other aspect of their lives.

Dina felt the slow burn of disgrace turning her ears scarlet. She wasn't offended by the probing personal nature of these questions. This was simply the way people in the *haredi* world dealt with each other. Everything was everybody's business. Knowing how much money you had, how you lived, was important information to be shared since it helped others to figure out how they, being in the same situation, held back by the same stricture of law and lore, could also manage. Nothing was too personal to ask.

She was mortified by the sudden realization of her lowly status as the wife of a workingman. "No, well, actually . . . my husband is not in *kollel* at all." It was an embarrassing admission of complete and utter failure. Only at this moment did she fully realize how far her own status had fallen as the wife of Judah Gutman, full-time, successful, self-supporting carpenter.

"Oh," the other girl said. "I heard he was very talented, a very wonderful man. But I thought he was at least learning part-time. . . ." Her tone wavered between polite embarrassment and self-congratulation.

"Judah has a *shiur* every day after work," Dina replied defensively, her tone apologetic, knowing this admission would only make matters worse. A *shiur* was just a mere study session, comparable with those dilettante, unaccredited courses given at night in the university to retired people beyond all hope of ever earning a bona fide degree. It marked you as one who would, at the most, reach the summit of a small hill, having abandoned the scaling of serious heights to those more competent. "And what about you?" Dina smiled graciously, trying to cover her chagrin.

"Oh, my husband learns full-time. I hardly ever see him," the other girl boasted. "Why, I'm working myself to the bone." She smiled happily. "*Baruch Hashem*, though, I have nothing to complain about. *Baruch Hashem*, he is doing well in his studies. How do you like your classes?"

"*Baruch Hashem*." Dina nodded, tired.

All day it was as if a cloud had descended and was swirling damp and gray around her head. She thought of her luxurious mornings in bed, of her wonderful, appliance-rich kitchen, of her long nights full of her husband's passionate companionship, and it became a bitter shame to her. She had it so easy because she was not going to achieve the heights in Torah her friends were, as they sacrificed on the home front for their husbands' gains on the battlefield of learning.

"And what did you learn today, my little dove?" Judah greeted her eagerly that day after work.

Instead of running to him and throwing her arms around his neck with a hug as she had been doing, she walked to him slowly and gave him her cheek for a kiss. He had no beard. It was suddenly shameful to her to be married to a beardless man.

"What did *you* learn?" she challenged him.

His eyes searched hers, surprised but not yet hurt. "Why, we are learning *Mesechet Kedoshim*."

"Temple sacrifices? Not very useful," she said unkindly.

"My dearest, every part of the Talmud is sacred and important! Even if we don't have a holy Temple right now, and cannot bring sacrifices to atone for our sins, still, it must be studied for the future." He looked at her, not wanting to bore her. Actually he found the topic fascinating. For the tractate dealt not only with the actual sacrifices themselves, but also the principles involved in deciding exactly which sins called for sacrifices and which did not. Had he been less afraid of boring her, he would have elaborated, telling her that as a basic rule a man could not offer any sacrifice to atone for a sin committed with malicious intent. Only the court could punish a man for such a sin. In the case where a court had insufficient evidence, such a man's punishment was left in the hands of G-d himself. A sacrifice was acceptable only in the case where a man sinned unintentionally—someone who, for example, was forced to disobey or who simply didn't know the law, didn't bear responsibility. In such a case he was required to offer a sacrifice to atone not for the sin itself, but for his forgetfulness and ignorance.

But like many pious men, Judah assumed the Talmud was boring to women. He didn't want to bore his lovely little bride. He wanted to amuse her, make her happy. So he changed the subject. "Shall I show you what I've made for you today?" Each day he brought her something, a habit she had found absolutely charming until now.

"I'm not a child," she said petulantly. "I don't need to be pampered and indulged. I'm not used to it. We are used to *kollel* men in our family," she added, wanting to be cruel.

His large, handsome face drooped physically, as if absorbing a blow. "Well," he said with quiet constraint, "I'll just put it here then and wash up for dinner." He placed a small box on the kitchen table.

Her heart ached at the dejected slow movement of his footsteps out of the room, the quiet click of the bathroom door.

How could she have been so spiteful, so horrid? That isn't me. I don't know who that is, she thought, walking to the hall mirror. The face reflected seemed odd to her, full of strange new compulsions, profligate, frightening in its capacity for doing the inexplicable. Yet she saw something that pleased her, too. The lovely face, the sparkling green eyes, the tender lips. A sense of her woman's power surged up, challenging and assuaging her guilt. He would forgive her. This she did not doubt. But would she want, or feel it necessary, to forgive herself? This she did not know.

She walked into the kitchen and picked up the little box, opening it. Inside was a little wooden dove, hand-carved and polished so smoothly that it seemed impossible it could have anything in common with hat stands or furniture. It was an exquisite little work. She studied the wings, beak, and eyes. Only someone who had held a tiny winged creature close in his hand and studied it could ever have pictured it so clearly and lovingly. A little dove, its wings closed comfortably, at rest, content.

A little dove, he called her. Her heart surged with rage at the presumption. Yet the work was beautiful, showing a sensitivity to beauty, a love of living things, that touched her.

He seemed distant all evening. She was extra solicitous in apportioning his dinner. She wanted to put her arms around him, to lay her head on his chest. She was thinking this as she picked the plates off the table. As he handed her his, she looked down at his paint-stained fingers, the broken, work-roughened skin, and felt a faint repulsion.

"Shall we go to bed now?" he asked almost plaintively. They always, until now, had gone to bed together, even if they had to separate the beds during her "unclean" days.

"In a little while," she told him, not looking up, her eyes fixed on the bright, illuminated page of a book in the lamplight, a page in which she did not see a single word. Had he come over to her and lifted her to him, she would have been his again. She would have forgotten everything. But he didn't.

She heard the door of their bedroom open, and then she heard it close.

CHAPTER 24

THE FIRST TIME NOACH SALTZMAN STOOD AT HIS LIVING ROOM window and saw Dina Reich, he was stunned. He absolutely couldn't move. He couldn't see her body, covered as it was by the modest, loose-fitting robe, but her face was very clear to him. Her forehead was white and smooth beneath the gorgeous light blond hair, her eyes large and soft, her cheeks pink and softly hollowed. She stood on her porch, the one that adjoined his own.

"New neighbors?" he casually asked his wife, Leah, later that morning. Leah, slow and ponderous, whose tendency towards sluggishness was exaggerated by the late days of her fifth pregnancy, had carefully laced up the shoes of her four- and five-year-olds, poured herself a cup of hot milk, and wiped down the counter before replying, "Newlyweds. She's just a baby, barely eighteen. And he is a carpenter." Her tone was critical, as would be expected from someone who had herself married with difficulties that had been overcome only at age twenty-four by her family's rabbinical *yichoos* and her father's prospering diamond business.

Like the biblical Leah, about whom the Bible can find nothing more positive to say than "Her eyes were soft," Leah Saltzman had few physical attributes that could be praised. Those that she had had at twenty-four—a clear, fine complexion, a slim, hourglass figure, a striking head of auburn curls—time and pregnancies and religious strictures had slowly eroded. With each child she had added a few wrinkles and ten pounds that had stubbornly refused to yield to any treatment or effort to remove them. Instead of her hair, she now wore the expensive and elaborate concoctions of the wig salon. Only her husband, in the secret spaces of their bedroom, saw her hair as it really was: drained of all vitality by constant covering, shorter than a man's, dusted with gray.

Like most men who marry for money, Noach Saltzman had also expected that his wife would remain at least as attractive as he had found her under the wedding canopy. That is, tolerably attractive. With the first child and the first ten pounds, he had found himself touched with annoyance. With the second, regret, and by the third he was close to despair. It became an effort to touch her at all. A chore. It was after the third child and the first thirty pounds that he had found himself actively pursuing other "opportunities," as he liked to call them.

It wasn't difficult. He was a very attractive man. Tall, handsomely broad-shouldered and slim-waisted, with thick black hair and deep blue eyes, he found women of all kinds only too eager to share his company. At first he had concentrated only on single girls, even insisting that they go to the mikveh before joining him for the long weekends in Paris, Amsterdam, or Eilat he added to legitimate business trips. After all, even though the sages frowned on relations between unmarried partners, *halachically* a man was not forbidden to have relations with an unmarried woman, no matter his own marital status. For a married woman, in contrast, such dalliance was considered a capital crime deserving of death. The inconsistency was explained as a realistic sop to man's weak nature. Also, since only the woman could carry a child, her crime was worse since her sin could bring illegitimate children into the world, *mamzerim*, who, according to *halacha*, could never marry into the Jewish people and would carry the taint of their birth for eternity.

Thus, a married man who took unmarried women to bed was actually not doing very much wrong. The women were simply considered concubines.

Actually it had worked out very well for Noach. His father-in-law's offices in Tel Aviv's diamond district were situated on a crowded trading floor full of young secretaries and diamond cutters, most of whom were from religious homes. They were very young, very innocent. They never even suspected until much too late that his interest and friendliness were not paternal. And by then most were so overcome by the first real taste of romance and danger that had ever touched their sheltered lives that they were ridiculously easy pickings. Most important, they managed to keep their mouths shut when it was over, since that was very much in their own self-interest. Occasionally, in the beginning, he had made a mistake and a girl had refused to cross over that thin line that separated cordial business relations from budding personal ones. Several times he had also miscalculated badly or found himself pushed into carelessness by a girl's loveliness, her youth and promise. But so far he had avoided exposure and true disaster because even the girls who had spurned him in shocked disbelief had not had enough self-confidence to talk. Or perhaps they had simply been restrained by the strict teachings of their upbringing, which taught them to judge each man leniently and to give each the benefit of the doubt. Most of the time such girls simply blamed themselves, searching for deficiencies in the modesty of their dress, their makeup, the way they smiled, or what they said. They took full responsibility and found jobs elsewhere, leaving Noach Saltzman free to go his merry way.

It was only after his wife's fourth pregnancy that the slow but steady erosion of all his remaining religious beliefs and scruples was finally complete, leaving him almost totally conscienceless. The teachings of the rebbes in the yeshiva, of his strict, sincerely devout parents, were first rationalized and then discarded. It was only then that Noach Saltzman experimented with a married woman.

Initially he had found this an enormous step. A man who took another man's wife would be punished by death. There were no ifs, ands, or buts about it. No mitigating circumstances. No way out. This was a very difficult hurdle for Noach, and one that took him a number of years to overcome. At the beginning he trembled at the very idea of G-d sealing his fate so utterly. At the time of the prophets, the judges, the great Sanhedrin, an adulterer accused by two witnesses would have been stoned to death. Nowadays religious Jews believed that all those upon whom the courts could not implement the rightful penalty for capital offenses would receive it from G-d personally.

But then, as is true with anyone who devotes much time and effort to satisfying his body, he found that his body became only more dissatisfied, more demanding. He was like a gourmet in constant, agonizing search for the most delicious food, whose every successful meal simply pushed the limits of the search farther off, requiring that much more effort.

And then he thought about repentance. One could always repent, he told himself, and save oneself from punishment. After all, who in the world did not sin? Even the biggest tzadik had his secret vice. Sometimes it came out and there was scandal, but most of the time no one ever found out.

He thought about that for a while. People could live their whole lives and never get punished at all. He took it one step further: Maybe there was no punishment for such things, because there was no crime. If a man and woman both agreed, who was harmed? The husband? Only if he found out. These things could be managed decently, he thought. And thought. And thought.

There was an excitement to an affair with a married woman that had no equal. It was similar to being one of those tightrope walkers who stretched wires between mountains and then rode bicycles over them. Part of the joy was the delicious excitement of contemplating failure. The risk was enormous, for such things were not tolerated in the *haredi* community. Once exposed, it meant automatic divorce for the woman, lost custody of her children, loss of all her property. As for the man involved, he would be disgraced publicly, thrown out of the community.

Yet there is that in human beings, the legacy of Adam and Eve, which longs for the thing denied. What was there about Mrs. L., his first married woman, which had surpassed the others, the young girls? She wasn't as pretty as some, or as supple. She wasn't as enjoyable company as a few. Still the experience had seared his soul. There was no comparison, he told himself, convinced himself. He simply longed for the next opportunity.

He pulled back the curtain and stared across at the vision of the young woman who combined everything he had ever sought, ever dreamed about. She had physical beauty that was at once that of a young girl's and yet with that added dimension of passionate experience that belonged to a married woman.

He found his heart beating in excitement each time he even thought he glanced some movement behind the curtained windows of the apartment across the way. Just a glimpse of hand, white and small, was enough to wipe his mind clean of all thoughts, to leave him throbbing with wonderful pain.

He took to waiting by the door in the hope that he might hear her open hers and thus arrange to meet her casually in the hall. This was very complicated, as the building was a noisy one, full of dozens of active children constantly tramping up and down the stairs. Also, since he left for work early each day, and returned only after her husband was home from work, their schedules were totally incompatible. He was not often successful.

"Why don't we invite the new neighbors over for *kiddush* on Shabbat morning?" he finally was forced to suggest to Leah.

Leah, with maddening slowness, looked down placidly at the newborn child nursing eagerly at her breast, slowly stroked its fine soft hair, languidly took out a tissue and blew her nose, then tucked in all her hair beneath her wig. Only then did she reply indifferently: "What for? We have nothing in common. Besides, I'm not up to company with the new baby."

"Well, it just doesn't seem very neighborly to me," he began, his tone rising with convincing righteousness. "After all, we haven't been very helpful, or hospitable." He went on, throwing in admonishing words like *chesed,* compassion; *hachnasat orchim,* hospitality; even "love thy neighbor as thyself"—until even Leah, who was not burdened with anything even akin to an imagination, looked up suspiciously and asked: "Why them? The neighbors downstairs have been there almost two years and we've never invited them for *kiddush!*"

"Well," Noach said, cornered, forced to back away and attempting to do so gracefully, "of course your health and the baby's is most important. I wouldn't, G-d forbid, want you to strain yourself. I just thought it would be a kindness. . . ." He exited quickly, closing the bedroom door behind him. He sat on the bed, shaking with frustration, finally pacing to the window. He stood there a long time. Once, he thought he saw the curtain across the way move a little, as if someone might have touched it passing by. A great thudding ache leapt up into his throat.

It was almost two months before he saw her close up. He was on the way home from the synagogue Shabbat morning. He held his two little boys' hands, waiting to cross the street, when all at once she and her husband came toward him from the opposite side.

He thought his heart would stop as she moved closer and closer to him on the broad sidewalk. She wore a slim-fitting silk dress of blue-green with flecks of gold that matched her eyes. He hadn't known! The color of her eyes! It was too much, too great to hope for! And her body, so exquisitely small and fine, like one of those rare, antique porcelain dolls he'd taken the children to see at the Israel Museum.

"Shabbat shalom!" he called out a little too eagerly as they approached.

"Shalom aleichem, Shabbat shalom!" Judah returned heartily, extending his hand warmly to the other man.

Dina kept her eyes shyly cast down at the pavement. Noach gave a bare, polite nod in her direction. Yet all the while he exchanged calm pleasantries with the other man, his neighbor, his body was tense, alert, gathering small scraps of precious information, storing them like some obsessed miser: the neat, fine curve of her nostrils, the slimness of her ankles, the intimate rise and fall of her breasts as she breathed. When they continued on their way, he listened intently to the receding tap of her pointed heels on the dry pavement as she retreated behind him, succeeding in isolating that faint and indefinite sound from every other in the entire city.

At home he exulted with a joy he had not known for years: He had been near her! He had nodded to her! Her modesty, the delicate sweep of her gold lashes on her cheeks as she looked at the ground, filled him with a wondrous gratitude. It showed that inside she was as fine, pure, and good as outside. She was the ultimate prize, the ultimate challenge. Just the idea of it made him feel like an explorer at the gateway to a great unknown continent full of unheard-of beauty, unimaginable dangers. It melted away the years, the disappointments, the failures. It made him forget his triumphs, his pleasures. They all seemed so paltry, so inadequate to his needs. His life until now had been trivial in all its aspects, he thought. Even the sins had been pale jokes and silly wastes of good time. All the women he had ever known seemed like bad fruit, overripe and slightly bitter. Juiceless. He had wasted his time, his passion, on things that were beneath him.

Only this, he thought, was worth pursuing without restraint, using every means at his disposal, everything he had ever learned or experienced. To accomplish this was to be alive at last. Was it even possible? He had no way of knowing! That was the beauty of it! Nevertheless, he felt his old confidence somehow overwhelm his doubts. He went to sleep, dreaming only of the morning, the next day, the next opportunity. He set small, manageable goals for himself: Today, I will see her hands, I will watch her fingers move. Or: Today I will catch her eye in the window without acknowledging it. Slowly, he thought. Inch by inch. Minute by minute, day by day. He would establish innocent contact, preparing the way for the use of his greatest ability: transforming innocent contact into something more, coaxing it slowly to the final extremity, where there would be no barriers, no safeguards, and no exclusions.

It might take years, he told himself. Somehow this thought did not discourage him. Quite the opposite.

CHAPTER 25

Faigie Reich sat down heavily on the worn easy chair that had served her almost all of her married life. It was late Friday afternoon, and the arduous, formidable tasks necessary to usher in the Sabbath had just been completed, as usual, at the very last moment. She sat back, wiping the beads of sweat from her forehead, feeling a tired satisfaction in the fresh, immaculate appearance of the whole house. Each possession, no matter its age or simplicity, had been cared for. The pillows of the couch, simple foam rubber-filled squares, had been beaten clean of dust, wiped free of any speck of dirt. Everything not nailed to the floor had been picked up, dusted, and polished. The floors had been washed and shined with many pails of hot, soapy water. And then, when the floor had dried to a hard shine, everything had been put back into its proper place. All the windows and mirrors had been sprayed with ammonia and rubbed to an immaculate shine with endless newspapers.

Then, of course, there was the cooking, enough for three major sit-down dinners for the family and a few guests, adding up to not less than thirteen or fourteen people each meal. Since no cooking was allowed from Friday night sundown until Saturday night at sundown, and even heating up food was forbidden, there was always a mad rush to get it all done. Of course, all the baking and some of the other cooking was done as early as Wednesday or Thursday. Yet there was always that temptation to add one more delicacy, one more delicious treat, to the Sabbath menu that constantly entrapped Faigie Reich and most good Jewish wives into that great, mad rush with the sinking sun that caught them exhausted and harried each Friday afternoon.

This had been going on almost all of her married life. Still the ushering in of the Sabbath never failed to cheer and refresh her. For once the work was completed, there was a whole, blessed day with hardly anything left to do (the little task of serving and washing up and minor clean-ups didn't reach the level that entitled them to be called "work," not in Faigie Reich's perspective). There was time to talk quietly with her husband on the long, slow Friday nights, a time that reacquainted them as intimate friends rather than just business partners. There was time to simply sit back and watch the children in pleasure as they sat around the table, all scrubbed and clean in their Sabbath best, a time to say, quietly in her innermost being: "Thank you, G-d, for all your gifts." Most of all, there was the luxury of time to relish the accomplishments and blessings of an uncompromising, austere, and frill-less life.

She wiped her eyes and was just about to get up when she felt the old, familiar pain shoot through her chest. She sat back, waiting for it to finish its stabbing work, to lift and disappear. She tried to get up again. That was when she felt the new enemy she had not met before. It was like having the building fall on her. She felt herself pressed back into the chair, smothered in debris, white hot steel slicing through her chest, ripping up and down her arms, from armpit to wrist. She tried to call out, but the breath had been sucked from her as if by a great wind. She saw a shining light that seemed like a sun rising from the black clouds after an intense and world-shattering explosion. Those around her seemed to be moving in slow motion, as if through some clear, viscous liquid. There was her husband peering into her face; the frightened, pale faces of the little boys; and Chaya Leah's flushed excitement. She felt herself trying to smile, then to point to the clock as she remembered that it was time to light candles. Was it time to light yet? she thought, drifting slowly past her family, slowly down some clean and quiet path just across from them, very close yet too far to hear them, or them her.

When she opened her eyes again, she was surprised and initially pleased. It was white, immaculate. Like the tablecloth on the Sabbath table. Yet as she tried to move, she felt pins and tubes in her arms bite back punishingly. All around were machines blinking in colored lights, with small incandescent numbers that changed before her tired eyes could focus. This frightened her. But then there was her husband's kind face. He looked at her hopefully. She tried to smile. So tired, so tired! she thought. Not even a smile can I manage.

She closed her eyes again, and suddenly she was a young woman transported to her first home. She almost laughed to see Dvorah as a twelve-year-old again, her long dark braids touching the tops of her hips, her serious little face straining under the burden of holding year-old Asher up to the sink to help him wash his face. And there was Dina sitting placidly in a corner, patiently retrieving her ball and jacks from Chaya Leah's relentless, marauding raids. And Ezra looking seriously over her shoulder as she nursed three-month-old Shimon Levi, who lay restlessly, heavy and warm in her lap.

She was back in the two and a half rooms in Meah Shearim. All beds, so many beds! Her head ached to think of them. The tiny half room with its three beds, the two boys in the living room with the couch that opened to two beds, her own bedroom with the twin beds and the baby's crib in the corner. And the living room filled with books. There was no place to entertain, since the boys needed to go to sleep by eight. The only visitor was her husband's learning partner, sitting by the living room table, both men immersed in the soft give and take of questions and answers as they struggled with the Talmud. And she, alone, in the kitchen, washing, cleaning, cooking for the next day. Alone, tired. And the dream that had come to her of the little store, of a little more money coming in.

Putting one *agora* next to another *agora*. Saving! All the time. Searching for cans that cost two *agorot* less or fruit a little less nice, a little cheaper by the kilo. Taking out the loans, opening the store. The bright colors, the salty smells of the wool in the cardboard and plastic.

She opened her eyes and saw her husband sitting in a corner of the room, his head bent over his Talmud, rocking gently back and forth.

"There isn't enough room for another child," she heard herself telling him. "Please, at least go look at the apartment. I know where we can get another loan!" She was begging him, and his face was mild, placid, skeptical. She hated him for that, for his acceptance. There was another child coming, a seventh, and no place to put it.

"I have seen it," she heard him say. "Three bedrooms. The man who lives there has twelve children. My darling Faigie, just think. If he can manage in four rooms with twelve children, why do we, who have seven, need more than two and a half?"

She struggled against her resentment, his acceptance.

Yet a moment later she looked up and he was there above her, her good husband. He held her hand, he patted it with love and concern. "We have four rooms now and only five children," she whispered, and she could see he did not understand, but was simply smiling back at her smile. But suddenly she was even too tired to do that, to smile. She, who had risen every morning at four-thirty, who had gone to sleep each night after midnight, who had given birth to eight healthy children, who had worked and supported a husband so that he might learn. Suddenly there was no strength left, not even to stretch her lips upward.

The girls were there and, magically, all grown. Dvorah, lovely, dark, with her two babies, pregnant yet again. She looked happy. And tired. So tired. She felt her daughter's smooth, cool cheek brush her own. And Dina, heavy with her first child. How much she wanted to see that baby! She searched her daughter's lovely young face. It was smooth, well cared for, yet the eyes were troubled and afraid to face hers. She would be all right after the baby. She would learn to love Judah, as Faigie Reich had learned to love the calm, pious, bearded stranger who had entered her life so long ago. I do love him now, she told herself.

He was my partner, she thought. I did not do it for him, but with him, both of us, together, struggling. And often his share seemed easier to me. His learning against my working. He leaned on me, and I had to stand up, not bend. And I stood, she thought. Always. She felt a touch of bittersweetness in her mouth that spread down her throat.

The small, cold hours of the morning, with a book in her lap, a baby in her lap. Trying to learn, desperately, to find some wisdom that would help her through the dark, cold, exhausting hours. And always the baby in her lap, the baby's cry. Fecundity, the hot, suffocating press of small, hungry, needy lives crushing against her. No help. Always being the helper, the giver—another mouth to feed, another beggar. Try to hold down the hot bile of resentment. Try to rise above it, to see the world with her husband's unworldly eyes. But yet, always the burden, heavy, unmoving, weighing down *her* shoulders, in order to leave *his* free.

The humiliations. The face of the woman who kept the books at the grocery. The end of each month. Another day and another day. Begging. The yeshiva had not paid its students their stipend yet. Her husband had not received his stipend yet. Please, just another day. Making over the girls' skirts, lengthening the boys' pants—another year and another year, until they had stains even her red, swollen knuckles could not remove with the violence of their desperate energy.

The housework—a constant foe—battling, retaking old territory, each day reclaimed by the endless incursion of the enemy: sticky fingers, food digested and spit up, little papers from crayons, little crumbs. The air itself an enemy, blowing through the windows, depositing the dusty debris from the new white stone houses going up in Jerusalem's hills.

The old, endless rage of work. The old, endless temptation to succumb, to rest. Oh, long awaited! Yet you cannot. The children wait. And your husband waits. And the house waits. And the friends and neighbors and needy strangers wait. For you. Only for you.

How was it, then, that there had been so much joy? Always, always. The Passover table sparkling red with wine, green with parsley. The Succoth booth fragrant with citron, myrtle, willow, and palm; the flickering row of Chanukah lights like a beacon in the window; the baskets of Purim treats wrapped up in gold foil and ribbons sent to neighbors. Around the year, more joy and more. Each step full of pain and yet painful progress. Higher, one joyous rung higher, and yet another . . . The redeeming beauty, indescribable, of believing. The faith, richer than the gold of the candle flames, the heart pounding full of benediction, the whole body swaying to the rhythm of prayer. The peace. The calm joy of G-d's nearness every moment. The prayers. Not extra work, but the only rest. The prayer, the brace, the foundation, the urging, the eagle's wing bearing you aloft in safety when you were so tired, so unutterably tired, that you could not lift your head.

There was Chaya Leah, who looked so much as she once had, gone suddenly slender and pale! A frightening stab went through her to see her this way, all the life drained out of her, totally subdued. Her father's words, his kindness and disappointment, were a bite harsher than a scorpion's, cutting deeper than any whiplash. There was no way to resist him. How well she knew that! His goodness, his piety, gave him infinite power. Chaya Leah must have what she wants, she thought suddenly. Not like the others, not like me. She felt a great wash of anger and pity. She motioned for her husband. He bent down quickly. "Sha, don't talk. Rest," he begged her.

"Chaya Leah," she said, almost choking. "Let her marry Moishe. Don't stand in her way. *Let her go where her heart is!*" She saw his face change color. "I know. It's a mixed marriage. He's a Hasid and we're Misnagdim. But we are all Jews. Please, promise me, if that is what she wants. I want her to be happy. Please, my dearest. *Let her go where her heart is!*"

"Sha, sha. Weddings!" He smiled at her, then was suddenly serious. "It's in G-d's hands." He shrugged. The boy was in the army, already an officer in a tank corps on the Golan Heights. Another disgrace.

"Promise me!" She shifted her body off the cushions.

The nurses and doctors were like birds, she thought, as they swooped down beside her, surrounding her. Too tired to struggle, she thought, and yet the vision of the family all around her, her daughters and sons. My work isn't finished yet, she begged silently. The boys are still young. But the momentary panic and resistance left her. She felt calm and strangely joyful as she closed her eyes.

Vulnerable, fragile, the flickering life within her. Always. And she had not known. It seemed so strong, like a mighty river flowing, like the inevitability of tomorrow, a gift, like rain hard and sure on the winter pavement. It had been there when she'd needed it to breathe life into the little soft bodies, wriggling red with life, pushed from her body with agonizing determination. All healthy—thank G-d. All mentally fit—thank G-d. All spiritually whole—thank G-d.

She closed her eyes. Her feet were little again. A tapping little girl's. And Jerusalem was at war. Would Rommel's troops break through? Please, G-d, help us! The Italians were bombing Tel Aviv. Please, G-d, help us! And the war of independence. Please, G-d, help us! And no water, no food. Please, G-d, help us!

We have won. The foreigners are gone, the ones who hate us. And still the trucks move through our streets, breaking the Sabbath peace. Jews driving on the Sabbath. Dear brothers, dear sisters, can't you see how He blesses us? Don't you see we will all suffer together or be blessed together? Keep the Sabbath holy. But you cannot tell them. Their eyes are black with contempt and anger. Create your own little world. Block out the cars, the movie theaters, the televisions . . . create a pure, good, holy world.

And yet so narrow! One step brings you across to their streets. The constant temptation to wander, to see everything. Hold yourself back, hold yourself higher. The struggle's constant, implacable force. All your energy against the enemy who stalks.

Who is the enemy?

Good-bye, my children.

I did not say that. My life is not shrinking. And yet the soul is expanding, even now. There would be a good reward. Yet the eyes of the boys still young, still needy, haunt her. The eyes of the girls, mourning yet reconcilable. They have their own lives. The eyes of her husband, worst of all. Desperate, full of fear. He will have to manage now. G-d will help him. She cannot anymore.

She closes her eyes. Too tired to think. She closes her eyes, and the darkness and silence descend. Yet within her the hub of the deepest blackness, within her the deep frozen soundless water, a new dim light begins to flicker, a soft murmur of hope beats like a heart, steady and joyous. The flame grows closer, an aurora of soft, golden-edged, dawn-bearing brightness. Her soul weaves upward, fascinated. He is waiting for her. The essence of happiness is waiting for her. Her job is done.

She is not afraid, still she shudders with terror. It is so hard. All she knows! And who will do the work now? Who will light the candles, visit the sick, comfort the bereaved, feed the hungry man at the door?

The flame grows brighter. It warms her cold, shuddering heart. It takes her hand like a father. She is not afraid. She is not afraid. She is finished. Her job is done, completed with honor. The husband, the children, all around her. And yet all alone except for the flame that flickers, the hand that holds hers like a father's. All alone, except for that. Everything else—a momentary dream, an illusion. This is the truth. The struggle was the truth.

She is calm. She is ready. The flame burns brighter, like the burst of a wick feeding from the last drops of holy oil. It rises, it grows into a great conflagration. But only she can see that. For them, it is simply extinguished.

CHAPTER 26

THE FAMILY GATHERED AROUND THE FRESH GRAVE. IT WAS ON A newly opened hill on Har Hamenuchot, the Mount of Rest. The newly dug hole, the moist smell of spaded earth, seemed lonely among the hard, level plots. The wind blew fresh and warm from the dark green forests that flowed down the gently sloping hillsides, and the sky was clear in the brilliant spring sun.

Wrapped in the flimsy, simple white winding sheet, the body of their beloved mother, wife, grandmother, sister, and aunt, the body of their dear friend and faithful, generous benefactor, was lowered into Jerusalem's whitish, unyielding earth. With the first dark shovelful of earth that fell, flattening the cloth, the boys began to cry: Benyamin and Duvid, the youngest, were taken farther back to where the women stood, barred by old Jerusalem custom from getting too near the grave. Ezra, his boyish shoulders rounded from trying to bear up under the unendurable burden of pain, said the kaddish prayer for the dead in a choking voice, joined by Asher and Shimon Levi, who seemed suddenly all grown up.

Dina squeezed Duvid's shoulders, too heavy with the child within her to attempt lifting him. With each shovelful of earth, she repeated the words: "G-d is my light and my salvation, whom shall I fear? G-d is the refuge of my life, of whom shall I be afraid?" She felt no comfort. It was not the right prayer for the moment. She was not afraid. She was empty, annihilated with the horror and surprise of death, which had come so suddenly.

There had been no warning, no time to go through the stages of fear, anger, acceptance, and mourning. A sudden hole had been ripped in the fabric of her life, wrecking her whole outlook, her whole philosophy. It was unfair! she shouted inside herself. Good people are promised a long life! Her mother had been the best person in the world. What could G-d be thinking of?

And the more she thought about it, the more her shock and horror grew. For the first time in her life she saw her simple view of life, her simple faith, for what it was: a deal between the created and the Creator in which you kept his laws in exchange for earthly happiness.

Her mother had been a saint. Yet she had died so young, only fifty-one! The world was not supposed to be run this way! The beat of anger, of impotent protest, sounded inside her like a hammer banging down the flimsy walls. Beat, beat, beat, she felt the neat, carefully constructed rooms inside herself suddenly crash, the lights going out. She needed desperately to talk to someone. Terror shot through her. There was no one.

Her father? What could she ask his pale, shell-shocked face? Her sisters? They too were in mourning; their world was as chaotic as her own. Judah? She looked at her silent husband standing over the grave, helping to pour earth over the body. His passivity, his quiet acceptance, enraged her. Never a word to say for himself! He would bring her more little carved animals, more little toys to play with, as if she were a child!

She wanted words, just words. She wanted someone learned and pious to make sense of it all with quotes from the Torah and the Talmud, to make her see where her faith had gone wrong that she stood now so defenseless. She wanted someone who could pour holy words over her wounds like a healing balm, who could use words like cement to magically reconstruct all her old beliefs, repairing the cracked foundations.

Judah would hold her silently. Judah would caress her silently. He would look into her eyes with understanding and pain and acceptance. He would plod along as if nothing had happened, she told herself, hating him for it already.

She felt the child within her move vigorously and felt sure she was going to faint. Only Duvid's small, quivering shoulders supported her, giving her consciousness meaning. *Ima!* I am lost, she thought. I can't go on. I have no one to love, she thought irrationally. I have no one who loves me, whom I can talk to, she mourned, near hysteria. She felt the endless anger rise in her like a shout, a scream of protest against a nameless and obscure betrayal.

In her whole, sheltered life, she had never felt this way before. It was frightening beyond words. She, the calm, good girl. The peacemaker. The good daughter, the good student, the dutiful wife. The pious prayer sayer. The obedient Jew. Perhaps I have never really known myself, she thought with morose satisfaction. Perhaps all along I have been faithless and full of doubts and hatred.

She saw the earthen mound rise with solid finality over her mother's grave. Is this the reward, then, for all our goodness? This cold earth on this windswept hill? She tried to calm herself, to think of the eternal soul now entering its golden peace. Yet the amorphousness of that image could not compete with the solid, yawning earth, the familiar flesh and form thrown down and buried. The horror —oh, the horror of it! How could one believe in anything? she told herself with limitless bitterness.

She sat in her father's house on a low footstool, remnant of the ancient mourning rite in which the mourners turned over all the couches and beds in the house and sat on them upside down. The whole family was there, day and night, through shiva, the seven days of mourning demanded by religious law, when it was believed that the soul of the departed flitted between heaven and its earthly home, mourning its lost body. Men and women and children the family had never seen before trooped through the house, paying their respects. "She gave me money for my baby's crib," one woman informed them. "She gave me free wool to knit skullcaps, which I sold for food money," someone confided. It went on and on. People their mother had visited in the hospital and people she had given food to for Sabbath and holiday meals. Every day more and more strangers crowded in, warming the hearts of Faigie Reich's husband, her sons and daughters, comforting them with the real evidence that their wife, their mother, now resided in the most beautiful part of the World to Come, all her good deeds shouting to G-d in her favor.

Only Dina sat silently, unmoved. So many good deeds, so many mitzvot, and yet still the cold, yawning earth, the windswept hill. And she had never had a moment's rest or taken an ounce of material pleasure. It was always work and duty. Work and duty. Why, her mother had never in her life gone to a hotel and been served a meal! Or sat in a concert hall! Or flown in an airplane! Dina cried until her eyes were red and swollen, mourning for the flinty hardness of her mother's short life. What had she enjoyed, what had given her pleasure? In her anguish she began to imagine or project secret unfulfillment and imperfection on her mother's life, ignoring the serenity, the quiet pleasure, the inner satisfaction, that had lined the coarse, practical material of that life with silk.

For weeks after the funeral she felt as if some dark, suffocating fallout billowed around her, poisoning the very air, dimming her vision. Judah thought he understood her. His heart ached with helplessness at her pain. His pretty, sensitive little bride. He brought her little carvings. He did the shopping and brought home ready-made food. He sat by her bedside silently (words could only hurt, he thought, could only belittle the enormity of her pain, which in time G-d would give her the strength to overcome), holding her hand as she wept. When she shrugged him off, or turned her back to him, he took the rebuff with equanimity, walking quietly out of the room. All pregnant women were especially sensitive. Insisting would only make things worse. Words would only make things worse. These things just had to be gotten over gradually, he thought.

So dim was her vision, so numb her feelings, that even the pain of childbirth did nothing more than ripple through them, a dark, battering wave slapping against her in the pale gray twilight. And there was the child, a boy. Joseph—Yossele—a firstborn son.

"This will bring her comfort," Judah's mother assured her worried son. "Treat her like a queen now. Let her rest, leave her be," she exhorted him.

Judah went slightly mad with happiness about the baby, and no one could blame him: he was such a happy, beautiful child. He looked just like his mother. His hair was so blond and so thick that even the overworked baby nurses couldn't resist fiddling with it, so that each time Dina went painfully down the corridor to fetch his little crib on wheels at nursing time, she found his hair had been combed differently, curled around his forehead or behind his ears. Yet the birth, the child, never seemed quite real to her. Only his mouth sucking at her swollen breast finally brought her some sense of vitality.

The pattern of existence that had been so mauled and

tattered by her mother's sudden death evolved slowly into a tentative new design that centered around the baby's waking and sleeping. It was good to be so tired you couldn't think, good to know each moment what was expected of you and to go through the motions.

She was in despair, and yet it was easy for Judah to mistake her mechanical motions for a return to normalcy, a healing plunge back into life. She loved the baby, yet he didn't seem quite real. Often she took him with her on long rides that wound up in Har Hamenuchot. There, by the simple white carved headstone, she felt the ice around her heart melt for a few moments. She pulled out the weeds and wiped the white dust from the carved letters. "A woman of valor, who will find? Her value is far above pearls," was written above her mother's name. It was the beginning verse of a song her father had sung to her mother every Friday night, a song praising the virtuous housewife who knits so that her family might wear warm wool in winter; who gives generously to the stranger; who has won by her good deeds her husband's implicit trust. Yet, reading the words, she felt her heart break anew. A woman of valor. And yet the earth and the windswept hill! Despite the spring heat, the stone was always cold. Only the living could feel warm, must feel warm, for there was nothing afterward but this icy earth.

I want to live, she told herself with shocking urgency, walking swiftly down the long stone-strewn path that led out of the cemetery. I want to feel warm. She hugged the baby with a new urgency. And yet it did not warm her. Her heart froze again as soon as she walked into her home.

She put the baby down to sleep and walked to the window, searching for some hope in the sky, the hills, the forests. In the window across the way, she saw the curtain pull back. The dark blue eyes met hers. She dropped her eyes, confused; then slowly, almost against her will, her eyes lifted. Abraham! But no. The beard was much darker, the eyes blue, slanted, and more intense.

Still, she felt a small thrill of connection before letting the curtain fall back into place.

She went about her work. The early morning nursing. The morning prayers. Breakfast for Judah, since she was up anyway and he was always so grateful. Laundry. The baby's walk in the park and shopping. More nursing. Lunch. Then a short nap before nursing again and beginning dinner. Nursing, then watching Judah play with the baby, laughing at his shameless antics to make the child squeal with delight. The final nursing, the cleanup in the kitchen as Judah and his learning partner filled the living room with their quiet Talmudical debates. Then bed.

They slept apart now. She would not be able to go to the mikveh until the bleeding stopped completely. It was going to take a while. She didn't mind not being able to sleep with him, as much as she minded his not being able to touch her. She needed warmth, a hug, a tender kiss. And Judah was distant. He had no choice, according to the law. She felt the irrational resentment towards him grow. He was never there when she needed him. Always some other excuse.

She began to look forward with a guilty thrill to passing by the window, almost holding her breath. Once or twice a day she noticed the eyes, the intense face and studied them. His brows were low and intelligent over eyes that were narrow, lifting at the corners in amusement. Yet they were not cheerful eyes, but rather demanding and knowledgeable with a guarded intensity. His nose was thin and fine, his upper lip narrow and definite over the sensuous fullness of his lower lip. The bones of his jaw and cheekbone were delicate and firm, giving the face a handsomeness and youth that made her wince at the shameful depth of her interest.

And then one day, their eyes met. And lingered. It was just a fraction too long, perhaps no longer than fifteen seconds. But it was long enough to belie the casualness, the accidentalness, of seeing him. Those fifteen seconds betrayed her. He could have no doubt she had been looking at him.

Afterward she felt shaken, as if she had leapt over some vast abyss and landed in a strange country. She would not look again, she told herself. It was indecent. Besides, she had revealed herself shamelessly.

She held out a week, and then, as if pushed by unseen hands, she found herself by the porch, helplessly staring at the house across the way. She stared a long time before turning her back dejectedly and closing the door behind her.

All the while, well hidden behind the curtains, blue eyes laughed with triumph and renewed determination. Not yet, he told himself with the relentless patience of an old, successful campaigner who senses the enemy's helpless restlessness to get the battle moving. He was too experienced for that. She wasn't ready. Not yet. But the progress was unmistakable.

Part Two

CHAPTER 27

AND THEN, SUDDENLY, EVENTS TOOK PLACE THAT CHANGED the flow of Dina's life. Her sisters wanted her to help out at the store. At first she resisted.

"But how can I? Who will take care of the baby? Who will serve Judah his dinner?"

"Dina, Judah's mother would like nothing better than to watch Yossele—you know how she dotes on him. As for dinner, I'm sure she'll put it in a clean plate for Judah if he can't manage himself," Dvorah went on sarcastically. "Besides"—her voice was suddenly wheedling—"it would do you good to get out. Having a baby doesn't mean the world stops. Anyhow, he's already six months old, not exactly a newborn! Everybody is worried sick about you," she scolded. "Especially Judah."

"What has he said to you?" Dina immediately went on the defensive, which surprised and slightly alarmed her sister.

"Why, nothing. He doesn't criticize you, you understand, so there's no use your making a *ganzeh megillah* out of it. He simply asked me if I thought it was normal for a new mother to stay at home so much, to be so pale. . . . Of course, I told him he was just being a typical new father. But I'm telling you that it isn't normal, it isn't right. You can't just lock yourself up away from the world. . . ." Her tone dropped into gentleness. "I know how hard it is. It's like being in a foreign country and not knowing how to go home again. There's not a day that I don't think of *Ima.*" Dina looked at her sister with a flash of hope. "But we've got our own homes now. . . ."

Dina's eyes took on the cold, glassy look of dejection that had been bothering Judah, alarming him, since Rebbetzin Reich's funeral. It was like some old dimming lens falling over her bright green eyes, clouding their beauty. "It doesn't feel like it to me. I feel . . . lost."

"Doesn't Judah treat you well?"

She nodded. "Too well. He treats me like I'm made of crystal and will shatter any minute. He works so hard, and he tries to make things easier for me. But I don't want things to be easier. I want to feel something. . . ." She stopped herself, afraid to say more.

"You don't love him. Not yet." It wasn't even a question, simply a statement of fact.

Dina felt her chest heave with relief. "When will I?"

"I don't know exactly," Dvorah answered honestly, troubled. "But if he is good to you, there will come some small moment when you see him for what he really is and begin to feel that connection to him that makes him family."

"Family?" Dina thought the word oddly deflating. Did you want your husband to feel like family, so comfortable and familiar? Was that the most she had to hope for? "But when do I start wanting to be with him, to lie next to him in bed, to spend the mornings with him and the afternoons and the evenings? When do I start caring if I see him or I don't?" Dina felt shocked at herself. This was a blatant exaggeration. Yet simplifying matters so drastically, so dishonestly, somehow made her feel better. The truth was far more complicated and harder to grasp.

The truth was that she felt abandoned and desolate, cut off not just from him, but from life itself. His silences, his fumbling, ignorant attempts to make her feel better, made her furious, made her want to feel to extremes. The truth was, she felt far more for him than she was willing, in her depression and anger, to admit.

"You're just upset," Dvorah said hurriedly, appalled. She'd had no idea. This was quicksand being spread all around her. She had no intention of stepping into it. She had her own problems. Another baby coming. The third in three years. There was no point in exploring the dark, evil-smelling stuff that lay just beneath the bright calm exterior of existence. You kept the lid on sewer drains, didn't you? Then why go exploring in such places? Another baby, another blessing, she told herself. *Baruch Hashem*, she told herself.

What right had Dina to be depressed? It showed a distressing lack of faith, a crumbling of the iron pillars that their mother had forged in all her girls. She had no right to collapse. She had no right to go whining after the moon like a spoiled child.

Dvorah, harried, hardworking, pregnant again, had learned not only to accept her husband, but to love that which was kind and generous in him. She had made her peace with the limitations of her life and in so doing had lost the ability to sympathize with those less fortunate. It was like being a paratrooper. Once you plunged into the open sky, once your parachute opened and you'd landed, your mind and heart were far from those still shaking with fear on the airplane. You hated those who wouldn't jump, those who forgot how to pull the string and open the parachute. They'd all received the same, harsh, detailed training for the mission. No one deserved sympathy for cowardice or for screwing up. Dvorah didn't want to remember how she'd felt at the beginning of her marriage now that she was truly happy with her husband—at least as happy as she was capable of imagining any woman could be with a man.

She changed the subject. "About the store, Dina. You can't be selfish. Without the income from the store, *Aba* wouldn't be able to keep paying Mrs. Weinstein to take care of the house and the boys, not to mention the debts on my mortgage, which *Aba* promised Yaakov's parents he'd pay when we married. You know that I've been working in the store every morning since *Ima* . . . and Chaya Leah's been taking over each afternoon. But she has exams coming up and can't manage. And I've got to be home in the afternoon for the children. Besides, I'll be giving birth soon, so you can't depend on me. Can you come every afternoon from four to seven?"

"I'll do it," Dina finally acquiesced, seeing no choice, a thick phlegm of shame and disappointment choking her. She felt cheapened and somehow tricked at having revealed so much about her marriage only to have been totally ignored. She felt as if all her feelings had somehow been invalidated. Worse, they seemed shocking, hideous. What had she been thinking of to have spoken so freely? She was angry at herself for having trusted Dvorah to understand, and even angrier at her sister for having somehow failed her. Most of all, her own openness was frightening. The hinges of the trunk were coming undone, she told herself. They would not hold much longer. "I'd be happy to help," she said a little more loudly and emphatically than was necessary, drowning out the other thoughts.

That was good enough for Dvorah. "*Baruch Hashem!*" she said encouragingly. "Come to the store. It will keep you occupied. It's not good to think too much." The two sisters' eyes met for a moment, then parted—accusing, guilty, and full of unwilling understanding.

"Judah, Dvorah wants me to help out at the store," Dina told her husband later that evening, wondering, even hoping a bit, that he might object.

He looked at her, his eyes filled with disappointment yet acceptance. He never resisted her. He tried to focus on her words. "The store? Your mother's wool store?"

"There is no one to run it. Dvorah has been doing it in the mornings and Chaya Leah each afternoon. But her exams are coming up. Her schoolwork, you know . . . piling up."

"Do you want to?"

"Well, I do want to help, but wouldn't it be hard for you to manage? I wouldn't be home to serve you dinner."

He looked up at her, crestfallen. He loved her serving him dinner! He loved her sitting across from him, reaching out for his plate, filling his coffee cup. "Well, I suppose if the family needs you and it wouldn't be too hard for you . . . What about the baby?"

"Your mother has been kind enough to offer to come and watch him. She'll see to your dinner. I won't be home too late. The store closes at seven each evening." His reluctance was oddly spurring her on, giving her a sudden urge to convince. It became important for her to go without her even knowing why.

"Are you sure it won't be too hard for you, my dove?"

His honest concern drove her mad with aggravation: "You act as if I am made of soap and will melt!"

"You must do what you think best, of course. I was just concerned," he added sorely, hurt by her rebuff, the way she contemptuously brushed away his care.

"I know." She kissed him on the cheek, slightly penitent. But the light in her eyes was oddly triumphant.

CHAPTER 28

It had been a disastrously rainless winter. The dryness had prolonged the warm late summer weather, and all through October and November the sky had been a bright, cloudless blue. Yet the sunny, warm, clear days had begun to feel like an evil omen, a portent of G-d's punishing anger. If the rains did not come between October and April, it would be too late. The crops would die, the reservoirs dry up.

Prayers for rain were intensified, and the pious flocked to the graves of saints in Tiberias to entreat heavenly mercy. Without rain Israel would once again become the barren desert it had been before the Jewish people reclaimed it. Nevertheless the face of heaven continued to look down, a blank, indifferent blue.

When by January the rains still hadn't started, there was a sense of foreboding and panic in the country. The reservoirs were reaching low points they had not known in years. The pumping stations that carried water to the Negev had been shut down. There was no rain. It was not weather. It was a personal tragedy felt deeply by every religious person. The prayers were redoubled.

And then G-d smiled, and the rains began—slow, gentle day-long showers that replenished the dry earth without flooding it. People went out into the streets and lifted shining faces to heaven, laughing at the water that touched their eyes and cheeks and hands like friendly kisses. Just the sound of the water tapping on the windows and pavement seemed like a melody, a sweet, youthful song.

Dina had suffered the barrenness of the dry spell, taking it almost as a personal punishment. And now, as the clouds filled the sky, she felt herself forgiven. The winter flowers, the cyclamen and iris, were blooming again. She felt a benediction in the cold rain, an odd pleasure as she made her way to the wool store.

The dampness of her soaking raincoat mingled with the salty warm smell of wool. It was pouring outside, the rain crackling against the store windows, sending a cool, steady draft under the ill-sealed front door. She put on the small heater and hugged her sweater close around her as she sat on a high stool, puzzling over scribbled pieces of paper and the backs of envelopes that constituted Chaya Leah's inventory control system.

The air in the little store warmed quickly. She took off the sweater and adjusted the shoulders of her pretty flowered blouse. Her figure had changed since the baby. Although she had lost all the extra weight quickly and easily, still, she no longer looked like a little girl. Her body was more womanly, softer. The milk in her breasts still lingered, giving them a voluptuous new shape over which she harbored a secret, proud joy.

The passion of her nights with Judah had opened a new world to her, a world in which she was not entirely comfortable. It didn't seem right to her to fall into such voluptuous abandon, such unrestrained intimacy, with the same person with whom she felt such estrangement during the light of day. In his daily words and acts, there was never any hint of his nightly passion, and she resented it.

Yet his boundless adoration of her body had made her treasure her womanliness with newfound satisfaction. No longer did she feel her body was simply a given, a functional machine whose purpose was to produce children. For the first time she focused on her body instead of her soul, welcoming her physical beauty as a good in itself, with no need for a higher meaning. She found herself becoming quite vain, quite proud, as she studied her body with increasing frequency.

She was grateful for the silence of the empty store. For the two weeks she had been there, the bell on the door had never stopped clanging, and customers had filled every empty space, clamoring for her attention. She had not found a spare moment to tackle the books or make some kind of ordering system. It was finally winter, and the cold, dark Jerusalem nights kept people home, knitting and crocheting through the long dull evenings in homes where no television, radio, or newspaper was allowed to enter. Women came in droves to the familiar little shop they trusted to buy the wool.

But tonight, Dina saw, the weather was too harsh for any but the most intrepid to brave the streets. She looked down at Chaya Leah's sloppy jumble of numbers, chewing pensively on a fingernail.

The doorbell gave a small jangle. She felt the cold gust enter the store. When she looked up she felt a shock rip through her bowels, beads of sweat sprout in her armpits. And at the back of her neck little hairs sprang up, as if pinched by intimate, icy fingers.

"Ah, hello, Mrs. Gutman, I had no idea . . ." Noach Saltzman said with friendly casualness.

To her dismay and fascination, she saw that he looked at her steadily instead of dropping his gaze modestly or looking over her shoulder, as every other man she knew outside her family would have done. He looked and looked. At that exact moment, she knew it had been his eyes behind the window. She also knew, with a knowledge more terrible and exhilarating than she had ever felt before, that he had seen her looking back.

"How . . . how can I help you?" she stuttered, pulling her sweater protectively around her shoulders. She saw his eyes flit down to her shoulders, to where the flowered silk molded itself to her arms and caressed her neck. She saw his gaze momentarily linger.

"Terrible night to be out. I'm soaked through." He laughed at himself, shaking drops of water from his coat. She was surprised at the deepness of his voice and the elegance of his language. He spoke Hebrew the Israeli way, with none of the guttural Yiddishisms that Judah and her father used. He spoke almost the way the *chilonim* spoke, the consonants crisp ("Shabbat," not "Shabbos"; "tallith," not "tallis"). There was a foreignness that made him sound distinguished and a bit dangerous. It excited her imagination. "My wife's been wanting to knit a baby blanket but hasn't been able to get out this past week. I pass this way from work anyway, so I thought I'd help her out." Again the dark blue clever eyes, amused and intent beneath the low, intelligent brows. She was glad for the solid counter between them.

"What kind of wool?" she asked.

"Well, it doesn't matter, does it? Just plain wool," he said, perplexed.

Her tense, tight lips relaxed into a little smile. "What weight do you want? How many ply? Cotton, acrylic, or wool? What color? How many ounces? And it would help if we knew what size needles she's using."

"I have no idea." It was his turn to be confused. Then his eyes focused on her smiling lips. He saw them tense again. "I just thought balls of wool were all the same! I guess I'll have to ask her again for more details. Thank you for straightening me out." He began to button his coat. "It can't have been much of a night for business," he said, laughing, as the wind rattled the door.

"Not much. But at least I have some peace and quiet to do the books. Not that I know what I'm doing." She shook her head, wondering why she was prolonging the conversation. He made her uncomfortable, yet she didn't want him to go. She found the contradiction stimulating. She found herself preening a little, touching her hair, smoothing down her brow.

"Why, it may seem difficult, but actually there is not much to it. When I began in the diamond business, I also couldn't make heads or tails out of inventory and profit margins. But I've actually become quite expert at it. Why, I'd be happy to give you a few pointers."

"It would be a great *chesed*," she said honestly, trying to fight down her apprehension at seeing him unbutton his coat. The apprehension won. "But I'm afraid I have to be getting home now. Perhaps some other time?"

"Of course. Why, it's lucky I came by at this hour. My car's right outside, and we live in the same building. . . ." He looked at her expectantly.

She hadn't actually meant to shut the shop so early. It was barely six-thirty. Yet she'd already told him she was leaving, what else could she do? How could she refuse the ride without practically admitting the unthinkable ideas that had been going through her mind and that she suspected in his?

In order to bring some normalcy and respectability to the situation, she had no choice but to casually accept, to go along with the fiction that his coming to the store had been an accident and his offer of a ride home simple neighborly kindness. She had no choice but to ignore the months and months of glances behind curtained windows that had passed between them, drawing them together in a dangerous, beguiling intimacy.

"I'll just be a minute. This is very kind of you." She kept her voice steady, but her legs felt weak. Even as she turned to pull on her coat, she could almost feel his eyes bearing down on the soft whiteness of her small hands as she lifted the long blond hair off the nape of her neck. With each button she saw his eyes move with surreptitious longing gradually, slowly, down the whole length of her body. She felt almost faint.

He held open the car door to the front seat for her. He was very tall and slim, and his black overcoat was a fine, pure wool, the kind she had seen on wealthy *kollel* men and yeshiva boys from England. As she brushed past him, she smelled the musky scent of something very male and very clean. The hands on the door handle were impeccable in their unblemished whiteness, unsullied by any physical labor. They were the hands of a scholar, she told herself.

The ride home took much longer than she thought it would. She was sorry she had sat on the front seat beside him instead of in the back, forgetting that it had not been her choice. He spoke little, except to tell her some general principles of accounting procedure. He was frank in his respectful admiration for her plunge into the family business.

"A new husband, a new baby, losing your mother . . . Why, most women would have just collapsed, but you, you are so brave, so resourceful," he said, making the intimate words sound respectable somehow. She listened to him gratefully, soaking up the words of understanding and praise like parched earth. He spoke to her heart, understanding what she had been going through. Yet he had not crossed the line into intimacy, she told herself calmly. That was all in her imagination. She couldn't help feeling a secret immodest pride in the way he looked at her. His longing was so palpable, so flattering. She felt a surge of inexplicable happiness, the first she had known in months.

"Judah," she called out softly, unlocking the front door. It was just after dinner. His mother had already gone. He came out of the kitchen, wiping his big, rough hands on a dish towel, buffing his broken, stained fingernails. She watched him with strange intensity. They were the hands of a workingman, rough and raw.

She remembered the first time she'd seen him in his workshop: the dusty pants, the stained, greasy apron, the head peppered with sawdust and wood shavings. The appalling thought: This is my husband. A small, secret swell of shame had washed up from her bowels.

She looked up at his kind, good face and blushed with guilt, feeling wicked and hardhearted. She took the towel from him. "Go, rest. I'll finish." She went into the kitchen and secretly watched him as he settled himself comfortably on his favorite chair beneath a circle of lamplight. His smooth forehead glistened with health and the oil of being young and contented. It was endearing to her suddenly, that broad, kind slope beneath his thick, unruly hair. Like a vulnerable little boy's.

She put down the towel and came to him, drawing her fingers across the light worry lines over his brows. He lifted his head in pleased surprise, his lips catching the soft, childish pads of her fingertips. He drew her toward him gently. "My little dove," he whispered, his caress becoming more forceful.

The house breathed with the hushed quiet of a peaceful evening among convivial people. She felt a contentment at times like these that went deeper than she knew. Her own home. Her own husband. Her own little perfect child. She wanted it to be enough for her, and in a very real sense it was. She owned the map to the good life. She knew just which roads would lead her to spiritual contentment, to a blessed and rewarding family life. That is what they taught girls in Beit Yaakov.

What they hadn't prepared her for were the sudden storms, the washed-out bridges, the detours, the side roads . . . The best she could do in explaining it to herself was to say: Just because things are supposed to be a certain way doesn't necessarily mean they are. Life wasn't the neat, tucked-in shirts, the ironed skirts, of Beit Yaakov. It was incredibly messy. Pleats came out. You had to squeeze into things so small you could hardly breathe or were forced to wear things so big they hung on you, looking ridiculous.

She closed her eyes and pictured another man holding her. It was his arms, his cheek. Her stomach leapt in shock and excitement. She opened her eyes, looking at Judah, and pushed away his hands. All he ever wanted to do was go to bed, she thought irrationally. He had no feeling, no delicacy. . . . To him it was all thc same. She wouldn't admit it was his love for her that knew no bounds, that never stopped. For her, things had bounds. A caress on the forehead was not the same as going to bed.

She got up abruptly. That was what was wrong with life. It was constantly surprised into chaos. The center didn't hold. Pieces went flying off like debris landing everywhere, shattering the windows and shaking the doors of people you hardly knew, connecting you to them with sudden strange consequences over which you had no control.

She could see his mouth turn down in hurt. He could never accept her resistance. He never resisted her. He wanted to remove every barrier between them, to be one life, one flesh. He thought the way to do that was to wait for it to happen. To hope. He felt helpless, like a calm port that can only spread the safe harbor of its jettied arms and wait patiently for the battered ships to return gratefully from the storms. He thought he understood her, that he knew her as deeply and intimately as possible. He knew, of course, almost nothing.

We never do. Fifty years people laugh and quarrel,

sleep in the same bed, buy each other food and clothes, create new lives that combine their very cells, and still they are strangers in every sense. They spend their lives groping for each other in the dark, their blind flailing causing injury and pain as they futilely slash at the impenetrable otherness that quarantines each man in a bunker of steel like that of some violent dictator, paranoid with fear, dug deep enough below the earth to withstand the explosion of two atom bombs.

She made herself busy tidying up the living room, picking up the baby's toys, until she heard Judah's complacent footsteps walk toward the bedroom. "Are you coming?" he called out to her.

"In a minute," she replied without looking up. She sat down on the rocking chair in the baby's darkened room and watched the curtains on the window rise and fall with each tiny breath of winter air. The window seemed almost alive and somehow sinister with its dark reflection, like the eyes of a blind man. She would not go near it, she told herself, looking at the baby. Yet, perhaps, it was too much of a draft. She walked over to it slowly, her hand trembling as she pressed it closed, her cheek crushed against the wall as she stood sideways, waiting, concealed by the darkness.

From across the way she saw a white hand move the curtain back. A chill so cold it felt hot gathered momentum down her spine. A nudge, like the devil's own irresistible hand, propelled her forward until she and Noach Saltzman stood facing each other shamelessly across the dark abyss.

CHAPTER 29

"COME, YOSSELE, COME TO *IMA,*" DINA CROONED TO THE baby. He smiled up at her angelically, with a fat, damp, satisfied grin. She felt a sudden wild convergence of terror and happiness in her chest, like two wild animals tearing at each other. She lifted the child and pressed her fingers into the silky fine down of his blond hair. Fat, fair little green-eyed wonder!

"*Neshamaleh,*" she whispered, her lips brushing against the child's warm, throbbing temple. My little soul. It was a term of endearment Israeli mothers used to express the inexpressible: the boundless, unending nature of their connection to their babies. "*Neshamaleh,*" she repeated, feeling the weight of his soft, round bottom, the frantic activeness of his little fat legs pushing off from her. She laughed and put him down. He crawled with reckless speed, like a newly wound-up toy, out of the door and into the living room.

She ran after him, laughing and breathless, sweeping him into her arms, saving him from a disastrous collision with a sharp-edged coffee table. He squealed and kicked in furious protest to find his feet once more off the ground. "Little destroyer, little spoiled one . . ." She laughed, a vibration of pleasure that chimed like large bells ringing deep within her.

As she walked past the hall mirror, she stopped to show the baby his reflection and found herself staring into her own eyes. They were dark green and sparkling. Her lips were curled into a shy, soft smile of secret joy. Her cheeks flamed dark pink, almost shameful somehow. Yet how pretty she looked in the long blond wig just back from the hairdresser's! Like a fairy-tale princess. She laughed at herself in the mirror, admiring the familiar yet suddenly strange image of the lovely, desirable woman, a woman who thought nothing of standing idly and vainly looking at her own image when she could have been cleaning up the house or ironing the clothes.

How suddenly sweet it felt to be alive! After all those months of despair, she felt like a young girl again. Anything was possible! The world was beautiful and unpredictably exciting! Dancing with the baby pressed to her shoulder, holding his palm and fingers formally, as if he were a gentleman and a dancing partner, she thought of what she would wear to the store that afternoon. The colors of her new clothes spinned around in her head. Dark, forest green and pale salmon and deep, sea blue. So many new clothes she had now, she thought proudly. None of them hand-me-downs. All of them made to order with lovely fabrics she chose herself. And she looked so beautiful in them, so very beautiful, she told herself in a strange ecstasy of careless forgetfulness and excited pleasure. Oddly, she did not think of this with gratitude toward Judah, whose generosity was almost foolish in this regard. The clothes were hers. The house was hers. Judah was somehow outside it all.

She put the baby in his playpen and twirled around her home. Everything she owned suddenly pleased her immensely. She felt rich and privileged and utterly spoiled. And she saw nothing wrong in any of it. What could possibly be wrong with being so happy?

She waltzed into her bedroom and opened the closet, flinging the clothes on the bed. She tried on a long moss green flowered dress that showed off her tiny waist, then rejected it because it seemed to flatten her bust and give her a childish innocence she found suddenly extremely annoying. She tried a navy blue skirt-and-sweater set with small crocheted flowers strewn across the top. "Too high-necked," she said critically. "Too 'dressed for the synagogue.' " All wrong, all wrong.

All the while she hummed to herself, a sweet little catchy tune she used to sing as a child. A song of flowers newly planted, spring growth, and the shade of river trees. She would see him tonight, she thought without guilt, as if in the midst of an uncomplicated dream where all obstacles suddenly vanished and the dreamer found herself involved in all manner of dangerous, pleasurable activities with strange ease.

Judah's mother arrived promptly at three-thirty, panting and heavy-footed from the climb up the stairs.

"Such a *shayneh maideleh!*" she said to her daughter-in-law, kissing her and hugging her. "This dress, pink-and-black paisley. This is a *shayneh*, *shayneh* dress. In such a dress you look like a movie star. My son is behaving himself, I hope? You know how men are, forgetful. You make him pay attention to you!"

"But Judah is very kind and always pays attention to me, Mother!" Dina laughed.

It was the old joke between them. Mrs. Gutman was ecstatic over her daughter-in-law and her grandson and never pretended otherwise. Everything Dina did with the house was beautiful and showed talent. The way she handled the finances was amazingly thrifty and praiseworthy. The way she cared for Yossele was remarkable in its devotion.

Yet despite the praise, Dina was a little uncomfortable with her mother-in-law. She felt as if Judah's mother, like her son, was constantly tiptoeing around her feelings, afraid to accidentally tread on them and make a mess. It didn't allow her to develop a real relationship with her, something she needed desperately after her mother's death. She enjoyed the praise but felt uncomfortable with its unfailing constancy. She missed her mother's fond yelling, her prodding, her caring reprimands, her wise cautionary tales. Mrs. Gutman's endless compliments fatigued her, and she found herself unaffected by them.

Besides, with the praise came a constant shrewd and unrelenting examination of her life with Judah. Mrs. Gutman, who in another incarnation may have been the chief inspector of Scotland Yard, had an uncanny ability to use the smallest shred of evidence to lay bare any and all domestic secrets of married life, especially those things you wished most to hide from her. She knew everything, always. A gain or loss of weight was immediately traced to its revealing source: depression, pregnancy, overwork, a dancing class attended twice a week . . . If Dina and Judah ever had a misunderstanding, her remarkable radar zoomed in on it immediately simply by registering the number and quality of sentences that passed between them. There was nothing she didn't know. There was no place to hide.

Yet she couldn't help liking her warmhearted, generous mother-in-law. Mrs. Gutman spent hours in the kitchen preparing complicated dishes like stuffed cabbage leaves, kreplach, and cremslach and bringing them over in little plastic containers. She was also a steady supplier of luscious home-baked cakes and cookies. Moreover she was constantly on the lookout for any lack in her son's household, which she was quick to supply. This ranged from a lovely set of silverware to bibs for the baby. As for babysitting, she truly rejoiced in the opportunity.

"Your cheeks are pink again, Dinaleh. I knew this getting out a few nights a week would be good for you! And I know you are doing such a wonderful job in the store. Everyone I meet tells me how organized you have it, and how they enjoy buying from you. Why, you'll have it doubling the profits in no time. Talented, so talented," she went on, all the while studying her daughter-in-law with a steady, appreciative, and slightly questioning gaze.

Dina found herself blushing under the scrutiny, her heart beating with a heavy knocking apprehension she couldn't define. "Thank you so much for coming! Are you sure the baby isn't too much for you? Don't let him bully you into letting him out of the playpen!"

Mrs. Gutman bent over her grandson and picked him up in her arms. The two beamed at each other. "That is what I'm for, to be bullied. Isn't that so, my little angel? Come to *Bubee*, let's wipe your little face, your little hands. See what *Bubee* has brought her little darling?" She carried the cheerful, round little boy in her arms.

Dina found herself sighing with relief as she closed the door behind her and fled gratefully down the steps to the bus that would take her to the store.

Of course, her mother-in-law would notice the dress. It was too expensive and elegant for every day. She tried to analyze the remark "Make him pay attention to you!" What would that have to do with the dress? Knowing Judah's mother, she had no doubt that it had some relation. Perhaps she thinks I am feeling neglected and the dress is to catch Judah's eye. She laughed inside herself. Judah always paid attention to her. Always showed her how beautiful she was. As if she would need to dress up for him to notice her! Why, no matter how frowsy she looked, his eyes had that eager, boyish delight in seeing her. He was so easy to please, she thought with a touch of impatience.

But the other (*Noach*, she whispered secretly into the cool back of her hand that brushed across her face, as if hiding something or wiping it away). He would notice if she was well dressed or not. He would appreciate it.

As she neared the store, she found herself hurrying on the slippery pavement. She had worn her best shoes, patent-leather pumps with unusually high slim heels, shoes she wasn't entirely sure how to walk on. As she turned the corner, she felt her ankle twist and felt with helpless panic her body hit the pavement. There was mud on her coat and stockings. Her hand was bruised. A group of passersby hurriedly surrounded her and lifted her to her feet. Even the wig had moved over to the left and hung with unnatural stiffness. She felt the humiliation crawl up her face. "I'm all right, all right," she begged them, quickly brushing off her soiled clothes. Finally they let her go. She could feel their eyes bore into her back.

Careless, foolish! Just look what you've done! she berated herself. She felt like weeping with rage and frustration. Her careful toilette! She surveyed the damage in a small back-room mirror, washing her scratched hands and straightening out her wig. As her eyes met those in the mirror, the thought came to her with stunning clarity: It was all G-d's will! His punishment! He, from whom nothing could be hidden, had seen her guilty joy, her vain primping. There was a phrase for what she had done. It was one of those sins for which one asked forgiveness each Yom Kippur: "the hurrying of legs to do evil."

The guilt and shame that had so far eluded her suddenly converged on her from all sides. She could fool Judah and his mother. She could even fool herself. But she couldn't escape from Him! The idea of His reading the shameful pictures of her mind, the disgraceful longings of her most secret heart, made her physically ill. She ran to the bathroom, retching and miserable.

Then, surprisingly, she found herself recovering with a new hardiness she had never felt before. Her eyes were steady and deliberate as she smoothed down her stockings, drawing them up tighter over her slim calves and young, firm thighs. They weren't torn, just muddied. She dabbed them clean with a piece of wet cloth. The dress wasn't damaged, either, she noticed. The coat had taken most of the abuse. Yet it too could be brushed clean. The wig was already back in place, as lovely and alluring as ever.

After all, she had just been running too fast, she told herself. Nothing more to it. Not so very bad at all, in fact. She hadn't done anything wrong after all. You couldn't punish a person for his thoughts, could you? What were thoughts, just flashes of light and color, intangible and thus not something for which one could be held accountable.

Except, of course, in the case of adultery. The commandment was, after all, "Do not covet thy neighbor's wife." To covet was not an act but simply a thought, a feeling in the heart. But that was to the man, not the woman. It didn't say "Do not covet thy neighbor's husband," now did it? She smiled to herself, cheering up. She was shocked at how quickly she'd recovered from the fall, from the idea of its being a punishment. Not so long ago such a thought would have left her wrung with guilt and repentance. She would have dwelt on it and prayed with parched and striving lips for forgiveness.

It was only then that she had some glimpse of how far she had traveled down that foreign, strange, unmapped road. She no longer had any signposts, any markers, showing her what to expect ahead or even how to get back to where she'd inadvertently (or perhaps not. Perhaps not?) turned off.

The bell jangled at the door, breaking her reverie. She looked up and smiled at the two sweet little teenagers in their Beit Yaakov uniforms, their hair combed and pinned smoothly back. The sight of them filled her with a sharp, almost painful pleasure.

The hours passed, enveloping her in a haze of confusion and mixed feelings that alternated between dreamy anticipation and harsh self-loathing. She forgave herself and punished herself. She tried to make the wild churning in her chest stop. I will close the shop early, she suddenly thought. Before he gets here. I will leave him a note on the door not to come ever again.

She felt an incredible release at the thought, a reprieve. She wrote quickly—a firm, almost harsh message that left no room for doubt or ambiguity. She spoke of conscience and G-d and warned him she would tell her husband and his wife if he continued to pursue the matter. She put on her coat and walked deliberately to the door. It was six-thirty. He was due to arrive at five minutes to seven. But before she could tape the paper to the opaque, patterned glass of the door, an older woman advanced towards the store. It was Mrs. Schwarzberg, a former neighbor and a good friend of her mother's.

"Not closing up? Too early, too early!" She brushed past Dina and into the store. "What would your mother say? A half hour before closing time? How do you expect to make ends meet if you don't work, *maideleh*, eh?" She smiled to show she didn't mean any of it. "And how is your fine husband, your little one?"

"*Baruch Hashem*. . . ." Dina smiled at her uneasily, crushing the note and stuffing it into her coat pocket.

CHAPTER 30

IT IS STRANGE ON WHAT INSIGNIFICANT AND FOOLISH TRIFLES whole lives depend. Accidents of time and opportunity, small last minute decisions, petty considerations not worth a moment's thought, may build or irretrievably smash a person's whole life. We worry about the future, plan for it, think of it in grand and abstract terms, when in fact those incidents that actually shape and define whether we shall live decent, satisfying lives or shameful wasted ones are often too silly to imagine.

Dina Gutman, respectable *haredi* wife and mother, would not even remember later, under the crushing weight of almost unbearable suffering that was to fall on her, that the entire avalanche had been triggered simply because an old woman had not been able to make up her mind whether to buy pink or yellow yarn. The woman's wavering indecision kept Dina in the shop just long enough to make it impossible for her to escape her fate.

She heard the clang of the doorbell like some dark omen as Noach Saltzman stepped over the threshold, bringing with him the tantalizing, cold scent of the dark night.

"I waited outside until your customer left," he explained, taking off his coat and hanging it up next to hers.

"You don't need to apologize. After all, it is you who are doing me the favor," she said, unable to take her eyes off the two coats that hung with such strange intimacy, the sleeve of her small, pastel tweed intertwined with his dark, fine wool. It was almost as if they were embracing. "I'll just get the books. I suppose we should leave the door open?" she suddenly remembered.

Noach Saltzman knew exactly what she was talking about. She was talking about *yichud*. *Yichud!* It was the well-known rabbinic prohibition of a man and woman other than husband and wife being alone together in any place where there was no chaperon and it was unlikely that they would be disturbed. It was a law that was very strictly defined and very closely adhered to in the *haredi* world. A woman was not allowed to be alone with any man except her husband, grandfather, father, son, grandson, or brother. The problem began when a girl reached age twelve and a boy age nine. Thus a twelve-year-old girl couldn't baby-sit for a nine-year-old boy. Nor could a boy over thirteen baby-sit for a girl over age three.

Situations that were particularly common and warned against included a woman being alone in the house with a salesman or repairman or a secretary being alone with a boss. Thus doctors treating *haredi* women left the examination room door slightly ajar; men taking elevators passed it up if there was a single woman inside; and women taking a cab opened one of the windows or avoided it altogether.

Yichud had in the past posed a not inconsiderable

stumbling block for a man like Noach, and he had become an old hand at dealing with it.

"Why, of course, leave it open if you like. I'm afraid, though, it might mean endless interruptions with people coming in thinking that the store is still open. I'm sure you want to get finished as quickly as possible and get back to your husband and son at some reasonable hour tonight. Why don't we just close the door and leave it unlocked?"

She hesitated. "Well, would that be enough? I mean, according to the law?"

"Yes indeed. The *Radvaz* and the *Ezer Mekudash* permit it. *Sefer D'var Halakhah* says this was the view of the *Chazon Ish* as well. Tropper's book, *Kuntres Yichud*, on page nineteen cites the decision of the Gaon Rav Eliashiv and HaGaon Rav Sheinberg, who both agree," he said with sober, rabbinic authority.

Dina felt herself flush, mistaking his practiced ease for scholarship. She felt ashamed of herself. He was a *talmid chachem*, a scholar! He even mentioned Judah and the baby and was concerned about them! Why, he was merely a good person, doing her a great selfless good deed, a true *chesed!* All the impure thoughts, all the dreaming, the passion, had been in her imagination. It was her sin only. The thought that she'd been but a hairbreadth from sending that note with all its horrible implications made her knees weak.

"I'll just put the 'Closed' sign up, then," she managed weakly.

"Fine. . . ." He nodded as if he didn't know full well that no rabbi would agree to such an act. For the moment she put up such a sign, no one would likely bother to check if the door was locked or not, leaving them in utter, forbidden privacy. Of course, he thought it better not to point that out to her.

She spread the worn books across the counter and pulled up a stool for him across from her, leaving the full length of the table between them.

"I can't make heads or tails out of it, and that's the truth," she admitted, fumbling with the books. "It's so awfully kind of you," she repeated, feeling rather speechless all of a sudden. It was the warmth of his physical presence in the small, dark room. She could almost taste his breath in the air. She shivered involuntarily.

"Cold?" His voice was low, concerned.

"A little," she admitted reluctantly, feeling instinctively that this was too intimate a detail to share.

"Can I get you a sweater, or perhaps your coat?"

"I forgot to bring a sweater tonight," she said, praying that he couldn't somehow divine that she had done it deliberately, not wanting to hide the clinging contours of the soft, silky material over her breasts and shoulders.

"It's a lovely dress," he said slowly.

She said nothing, watching his eyes linger, as if hovering over her body waiting to land. She felt the odd sensation of having suddenly been bathed and rubbed dry a little too hard. All her body tingled painfully, but with heady refreshment. Perhaps, then, not imagined? Perhaps, then, all true? She glanced at the clean, long fingers, the thick scholar's beard. Was it possible? Someone like him? She felt a sinful humiliation; she felt a satisfied pride.

A strange silence then settled over them, broken only by the whispery flap of pages being turned, the labored clicking of a cheap battery wall clock, and their slow, measured breathing. Far away, as if from another world that had nothing to do with them, a car's horn sounded, footsteps advanced and retreated, a dog barked.

"You've got it a little confused. . . ." He finally looked up and smiled. Their eyes met. His were cool, like a blue lake, with a black defining rim. She found herself mesmerized by his intensity, or perhaps her own reckless longing. "Here, let me show you." He pulled his chair around the table, putting it very close to hers. He did it in a very nonchalant, businesslike way. After all, how could he possibly explain the books to her if one of them were looking at them upside down? She tried not to look at him again, to still the almost painful excitement at the center of her body that throbbed so shamelessly. "If you would just make these two columns one, just add the numbers together, it would simplify matters for you tremendously."

"Yes," she whispered, understanding nothing. "Yes, of course, how stupid of me."

"Not stupid." He smiled at her. Something strange was happening to him. He felt himself trembling. He had never felt like this before, and it frightened him. Things were totally out of control. He resisted an almost uncontrollable urge to rub his shoulder against hers. It would be so easy, just a tiny, accidental half step closer and it would be accomplished. He resisted with all his might. No, it would scare her away. She was like a lovely little bird eating out of his hand. One harsh, sudden movement would send her flying high and far. And he did not want that. No, now more than ever, he did not want to do that.

It was almost nine when they finished. She entered his car naturally, forgetting her earlier awkwardness. Already she felt comfortable with his holding open the door for her, felt at home in the gray upholstered bucket seat. As she adjusted the seat belt, reducing it to half its length, she gave a brief thought to Noach's wife. Heavy and unattractive. A sly, humorless woman who squeezed all the joy out of observance, leaving the mitzvot as dry and hard as parched desert earth. Dina was astounded by the harshness of these thoughts. After all, it was wrong to think badly of others, especially those who had not harmed you in any way. Causeless hatred, it was called. And she had no reason to hate Mrs. Noach Saltzman. At least not any she could admit rationally.

Noach got into the car. His sudden presence, so close, was exhilarating and yet somehow exhausting as well. She felt she was fighting some intangible foe each time he was near her. All her senses were alive, alert to the danger. Yet what happiness! It was like being reborn to all the feelings that had lain so dead in her for so long. The car began to cruise smoothly into traffic.

He inclined his head to her, speaking in soft, low tones: "Look, I know it's late, but there is something I want to see. Would you mind if I took a small detour? I really hate to miss it."

What could she say? It was his car, and he had spent all evening helping her. It seemed so childish and petty to object, her mind scolded her, while her heart beat with joy and excitement. She wanted to go with him.

She nodded wordlessly, looking at her watch. What would Judah think? Yet somehow the idea didn't frighten her. Judah would be kind and understanding and sweet. He would accept whatever explanation she gave him, she told herself a little smugly.

They rode quietly for twenty minutes when he suddenly pulled over.

"Come out for a minute, won't you?"

A small prick of fear entered her heart. Yet she did as he asked. She could not believe her eyes. They were in some dark, high spot—she had no idea where, Talpiot, perhaps. She found the whole city spread out before her: astonishing, enchanting, luminous, yet suffused in mystery. It had all the elements of a great work of art. For the first time she grasped the full significance of this place she called home, her birthplace, its familiarity replaced by an overwhelming strangeness born of new insight.

It had been here, this earthly Jerusalem, for thousands of years. Her footsteps followed those of ancient ancestors who had never ceased to cling to its hills and valleys, to call it home. Their bones, long turned to dust, infused the very earth with meaning and obligation. It was a holy place.

She went back into the car and sat on the other woman's seat, her face white with shame.

Noach joined her hurriedly. "Beautiful, isn't it?"

She only nodded. "It's late," she told him coldly. "My husband will be waiting."

His head swam in confusion. This was his romantic spot. Women usually grew all soft and sentimental here. Dina's sudden coldness filled him with confusion and a sense of failure. He started the car, then let the motor die. "Why are you angry?" he asked her, peeved.

"It's not. I'm not. . . ."

"You are," he insisted, "and I think I have a right to know why. What have I done?"

"It's not that. . . . I've . . ." She couldn't find the words.

"Is it so wrong to try to find a little happiness? Is it so wrong to try to be with the one person in the whole world who makes you feel it's worthwhile to be alive?"

His words were electrifying. If he had punched her, she could not have felt more horrified, surprised, or helpless.

"You mustn't say these things to me!"

"I love you, Dina. You must know that."

"How can you say that?! It's wrong, evil. It's a sin. We don't even know each other."

"I know you." He reached out as if to lift her chin, yet at the last moment curled his fingers back without touching her. It didn't matter. He didn't need to force her. Her eyes had no place else to look but directly into his.

She was completely shaken by the unexpected intimacy, the way he had reached out to her, and most of all, his astonishing words. She felt like a willing captive in some tale of romantic piracy spirited off to some faraway island with no clue as to how or why she was to get back.

He smiled, yet his eyes were so full of pain.

"Are you very unhappy?" she asked him as if he were a child.

"Do you know what it is to live so many years without love, without passion? It's like being dead."

"Don't you love your wife?"

"My wife . . ." He had many cleverly bitter things to say but shrewdly thought better of it. "She is a good person, a very pious woman. But right from the start, I had no say. It was a *shiddach*. I was nineteen years old. I was considered a promising scholar then, and I was active in politics. My family are known as *geonim*. My father-in-law, a wealthy and persuasive man, was very anxious to talk my parents into a match. What did I know? I was nineteen years old. I didn't even know what a girl was. I had never in my life even talked to one who wasn't a close relative. Before they set the wedding date, I saw her for ten minutes, and even in that ten minutes my father walked in and asked: 'So *nu* already?' But even in only ten minutes, my future wife made it clear what she wanted: Torah, Torah, and more Torah."

"There's nothing wrong with that!" Dina felt herself near tears. He was coming too close to her, his words burrowing down deep beneath layers and layers. They were setting something free, a heavily chained trunk was suddenly flying open. It was terrifying.

"You don't understand, and yet you already judge and condemn! You see, I thought I wanted that, too. I wanted with all my heart to be like my father. But I'm not my father. I can't be my father." His fist struck firmly against the steering wheel, like a gavel used by a judge just before pronouncing sentence. "Even before I married, I was different. I liked to know things. I used to read newspapers, and listen to the radio in town inside some cafe. I even went to the movies once."

"What was it like?" Her tone was dreamy, forgetful, her anger past.

"It was . . . fun."

She didn't even know what that word meant anymore. She wondered if she had ever known. She wanted to weep. She was only eighteen years old.

"I told my father-in-law I wanted to leave the yeshiva and go to work. Ho, what battles! My wife was furious.

You'd think I'd announced I wanted to open a massage parlor! Her family was furious. They'd expected me to go on learning, to become a *rosh yeshiva*. But I wasn't making a decent living. Is it wrong to want to support your wife and children, to want nice things?" His tone turned acid. "So, finally, my father-in-law agreed to find me a position in the diamond business. His family has connections.

"Tel Aviv is different from Jerusalem. I feel free in Tel Aviv. I used to bring bathing clothes with me and go to the beach after work or early in the morning. I'd put on a bathing cap and tuck my *payess* inside and just walk down to the shore. No one would stare at me. I felt like everybody else."

"You could have gone to the separate men's beach in Tel Aviv," she said with a try at severity.

"But I liked the women." His eyes caught hers boldly. "I liked to see them in their bathing suits. The human body is so beautiful. Like a work of art. G-d made it so. What is wrong with appreciating that?"

How was it that she could not think of an answer to that, an answer she knew so well? Lust, wandering eyes, it all led to evil and *gehinnom*. Why couldn't she think of that?

He looked at her, monitoring her response carefully. Satisfied, he continued. "But I wasn't happy leaving it at that. I wanted companionship. Someone to share my life with. My wife is so closed. I can't even talk to her about the slightest thing that means poking your head outside the synagogue or the kitchen."

"Did you find companionship?" Dina asked with stunning accusation.

Noach Saltzman was not prepared for such a direct question. It hit him in a sensitive spot for some reason, a place he was not aware still existed in his callous, well-experienced body and mind. But nothing about this girl was typical. He had waited for her with unheard-of patience. He wanted her desperately, and this gave him a new weakness he did not know how to handle.

"Yes, I found it," he said frankly, shocking himself. "Again, again, and again. I'm a womanizer, I guess you'd call it. A skirt chaser. I am looking for love, for the one great love of my life. And now that at last I have found her, she's going to spit on me and throw me out. Isn't that right? Because I am not clever enough. I could lie so cleverly to all the others. I was so wise and practiced. But with you, with the one woman in the whole world . . . I do everything in the worst possible way. . . ."

He started the car, overwhelmed by the stupidity and hopelessness of his performance. What had gotten into him? What devil? To tell her the truth? It was all over, hopeless.

They rode all the way back in silence. He opened the door for her, afraid to look her in the face. To his astonishment, he felt cool hands burrow into his thick hair, just at the back of his neck. "You mustn't think these things, Noach. For your own good, we must both forget." Her breath was cool and fragrant over his eyes and cheeks as she whispered the words. Her little hand burned against his skin. Then he heard her delicate small footsteps, hurrying and anxious on the stairs.

CHAPTER 31

DINA OPENED THE DOOR SLOWLY, WITHOUT KNOCKING. Perhaps Judah would be asleep, she hoped dully. I can't face him right now. In the morning it would be better. It would be easier. I won't remember so much. Her fingers still tingled deliciously. She felt enveloped by a new power, a force outside herself that was suddenly pulling the strings to which she had no choice but to dance. It seemed all preordained somehow. Her choices seemed suddenly to have been taken away from her.

She knew, and had always known, that one day it would happen. The illegitimate feelings she had given birth to and tried to smother in infancy would spring up fully grown, monsters of her own creation. And in a strange contradiction, she welcomed the horror, longed for it. Anything passionate was better than this quiet, dull contentment, this correct, proper half living that had been forced on her.

She thought in overwrought, schoolgirl clichés straight out of the romance novels she had never read: he had come for her, the true man of her heart. He had swept her off her feet in passion. He would risk the world for her. She found herself wallowing in joyous pride. To mean so much to someone else! Someone so handsome and learned. Someone with clean, immaculate fingers. A *talmid chachem!* All his faults she easily forgave. They made him, if anything, even more glamorous. He was living out all the sins she knew she wanted to try.

What would it be like to go swimming at the beach surrounded by men in bathing suits who would look at your skimpily covered body with interest and appreciation? What would it be like to sit in a darkened movie theater and watch forbidden, enticing stories acted out larger than life in front of your eyes? Most of all, what would it be like to know? To read and hear and see whatever you fancied?

Without knowing it, by telling the sad and unfortunate truth, Noach had established a deeper bond of intimacy with Dina than he could possibly have done with the most accomplished and well thought out of lies. His sins coupled with his uncharacteristic honesty had won her over. Here was a man who dared all for love! He had tried many women and wanted her! While Judah . . . why, she was probably the first girl he had ever gone out with! What value did his adoration have, based as it was on so little? With Noach she felt for the first time in her life the perfect fullness of being a woman, the amazing power.

If she had been perfectly honest with herself, she would have had to admit that what she was feeling most was a perverse sense of personal accomplishment. Until now she'd felt she had done nothing on her own. Even her good deeds, her piety, were somehow a legacy, not a personal choice. She had not known evil, and thus the good had fallen into her lap. She had not had to choose. Even in love, in marriage, she had not achieved any triumph. She had not married the man she really wanted, but simply someone who had been chosen for her and who wanted her.

And yet . . . he was such a good man. She could not be indifferent to that, to his joy in her. Physically she had to admit she loved Judah. But he was no challenge. His love for her proved nothing, neither her beauty nor her goodness nor her rise to a new social status. He had to love her. He was her husband. Whereas Noach, Noach had chosen her from among the many. Noach, who had endless choices. Noach, who was immaculate and learned. He had courage she admired because she could not see its dark roots.

Despite the lateness of the hour, Judah was still up. At the first sight of her husband bathed in golden lamplight, sitting on his comfortable chair, an open Talmud on his lap, she felt a heavy thump of foreboding go off in her head like the sickening noise of an accident. He looked up slowly, a familiar loving smile crossing his warm, gentle lips. "Dinaleh!" He closed the book and put it aside, motioning for her to come. She walked to him, feeling the nauseating sea of guilt break over her insides.

She slipped onto Judah's lap and laid her head against his shoulder like a little girl.

"Did you have a hard time in the shop?"

She nodded, not looking at him. "Were you worried? You didn't have to be, you know. I'm not a child." Her tone was peevish.

"No. I know that, my little darling wife. My little dove. . . ." He stroked her cheek, which grew warm and pink from the caress. "But I can't help being concerned."

What was she going to do!

"Judah," she whispered.

"Yes, my little dove?"

"Judah, did you ever think about going to the movies?"

"The movies?" He was thoroughly puzzled.

"Or reading the newspaper, or listening to the radio?"

"Not really. My life is fine as it is. I have you and the baby and my shop. What would I need those things for?"

"Just to try them. Just for . . . fun!"

"Fun?" He seemed puzzled. It was not a word *haredi* adults ever used, except perhaps to describe events on Purim, the holiday in which merrymaking, overdrinking, and overeating were considered a positive commandment. "Fun is for children," he scoffed. "I like my pleasures deep, not shallow. You are my dearest pleasure, my love. You know that. I could never treat that lightly. It means far too much to me."

She found this answer annoying in the extreme. He took all the small, frivolous pleasures and discarded them because he wanted the big, serious ones. She felt absurdly threatened and defeated, as if he had physically taken something away from her. "But don't you sometimes wish you could try something new?"

"New is forbidden by the Torah," he said with a half smile, partially mocking the oft stated rationale behind some of the more extreme *haredi* sects that saw in their fight against the modern world a glowing ideal in itself.

"Why didn't you call the store if you were worried?" she complained.

"I didn't want to disturb you. I figured that you must be up to your neck in work." He found himself surprisingly defensive.

She jumped off his lap. "You might have called just to see if I was all right," she said unreasonably, with irritation.

"Would you have wanted me to? Wouldn't it have felt like I was checking up on you?"

She was struck by the truth of his words, which made her even angrier. "And what would I care if you wanted to check up on me? Do I have something to hide? Oh, this is intolerable." She went into the bedroom and slammed the door.

Judah sat motionless, feeling the sudden cold where her thighs had rested against his legs, her head against his shoulder. He slapped his palm against his head. Dummkopf! Stupid head! But he had been grossly misunderstood. How could she have misunderstood him so perfectly, with such perfect injustice? He chalked it up to his usual clumsiness. My mother was right, he thought glumly. I don't have any idea about how to treat a woman.

He walked slowly toward the bedroom, opening the door diffidently. But the lights were already out and she was already in bed, thoroughly covered up.

"Dina," he whispered, sitting beside her on the bed, his large hand resting on the covers. He felt a faint stir. "I'm sorry, forgive me."

She made no move, feeling his hand warm and heavy above her, holding her down. If I am still, he will go away, she told herself. She hardened her heart against his pleading. Leave me alone. Just leave me alone already, she thought a bit desperately. It was too degrading to see him apologize so abjectly when the fault had been all her own. But her heart was closed now, encased in something hard and cold. He was a nuisance. Soon he would go away. She kept perfectly still, as if her life depended on it.

Nothing changed. Everything changed. She woke up in the morning and did her ablutions, but when it came time to pray, she couldn't say the words anymore. When you prayed, your mind and heart were open, vulnerable. You conversed with G-d. For the first time in her life, Dina Reich Gutman was afraid of this conversation.

Even the baby seemed suddenly abstract. His cries, his smiles, in which she had taken so much joy, seemed strangely distant, a kiss behind glass. Her mind and heart were elsewhere. She was already in the shop. It was already six-thirty. The little bell was jangling, the door was opening.

A few times she found herself walking toward the window, even though she knew Noach usually left for work around nine. Yet there was this almost irresistible urge to go there, to stand and search for him; to see the longing in his eyes, the white, promising fingers pulling back the white curtains.

Judah left a little later than usual. She had found the right face, the right voice, for Judah. She was bright and careless and hard as stone. She smiled at him without warmth and chattered to him nonstop without interest. A few times he had tried to break through to her, but she had blocked him with that pleasant, hard brightness that was as impenetrable as hatred. She was already dreaming of what life would be like without him.

It was an irrational dream. Always he seemed to just disappear into thin air. There was no unpleasantness or recriminations. No rabbis or divorce courts, no handwringing neighbors or relatives. Just a magic fairy wand floating over her life, taking Judah out without harming him or anyone else, leaving behind Noach and a clear path.

It was like her dreams of being in the army, she thought. She would never do it. She walked idly to the window and stared out at Noach's curtained windows. What was it like inside his house? she wondered. What did his clothes look like in the closet? The shirts, the intimate undergarments? Folded neatly, white? Or a jumble? What kind of chairs did he sit on, and how did his legs look when he was relaxed? And how would his chest look if you unbuttoned just the very top button or perhaps the one after that? . . .

She shivered and hugged the baby, who wriggled in mighty protest. She held fast to his warmth, his living motion. She was still a good mother, she told herself. A good wife. No one could prove otherwise. She hadn't trespassed any commandment. Even *yichud!* Her mind was her own.

As in the past, she told herself, there was no harm in dreaming. But somehow there was more to it this time. The dream was frighteningly close, terrifyingly real, almost as if it weren't a dream at all.

And the clock ticked on, relentlessly moving her life toward some goal she didn't dare predict.

CHAPTER 32

There was a horde of customers, all impatient, all demanding. The store was in an uproar, packed. She felt she could hardly breathe. So many were women who knew her or had known her mother. It was almost personal, like social visits. And each time the bell chimed, she lifted her head in panic toward the door. What if he should walk in on her now, surrounded by all these witnesses? They would all know immediately! Her face would beam the message out to them like a garish neon sign. Yet as the evening wore on and there was no sign of Noach, her panic in seeing him was replaced by an awful dread that he might not come.

And then the store emptied out. She looked around at the old, chipped walls, the stacks of yarn boxes that reached almost to the ceiling. Everything seemed to be waiting breathlessly, with that harsh, in-held breath of dismay that preceded some terrible crisis. She put on her coat slowly, wondering where she would go now, forgetting completely that there was no choice involved. She would go to the bus stop. She would ride the number four bus to a block away from her home. She would walk down the quiet street, up the quiet stairs, and enter her quiet house. Judah would be there, solid and loving, waiting for her. The baby would be there, sleeping his deep, healthy sleep. She would change her clothes and crawl in beneath the familiar clean bedcovers.

Yet it was impossible! How would she live through it?

She locked the shop and began the walk to the bus stop with heavy, reluctant steps. She waited dully for the bus, watching its tiny yellow lights, bright and predatory in the distance, grow brighter and more dangerous each moment as it drew relentlessly closer.

Yet, instead, there was his car. Noach rolled down the window and leaned over. Her heart leapt just at the sight of him. She felt an inexplicable relief and climbed in easily. This time the seat belt didn't even need to be adjusted.

"Where are we going?" she said gaily, moving over the difficult transition without hesitation. There was no longer any pretense of a working relationship, innocent excuses, or pretended moral outrage. She had climbed into the other woman's seat with alacrity, as if it were the most natural thing in the world.

All Noach's explanations, made unnecessary, dried up in his throat. He wasn't sure how to react, whether to be glad or dismayed. He had had other expectations of her. He couldn't decide if this behavior made her more or less desirable to him. He thought about it as he drove, throwing cautious glances at her, reminding himself of how lovely she was. Her eyes shone with a special light. Her whole face seemed to blossom in happiness.

His misgivings faded. He wanted to reach out for her

small hand, yet some instinct prevented him. Her touching him didn't count. Once he touched her physically, she might wake up. He had to do it so slowly and cautiously, she would never know how it had all come about. Noach Saltzman knew just how to accomplish it. He was a man with experience.

He drove down a long, deserted road that crossed over into the eastern, Arab half of the city. It was a bit dangerous, with the *intifada*. Many cars had had their windshields smashed by Palestinian teenagers—political delinquents, full of hatred and idleness. But what else could he do? The only hotel in which he could be absolutely sure neither of them would be recognized was the Hotel Inter-Continental in East Jerusalem, an Arab-run hotel full of foreign diplomats, the only major hotel in Jerusalem that did not have a certificate of kashruth from the chief rabbi's office simply because their customers were the kind that wanted ham and eggs for breakfast.

The danger of the road winding past the little, darkened Arab villages, their mosques sounding the ancient call to prayer, made Dina quiver with a dark thrill. Yet how could she fear rock-throwing Arabs when she had chosen to do something as incredibly dangerous as keeping a liaison with a married man behind her husband's back? The dark road, the uncertainty on every side, seemed a perfect metaphor for her emotional life. Once you defy G-d, there is nothing to be afraid of since everything is equally dangerous. Whether she walked to her own back porch or down this unguarded road, G-d's mighty hand of justice lay in wait for her. Of this she had no doubt. She could either repent and beg to be forgiven or go on and just not think about her fate. She chose the latter.

The hotel, with its famous seven-arched windows overlooking the Old City, was a breathtaking place. As they walked up into the lobby, a ray of light came through its great doors and fell on Noach. He had taken off his skullcap, she noticed. She stood motionless. The act, which could not be excused *halachically*, suddenly colored everything differently. He was ashamed to be seen with her with his skullcap on. He had no trouble just taking it off.

"Noach, put it back on! How can you?"

He looked at her as if she'd gone mad. He pulled her arm toward him with a little jerk. "Don't make a scene, Dina. The last thing we need is for people to think we are coming from Meah Shearim. The word would spread like wildfire."

She stumbled up the steps after him. Of course! How stupid! What would a religious couple be doing in a hotel that wasn't even kosher! Yet it bothered her. It was a concrete act, a throwing off of the yoke of heaven that was small and measurable, whereas the other, the act of being with another man, was too big and amorphous to be considered in all its ramifications. Kill one person and you are a murderer to be executed. Kill millions and you go down in history.

He led her to an elegant patio cafe. The gently lit city shone on them with a strange, beckoning light. But the more she looked at it, the less familiar it became to her. She had never seen it from this side before. It was a foreign place, full of Arab villages, mosques, and minarets. What had it to do with her?

"I'll have a beer," he told the tall, polite Arab waiter who bent his head diffidently in their direction.

"A cola," she wavered. Even the glasses would be *trayf*, washed together with plates holding forbidden meats and cheeses. She would not pour it into a glass but drink it from the can, she told herself.

"Do you like it here?" he asked her, smiling.

"I hate it," she answered him brutally.

"But why?"

"Because you had to take your skullcap off. It's degrading."

She was an odd one! But it intrigued him. "Why is that?"

"I haven't done anything wrong! We were working together, that's all. The door wasn't even locked. It wasn't even *yichud!*"

"So my taking off my skullcap is the first wrong thing we've done, is that it?" He tried to keep the amusement out of his voice but failed.

"You're mocking me." She got up abruptly. "Take me home, now!"

"But, Dina, please. Just have your drink. Look, I'll put my skullcap back on." He took it out of his pocket and placed it on top of his head. The black velvet material faded into his jet black hair. He looked around uncomfortably. "Don't you think it's worse for me to be seen eating in a *trayf* place wearing a skullcap? Why, people might think that the hotel suddenly went kosher! They might order a whole meal on the basis of seeing me here with a skullcap!"

She sat down as if all the air had gone out of her. Of course. It was *marit eyin*, visual deception. A person had to make sure he didn't even seem to be breaking a commandment. Thus, even if you ordered a Coke in McDonald's, drinking it there with a skullcap on your head might give people the impression that you were eating a Big Mac, fries, and a milkshake. Of course he was right. She felt very foolish.

"Why do you constantly suspect me? Do I seem to be such a worthless infidel in your eyes? Such a *kofer?*"

"No. It's me. I don't know what to think. I'm so ashamed. I shouldn't have come."

He reached out across the table and held her cold, trembling fingers until they were warm again. "We are just talking, Dina. That's all."

She looked down at his hand on hers, feeling some barrier shatter, the shards cutting deep into her soul. The tears swam in her eyes. The touch of his naked flesh on hers was so wrong, so degrading. Yet she felt she wanted it more than anything. "There is no hope for me. G-d will cut me off. I am lost."

"It's a terrible thing to be lonely. And we're not doing anything wrong. I am a religious, G-d-fearing man. But what . . . It's the community that decides the rules. They make a big thing out of the idea of 'Thou shalt be holy.' But what about 'Thou shalt not steal'? Who does the community honor with seats by the eastern wall of the synagogue, with the sixth aliyah to the Torah? Why, all the rich, crooked businessmen! And nobody minds! What is my crime, your crime? That we were married too young to the wrong people? That we are lonely and desperate for love? I do not steal. I am simply a lonely man tied to the wrong woman—a man who needs love, companionship. Passion. Is that so terrible, to have finally found, after all my years of searching, the woman I love? The one I want to spend my life with?"

She had never been wooed by a man before with such thrilling words. She was an innocent who took each worn phrase and folded it into her heart as if it were an original. As if she were the first woman in the world to be told "My wife doesn't understand me!"

"You know, *haredim* think that it's easy to get a girl," he went on. "Among themselves, the men talk. They think that if a girl agrees to talk to you, she'll agree to everything else. It isn't so. I want to tell you about my first girl."

"Why?" She was amazed.

"I don't know. I just want to. Can you understand that, the relief in not having to lie anymore? I want everything to be straight between us. This girl I met in the office. She was about eighteen, the daughter of the head of a yeshiva in Bnai Brak. For some reason, she hadn't yet married. They said it was because she was too pretty, too well connected. No one was worthy of her. I could see that she was lonely. I saw it in her eyes and she saw it in mine. We began to talk, just—you know, nothing special. She stayed late one night—I never knew if it was on purpose or not—and I decided to stay with her. I have a television set in my office with a video recorder and some movies. Nothing terrible. Little romances like *Gigi*, musicals. I asked her if she wanted to watch one with me."

Noach paused and looked intently into the lovely, fragile face of Dina Gutman. Perhaps it was her tears that made her lovely eyes a bit red. Or perhaps it was the worry lines of guilt that suddenly sprouted on her forehead, making her a little less lovely. Whatever the reason, he began to think like his old self. Like a man in a new suit who changes back into comfortable work clothes, his old self fell over him with curious ease. He squeezed her hand a little tighter.

"What happened?" she finally asked.

"Well, it went on for months. I never slept with her," he found himself lying with strange ease. "I swear it! I know those who found out will never believe me. But the sex wasn't important. It was the feeling, the communication, the caring between us. We hugged a little and kissed. She used to like to cry on my shoulder. I don't know, it made her feel like she had a life of her own. At home they were so strict with her."

"What happened to her?"

"They married her off to some yeshiva *bocher* quickly." He drained the last drops of beer. "I swear to you by all that is holy that I never slept with another woman other than my wife. I have never even been tempted before, until now." He looked into her eyes meaningfully until she felt herself going blind and lost. His words fueled her pride. She was special. She could make things happen. She had some control over her life. And he wasn't bad. Not really. His palm over hers began to burn into her skin. She pulled it away, pouring the can of Coca-Cola into the clean glass, forgetting she hadn't meant to use it. She remembered, in the middle, about the glass but didn't stop. She drank it down, her lips eager, straining for the final cool drop. Then she waited for something to happen.

Through the long, quiet moments sitting beside Noach in the elegant lobby, through the long, slow ride back to the city, she waited breathlessly for something to happen, some terrible accident, some sudden, painful smash-up. But the air was benign. The roads clear. The silence innocent. Perhaps, then, she thought, nothing would happen? So many good people suffered. So many bad ones prospered. Who was to measure G-d's justice? She had drunk from a *trayf* glass. She had touched another man behind her husband's back in the full sight of G-d, from whom nothing could be hidden, and still she breathed, safe and unharmed.

It was so late when they got back that he didn't bother discreetly leaving her off a block away, as he had been doing. He pulled up in front of the apartment building. He stopped the car. And then with stunning release, she felt the rush of his arms around her, the press of his lean, eager body into her soft, yielding one. His cheek, the soft hair of his beard, brushed against her eyes and temples. She reached up and found the back of his head. He pressed his lips full on her mouth with reckless, careless passion.

Outside in the darkness white gloves flashed like exclamation points in the night. Dark men stood silently, watching.

CHAPTER 33

SHE WAS TRAVELING TOWARD THE BRINK. SHE FELT IT, SAW IT, like a bold and dangerous new frontier that loomed solid and immovable in the distance. Yet it was hard for her to believe in its reality. At home everything remained virtually the same. Judah asked no questions, demanded no explanations of her comings and goings. He was calm, steady, and warm in his love. He continued to shower her with his odd little gifts: wildflowers, drawings of birds, little wood carvings, pretty scarves, packages of exotic teas. Only, perhaps, his young, smooth brow had begun to lose its flexibility, springing back slower as, increasingly, he kneaded the skin in thought.

Her time together with Noach was becoming less frequent and more difficult to arrange. Chaya Leah had finished her exams and taken over the shop once again in the afternoons and evenings, giving Dina little reason to be out after dark.

She had taken to meeting Noach after visits to her father and Dvorah. But lately she was finding the transition from honest family visits to illicit, secret liaisons increasingly loathsome and degrading. More and more, with sickening results, the question kept repeating itself to her: "What if they knew?" She felt as if she were carrying the germs of some vile contagion deliberately into their healthy, innocent homes.

She began to see him less often, yet her thoughts were never far from him. Her dreams took on new urgency, new color, and an almost violent passion. Often she was in his arms, their bodies tangled inseparably. She could not get free of him. She did not want to. With him, even only his image in her mind, the whole world was charming and light, with an unpredictable newness, a variety, she found irresistible.

No, it was not her husband who was transforming the familiar landscape, turning it into an unknown, unexplored country. It was Noach.

He was constantly pushing, convincing, wooing. Even when her eyes were closed, his silent face pleaded. His eyes implored from every window. His hands were urging, insistent, and on the brink of rage. He wanted her to go away with him to Tel Aviv for two days. His wife was going to Haifa for a cousin's wedding, and he had convinced her to stay on at the hotel with the children for a few extra days' vacation while he went back to work. He wanted Dina to join him in Tel Aviv overnight.

"We have no privacy," he argued convincingly. "We'll be able to swim at the beach. To watch TV and videos, with no one to bother us. . . ." The rest he left unsaid. The ultimate act of intimacy, the complete joining that would officially unite them and damn them forever, they never discussed. So far, their intimacies had not gone beyond long talks, long walks, some hand-holding, and a few kisses. "In Tel Aviv, in a five-star hotel, no one will suspect we aren't man and wife," he whispered to her, his breath warm on her neck and ear.

In the light of day, or sitting with Judah in the lamplight, the idea seemed an impossible, vaguely repulsive fantasy. Yet at other times—after hours of romantic conversations, with Noach's hands caressing the small of her back—it seemed like the most delicious, wonderful, exciting experience life could ever offer her. She hated the swift passing of their stolen moments together. If two hours left her breathless with joy, then what would happen in two days? she exulted, brimming with a reckless elation, a joyous, in-held laughter so loud that it deafened her to all other voices, like a tremendous thunderclap.

Then one morning, after a week and a half of not being together, she returned home from the park with the baby and found Noach standing in front of her door.

"Noach!" It was broad daylight. People were walking up and down the stairs. She even thought she heard his wife's voice coming out of his apartment. It was insane!

He pressed his body against hers, backing her up against the door. "Let me in," he said in low, urgent tones. His pupils were dilated, his lips closed together firmly.

Little Yossele was still sitting in the carriage, his eyes wide with surprise, watching his mother and the stranger. She fumbled for her key, wanting only to get into the house, away from the neighbors who might pass by. The door opened. She backed in slowly, holding the baby against her chest, as if for protection. Noach followed her swiftly.

"I have to talk to you." He was pacing up and back, agitated.

She ran to close the curtains. She put the baby into his playpen, then walked back into the living room. He was sitting on Judah's chair. The sight of him there filled her with a sickening guilt.

"Don't!" She pulled him up.

His arms enveloped her. She felt herself thrown back against the wall, crushed, overpowered. Yet her body responded with odd joy, more to his enthusiasm, his passion for her, than to anything else. They were two bodies, nothing more. She didn't think. There was no such thing as right or wrong. The longing was so strong, it obliterated all other considerations, all restraints.

Strangely, it was Noach who pulled back. He didn't want it to be quick. He had plans that took time, long, slow, unhurried hours of absolute privacy. Like a gourmet, he was not willing to take his meal, no matter how delicious, without the proper surroundings. Her baby calling from the playpen, his wife just across the hall, was not what he had in mind. "I want you to say yes. I want you to agree! To promise me! June twenty-ninth at the Tel Aviv Hilton. For two days!" Before she could answer, his hands pressed her back toward him, his mouth covering hers. She felt his fingers slipping inside the collar of her dress, caressing the back of her neck.

He took his mouth off hers, waiting for her to speak. He felt her fall against him, burying her head on his shoulder. "I want you to answer me," he cajoled. "Please. . . ." Tears sprang into his eyes.

She looked up at him, shocked. With her small, childish palm, she wiped away the tears, drying her hand on her own cheek. "Yes—" She stared into his face, overpowered by the intensity of the moment, the overwhelming relief at having come to some decision. "Only go now. Before someone sees!" She almost hated him suddenly for being there. And yet her body! What was she to do with its longing, its shameless, unequivocal response?

"So you swear?"

"No. I promise. You know one is not allowed to swear," she admonished him.

It made him smile cynically, as always, this evidence of her small pieties in the face of her very large sins. Then he released her. He listened by the door a moment, then swiftly made his exit into the hall.

She locked the door, then leaned against it, feeling annihilated. And glad.

CHAPTER 34

B"H

Dear Moishe,

Your cousin Mendel held on to your letter two weeks before getting it to me, so that is the reason for the delay. As always, the minute I open it up I smell it. But it doesn't smell particularly like you. It smells like the army, all sweaty and oily.

How I wish I could see you!

I was surprised to hear about the payess. *Are your parents aware you've cut them off? Or are they still refusing to see you? It must be very awful for you on the holidays when the other men go home. Holidays at home are not the same for me either. Not without Ima. The housekeeper tries her best, but she is no cook, and the boys still ache for Ima. I try to substitute in a little way. It comforts me too, to hold them. I'm so lonely most of the time, I could die.*

Don't pressure me, please, about Aba. He doesn't understand about us. He's pretending nothing has happened. He's talking about calling Reb Garfinkel. . . . Don't worry!! They will never, never pressure me as they did my sisters. No matter what it winds up costing, we will be married one day. I defy them all! But I can't fight with my father just now. He is so exhausted most of the time, so weak. I just can't aggravate him.

My final exams went all right, I guess. I wasn't trying very hard. And Morganbesser watches me like a hawk. How I detest that woman, with her phony little sermons, her sickeningly sweet smiles. Maybe in your fantasy of rounding up the Morals Patrol in your tank, you could include her, especially in the part where you start dumping them over the Syrian border!

I know you mean well when you tell me not to feel responsible for my mother's death. But I can't help connecting the grief I gave her to what happened. My heart is broken over it, as you know. I can't promise you it will ever heal. That is why I must be the biggest tzdakis from now on. You would laugh if you could see me cleaning the house, tending the boys, making chicken soup for sick neighbors, bringing warm clothes to old people. But the work is good. It feels as if I'm working off some enormous debt. I don't really know if I will ever be finished.

No, I haven't gotten all pious on you. I'm still myself. Just older, and sadder.

How I long for you!

Chaya Leah

B"H

Dear Chaya Leah,

I don't think you would recognize me. The uniform fits better now than it did in the beginning. I've lost weight, which is not surprising, since the army isn't exactly a place where the food is tempting to begin with. Besides, even though the food is supposed to be kosher, and in fact there is even some little knitted skullcap type that is supposed to be the mashgiach, I still don't trust the kitchen. People are constantly in there. They use the meat knife to cut the cheese, and put cereal and milk into the meat soup bowls. So, I'm pretty much subsisting on raw fruits, vegetables, bread (mostly two days old), and lots of leben and yogurt. Can I manage two more years of this? Do I have a choice?

The problem I had with the other recruits at the beginning is getting better now. They no longer call me kuni lemel, *and have come to see the wisdom of having a beard (otherwise you have to shave every morning, even out in the field!!). The men have also come to see the advantage of having a* "dos" *(that's how we are nicknamed here, from* Orthodos) *in the unit. I am very popular when I volunteer for guard duty every time they are dying to see some soccer match on TV. On the other hand, they use me as the official whipping boy for anything that happens anywhere in the country which puts religious Jews in a bad light. You know, that whole disgraceful thing with Reb K., the Rabbinical* Court *judge, who was getting the women who came before him to sleep with him in exchange for granting divorces. Well, you'd think this perverted creep was my twin brother, the way everyone jumps on me! See, see, how can it be? they constantly demand. You see, how all the religious ones are just as bad as we are! Reb K., the pervert, may he drop dead for all the problems he's given me. But I've learned not to fall into that trap. I just shrug and say: "How should I know why he behaved the way he did?" That sort of takes the wind out of their sails and they leave me alone for a little while. Until the next religious scandal.*

My *master sergeant* (RASAR, *they call him, everything in the army is an acronym) has let up on me and given me the time I need each morning and afternoon to put on tefillin and pray. Also, I told him that if he didn't give me the time I needed, I was going straight to the colonel. I would have, too.*

Army rules are pretty generous when it comes to keeping religious beliefs. Who would have believed it, in Israel of all places?

The first part of the training was the worst. I figured out that the only purpose to most of the things we did—all the midnight marches, the two A.M. inspections, the minute examinations of how we folded our blankets and cleaned our guns—was to break our spirits. That is, to take away any lingering ideas that we were still independent, thinking human beings. In the army, you are not supposed to think, but to do what you are told. I guess, in a way, being a Hasid is pretty good training. But combining being a Hasid with being a soldier in the Israel Defense Forces is pretty near impossible. I'm happy I did it, though, despite everything. I'm glad to have escaped Meah Shearim.

Most of my scars have healed, although one or two still ache whenever it rains. That's when I think of Kurzman and the Morals Patrol the most. I'll be happy to add Morganbesser to my dream of rounding them all up at gunpoint in Meah Shearim before dragging them in my tank to the Golan Heights. A boy can dream, can't he?

But most of the time, I dream about you. I worry when you don't write. I hope you're feeling a little less depressed than the last time. It's insane for you to blame yourself for your mother's death. A heart doesn't get weak and give out overnight. Besides, some say it's genetic, that your heart is just born with that little built-in recorded message when to give out. I regret that you got into trouble. But I don't regret anything else.

In another year and three months, I'll be out of the army. Please, wait for me. We'll think of something.

All my love,

Moishe

CHAPTER 35

THE STRANGEST THING ABOUT THE DAY WAS ITS LACK OF strangeness. The sun rose, the baby smiled. Judah ate his breakfast and kissed her good-bye. She even sat down and buttered herself a slice of toasted challah bread left over from Shabbat. She ate it with amazing slowness, but with no appetite. In fact, although she felt the crumbs on her tongue, in between her teeth, she couldn't taste anything. Or perhaps she just couldn't remember she was eating and so forgot food was supposed to have a taste.

He would be waiting for her at two P.M. in a Tel Aviv beachfront hotel. Judah had hardly seemed to listen as she'd begun her casual but long explanation of how she had to stay overnight in Bnai Brak with an old friend to help her over a difficult pregnancy. "She's so depressed.

She just begged me to come," she'd said fairly easily. Only when she'd added, "It would be a mitzvah," did a small ache at the back of her throat almost strangle the words in her chest. Judah hadn't asked her any questions, just looked down at the floor as if he were studying something broken or dirty that needed to be taken care of, making a mental note to take care of it. But he'd nodded his assent pleasantly enough, she'd noted, as his look began to prick her ballooning sense of confidence and well-being.

That had been a week ago. She wasn't thinking about it anymore. It was all arranged, she told herself now. His mother would watch the baby until Judah picked him up after work. And she'd be back by the next evening in time to make her husband dinner.

They'd just left, her husband and little son. Judah had agreed to drop the baby off at his mother's on his way to work. "So you can get to your friend faster," he'd said, making her heart thump with a sickening sense of guilt. She'd searched his eyes as he stood by the door, the baby cradled in his big arms, tugging at his mustache. Her husband and son, she'd thought, studying them as one sometimes studies the minute, precious details of a rare photograph of loved ones long gone. A little panic shot through her as Judah inclined his rough, thick head of hair down to her to accept her customary kiss. His complexion was as smooth and pink as an innocent little baby's, she noticed, wondering why she'd never seen it before. . . . She held the baby's round, active little fist, kissing his tiny fingers, which continued to pummel the air in aimless fury and joy.

"I'll miss you both," she said without a trace of irony. It was absolutely true. As she heard Judah's footsteps descend, growing softer and more distant, a cold panic began to grow, spreading in concentric circles to every part of her body. A part of her wanted to run after them and weep, tug at their clothes and beg them to stay with her and never leave.

She ran to the window and opened it. But no sound came out as she watched Judah's large, powerful body stride away, his back to her. Perhaps if he had looked up. Perhaps if the baby had looked over his father's shoulder and caught her eye and waved, perhaps everything would have been different. But that is not what happened. Judah disappeared, never seeing her white and pleading face staring at his back. The baby played, totally absorbed in his father's shirt buttons, oblivious to his young mother's desperation. Then they were both gone. She closed the window and turned her back to it, heading toward her bedroom.

She began to pack a small suitcase. As she went through her lingerie, a knot grew in the back of her throat, an ache of shame and excitement beyond anything she had ever known. She felt the silky material of the skimpy gown flow over her fingers. She felt the soft cotton of the clean underwear, the bra. Her shame began to grow until it mushroomed into an explosive silent shout of disgust. She didn't want to do this! How had she gotten herself into it!

Then she packed her bathing suit. It was a new one—green and yellow flowers on a white background. She closed her eyes and felt the lids tremble. The sun, the sparkling waters, the joy of doing something new. And Noach waiting. She wanted to do it with all her heart. Yes! How lovely it would be! What a pleasure it would be! She folded the pretty suit, trying to imagine herself in it, diving under the waves, all the while her fingers working mechanically, folding, tucking in loose ends, making the final closure. The suitcase, a little overnight bag, closed with difficulty. Now if I can only keep it closed until I reach the hotel room, she mused, trying to forget the intimate things inside; to forget that she would have to open it and put them on in front of Noach Saltzman, a man who was not her husband.

She finished the final straightening of the bedroom, picked up a few of Yossie's toys, washed the last of the breakfast dishes. Then, automatically, almost thoughtlessly, she picked up her prayer book to say the morning prayers.

The pages felt cold and strange on her fingertips. "I am thankful before Thee, King Who lives everlasting. . . ." The words came slowly, falteringly. They felt sour and disgraceful on her tongue, as if she had bitten into something rancid. She felt a flash of sudden fear. There was a third party involved in all her plans. She could not keep Him out. He was there, looking over her shoulder, inside her head. She blushed with shame in an agony of painful revelation. Yet she felt beyond choice. She had made the commitment. Noach was waiting. His pull was stronger.

She kissed the worn, familiar pages, the front and back cover between which was stored the lifelong conversation she had kept up with her Creator since she was little more than a baby. Then she put it aside, picked up the suitcase, and locked the door behind her.

She walked thoughtfully down the first set of stairs. Yet by the time she'd reached the second, her footsteps were already growing lighter and swifter. In the end she flew down the last landing to the street, happily, carelessly, recklessly.

CHAPTER 36

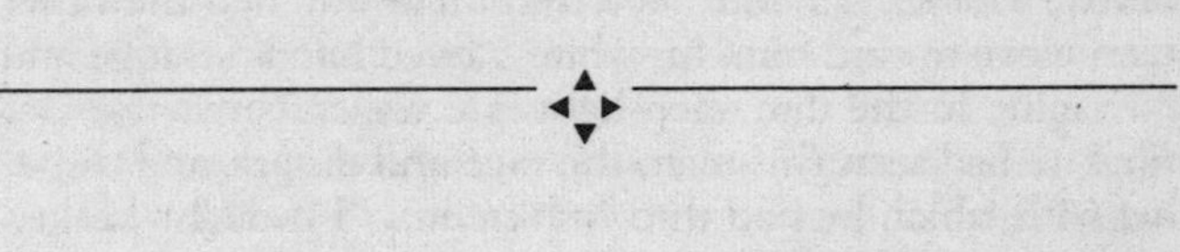

OF ALL THE TYPES OF WOODWORKING THAT HE DID IN THE SHOP, turning the wood gave Judah the most satisfaction. There was something magic about the way a rough, clumsy board without shape or character was transformed in seconds on the turning lathe into an object of smooth, delicate beauty. Sometimes he lost himself in thought, watching the furiously spinning wood as it turned with dizzying speed, an object to be molded in his hands to his satisfaction. And sometimes he identified with it, thinking of himself as just such a blunt and ordinary human stick who was whirling helplessly in a maelstrom of confusion as G-d chipped away at his imperfections, turning him out to His satisfaction.

The night before had been the first in his marriage without Dina beside him. The house had seemed cheerless and dark and oddly hollow. He was anxiously anticipating her return that evening, his eyes light with expectation as he watched the turning lathe. The wood was beautiful, soft, shapely.

He felt it before he saw it. There was someone in the shop. A flash of white peeked out of the darkness. Judah felt his heart drop with strange foreboding. He turned off the machine and looked up, expressionless.

"*Boker tov*, Reb Yid."

"*Boker tov*, Reb Kurzman," Judah answered reluctantly, wiping his hands on a towel. He watched the other man move toward him, his white-gloved hands strange and menacing in the dim shop light. He remembered the first time he had seen this man, the rage and disgust and disbelief with which he had thrown him out. "I thought I asked you not to bother me again."

"No, my good friend. You asked me not to come again without proof. If you had listened to me months ago when I first came to you, then I would not have the unfortunate honor of bringing you such proof as I bring you now. G-d forgive you for not heeding my warning!"

Judah found his legs suddenly weak. He stumbled against a stool and sat down. "You've brought me . . . proof?"

The other man nodded. "Pictures. Everything. We don't like to do this. But you gave us no choice with your blindness, your obstinacy, all these months. It is G-d's will that the homes of his people Israel be pure. You must purge the evil, the sin, from your midst, even if it is the wife of your bosom."

"You've brought proof?" Judah repeated in a voice so pitiful it would have broken the heart of any man less self-righteous and firm in his belief than Rabbi Kurzman. With the eyes of a condemned man who first glimpses the gallows, Judah watched the white glove vanish into a pocket and reappear with a stack of photographs. He felt his stomach heave with fear and disgust. He got up and backed away. He flipped the switch, and the little shop once more was filled with the roar of the lathe, turning and turning. He picked up the wood and carefully mounted it.

The noise covered all the other voices which suddenly filled the shop, five or six sturdy young men in their black outfits. He listened to nothing, to no one, save the still, small voice in his own head. It told him to turn off the machine. It told him to look at the photographs.

Again, with slow precision, he turned off the machine, wiped his hands, and reached out, touching the cold, almost slimy surface of the pictures. His eyes grew dim with hot tears of anguish. There, walking hand and hand on the beach, her thighs white and shameful in the bathing suit, her hand clasped in the other man's. His neighbor's. Noach Saltzman. The other man's arm around her shoulders. The two of them at the entrance to the hotel. He flipped through the stack, more and more and more. Yet all basically the same.

He rubbed his sleeve roughly against his eyes, took the pictures. "To whom have you shown these?"

"No one but you," Kurzman answered, watching him carefully.

"And they have no negatives?"

"No. They are Polaroids," the other man replied. The questions were neutral. He had seen many men react in exactly the same way. First they ensured privacy, then they gave in completely.

"What must be done?" Judah asked, but he wasn't talking to the other man. It was a question he was asking himself in the depths of his heart.

"Death by stoning, for both of them," Kurzman replied, misunderstanding. "This is the law. But since we have been cursed and punished by our Creator with the terrible Exile and the destruction of our holy Temple and Sanhedrin, and have no courts to enforce the law, we must satisfy ourselves with allowing G-d to visit such punishment upon them. What is left to us is the pale residue of our duty. You must divorce her, immediately. She is forbidden to you and to her lover forever. She must be thrown out into the street. She gets no marriage settlement. Nothing. She cannot see the child, she takes nothing with her. This is the law."

"There must be witnesses," Judah began.

"We are all witnesses," Kurzman answered.

"But to what? You did not see the act itself. You bring me pictures of hand-holding," he said contemptuously. "If this is all you have, you have nothing."

Kurzman stood up. "You are a man who makes holy things. The very wood that holds the Torah scrolls themselves. You are not blameworthy. She is entirely at fault. But if you do not act, the word of your sin will spread. Do you think anyone will allow you to make them holy objects, a man like yourself? You will be ruined. And your son, do you think they will take him into any decent yeshiva? Do you think he will ever find a wife with such parents? You will be an outcast." He put his arm around Judah's hunched, dejected shoulders. "You cannot save her. Save yourself, my good man."

Judah straightened his shoulders slowly, releasing the grip of the other man's arm, then he got up and walked toward the little stove where he kept a small kettle always humming. Before anyone could stop him, he threw the photographs into the fire, blocking the angry rush of men with his broad body. One grabbed Judah's arm and another his shoulder. With a push of enormous strength, the carpenter sent them slamming against the wall with a violence that nearly shattered the glass storefront.

"Enough!" Reb Kurzman said with commanding menace. "Leave us!" The young men picked each other up, dusting the sawdust sullenly off their immaculate black coats and pants. Together they filed out of the store, congregating around the entrance.

"Are you still not satisfied, Reb Yid?" Kurzman said softly.

"You have no proof," the carpenter repeated dully, his passion spent. "To hold a hand is not the other thing. You have no proof."

"There is only so far we can go. We don't hide our boys underneath beds," Kurzman said, his voice gaining menace.

"Then she's a *sotah*," Judah said. "We must take her to the holy Temple and have the high priest give her the bitter waters to drink. If she's guilty, she will die. And if she is innocent, nothing at all will happen, will it?"

"But there is no holy Temple. There is no high priest."

"And you have no proof," Judah said doggedly.

"Why don't you just ask her?" Kurzman said with deceptive mildness. "Discuss it with her."

"Yes," the carpenter answered, shocked that he had not thought of such a thing earlier. All these months. All those late nights waiting up. And never even the smallest suspicion until Kurzman had come to him the first time. And then he had waited and waited, refusing to believe. It had been unthinkable. Until now.

"*You have no proof!*" Judah got up, throwing his shoulders back, his powerful chest and arms, corded with muscles from the honest physical labor he had toiled at his whole life, pushing toward the other man, who was pale and delicate from a life spent in study, in pursuing ideas.

Reb Kurzman backed out. "It is the law. You must throw her out. She is forbidden to you," he said loudly, once outside the door and once again surrounded by his burly entourage, who closed ranks around their leader.

Judah closed the door behind him and locked it. He went to the back of the store and swept up the ashes where they had fallen from the stove. Only one photograph remained. Charred by the fire, only his wife's delicate blond head was still visible. His big thumb caressed it. And then he sat weeping, his soul a heartbroken lost child's within a grown man's powerful, helpless body.

CHAPTER 37

DINA WALKED GINGERLY INTO THE HOUSE, FEELING THE GRITTY pillow of sand press against her soles with each small step. Her clothes were full of sand. Her hair was full of sand. Even the wig was full of sand. Not to think, she told herself. Not to feel. Just to move, one foot in front of the other. To do. Wash out the clothes. Bathe. Then go pick up the baby from her mother-in-law's. She was home hours earlier than she'd planned. She wanted to see the baby, to feel him safe and whole, solid against her breasts. But most of all she wanted, she longed, to see Judah. She wove her way through the house, drunk with tiredness and the confusion of wandering through a desert storm which leaves one helplessly lost, directionless.

Each time she paused the images would start up again,

the feelings, violent, shameful, and joyful beyond imagination. Each time she felt it, she pressed her palms against her face, trying to wipe it away, to suppress it.

To wash off all the sand, all the dirt. To be clean and pure and without thought. That was what she wanted. But the sand was so pervasive. There was no place so secret and intimate it had not penetrated and touched. It was so difficult to rub it away. She tried, scrubbing and scrubbing and scrubbing. There was always a tiny speck she'd missed—beneath her breasts, in the corner of an eyebrow. Never, never clean enough.

The skin on her hands was wrinkled from the long immersion when she finally dried herself off. She wasn't entirely satisfied. She knew, in small, hard-to-reach crevices, the sand still lingered with irritating permanence. She put on clean underwear, a pretty flowered dress, clean stockings, and a newly cleaned and set wig. She was about to leave when the doorbell rang. Through the peephole she saw them. It was an odd group, the *spodiks* of Hasidim and the felt hats of Misnagdim mingling strangely. She opened the door without hesitation, thinking they were collecting money for some yeshiva.

"Mrs. Gutman?"

She was startled they knew her name.

"We have some business to discuss with you. May we come in?"

"My husband isn't here. I don't think . . ."

But they were already inside, the stocky one with the thick beard and white gloves, the burly, sullen younger men. She felt a sudden flash of inexplicable fear.

"We've already spoken to Judah," the white-gloved one said.

Judah? They knew who her husband was? she wondered, feeling strangely queasy at the way they said her husband's first name. It was so intimate, so personal. And these men were strangers. Yet they were in her house, hers and her husband's, without her permission. She felt a helpless rage.

"Before you start to be alarmed, I want to tell you that despite the horrible, disgusting crime you have committed —may *Hashem* have mercy on your soul, which is forever damned!—we are here not to punish you, but to help you."

She felt her hands trembling and groped her way to the couch. They grouped around her, their hands clasped behind their backs or in hard, white-knuckled balls before their stomachs. She had no way to escape.

"We know everything, from the beginning. The trip to the American Colony . . ."

She felt her face flame. They knew everything, everything! Even that! All this time! . . . She covered her face and sat absolutely still. "I want to see my husband! I want to talk to Judah, to make him understand what really—"

"Don't cover your eyes, it won't help you. Open them for a change! 'Her faithlessness was in her skirts; she was not mindful of the end'; 'and the land became full of lewdness,' " he shouted at her with stunning cruelty. "Open your eyes, take a look at these." He handed her the photographs, taken seconds after the ones Judah had seen (they had taken triple of everything). She looked at the first one, recognizing her thighs in the bathing suit, white and vulnerable and unspeakably licentious exposed to these men in the privacy of her home. She didn't cry. She didn't say anything.

"Judah has seen them also."

She felt hypnotized with horror as she thought of these photographs in Judah's familiar hands, his unruly head humbled over, studying them. She wanted to die. She covered her face with a pillow and wept until she thought her heart must stop or else beat in separate pieces.

"Good, my daughter, cry." The voice went on with mild approval. "Repent. But there can be no repentance without justice. Without punishment. After all, your sin endangers the whole community. Didn't Achan the son of

Zerach sin, and wasn't the whole community punished for it? Isn't it written: 'Thou shalt surely rebuke thy neighbor and not bear sin because of him'? Your sin is great. And the punishment for the adulteress is death."

She hung her head, unafraid. She agreed with everything he said. She was grateful for the words. They were true and good. She deserved to die. It was just.

"But only G-d can decide such a thing. The power has been taken away from us, along with the Sanhedrin and the holy Temple. But this is our power. You are forbidden forever to your husband and your lover. Your husband will divorce you, and he will get the child. All property is his. You have forfeited your marriage settlement with your behavior. And forget about seeing your husband, beguiling him with any more lies. The sooner you leave, the less disgrace will fall on your family. If not, then by tonight there will be posters all over Meah Shearim with the whole story. Every child who goes to *heder* will know what Dina Reich Gutman has done—"

"No! *Please!*" Her family. Her father, her mother's memory, her sisters and brothers. The disgrace that would fall on them all! And it would never end. It would go on and on and on. Like Sruyele's. Her body was frozen. No blood flowed, the roaring in her ears made her faint with a growing sickness. "Please," she begged softly, falling to the ground, utterly boneless, like a newborn too weak to hold her head erect. "Does everyone . . . do they have to . . . know?" she begged humbly, utterly crushed. She felt powerless, dangled high above a dark canyon of treacherous rocks, in the hands of a great, implacable force. "Why do they need to be disgraced? It was me, only me! They are so good. . . ."

There was silence as the men glanced at each other meaningfully. "While you are still here, we will have no choice but to publicize the matter, as an example to the community, a warning. But if you should leave right away, simply disappear, leaving only a note behind to your husband, admitting your guilt, telling everything, then I suppose justice might be tempered with mercy." The last words rose in the form of a question addressed to the general group, which nodded in reluctant approval.

"Thank you, bless you," she wept, heartbroken yet with a sense that the worst had not yet happened, that she had the power to prevent it. They placed a pen and paper in front of her, being scrupulously careful not to hand it to her lest their hands accidentally touch hers. She picked it up, trying not to think of Judah or the baby. If I think of them, I'll scream, she thought. I can't think of it now. Now I have to do what they ask me to. To do it blindly.

If she had only done what G-d had asked her to, blindly! If she had never questioned, but simply followed the good life of her mother and sister! She forgot Noach. What was he to her? Where was he now? She picked up the pen and began to write. When she finished, she handed it to Kurzman.

He read it with unrushed concentration, his brows furrowing, his white gloves meditatively stroking the full length of his dark beard. Then, with surprising violence, he crumpled it and threw it on the floor.

Dina watched him, terrified.

"Now . . ." He placed a clean sheet in front of her. "Now, my daughter, for the last time, will you write the truth?"

"Wasn't that the truth?" she asked, mesmerized by despair. She had written what she understood. But perhaps he was right. Perhaps there were other things she had overlooked that he knew about, as he seemed to know about everything. Like G-d. Why else would he be so angry?

"You know it wasn't. Tell about the hotel room, about how you took off your clothes, how you got into bed with Noach Saltzman, how you let him have you the way only a husband should have a wife." His voice grated with a harshness that made her want to scream with fear.

"I can't write that, please!" she begged.

"You can and you will, or everything I have warned you about will come to pass."

She hesitated, looking him over in shock. He was dressed in the immaculate dark clothes of the *kollel* man. He was a man, a rabbi, a scholar, the kind of authority figure she had been taught to respect and obey unquestioningly. All her upbringing, all her understanding, combined to defeat her, to take away all her resistance. This was what he wanted her to write. This was what he insisted was the truth. What did it matter what she knew, what had really happened?

Like a prisoner who has been drugged and beaten, she took up the pen. She wrote and wrote and wrote, until everything he told her had been clearly described.

She handed it to him obediently.

Again the slow, meditative stroking, the careful examination. But this time his forehead was smooth, his eyes light with satisfaction. He folded the letter and placed it on the telephone, where Judah was sure to find it. "Good! Progress!" He rubbed his hands together briskly. "Now you may pack a small suitcase," he ordered her.

"A suitcase," she repeated numbly. "But where will I go?"

"My child . . ." His voice was suddenly, strangely accommodating, even fatherly. Her heart, like parched and battered earth, welcomed the stingy drops of mercy. "We will not abandon you. You too are our sister, a member of our people. We have made arrangements for you to leave the country. You will work for a Jewish family in New York as an au pair. They have children and a big, comfortable house. You will have shelter, food. You will not be in the street. We are not entirely heartless, as our Creator teaches us: 'Thou shalt not harden thy heart nor shut thy hand from thy needy brother.' 'If one is merciful toward his fellow creatures, Heaven is merciful to him; and if one is not merciful toward his fellow creatures, Heaven is not merciful to him.' "

If the *halacha* had not forbidden it, Dina Reich Gutman would have gone down on her knees in gratitude and kissed Reb Kurzman's white-gloved hand.

CHAPTER 38

DINA LOOKED UP AT THE SKY, SHOCKED. RAIN! IN SUMMER! She, who had never known anything but the brilliant blue of Mediterranean skies from April to October, stared at the dark clouds that pressed heavily against the rim of the horizon, the smoking wetness that boiled around her, obscuring her vision. She stepped out of the cab onto the New York City pavement, feeling that the whole world had undergone a frightening, cosmic transformation. This was not merely a new place. It was an unpredictable new planet.

"Well, what do you know. Here already. Wasn't a bad trip, was it? You're going to love this location, dear," Bertha, the agency woman, said warmly. "Upper East Side, right near Bloomie's . . ."

Dina strained to understand, but the woman's heavily

accented English was almost impossible for her to follow. What was "whadayahno"? What was "wazinabadtrip"? What was "yugunna love"? The words ran together like boxcars, leaving behind only an incomprehensible rumble.

"Idgivya a little tour, but whacanyudu? This weather," Dina heard. She smiled gratefully anyhow, giving up her effort to understand the words, relying on the earnest friendliness of the tone. There was no mistaking the woman's goodwill.

Besides, it was too terrible to even imagine what would have happened if the agency woman hadn't been at the airport to meet her. The noise, the crowds, the confusion . . . Why, she would probably have still been there, like some abandoned and forgotten suitcase, an inanimate object weighted down by fear.

Bertha put an arm around the shivering girl and ushered her quickly beneath the shelter of the porte cochere.

"Home sweet home!" Bertha said gaily, her eyes filled with concern and no slight guilt. She was delivering the goods, as promised. But she hated these Israeli deals. More and more often lately the girls were arriving barely out of their teens and scared to death, not at all like the Israelis they used to get: tough, adventurous young women who'd been through the Israeli army and were ready for a good time. Those types had bounded off the plane in tight jeans, their eyes shining with eagerness, full of a million questions. But these girls, with their long dresses and shocked, painfully shy eyes, reminded her of little netted sparrows, too exhausted even to beat their wings. Most of them didn't stay more than six months to a year. There had been rumors of pregnancies terminated as well as babies born and spirited away. She didn't check into rumors. And of course there were the ones who stayed on and on and on with a grim kind of hopelessness.

It had been going on for about two years, ever since those mysterious phone calls from Jerusalem and the meetings between her boss and those Hasidic types. And it stank, Bertha thought hotly. But she wasn't being paid for her opinions. She was being paid to match maids, cooks, and au pairs with the wealthy New York families who needed and could afford them. Usually she did it quite efficiently.

But there was an added problem with this one she had not been able to overcome. The application had been done hastily, over the phone. The callers had specified, as usual, an Orthodox religious home for the au pair. But then, without waiting for an answer, they had simply put the girl on a plane and sent her over.

Well, it so happened that there weren't any Orthodox Jewish families who needed an au pair at present. So she had done the best she could.

Joan Rosenshein needed a maid, not an au pair. But she was a nice person. And the town house was beautiful. Besides, the Rosensheins were good, longtime customers who just happened to be at the top of the agency's waiting list. As far as religion was concerned, that wasn't one of the things agency applications got into. The Rosensheins were Jewish. At present, Bertha told herself, gnawing her lower lip, that was the absolute best she could do. She knew it was not nearly enough.

Extremely sophisticated and expensive wiring succeeded in turning the pleasant chiming doorbell of the Rosensheins' elegant Upper East Side town house into a shrieking buzz in Joan Rosenshein's office, breaking her concentration. Reluctantly she put down her paintbrush and slid off the drafting stool, her warm brown eyes fixed with critical scrutiny on the illustration on her drawing board. She felt a sinking sense of failure. The colors were all wrong! Gophers were brown, even if they did have names and wore trousers and pink ruffled blouses. But James, beautiful, slim, blond James, Mr. Art Director, god of the free-lancers, was insisting that yellow was a happier color. That it would sell more books.

The yellow didn't look happy. It looked hideous.

"Yes?" she sighed deeply into the intercom.

"Joan? It's Bertha. I've got the new maid with me."

"Stupendous. I'll be down in a minute."

Joan ran down the staircase, making a halfhearted attempt to tie back her thick, curly brown hair. It wasn't long enough for a ponytail and yet not short enough to just shake and forget. A style only a hairdresser (who didn't have to wear it) could love. Why, oh, why did she always let her hairdresser talk her into these things! She always came with an exact idea of what she wanted, and he always succeeded in making her feel that he couldn't be responsible for the results. The outcome was always something she mildly disliked, which he loved. And no matter how many times it happened, she always smiled and gave him a big tip. Well, what could you do? He always looked so absolutely thrilled at the results. Why should both of them feel bad?

The impact of the hard wooden steps on her bare feet resurrected a nerve buried deep beneath a wisdom tooth. It awoke with vicious suddenness, the pain thrusting up like a dagger through her jaw to her temple. She had no time for dentists. She pressed her palm against her throbbing jaw, then glanced at her watch. The illustrations were due by the end of the week. Her aerobics class was in half an hour.

At the sight of the kitten slipping and sliding up the polished wooden steps toward her, she slackened her pace and forgot her teeth. Maury would be furious. She'd absolutely sworn the last time that it was absolutely the very last time she'd bring some dirty, flea-bitten thing into the house. . . . But this one . . . nobody with an ounce of human feeling . . . she simply couldn't help herself. It didn't look too bad, she thought hopefully, considering its traumatic and nearly fatal recent past: some upcoming members of the younger generation had been expressing themselves creatively by tying rubber bands around its neck. The bands had been so tight, buried so far beneath the fur, that they had almost been invisible. The poor little thing had been wild with pain until the vet figured out what was wrong. (One hundred and fifty dollars. Wait till Maury got the bill.)

Right, Joan, she told herself dryly, that's what we need. A little cat to pee on the Aubusson, knock over the Lalique vases, and scratch up the Chippendale. She crouched down a moment, rubbing the homely little flea-bitten creature between the eyes. It responded by pushing up affectionately against her fingers.

A slow smile spread across her face.

The doorbell rang again, and her smile faded. She hated meeting new help. In fact, even though she had had some kind of live-in maid for the last ten years (ever since Maury had made his first Wall Street killing and bought the town house, the Aubusson, etc., etc.), she had never quite gotten used to having someone else do her housework.

In the beginning she'd felt guilty and almost nauseated about asking a stranger to clean her toilet bowls and polish her silver. She'd wound up tagging around after the woman, practically begging her to sit and rest and drink coffee.

Lonely and bored after quitting her job as a book designer for a publishing house (Maury had insisted on that too when he'd made his killing and bought the town house, the Aubusson, etc., etc.), with nothing to do but go shopping and no one to talk to but five-year-old Stacey and one-year-old Steven, she'd found herself using the housemaid as a companion, pouring her heart out in long, revealing conversations. And the woman had been only too happy to put aside her cleaning fluids and listen. At the end of the day Joan had found herself frantically cleaning up the house before Maury got home.

As time went on, the woman had lingered longer over

her coffee, had known just where the good cookies were, and had waxed long in meditative, sly advice, until finally, painfully, Joan had realized that no matter how nice she was, or how magnanimous, the woman's heart burned hot with contempt and resentment that their relationship wasn't reversed.

After that she'd learned to be more cautious and aloof, to get, as Maury constantly chided her, her money's worth. But it went against her warm, trusting, egalitarian nature.

The last maid had left suddenly three weeks before. The house was a wreck—the tall bookcases were covered with dust, and the odor from eleven-year-old Steven's bedroom and bathroom was beginning to go way beyond environmental air pollution standards. She would certainly get "her money's worth" from this girl, poor thing!

She was enormously relieved Bertha had come up with someone, particularly since The Rosenshein Show was in just three days. As usual, The Rosenshein Show, a monthly event, must find the house, the garden, and the food (not to mention the wife, which was hopeless) perfect. "In my business, nothing puts valued potential clients off more than a hint that Maury Rosenshein, investment counselor, is low on cash and letting things slide." And nothing made her life more difficult or complicated than when Maury Rosenshein wasn't happy.

She gave herself one last nervous look in the hall mirror, going through her usual rapid litany: You look much younger than forty-two, even without a drop of makeup, but the body needs serious work. She practiced one this-will-all-work-fine-you'll-love-me-the-house-the-kids smile. Then she pulled her off-the-shoulder, paint-stained sweatshirt over her shoulder, checked the zipper on her jeans, and opened the door.

CHAPTER 39

SHE HAD EXPECTED TO SEE A STURDY POLISH BLONDE OR ONE OF the little, efficient Filipinos. Certainly not a child refugee with shocked, exhausted eyes in a long-sleeved, wrinkled dress and a matted, damp blond wig. The girl looked exactly like one of those "huddled masses yearning to breathe free," she'd tell Maury later that night, trying to win his sympathy. Like one of those daughters from *Fiddler on the Roof*, the one with no luck. Really, she seemed just about ready to faint.

"Please, come in, sit down."

Bertha walked slowly into the living room and settled herself comfortably on the pretty little sofa with its blooming glazed chintz pillows. Dina followed with small hesitant steps until she was barely inside the door. She put down her suitcase but clutched her purse tightly under her arm.

It was a beautiful room by any standards. The wall paneling glowed with calm, unshowy richness. The tall French doors let in the dappled shadows of the blooming garden. And colors, subtle oranges, deep pinks, vibrant roses and violets, rioted on fabrics and in lovely fragile vases full of real flowers. "This place is such a gorgeousness. I could stay here forever." Bertha leaned back into the plump, downy softness, giving her words substance. Then she seemed to remember herself.

"Let me introduce you two. Joan, this is Dina."

Joan offered the girl her hand, but Dina seemed confused and just stared at it.

"She's just tired," Bertha said quickly. Maybe it was true, and maybe it wasn't, she thought. Go know. "She's been on one of those horrible group flights for twelve hours, the kind where they pack you in like herrings in sour cream. Maybe you should just show her to her room, Joan. We can talk later."

For one moment the sensible question of what possible use this pathetic refugee was going to be with the housecleaning went through Joan's mind. But it was pushed out rapidly and completely by the worthier and more foolish instinct to lead the little tired thing up the steps, wash her face with a warm, soft washcloth, and tuck her into bed.

"Come, Dina, it's just up the steps."

The maid's room had just been redone in pine with pretty Laura Ashley wallpaper. It was small but cozy, with its own bathroom and a pretty dressing table. The big, old-fashioned windows let in generous light, and on a fine day one could even make out the lovely old oaks of Central Park. It was a place that had never failed to evoke a little gasp of pleasure from those seeing it for the first time.

But there was no reaction on this girl's face, Joan noted with disappointment and a growing concern. She seemed frozen into an attitude of dull, sorrowful acceptance—an attitude, Joan realized with sudden insight, that would probably have remained the same had she been ushered into a dungeon under the stairs filled with bats.

"Are you hungry, dear?" she asked gently.

Dina shook her head.

"Then I'll let you get some rest. We can talk later." She closed the door behind her with the respectful gentleness of one leaving a sickroom.

Joan walked meditatively down the steps. She sat down next to Bertha on the sofa, pulling a pillow onto her lap and clasping her hands together until the knuckles showed white. "Bertha dear. We've known each other a long time."

"This is true." The older woman nodded with vague unease.

Joan unclasped her hands and spread them out beseechingly: "So what is this we have here?"

"I understand your concern, Joan, believe me I do. I can only tell you what I know. She's twenty. An Israeli. Arrived this morning. Wants work as a maid or au pair. Likes children . . ."

"That's not what I mean. . . ."

"Maybe she's just tired."

"She looks more than just tired, Bertha."

"Then maybe it's the language barrier."

"Does she know any English?"

"They all do. They learn it in school. But of course, I can't say for certain. We haven't, uhm, *conversed* much. But she's sweet. You can see that."

"I don't know." Joan shrugged.

"Look, Joan. I can see you have doubts, and I know that this is a business, but I want to be honest with you. If it doesn't work out, I'll take her back. I'll find you someone else. But honestly, I wanted this girl to come to you first. Lots of people—I don't have to name names, but people you wouldn't expect—are trying to cut corners these days.

They're turning these girls into slaves. They're giving them floors and windows and laundry and cooking and the kids. They're making them serve dinner and do the ironing and plant tulip bulbs—you name it. I think she's had a bit of difficulty back there. Some kind of trouble. Not legal, of course. Family, something. She's just tired, I think. And I know she'll be in good hands with you."

Nobody spoke. The kitten jumped up and sat on the pillow in Joan's lap.

"Cute," Bertha said. "Needs a bath, though."

Joan stroked it behind the ears. "Nothing's perfect."

"Look, in a day or two if she's not all right, you'll let me know. I'll take care of it. Unless you've already decided you don't want her. I could take her back with me now."

The kitten snuggled against her, its memory short, its nature forgiving.

"No, leave her. Just leave her. We'll work it out."

Perhaps it was Joan's own kind nature, her honesty and open goodness, evoking the agency woman's own best instincts. Or perhaps it was simply good business practice or G-d himself watching over Dina Reich. How else can one explain that despite Bertha's panic at having Dina left on her hands, and despite having achieved the perfect cue to beat a hasty retreat, she nevertheless found herself bringing up the most potent problem of all. She took a deep breath. "Before you decide, Joan, there is something you should know."

Joan looked at her steadily.

"The girl is very religious. I mean extremely, extremely Orthodox. The agency gets them every once in a while. They are good workers—the best. Very reliable, hardworking. But you have to know their rules."

"Rules?"

"Well, religious stuff. Like Saturdays. They must have Saturdays off, and that means stopping work before sundown on Friday."

"I can live with that."

"Fine. Okay. But there's also the business with the food. You know. The kosher business. Were your parents religious at all? Grandparents?"

Joan shook her head. "There are no beards in my family at all. Even my grandfather—I've got this great picture of him looking like Ronald Colman in this dapper-looking suit, sitting outside his family's country villa—even he was a rich Polish businessman who thought religion was for poor Jews. And my grandmother was sent to a Polish Catholic girls' high school because it offered the best French lessons. Half the other girls were Jewish, too. She thought Yiddish was embarrassing. She thought Jews who looked too Jewish were embarrassing."

"Did they get out of Europe in time?"

Joan hesitated at the painful subject. "My grandmother did. But he . . . the Germans closed down the factory one day and he just disappeared. I think that's why my mother at least kept Seder night. I mean, in the end it didn't matter what he believed, he died for his religion anyway. We do go to the Reform temple for New Year's and Yom Kippur, although the kids spend most of the time playing tag down in the basement. I myself don't really see the point in any of it."

"Well, Dina is from Jerusalem from a very traditional home. She's got to have kosher food."

"You mean like Hebrew National salami and Levi's rye bread?"

"I guess." Bertha shrugged, feeling like someone legally blind leading someone totally blind. "Oh, and not to put milk in her coffee if she's eaten meat. And no crabs or clams, or ham."

Joan listened, fascinated. "Maybe I should write this down." She jumped up to get a pencil and a large notepad. She glanced at the clock. There went aerobics. She shrugged. Who had the energy, anyway? She settled herself comfortably next to Bertha. "And what about things like

Coca-Cola and milk? Is that all right? And eggs and rice. Please. Go on. . . ."

The truth was, Joan didn't need a big notepad. Everything Bertha knew would have fit on one small Post-It note.

Dina could hear the voices of the two women rising and falling. She stood, exactly where Joan had left her, unable to make the slightest decision. Finally she put her purse down for the first time since leaving Jerusalem.

She still couldn't believe how fast she'd gotten a passport. It seemed that Kurzman had connections in the Interior Ministry now that an ultrareligious party member was minister of the interior. It had taken hours instead of the usual two weeks. The visa, the ticket, everything had been arranged ahead of time. In the midst of her near hysteria, she had not had time to wonder why or how this could be. After all, her decision to go had been so sudden, shockingly sudden. At least it had seemed so to her.

Her head swam with potent images: Judah, the baby, her father . . . Jerusalem rooftops gleaming silver after a rain, the silver-white sky. The old stones of the houses in Knesset Yisrael, pink as dawn, the green of hardy little plants sprouting impossibly between the mortar. She lay down on the strange bed in the unknown room in the foreign house without even taking off her shoes. The ache in her head spread to her stomach and then to her womb. She pulled her knees up to her chest and hugged them, trying to take up the smallest possible space, trying to disappear completely.

When she awoke, she felt her mother's kind hand shaking her awake. She expected to see Dvorah's small, dark, neat head in the next bed, Chaya Leah's red, unruly hair; to hear her little brothers rioting in the next room. She smiled to herself, relaxed, until she opened her eyes and heard the raised voices just outside her door. "I never liked it before, so why should I start liking it now?" It was a man's voice, low and insistent.

"But I thought, it's such a pretty color. Listen, Maury, I don't have time to get a new dress!" a woman's voice pleaded.

"Well, excuse me. If you didn't waste it, you'd have it for things that are really important."

"What do you mean by that, by 'waste it'?" she said levelly.

"Like drawing pictures for nickels for some fag art director. Like washing windows and letting the maid sleep!"

"Keep your voice down! You don't know the first thing about my work. Not everything is money, Maury. We agreed this is my choice, my decision. So just butt out. As far as the maid's concerned, she's exhausted. Anyway, she isn't supposed to wash windows. The Polish girl washes the windows and the floors. . . ."

"Oh, excuse me. The Polish girl. And she's the Israeli girl. And all I know, because obviously I'm an idiot, is that I write the checks for cleaning help and maids and I wake up in the morning and my wife is washing windows. So where is the Polish girl?"

"She's got the flu!"

"It's spring. Nobody gets the flu in the spring."

"So she's got an allergy. What difference does it make what excuse she gave me? She didn't show up."

"Call another service! I don't have to remind you about the party, do I? I mean, there's no question that the house will be ready by then? Assure me that I'm right about this, Joannie. . . ."

"I assure you."

It was Joan's voice, Dina recognized. And although such a conversation between a married couple was inconceivable to her, the man was no doubt Joan's husband. Dina listened, frightened and appalled, and yes, a little exhilarated at the frankness and harsh honesty of such an equal exchange of views.

Dina heard a short, tentative knock at her door.

"Come in."

Joan walked in slowly. She sat down on the side of the bed. Dina pulled the covers up, ashamed. She had not changed into a nightgown. Even her shoes were still on her feet. "You are angry?"

Joan shook her head. "Not angry. It's just . . . We have guests coming for a party in two days. There is so much to be done. And the other cleaning girl didn't show up. . . . Do you understand me?"

Dina shrugged. She knew English from school. From the letters from her American relatives. She was good with languages. But this was so fast!

Joan repeated everything patiently, slowly, wondering at the desolation in the young girl's lovely blue-green eyes.

"I understand." Dina nodded, filled with the same kind of courtesy that made her give her seat on a crowded bus to an older woman struggling with packages. She wanted to get up, to help. Still, she felt uncomfortable and embarrassed as she glanced at Joan's fashionably tight jeans, which seemed to outline her legs and crotch in indecent detail. Dina felt her skin prickle with disgust.

"Are you feeling all right? I mean, you haven't even undressed, or washed, or eaten . . ."

Dina heard the slight, nervous edge to Joan's voice, the edge of distress and more than a little concern, and suddenly she saw herself through her employer's eyes. She sat up, blushing. "I'm . . . so . . . sorry," she said in slow, halting high school English. "I was just . . . like . . . you say . . . tired. I will try better. Yes."

She hurried out of bed and into the bathroom. Automatically she poured water over her hands from a cup, three times on each hand to wash away the evil residue of sleep, but somehow she didn't feel herself rid of it. She looked at herself in the mirror, shocked. The wig was all matted and awry, the face dull and creased from sleep, the dress wrinkled and stained.

"I'm sorry, really. I feel badly about getting you out of bed. It's just that, as I said, we've got these people . . . company—very important company—coming in two days," Joan's voice pleaded through the bathroom door. "I'll wait downstairs for you. We'll have some breakfast. We'll talk."

Dina heard the door close. Hurrying, she changed into clean clothes and automatically reached for her prayer book when the radical change in her status suddenly struck her: she was their maid, and she had no right to time. She had slept it all away. She kissed it and put it away, making her way quickly down to the kitchen.

"Dina, my dear. First sit down. Have some breakfast. Now I know all about 'kosher.' I even called the rabbi at the temple," Joan said with pride. "I've got this wonderful Jewish rye bread and some fresh butter. Or you could have cornflakes and milk. . . ."

Dina looked at the package of bread, turning it over slowly, searching for the stamp of kashruth, the Hebrew words that would tell her which rabbi had supervised the preparation of the dough, making sure all the ingredients were kosher and that the flour had been properly sifted, and that a portion of the unbaked dough had been taken off and burned as a remembrance of the dough portion owed the priests in the holy Temple. She looked at the cornflakes box and at the container of milk, seeking to know if proper rabbinical authorities had seen to it that the ingredients in the cereal were permissible and if the milk was *cholov Yisroel*, milk that had not been touched by gentile hands, an added stringency that was meant to prevent the remote possibility that cow's milk had been mixed with unkosher donkey's or camel's milk.

On the bread she found only the word *Jewish* without any rabbi's certification. And on the milk she found nothing. Only the cereal box had a little symbol, an "O" with a little "u" inside. She had heard of this. It was the stamp of America's Orthodox Union of Rabbis, and although they were certainly not as reliable as *badatz*, she remembered hearing that they could be relied upon somewhat.

"I'll take this." She picked up the cornflakes.

"Fine." Joan smiled, bubbling with nervous relief. "And here's a bowl and a spoon."

"I'm sorry to say . . . to ask . . . but is this your milchig set or your fleishig set?"

Joan felt a little sensation of distaste at the sound of the Yiddish words. She felt ashamed of herself. After all, she was a liberated, open-minded American, a sophisticated New Yorker brought up to respect other cultures and religions. So what was it about her own that made her cringe? "I'm afraid I don't speak Yiddish, Dina."

"Is it your dish for the milk or for the meat?" Dina repeated.

"It's my everyday Noritake willow pattern," Joan answered, bemused.

"Only one set for both? Milk and meat both?" Dina's eyebrows lifted in horror, pushing the bowl away. "Can't use it." She felt a sudden irrational anger that there were Jews in the world who only had one set of dishes for meat and milk.

"Does that mean you can't eat anything?" Joan asked, chagrined, feeling like a student who has prepared carefully for an exam only to find out it was on a different subject altogether. "Well, what about paper plates and cups? Plastic." She hurried to get out her picnic supplies and was rewarded by Dina's first, hesitant smile.

Dina shook some cornflakes into a plastic bowl, took a plastic spoon, and began to eat.

Joan watched her, appalled. "Don't you want some milk with that?"

"Not good. Gentile milk. Not *cholov Yisroel*."

Again, those horrid Yiddish words! Joan felt them explode in her ears like some embarrassing secret.

"Just get out of my face, you little brat. Mom, Suzy is in my room again," her fifteen-year-old's voice rang through the halls. The usual morning bedlam was beginning.

"Just a minute, Stacey. I'm in the middle of something here," Joan called up to her eldest. "Please, just give your little sister a hand getting dressed this morning, Stacey, honey."

Stacey, a tall, slim redhead wearing a sweatshirt that left one shoulder bare and a short tight skirt, walked casually into the kitchen. "She's your responsibility, Mom, not mine. You were the one who decided to have her. Don't try to push it off on me, like you're always doing. What's for breakfast, anyhow? Oh, hello"—she turned to Dina—"who are you?"

A young boy, his hair wet, his eyes barely open, shuffled morosely into the kitchen. His hand shot out automatically to turn on the television. Without moving his eyes from the screen, he took down a bowl and filled it with cereal and milk. Then, his eyes all the while fixed with dull, steady interest on the tube, he ate.

"And good morning to you, Steven dear," Joan said dryly, switching off the set. The act evoked a sudden surge of life from the child.

"Hey," he cried in outrage. "That sucks! What you do that for, jerk?"

"Stacey, Steven, I want you to meet Dina, our new maid. She's from Israel. . . ."

Steven turned the set back on. Stacey turned it off. "Your mother's talking to you, cretin," she told her brother.

"Die," he answered her, switching the set back on.

"After you," she replied sweetly. "Hello, Dina, and good luck," Stacey said, grabbing a doughnut and sailing out the door.

A little girl wearing a dress backwards walked sleepily into the room.

Joan lifted the plump little cherub, kissing her soft cheeks until they glowed pink.

"No more kissing, Mommy."

"Maybe just one. Just a teeny, tiny one," Joan teased her.

"No more," the child said grumpily, wiping the kisses away.

"Suzy, sweetie, this is Dina. She's going to be helping Mommy keep the house clean. Won't that be nice? Isn't she pretty? Say hello, then have your breakfast before you miss your ride to school." Joan sat her down and poured her a bowl of cornflakes and milk.

"Don't want cornflakes."

"But, honey, you always eat cornflakes."

"But I don't want cornflakes."

"But I've already poured them for you. See, I've already added the milk, Suzy sweetie."

"I want Frosted Flakes."

"Now, honey, you know Mommy doesn't buy that anymore. That it's too full of sugar. Remember what Dr. Meyer said about cavities. Now, just eat your cornflakes."

"No cornflakes."

"Shut up, brat," Steven told her.

"Mommy! Steven called me a bad name! He said 'shut up,' too."

"Beam up," Steven told her, his eyes still fixed on the set.

"Well, why don't you just have a doughnut, then, Suzy." Joan sighed.

"A chocolate doughnut?" the child interrogated.

"No, a sugar doughnut."

"I only like chocolate doughnuts. . . ."

"Suzy, you're going to miss your bus, dear." Joan smiled sweetly through gritted teeth. Every morning was usually a little bit like this, but never *so much* like this. Or maybe she was just more embarrassingly aware of how it looked and sounded because of a stranger's presence.

Actually, Dina did seem a bit surprised. Her eyes were wide and confused as she surveyed the family goings-on.

But, aside from that, she didn't seem unduly upset. Joan had no way of guessing that behind Dina's uncomprehending stare lay a shock as profound as any the young woman had ever experienced.

CHAPTER 40

After all the children had gone, the house took on an unnatural stillness that magnified everything that had come before. Joan experienced an odd sensation of heaviness, as if her very limbs were weighing her down.

"Well. That's nice. A little quiet. They're usually not so . . . well, they *are* usually, but today they were especially . . ." she apologized, strangely flustered by Dina's silence.

Dina didn't look at her. Her eyes were gazing out the window at the angled cut of the city sky visible through the skyscrapers. It was the same blue she remembered. And the trees and flowers seemed to bloom in those same colors familiar to her from her former sojourn on earth. Yet the distance she had traveled from her home to this one seemed at this moment no less than interplanetary.

She looked at Joan with frank astonishment that bordered on horror. "Never, never in my life," she said with quiet but intense passion, "have I seen a family where the older children did not help the little ones! Never have I heard a brother say such things to his sisters! Never, never have I . . ." She paused, pushed beyond shyness, beyond politeness by outrage and grief, struggling vainly to find a word that would fully express her total inability to comprehend anything that she had witnessed. "Never have I *dreamt* of such a thing as a CHILD WHO TREATED A MOTHER WITH DISRESPECT! And such a mother! So kind, so nice, so generous, who does so much for her children . . . who gives them everything in such a beautiful big house!" She shook her head, distraught.

Joan's mind swam. She was at the same time both grateful and bitterly offended. I do do an awful lot for those kids, she thought, pleased at the recognition. But on the other hand, she couldn't very well ignore the implication that her kids had been poorly brought up, badly educated. She felt herself careening wildly between thinking: She's absolutely right! to How dare she!

"Joan, I do not mean to hurt you. But in my home, nobody ever raised his voice. I never heard my parents raise their voices to us or to each other. In a religious home, the children say softly 'Mother, please,' or 'Thank you, Mother.' We were ashamed not to help our parents. We fought only over who could do more."

Joan felt herself shrinking, as if the hard substance of her ego were being sucked out of her, leaving behind a thin, fragile shell. But then the humor of it struck her. She looked at Dina's matted wig, her sleep-creased cheeks and tired eyes. This, after all, was the result of such an exemplary upbringing. Yet she suppressed her smile not just out of politeness, but from a sober recognition of some sad truth. "You don't understand Americans, Dina," she defended herself weakly. "American mothers are not in the business of producing perfectly behaved little angels. We believe in creativity, spontaneity, independence . . . You sound like you were raised in a pressure cooker and you're too repressed to even realize it. . . ." A knot formed in her throat. She wasn't even convincing herself.

Dina took a hesitant step toward her. "You feel bad . . . angry. I'm sorry. I didn't mean. My English. It is not so . . . very good. I hope you understand. I hope I did not . . . Perhaps you did not understand."

"Oh, I understand all right."

"I hope I have not hurt you."

Joan summoned up all her anger, preparing to go on the offensive again, to tell this *employee* not to presume to think . . . to tell her where to get off, when all of a sudden, without warning, her eyes overflowed with big salty tears that gushed down her cheeks.

All that yelling, all that abuse, from everyone, all morning! And so much work. And tension. Ho, boy, let's talk about tension! And talk about fulfilling everyone's expectations! And it never being good enough . . . Even all that kosher food she'd gone to all that trouble to find and buy (precious little appreciation she'd gotten for that!). And for a maid, for goodness' sake, who'd been sleeping all day! And on top of it all, to get a lecture from her! "You wouldn't be so smart if you had any children of your own!" Joan sobbed.

The words affected Dina like a blow. She seemed to totter and lose her equilibrium. A look as tragic and heartbreaking as any Joan had seen on any human being passed over the girl's face. She seemed to age almost visibly. A single tear rolled down from the corner of each eye.

Joan, even more upset at having upset Dina, and Dina, feeling the full shock of her loss, both sat there, crying their eyes out, unable to regain control. It's the last straw, the last straw! both women thought, totally absorbed in their own pain.

After a while Joan finally looked up. She rummaged around in her pocket for another tissue and silently handed it to Dina.

"I've never made anyone cry before. I mean aside from family. I've never made a stranger cry. I feel awful," Joan said.

"I never did, either." Dina shook her head. "I ask forgiveness." What right have I to judge anyone else after what I've done?

"I forgive you, Dina." I forgive you because you haven't done anything wrong. The kids treat each other like dirt and have precious little respect for me or their father. A lot of it is my fault. I was too busy, too tired, too full of psychology textbooks, to educate them when they were little, and now I let them get away with murder because it's the path of least resistance.

I've given up hope that I can change anything.

There was silence as the two women sniffed back their last sobs and made their last blows into their tissues. Surprisingly, both felt better, almost refreshed from the sudden emotional outburst. And, strangely, it brought them closer together, like strangers on a camping trip who have crossed in each other's company some arduous terrain.

"Joan, I will work for you. I will do a good job for you."

"Do you feel up to it?" Joan said doubtfully.

"I am ready," Dina assured her, standing up quickly.

"Well, first off, we'll put you into a pair of jeans," Joan suggested, looking over the girl's long silk skirt with dismay.

Dina shook her head. "I don't wear jeans."

"Well, a lot of women who shouldn't, do, but you're so small, they'd look great on you. Not to mention practical. . . ."

"I must not wear jeans," Dina repeated, wondering if she'd gotten the English words mixed up.

"Well, it'll be a shame to ruin that nice little outfit."

"It's not modest to wear pants. It shows the legs and where the legs meet." Dina blushed.

Joan looked down at herself. Now skirts that hardly covered your butt, tank tops that looked like bras and see-through blouses, *that* was immodest. But jeans? Even born-again Christians wore jeans.

Joan examined Dina's skirt to hide her confusion. The material was silk, she was sure of it. Scrubbing toilets in silk. Jewish milk. She shrugged helplessly. "Well, maybe tomorrow we'll take you shopping, get your hair cut and styled, get you some kind of uniform," she said, trying to be kind. "But today there is just so much work that needs to be done. I don't even know where to tell you to begin. . . ."

"I will begin and I will finish," Dina said firmly. "I will do everything."

Joan felt herself smile, touched by Dina's desire to prove her worth. "I don't want a corpse smelling of Ajax on my hands when I get back, so take it easy. Besides, there's a girl coming this afternoon who'll do the floors and windows. So don't touch that."

"Another girl?"

"Not to worry." Joan laughed. "There's plenty left."

Dina was worried. The cleaning products, the equipment, were all so new and unfamiliar to her. Although Joan had explained them all to her before leaving the house, she found she couldn't keep straight which was for sparkling toilet bowls and which for greaseless stovetops. At home she had used bleach and ammonia from huge plastic containers for almost everything. She faced the cornucopia of brightly colored little cans and bottles with hopeless confusion.

She was suddenly very glad she didn't have to do the floors because the mop didn't look anything like the Israeli kind, either. It seemed like a big sponge. She had no idea what to do with it. In Israel one threw buckets of water on the floor and simply swept all the water and dirt out the front door or porch with a *sponga*, a sharp rubber blade on a long wooden handle. But here in America, they used a *sponga* to clean the windows!

There was no way to throw water over these floors anyway, she realized, with so many rugs, plants, vases, baskets, lamps, and sculptures all over the place. Not to mention wall-to-wall carpeting in almost every room.

So she rolled up her sleeves and began from the top working her way down, as she had seen her mother work; as she had worked in her own spotless home. She moved everything and cleaned thoroughly beneath and behind. She scrubbed and polished and straightened and dusted. She carried the bag full of bottles and sprays into the bathrooms, trying out each one to see which seemed to do the job best. Down on her knees, she scrubbed the toilet bowls of strangers, breathing in the unfamiliar, intimate smell of unknown bodies, of people who were not her own family. She tried not to think. To just move one foot in front of the other. She felt sick. Don't think, she told herself. Don't feel. This is your punishment. What you deserve.

The house was enormous. It was as big as an apartment house in Jerusalem. Dina kept wondering where all the other people were. It couldn't possibly be that one small family owned and used all these rooms. She kept thinking that there might be more children, but the bedrooms showed evidence of only the three she'd already met.

Stacey's room was striking. A series of unique collages covered the walls, as if someone had cut out pictures from magazines and put them together with a wonderful sense of humor and a perceptive eye for color. There was a sense of order in the room, yet not a sterile cleanliness. A distinct personality came through: fun-loving, intelligent, talented . . . Dina tried and failed to reconcile it with the badly dressed, disrespectful young woman she had met in the morning.

The young child's room was also lovely. The closet was enormous. Why, you could actually walk inside it! And the clothes—it seemed like a store, everything hung on hangers and covered in plastic. There were exquisite little party dresses trimmed in lace and velvet, matching tiny skirts and sweaters. And the shoes! Tiny patent-leather T-straps and small Nike jogging shoes lined up in boxes filled with tissue paper. The bed was canopied with yards of pink calico that matched the curtains and the bedspread. A thick pink rug warmed the floor. There were shelves and shelves and shelves of gorgeous dolls and stuffed animals, a vanity with a large mirror, and a bay window with a beautiful view of the private gardens.

Dina sat on the bed, trying to reconcile the exquisitely privileged child who had such a room with the unhappy, whining little youngster named Suzy. Yet she could not fail to be grateful to both girls for their neatness. There was hardly anything to do in either room.

But if the girls' rooms were unexpected fairy tales, the boy's was a predictable nightmare. At first she couldn't believe her eyes. It was like a place ransacked by brutal criminals who felt no respect of any kind either for things or for the human beings who owned them. She began the horrific task of making order.

All over the room were expensive electronic gadgets: video games, a television set, everything covered with debris so that they were practically buried. She picked clothes off the floor, touching them gingerly. Everything was well made, the most expensive quality, and practically brand-new. Yet there was no question that these things had not only been thanklessly worn and thoughtlessly discarded, but positively trampled underfoot like so much garbage.

A desk drawer had been emptied out onto the floor, and little pieces of paper from crayons and Magic Marker labels mingled with Yo-Yo's and stamps and stickers. Had she been more experienced, she would simply have swept the whole mess back into the drawer and replaced it. But she was thinking of her own home, her parents' home. She tried to treat the things with a respect their owner obviously lacked. She had almost finished the sickening task, exhausted, when she suddenly spied another door. She opened it and found the boy's closet. It made her want to cry.

Then the phone rang. From what she could make out from the voice emerging from the answering machine, it was a cleaning service and they were very, very sorry, but the girl wouldn't be coming this week after all to wash the floors and windows.

Dina stood in the huge dining room, her sleeves rolled up, the pail and brush in front of her. This was the last one. She had already done the kitchen floor and the patio. She had vacuumed every inch of all the other floors and cleaned all the windows. And now, practically numb with tiredness, she surveyed the vast, tile-covered floor.

It was as large as all the floors in her parents' home combined. There was a fraction of an instant, just before she fell to her knees, that she felt her soul ache with humiliation. Then she dipped the brush in the soapy water and scrubbed until her arms and back ached. Her soft, delicate hands turned rough and red in the hot, soapy detergent, her pretty sleeves and skirt soaked through, wetting her underwear, her skin. She felt dirty and degraded. When she was finished, she crawled into a corner and looked at her reflection on the floor. It shone with an indistinct, distorted glow. She was a stranger to herself.

Maid, she thought. In Hebrew it was an *ozeret bayit*, usually a heavy Arab woman or a poor middle-aged Moroccan or North African Jew. Poor and uneducated, she cleaned other people's homes because she needed the money for food and did not know how to earn it any other way. And now that's what I am, Dina thought, a little flash of anguish prickling through her raw, newly ragged cuticles. They felt like burned flesh.

At four o'clock the boy came in. He threw his books and sweater on the floor, went straight for the refrigerator, which he held open as he grabbed and ate things off the shelves. Then he put his feet up on the living room couch and put on the VCR.

"Shalom," Dina said.

He looked at her, puzzled. "Oh, the new maid." He nodded. "Hi, new maid," he said, his eyes returning to the screen.

She felt humbled by his arrogant tone. Yet he was only a child, and she was an adult and a mother. He was just a little boy, like one of her brothers who would have never dared speak to an adult, any adult, with such disrespect.

"Where is your sister?"

"Who cares?" he answered, his thumb pressing the little buttons on the remote control, a slow smile spreading over his face.

She walked around, curious to see what he was watching. The old taboo against watching TV or movies seemed so far from her now. She sank onto the sofa and tried to understand what was happening on the screen.

Her eyes grew wider and wider, her heart pounding with distress. A young couple with a small child were walking down a city street when someone brutally smashed the young father in the head, then brandished a gun in the face of the terrified mother and child. Then the screen switched abruptly to a man screaming as he fell into a bubbling vat of acid, and then again to a man, his face horribly deformed, pumping bullets into another man to the accompaniment of happy carnival music. And then suddenly a man was caressing a blond woman, kissing her passionately. And then they were in bed together. . . . And then one man burned another man alive and laughed uproariously at the burned corpse. . . .

It was horrible, horrible! She had never in her life witnessed such terrible things!

A little boy should not see such things! she thought suddenly, looking at Steven. He laughed at intervals, but mostly he sat smiling impassively as his practiced fingers fast-forwarded and rewound, manipulating the images on the screen, pinpointing his favorite parts.

She had to protect him, she thought wildly. After all, wasn't he just a child, a little boy like her small, innocent brothers? . . . Her breath caught in her throat at the idea of any of them seeing the sickening things she had just witnessed. She rushed over to the set and began to frantically press the buttons, trying to shut it off.

"Hey, dummy, what's the idea!"

"Your mother would not like it! For you to watch that!" She had no idea how to turn the thing off, so she stood in front of it, blocking the screen with her body.

"Hey, you're not my mother. You can't tell me what to do! It's a free country!" he screamed.

Dina stood her ground.

The boy got up and walked over to her menacingly.

"You can't tell Mom I didn't ask you nicely. I'm asking you nicely to please move."

Dina shook her head. "It is wrong! You are just a child!"

Joan stood in the doorway. The wisdom tooth sent throbbing waves of agony down her jaw. Her head ached. Her tired feet throbbed.

"What's going on here?"

"Oh, Joan, it was terrible! The things the boy watched! I tried to stop him, but I did not know how to—"

Joan slammed down her packages. "Steven! Have you been watching the R-rated stuff from Daddy's room again? How many times have I told you never . . ." She grabbed his arm, shaking him.

"Leave me alone! Stinking liar!" he yelled at Dina. "I haven't done anything wrong! I was just watching *Batman.*"

"*Batman?*" Joan dropped his arm, looking up at Dina in confusion. "*Batman?* That's a children's movie! Anyhow, he's seen it about two million times. . . ."

"You allow it? You permit this?"

"Well, yesss, I suppose." Why did she feel so uncomfortable? Why did she need all this aggravation?

It was all wrong, terribly wrong, she decided with a twinge of helpless fear. Definitely, definitely wrong. She took a deep breath, then she looked up grimly, turning her attention to her belligerent son and her frantic new maid.

"She can't tell me what to do!"

"Just calm down."

"But, Joan, the things on the screen! Murders and . . . and . . . men and women . . . together . . . in bed!"

"Dina, I really can't have you going around disciplining the children like this. Please mind your own business," she said harshly. "You just don't understand. It's different in America." Were there scenes of murders, sex, in *Batman?* Honestly, she didn't remember.

"I will go to my room now," Dina said stiffly. "I will lay down in my bed."

Joan read the tired defeat in the girl's shoulders as Dina slowly climbed up the stairs, and she felt a twinge of inexplicable remorse.

"Steven, don't watch that," she told him abruptly. "Go do something."

"Sh . . . ugar!" he screamed, bounding up the stairs.

The door slammed. She sighed, walking into the kitchen to prepare dinner. It was gleaming. Slowly she walked into the dining room. The house was sparkling, immaculate. The floors had never looked this good. A surge of hope went through her. Maury would be thrilled.

The party would be fine. She would have the time she needed to finish the illustrations!

Dina and that Polish girl had done an incredible job! Her regret for the harsh words of a few moments before expanded rapidly. Then she listened to the messages on her answering machine and found out that there had been no Polish girl. Just Dina.

CHAPTER 41

"I'M GOING TO CALL THE RABBI," JOAN TOLD MAURY AFTER dinner.

"Why?"

"Well, Dina . . ."

"Dina?"

"The new girl from the agency. The Israeli. I tried to get her some of her own kind of food, she only eats kosher, but she wouldn't eat anything I bought except the cornflakes, so this afternoon I stopped off at Green Meadows—you know, that vegetarian place near Fifty-ninth—and bought her some salads. I thought, What could be wrong with lettuce and tomatoes and some brown rice? Well, guess what? She won't eat that, either."

Maury put down the *Wall Street Journal* and looked up curiously. "Why not?"

"Well, she says she can't be sure someone has checked the lettuce and rice carefully enough to make sure there aren't any bugs or worms! She says if she can't be sure of that, it isn't kosher, either! I'm at my wits' end! I mean, she worked *so* hard all day today, and all she's eaten are some dry cornflakes. I think I'll call the rabbi."

"Whose rabbi?"

"Ours. You know, the one at Temple Shalom where we go for the High Holy Days."

"Do you even know his name?"

"It should be on the receipt for the seats. Anyway, Isabelle would know. She's very religious."

"Your sister Isabelle is not very religious."

"She goes every Friday night! Her kids are all in Sunday school there!"

"As I recall, your sister is a radical feminist, is into est, chants mantras, dances to Hare Krishna, has been through body realignment, primal scream therapy . . ."

"So she's a little confused. Her soul is searching. . . ."

He shook his head. "You know who was religious? My grandmother, may she rest in peace. Five o'clock in the morning she got up Fridays to bake challah and make kugels. I remember their house, *Bubee* and *Zaydee*, the candles burning, the little Yiddish songs around the big table. I remember—I must have been just a baby—the smell on Saturday morning in her kitchen. That heavy stew, and that chicken fat smeared over bread! I know, I know—cholesterol. But was that delicious! And then, my grandmother sitting with her kerchiefed head and reading all afternoon. . . . It was so quiet. Such a strange, funny kind of peace. . . ."

Joan stared, bewildered and pleased. In the past few months their communication had resembled a tennis match between two tired, vaguely hostile players vying halfheartedly for points. They hadn't had anything remotely resembling this kind of conversation. "You never talk about them. . . ."

"Well . . ." He cleared his throat, a bit embarrassed. "It's so long ago. So what do you want to call the rabbi for?"

"To find out where to get her some food she will eat! I want her to feel comfortable, but I don't know where to begin."

"She did a great job." He looked around appreciatively. "She deserves to be comfortable."

This, coming from Maury Rosenshein, a genuine compliment? Joan went over to him and kissed him on the top of his terribly thin hair. He was always so busy. There was so much tension in their lives. There was never any time, any peace and quiet. "This," she told him, patting his spreading midriff, "this I might marry."

"Yeah?" He smiled at her, pulling her down into his lap.

Marriage, Joan thought, is like a long car trip. At first you start out buying and packing—all fun and excitement. But then the road is long and the scenery boring. You get a little nauseated. Then unexpectedly the scenery suddenly changes. There are wonderful surprises and little imagined disasters. And in the end, she thought, her arms around her husband's comfortably familiar shoulders, you can't imagine not having gone.

The rabbi, Isabelle had warned her, was a terrible *yenta*. "If you want it broadcast throughout the tri-state area without the expense of a full-page ad in *The New York Times*, just whisper it privately to Rabbi Engst," were her exact words.

"But will he know all about Jewish milk and everything?"

"I don't know about Jewish milk, but he sure knows about which Jew is milking which. . . ."

• • •

"Rabbi Engst, thank you so much for agreeing to see me. I've got a . . ." Joan hesitated. She somehow didn't want to call Dina a maid. "A cousin from Israel staying with me who's very religious. She won't eat anything. Even the milk . . . she says she wants Jewish milk! I mean, where does one get . . . how should I . . ." she began.

"Tell her," Rabbi Engst said calmly, "that she's being ridiculous. Tell her she's in America now. That she has to compromise."

This, Joan thought, was really the easy answer that she had been hoping for. Or something close to it. Yet as she looked over the rabbi's passive face, the calm grip of his placid lips on the pipe stem, she couldn't help contrasting his easy complacency with Dina's unbending struggle.

Compromise. From what she'd heard, it was Rabbi Engst's middle name. When the congregation had wanted an organ, he'd brought in an organ. When the women had decided they should sing folk songs on the High Holy Days instead of hiring a cantor, he'd brought his guitar. And when Helen and Marty Morgenstern's daughter had wanted to marry an Italian Catholic, he'd agreed to go to the church and shake hands with the priest.

Rabbi Engst was nothing if not compromising.

She had always considered that kind of rabbi the best kind: liberal, progressive, willing to accommodate himself to changing times. . . . Yet, Joan observed with sudden perception, that could also mean he didn't really believe in anything. "Uhm, I agree with you. But she's very, very Orthodox, and she's my guest, and I just want her to feel at home."

"Well, you might go to the Upper West Side, or even," his mouth pursed in distaste, "down to Williamsburg, or the Lower East Side. They have stores that cater to that kind of clientele." He shook his head disdainfully. "Still back in the Middle Ages, these people."

"Well, I remember you once hosted some African folk healers. And then there was that whole discussion about alternate life-styles and supporting the PLO. I'm surprised you can't take a little of that tolerance and send it in my Israeli cousin's direction." She waited to see how long it would take for his pipe to fall out of his open mouth.

Not very.

"I thought we'd go shopping today, get you some new clothes," she told Dina the next morning, wincing as she watched the girl's red, dry hand grip a plastic spoon filled with dry cornflakes. "I also think I know where we can get you your milk and some other things. Maybe we'll eat out for lunch, too, just make a day of it. You sort of overworked yesterday, Dina. In fact, I'm relieved you're still breathing."

Is it the next morning? Already? Dina wondered. She sat in the kitchen, her knees bruised, her arms and fingernails aching. She saw Joan's kind face as if through opaque glass, heard her words as if through a long tunnel. She was exhausted, disoriented. Then, in what seemed to her amazing swiftness, she found herself strolling in the center of the city.

Everything amazed her: the black-veined highways swollen with sleek metal, the mirrored monoliths reflecting the golden morning sun, the brisk, joyful click of countless shoes against the pavement. The endless activity.

Dina stopped at every store window, staring at luxurious linens and bedspreads, colorful vases and elegant furniture. Everything was displayed with such extravagant exuberance. It seemed like each window held not only goods, but an announcement, an important revelation about life. She felt a new energy, her head growing light, dizzy, with the sudden avalanche of such undreamed-of riches all piled up in one place.

Like every foreigner seeing the incalculable wealth of America for the first time, she felt almost drunk with a strange happiness. It was like a great mountain that only the natives born in its shadow can ever take for granted. She was pierced with the pure joy of knowing that such abundance, such material riches, existed.

Tears of wonder came to her eyes.

"Why, what's the matter, dear?" Joan asked her, alarmed.

"I've never . . . such a . . . beautiful . . ." she said haltingly.

Joan's eyes opened wide with surprise, and she smiled a little, looking around her. It was all so familiar that she really didn't see it anymore. It was just the city, that's all. Yet Dina's exultant wonder was like a great snowfall that suddenly transformed everything familiar into something fresh and unexpectedly marvelous.

"Beautiful," Joan heard herself repeating thoughtfully. Perhaps.

Bloomingdale's on a summer's day! Deliciously cool, perfumed by exotic scents and the crisp, clean odor of new clothes. The overhead chandeliers blazed. The counters gleamed. And everything was so lovely to look at, to touch. Dina didn't know where to begin.

She wanted everything. More than that. She *had* to have it. There was no possible way she could leave the store without it. . . . And each time, the object changed. First it was a small red ceramic box with a golden ceramic bow holding a scented candle. "Free with purchase," the Arden saleswoman said, beaming. She held it up to the light. The beautiful little thing, so shiny and delicate. Once you knew it existed, how could you ever be happy without it? But then she was distracted by a perfume atomizer: sparkling crystal with a stopper like a dove. She caught her breath. Why, she had to have that, too! She walked from aisle to aisle, entranced, while Joan followed behind her like an indulgent parent going through Santa's house with a small child.

Finally, as her feet began to ache, Joan suggested they go upstairs to look at some clothes.

"Upstairs?" Dina said, amazed.

"Why, Dina, this is only the ground floor. There are quite a few more." Joan laughed gently at Dina's look of utter wonder. "You're so small, let's go to petites first."

Racks and racks and racks of clothes. All displayed, all amazingly her small size. And the dressing rooms! Large and private with not one, but two mirrors to see both the front and back. You could look at yourself for as long as you liked in privacy, with no pressuring saleswomen. This seemed an almost sinfully delightful freedom.

Joan brought her casual clothes to try on. Light cotton skirts and short-sleeved tops. Jogging suits. Everything felt so loose and comfortable. And she looked so different. Lighter. Younger. Less tense and formal than in her own clothes. She tried to find some that fit Mrs. Morganbesser's standards, but it seemed very strange. Like looking for a river in the desert. After all, she was on another planet, wasn't she?

"Dina, just try on the jogging suit. Just let me see it," Joan pleaded. "It'll be so comfortable for you to work in."

Well, it was just in the dressing room and they were both women, after all. She walked out of the dressing room hesitantly. The material felt strange between her legs. She felt positively naked.

"It fits perfectly. And it looks very nice on you."

"Oh, I could never wear such a thing, Joan. Never. It is very immodest."

"But why? After all, isn't it more immodest to be in a skirt when you're standing on stepstools dusting, or bending down to mop? I mean, this keeps a lot more covered up, doesn't it?"

Dina couldn't think of any answer for that. A small worm of doubt began to nibble away at her.

"But, Joan, how will I pay for all these things?" Dina

protested as they stood with the jogging suit and a pile of other clothes at the cashier's.

"Well, these are sort of uniforms. I have to give you something to work in," Joan said rather unconvincingly.

"You must take it from my pay," Dina insisted.

"All right. But remember, you worked extra yesterday. You weren't supposed to do floors and windows. So let's just say this is payment for that."

She's nothing like any woman I've ever known, Dina thought. She has one set of dishes. She wears immodest clothes. She allows her children to behave with terrible disrespect. Why, in Meah Shearim she would be shunned and chased out of the neighborhood. Then how can it be, Dina thought, truly confused, that she is also one of the kindest, nicest people I've ever met?

As they walked through the streets of the city, Dina tried to see beyond its luminous surface, to understand what it all meant. But it eluded her.

In Jerusalem it had all been so clear. She had felt the beating heart of history, thousands of years old. She had been involved in the slow march toward the Messiah, redemption, the end of illness, war, poverty; the triumph of justice, compassion, and brotherly love. Jerusalem was so simple: the small stone houses were ribs that closed around the Wall at its heart.

But this, it was so incredibly complex. She looked at the rushing crowds and thought of the millions and millions of individual lives that pulsed through the veins of office corridors and apartment complexes like corpuscles, giving the city life. But what were they keeping alive?

A terrifying thought occurred to her.

What if it had no meaning?

She dismissed the thought, feeling ashamed and rather stupid. It wasn't possible. It was just her small mind that could not grasp the grand design. It simply wasn't possible that such power, such activity, so many millions of lives, had combined to produce nothing at all of meaning and value.

"Here we are. I hope they're not too busy," Joan said, pulling open a heavy wooden door. Inside, the air was chokingly sweet and moist, like an unbearably humid summer day; and the noise of so many hairdriers buzzing simultaneously was menacing, like locusts swarming in for the great invasion.

"Hi, Joan, aren't you a day early?"

"Hello, Monica. I'm not here for me. This is my friend Dina. Can you fit her in?"

"We don't do wigs, Joan dear. But Maurice does. He's just across the street."

Joan looked at Dina. "Well, I think Dina wanted her own hair done. Is that right, dear?"

Dina looked around, appalled. It was full of men with their hands in women's hair. Strange men involved in such an intimate act! She felt a large ball of accumulated humiliation rise from her chest to her throat. There, in front of these men and the curious eyes of many strangers, she would have to pull the wig off her head and allow herself to be touched publicly by a man who was not her husband.

"*And the priest shall set the woman before the Lord and let the hair of the woman's head go loose*." It was beginning, she thought, the ordeal of the *sotah*, the ordeal that began whether or not you were guilty and ended only with your death or with total vindication. She had brought herself to this. This was part of her punishment. She bowed her head in horror. There was nothing to do but submit.

"I mean, you do *want* to have your hair done, don't you, dear?" Joan asked, unable to conceive of what was the matter now.

The hairdresser, a slight, effeminate man named Clark, wrapped a towel around Dina's frightened, shaking shoulders and led her to a chair. She reached up, closed her eyes, and pulled off the wig.

To her utter shock, nothing happened. Nobody even seemed to notice!

"Now just lean back and relax, honey."

The hairdresser's voice, gooey and harmless, was distasteful but oddly compassionate. Still, the touch of his hands on her scalp felt like a violation, a forced unwilling intimacy. She closed her eyes, feeling shame wash over her like the spewing jets of water.

"I've got to make a phone call, Dina. I'll be right back."

Joan pulled closed the booth door and drummed on the glass, deciding what to say. Then she straightened her back and dialed.

"Hi, could you put me through to the art department, please? . . . Hello, could I speak to James? It's Joan Rosenshein. . . . James? Uhm, glad I got you in. James, the reason I'm calling is that the illustrations aren't going to be ready by tomorrow. I really apologize. I'm awfully . . . What was that? Well, I know that. I realize that, and I'm sor—No, Monday the latest. I really appreci—Oh, yes, of course. No later than Monday."

She hung up and stayed in the booth a few minutes, leaning her trembling back against the cool glass. Another weekend marathon, she thought. No rest for the weary.

But when she came back to get Dina, she was not sorry she'd invested her time in helping the girl instead of coloring blond gophers. Dina looked so much better. So young and fragilely lovely, her clean, light brown hair falling softly around her face and shoulders.

"And now may I put my wig back on?"

Joan couldn't believe her ears. After all this! "But your own hair looks so nice, and the wig is so dirty. . . ."

"But, Joan, I cannot walk in the streets without something covering my hair. I am a married woman. Married women must cover their hair."

The girl was married! Where was her husband? she wondered. Had she been abused? Joan felt her head swim in frustration and confusion. "But Dina, why does a married woman have to cover her hair?"

"Because it isn't modest not to."

She took a deep breath. "Look, Dina. We'll go across the street and get your wig cleaned and set, too. Then you can put it back on feeling much more comfortable. Is that a good idea?"

"But I must cover my head with something. I cannot walk bareheaded in the street. . . ."

Oh, Joan moaned inwardly. I am never going to figure any of this out. "Here, take my scarf. Would that be all right?"

Dina tied it around her head. It actually looked rather nice, they both thought.

"Here, this place looks fine," Joan began. They were in Williamsburg outside a busy takeout food store. It had large, gleaming refrigerator units, clearly labeled packages, shopping carts . . .

"It isn't kosher," Dina pronounced.

"Why, of course it is!" Joan fumed, at her wits' end. "Just look at the sign, Dina. It says so right there!"

"It isn't *glatt* kosher."

"You mean kosher isn't kosher enough for you?" she asked, her goodwill fading. Is she deliberately trying to provoke me? Joan wondered, strangely hurt. Was she testing how far she could go? "I mean, the rabbi's beard isn't long enough, is that the problem?"

"Joan. Maybe we should just go home. You have been so good. You must be so tired. . . ."

Joan felt ashamed of her impatience. What did she know about these things, anyway? Besides, they were here already. She swallowed hard and took a deep breath. "Why don't we just walk some more. I'm sure we'll find someplace else you'll like."

The streets were bustling, dense with buildings and

people. Men in Hasidic dress. Women in long dresses and wigs. Joan could see Dina's face light up hopefully.

"Wait here, Joan. I will ask someone."

Dina stopped one of the women. Joan saw her whole body relax as the Yiddish words poured out with fluent ease. The dull confusion and pain, the sadness Joan had thought was her natural expression, lifted, leaving behind a youthful, clear-eyed sweetness. Joan felt a sense of déjà-vu, then realized why: it was like that moment when the vet lifted the rubber band off the kitten's fragile neck.

"Come, Joan. I have knowledge of the perfect place now."

The perfect place was the dingiest, sorriest hole in the wall Joan had ever seen. The windows were blurred with a slovenly gray ash, and the only display was a plastic chicken that had surely seen World War II come and go.

The food looked weird. But it was nothing compared to the man behind the counter. He had a long white beard and wore a white-and-black-striped *thing* with little fringes over a dingy white shirt. His pants were absolutely *tucked* into his socks. Joan felt the perspiration beading her forehead and trickling down her underarms and between her breasts.

But Dina was thrilled: "Chicken liver, herring, knishes, kishke, cholent!"

"I think I'll sit down, dear. Why don't you order lunch for yourself."

"But, Joan, you also must eat!"

"I don't think I really could. . . ."

Dina seemed crestfallen.

"Oh, well, sure. Order something light for me, too."

There was no air-conditioning. Joan took a table as close to a little noisy fan as possible.

The waiter brought two orders of kishke first. It looked like brown stuffing. Without the chicken.

"Uhm, what exactly is this, dear?"

"Oh, Joan, it is very tasty. Very good. You must try it," Dina urged.

Joan took a small forkful, prepared for the worst. It was . . . actually quite good. Savory, full-bodied. Before she knew it, she had finished it.

"It *was* good. But, tell me, what exactly—"

"It's stuffed intestines," Dina said matter-of-factly.

Joan took a long drink of water.

The next course was a plate of roast chicken with little doughy balls called shlishkes. The chicken was nicely brown but not quite fully plucked. The shlishkes were delicious.

"You like it?" Dina asked hopefully.

"Well, Dina, I don't think *Gourmet* magazine will be contacting this place for their recipes, but as Jane Fonda says during stomach exercises: We did it! We got through it!" Joan laughed into the girl's puzzled face. "Good thing you don't know what I'm talking about!"

"Thank you. Oh, thank you so much! I have not had such good food for a long time. It was a great *chesed*."

"*Chesed?*"

"A *chesed* is like . . . it's the greatest kind of good deed. It's something you do for someone else when you get nothing out of it, and it doesn't really matter if the person you are doing it for deserves it or appreciates it or even knows about it. You do it to please G-d, because it is the right thing to do."

"Well, you're very welcome," Joan replied, oddly touched by the words.

They walked through the hot summer streets, carrying the kosher milk and cheese, Dina's mood growing more and more buoyant so that she almost skipped down the pavement, humming songs to herself. "It is almost, almost like being home. As if I will turn the next street and find a bus that will take me home," she said, smiling.

"It's so wonderful to see you happy for a change," Joan said with real satisfaction. "And Dina, about the video, the other day." She took a deep breath. "Honey, you just don't understand our culture, and I can't have you impose your own very different standards on the children."

"Joan, you are such a good person." She hesitated, her natural shyness and good manners once again overcome by an outrage that she could not keep hidden. "But so cruel? How can it be? To your children, your own children?"

Joan stared at her, flabbergasted. "Cruel?"

"To let a little boy see such things? Horrors. A child should be saved, protected from. So much pain, so much cruelty . . ."

"Really, Dina. A kid's movie?"

"Have you seen this thing, this *Batman?*"

Joan thought a minute. She didn't remember *actually* watching it, but *everybody's* kids had seen it. . . . A small doubt crept into her certainty. Perhaps there was some truth to Dina's claims, some basis for her passionate disapproval. The truth was, she had no idea what kind of things her kids saw most of the time. "You see, Dina, there's just so much, such a bombardment. Movies, cable TV, MTV. It's impossible to fight it, to screen everything."

"I don't understand, Joan. It is just a machine. A little screen that brings it into your home. You could just pull out the plug, no?"

Pull out the plug? Joan thought, charmed and amazed by the wonderful simplicity of the idea and that it had never once occurred to her. "Is that what your parents did?"

"Oh, no. In my home there was no TV, or video, or radio. And we were not allowed to go to movies, or plays or concerts . . ."

"But then you've missed so much that's good! Plays by Shakespeare, *Les Misérables*, *Death of a Salesman*, *Anne of Green Gables*, *The Sound of Music*, *Citizen Kane*, *Cinema Paradiso*, *It's a Wonderful Life*. Beautiful, enriching stories . . ." Joan couldn't imagine such a thing. She was full of pity. "Dina, while you're here, you should try to be a little more open-minded. You should make use of your time to learn about things. There are so many movies, concerts, plays, museums, you could go to! So many courses to choose from in the evenings. Japanese screen painting, playwriting, Baroque music . . . I just finished a course in weaving. . . ."

Dina shook her head. "I couldn't! It's impossible!"

"But why not?"

"Do you think I never heard of these things, that I come from a jungle or a desert?" Dina said with quiet passion. "Israel is full of movie houses, universities, theaters, concerts. . . . We, our kind of people, don't participate in these things because secular knowledge corrupts, because men and women sitting together, mingling in theaters and concerts, leads to wantonness, sin. We deny ourselves because we are struggling to live holier lives."

"And do you? Does denying yourself all these things help you lead a holier life?" Joan asked with sincere curiosity.

Dina reddened.

All the things she'd been taught you couldn't do because of men and women mingling. All the things denied! Yet pure, pious Dina Reich who had never been to a course outside of Beit Yaakov, never seen a movie or a museum, a play or a concert . . . still, it had not saved her. It had made no difference at all! She felt the worm of doubt, larger now, gnaw with a greater intensity.

Joan saw her confusion and reached out for her hand. "Dina, honey, I don't want to force anything on you, just . . . well . . . there are so many choices out there. So many things you can learn to appreciate and understand if you'll give yourself half a chance instead of clothing yourself in this medieval armor. What are you afraid of?"

Dina said nothing.

"After all, it was your idea to come, wasn't it? Why not just relax and enjoy yourself for the time you'll be here?" Joan went on casually, her eyes looking at the colorful sights around her. "I'm sure that's what the people who love you are hoping you'll do before you go home." She turned to Dina, and her smile faded into alarm.

A sudden darkening change had come over the girl, like a cloud drifting across the sun.

Oh, for Pete's sake, Joan thought. What have I gone and done wrong now?

CHAPTER 42

IT WAS THE NEXT DAY. DOWNSTAIRS, THE CATERING PEOPLE were already getting the house ready for the party.

"Joan, I want to help!"

"Are you sure? You did so much running around in the heat yesterday. And the catering people will bring their own staff. Not enough, of course. . . ." Joan hesitated. Dina's help would be a wonderful boon.

Dina, who couldn't imagine not working when everyone else was, didn't think twice. What did being tired have to do with it? You worked until the work was done.

"Well, if you really feel up to it, it would be great! And Dina dear, perhaps you could wear one of your new outfits? That pretty apple green dress?"

The short one, Dina remembered. The one whose little sleeves could not be pulled down to cover her elbows, whose skirt barely brushed the tops of her knees. She remembered the mortification on her face as she'd looked at herself in the mirror. Joan had bought it. And now she expected her to wear it.

"It would make me very happy, and it would help my husband. These guests are important clients of his. It never hurts to have a pretty girl around."

Untrained in the art of throwing gifts back in the giver's face, Dina experienced a sense of defeat, of powerlessness. So she tried to compensate by turning to a different battlefront. "But I must wear my wig, Joan. It would be immodest, a sacrilege, not to!"

Joan looked at the wig. It had been washed and combed and sprayed into a glamorous blond dream. "Dina . . ." She hesitated, reluctant to cause offense but pushed beyond the limit of silent acceptance. For days she had watched Dina doing strange, incomprehensible things, but this business with the wig was the weirdest. "I know we haven't known each other very long, but I can tell you're an intelligent girl. So tell me something. How can you put on that flashy, Barbie-doll wig and think you're being modest! Why, your own hair—and mine, for that matter—is much less attractive. Don't you think that it's a bit ridiculous?"

Dina opened her mouth to speak, then walked slowly to the mirror. She studied herself for a few moments, then took the wig carefully off the wig stand and put it on. The change was startling and instantaneous. She went from a pretty young girl to a flashy, provocative woman.

She felt the blush rushing up her throat. It was, she thought with great surprise, more than just a bit ridiculous. But everyone did it this way in Meah Shearim and Bnai Brak! All the religious women. And all of them considered themselves paragons of modesty.

"I can't explain it. I don't know," Dina said miserably, feeling her last sense of confidence, of superiority, begin to disintegrate. Joan shrugged helplessly and closed the door behind her.

Dina sat down on the edge of her bed, trembling. All this time, despite her gratitude, she had viewed Joan's shameful ignorance of her own religion and culture as both pitiable and contemptible. Yet more and more Dina began to realize how little she herself really understood about so many of the things she did.

Could you really win G-d's blessing with empty gestures and mindless rote? Was she really any better than Joan, who did so many things wrong yet was so full of such sincere kindness and generosity? Who was a good wife to her husband and a caring if misguided mother to her children? What right did Dina Reich Gutman—child abandoner, husband deceiver—have to feel superior to anyone?

Slowly she unbuttoned her long-sleeved white blouse, button by button, feeling a little part of her self-respect bleed away with each one. She unzipped her calf-length pleated skirt and laid it neatly on the bed. She sat there, unmoving, the green dress beside her.

The ordeal, she thought, finally, dully, remembering with a stoic ache the joyous abandon in which she had once slipped into a pretty new bathing suit as her lover waited for her on warm white sands. And that sin had led to this one, she thought helplessly, slipping the dress over her uncovered hair. She felt no joy, no abandon, now, just self-loathing. With great effort she opened the door and walked out into the hall. She might as well have been naked.

She watched the unself-conscious mingling of the men and women, their easy equality and mutual respect. It was so different from the awkward social gatherings she knew, where the men and women segregated themselves in different parts of the house, never dreaming of having any kind of conversation.

She took in the trays with little hot canapes and then heavier trays with drinks. She balanced them carefully, walking among the strangers in the large living room. Some smiled at her politely, others ignored her, which she preferred. And then there were the other ones. The men in the catering staff whose hands strayed accidentally to her chest, and a few of the guests who stared at her with a look she couldn't mistake. There was one, especially. A slim, blond man with cynical blue eyes and a loose, sensuous mouth. He looked at her under half-lowered lids, as if each movement of her body were meant for him alone. His eyes sought hers with mocking but unmistakable interest. She felt her hands tremble each time she approached him. His big pasty white hands smelled of talcum powder. And always, his fingers, taking the morsels or the glasses off the trays, slipped and touched hers.

She refused to look at him, refused to know. She hurried into the kitchen and pressed her back against the wall, closing her eyes. She envisioned the world she had left behind, a world in which strange men lowered their eyes in respect and modesty when a strange woman passed them on the street. A world in which a woman, even alone on the streets at 2 A.M., was perfectly protected, perfectly safe. And then she envisioned Judah, his big arms around her, protecting her. She opened her eyes, and the visions vanished with heartbreaking swiftness. She had lost her right to even think of either one.

Joan walked over and put an arm around her. "You're doing a great job. Thank you, Dina! So what do you think of all this?"

"The men are so . . . so . . ."

"The men are rich, power-hungry bores," Joan whispered.

"No, not that, exactly." Dina blushed, thinking of the white hands. She was too ashamed to speak of it. "But the women are beautiful. They talk with men who are not their husbands?"

"Oh, Dina! Of course! And some of them—actually, most—don't have husbands, at the moment, anyway. They're an interesting bunch. You see that one in the stunning red suit standing by the window? She's got her own chain of minimarkets. And the blonde by the door—she's opened her own law firm. And take a look at the one by the piano—she's got the hottest art gallery in SoHo. What do you want to be when you grow up, Dina honey?" Joan laughed, throwing back her head and draining the white wine from the goblet.

Dina felt a little dizzy. What do you want to be? It was a question never asked in the *haredi* world, to boys or girls. What you would be was ordained the moment you were born: the boys would be scholars, if they did not fail. And the girls would be wives and mothers with some little, unimportant work on the side to help pay the rent, the food money. She had never even imagined the question. She looked over the women around her with fresh respect and a little awe and not an inconsiderable pang of envy.

The meal was long. The work was tiresome. Her feet throbbed. Her arms ached. Her head felt as if a sledgehammer were slowly working its way down the middle. And then thankfully, joyfully, she was at the door, giving out the wraps and hats. They were leaving. She looked up briefly at each one, waiting with dread and anxiousness for the cynical blue eyes to be safely on the other side of the door. But he never turned up.

Finally the room was empty. Joan locked the front door behind the catering staff and disappeared upstairs. Dina began emptying the ashtrays, almost sleeping on her feet. She went into the kitchen to load the dishwasher yet again. And there he was, leaning against the counter. She let out a little gasp of surprise.

"Pretty little thing," he said, not taking his eyes off her, not moving. She stood, shocked into stillness.

"Like a little flower waiting to be plucked," he crooned boozily, his mouth loose again.

"All the guests . . . they went home," she said. "Time to go."

He moved toward her now, too quickly for her to protect herself. His hands encircled her waist and roamed appreciatively lower.

"Dina!" Joan called.

"In the kitchen, please," Dina managed weakly, like a badly mauled small animal trapped by an experienced predator. She felt the hands withdraw, the heavy talcum smell waft farther away.

"Oh," Joan said, giving Dina a curious, troubled look that darted from her pale, petrified face to the man's calm, cynical one. "Mr. Weill, you're still here! I'm almost certain I saw your wife leave a while ago."

"Yes," he drawled easily. "She's an early-to-bedder. But the night's still young. Thought Maury and I could spend a few more minutes going over those figures he mentioned."

"Why, I'm sure he'd be delighted," Joan said with a frozen smile, steering him firmly out of the kitchen. "Dina, that'll be all this evening. Why don't you go to bed, dear," she urged, casting a worried look in her direction.

At this he stopped and turned, giving Dina one long, questioning look.

Dina stared back at him wretchedly. Then all at once a strange understanding flowered with horrifying clarity in her heart. A husband who chased after other women; a man whose hands sought intimacy with strangers even as his wife stood nearby, deceived and secretly humiliated. A man not unlike Noach.

She lay awake all night, unable to stop thinking.

She thought of Joan's words: "After all, it was your idea to come, wasn't it? Why not just relax and enjoy yourself for the time you'll be here? I'm sure that's what the people who love you are hoping you'll do before you go home."

The people who love me. Home. She missed it with every fiber of her being. Yet had she really been happy there? She thought of the easy confidence of the women she had seen, women who were able to move through the world with strength and independence toward some self-defined goal. She had never been able to choose anything, even her own husband.

Then she thought of the man who had dared to touch her, to force intimacies on her, because she was a woman and a servant and a stranger. A woman in Meah Shearim was respected. And safe.

Nothing was simple or clear-cut.

She went through the next day like a robot. The ache in her heart, so long numbed by the anesthetic of shocking change, now sent unbearable tremors through her whole being. The only idea that kept her from collapsing with grief and despair was one thought: The Sabbath was coming. Only one more day to the magic, healing balm of its peace and rest. Only one. Then she would have the time she needed to make some sense of all the contradictions, to meditate, to pray for understanding and forgiveness.

She got up two hours early Friday morning, wanting to get all the chores done as soon as possible. She polished and scrubbed and dusted. She made breakfast and prepared the children's sandwiches for lunch.

The day passed. The pale morning light waxed into the white-gold heat of midday, then began the gentle, subtle wane into dusk. She waited for the familiar soft glow of serenity to begin. Yet there was no change. The TV blared. The telephone rang and was answered. The kitchen appliances kept up their ordinary voices of rumbling activity. And outside in the street, cars and buses crisscrossed the restless face of the city.

With a growing dull pain of recognition, Dina felt her

heart would finally break: here, in this house that had all the riches a human being could ever dream of, in this great city of overwhelming wealth and abundance, there would never be either peace or rest. The Sabbath would never stray through its heavily carved and polished mahogany doors, never weave its magic healing grace around its great streets and roads and thoroughfares. They were condemned to an eternity of weekdays, each one the same as the next, and she along with them.

"We're going to the movies tonight, Dina. I thought maybe you'd like to come with us," Joan asked her.

She shook her head miserably. "I can't."

"Well, maybe you'll join the kids tomorrow. Maury and I, unfortunately, will have to work all day. But the kids are going to the country for some horseback riding and tennis. It'll be fun. Why don't you join them?" Joan urged her.

"Joan, both you and your husband will work on the Sabbath?"

Joan felt distinct discomfort under Dina's incredulous gaze. "Well, Maury usually does. But this is just one of those things for me. A rush job. Otherwise I'd join the kids, too," she began, feeling strangely apologetic.

"I thought American women were strong, independent! That they were free!" Dina cried.

"This is my choice. This is what I want to do!" Joan raised her voice in a counterattack.

"Oh, Joan, you mustn't work on the Sabbath! The Sabbath is precious and holy! It's a gift from our Creator. A day of rest! I cannot ride on the Sabbath, or see movies, or . . ." There were so many things! It was easier to say what she could do. "I must light candles and pray, eat a festive meal, and go for a walk or read . . ."

A lecture! This was too much! "Well, of course, it's

your day off. It just seems such a shame to waste it that way," Joan said stiffly.

"You do not understand anything, Joan. You know nothing," Dina said sadly.

Joan swallowed hard. Dina's calmness. Her calm assumption that she knew something Joan knew nothing about (and had managed to live quite nicely without, thank you very much!) made Joan want to scream.

It was ridiculous. She was the maid, simply the maid! A backward, uneducated foreigner. But somehow, somehow . . . What was it? Pity, a strange mothering instinct, or just simply curiosity, kept her from throwing in the towel. After all, there had been no arrogance in the girl's tone, just sincere regret. But it was so hard to keep bumping into this mysterious secret knowledge! It made her feel like a stupid child.

This was a whole new world, Joan began to realize. It was going to broaden the scope of her understanding and test her real tolerance and respect for other cultures, other life-styles. It was easy to respect Hindus, Buddhists, Baptists. After all, they couldn't threaten or compel you. They had no claim on you.

But this, this back-to-roots Judaism, it did all those things. It was in her blood and genes and history. It had to be dealt with. Even rejecting it meant some kind of emotional upheaval fraught with self-justification, denials, rationalizations, philosophy. It was a threat and a pain in the butt, and most of all it was a challenge.

Hurt, Joan walked away and sat down in the garden. She would have to spend the whole day slaving over those horrible blond rodents! She looked back at Dina. No power on earth could force her to work on Saturday. Which one of them was really strong? she wondered. Really free and independent!

She looked at the old fern. As it did every summer, it had gotten sort of dry and brownish and rather sad-looking. But this year, she thought, it looked even worse. It looked weary. Old. Her eyes shifted to its offshoot, a spontaneous growth thrust off from the mother plant sprouting nearby. It was so fresh and green and strong.

She had a sudden insight. Offspring. Children. We replace ourselves when life wears us down. We pass on the torch. You don't have children just to dress up and cuddle and play with. You have them to make sure you give over your most cherished values, your carefully sorted-out place in the great chain of being. And what were those values? What was that place? Did religion, culture, history, the ties of birth, play any part in it?

In a way she pitied Dina, as one would pity a Samoan tribesman dancing to drive away evil spirits in some apartment in the Bronx. She had come from a world where it all made sense, the rituals, the strict adherence to strange rules . . . It all seemed so terribly pointless in America—land of the shopping mall, home of the aerobic dance class.

Yet, Joan also had to admit, she also envied her. Her world seemed such a clean, orderly place, not the incomprehensible maelstrom of random violence, disease, and human waste it often seemed to Joan. She seemed to know every moment of the day what G-d expected of her and how to please him. It was all too ridiculously simple, of course. Life was not a sewing pattern where all you had to do was follow the instructions to clothe yourself in goodness. But perhaps, just perhaps, there might be a kernel there, something she could learn from.

In the kitchen, Dina placed two candles in exquisitely carved wooden holders. She lit them. They flickered, pure flames, tiny golden lights. Then she covered her eyes and blessed the Lord of the Universe, Who had sanctified her and commanded her to light the candles of the Sabbath day.

Joan stood there watching her, some deeply buried longing tugging at her, making its ancient claim.

CHAPTER 43

THE DAYS WENT BY SLOWLY. DINA FELT THE WORM OF DOUBT grow within her, becoming a monster whose heavy jaws were slowly devouring all her beliefs, all the careful teachings that had sustained her life so far. Questions that had lain locked within her since childhood rose up like specters, frightening and torturing her. What did she really believe? What kind of life was truly holy? Who was she, really? And who might she be with the right education, the right opportunities, the right to choose?

And more and more she thought with sickening guilt and longing of Judah and Yossele. Who, she wondered with almost unbearable envy, was tucking in her little boy's shirt, smoothing down his soft curls, washing the milk from his chin? Judah. My husband, she thought, sometimes convinced that his kindness, his tender care, were the only things she needed or would ever need. How had she not understood that? He seemed so real, so substantial, compared to Noach. Noach was a ghost, she told herself. Why, why had she done it?! It could never, ever be forgiven. The words beat inside her like the ominous drumroll before an execution. There was no compassion, no forgiveness in the universe that would cleanse her. Only punishment, she thought. Only suffering.

Like a prisoner shuffling through his days, paying off his debt to society, Dina walked through the hours from daybreak until nightfall like a machine, working, working, working, the harder the better. The house shone. The floors and windows and furniture and endless knickknacks gleamed, dustless. And each night she wondered: How will it all end? She tossed, sleepless, her mind a cauldron of anger, regret, homesickness, despair, and confusion. She felt bloated, deformed with the heavy guilt of unatoned sins.

She did not mind the work, even its humiliation. She wanted to suffer, because it would mean G-d's anger was being wrecked and the time for His compassion was drawing near. But what was she to do with the burden of Joan's kindness, her constant generosity, which faded her hopes as colors fade beneath the relentless benevolence of the shining sun? Like one who has borrowed from a usurer, Dina felt her debt simply increase from day to day. She did not want kindness. She wanted to be punished.

And then, one day, just after eleven P.M., when Joan and Maury were out for the evening and the children were asleep in their beds, the doorbell rang.

"Hello, dearest," Noach Saltzman said, his voice as smooth and thick as honey pouring over the sides of a jar.

Dina backed away near the wall, her eyes darting, panic-stricken, in all directions.

"Dina," he whispered. "Please, dear. Don't make a

scene. I only want to talk to you. Please," he begged. "Is there somewhere we can go to talk?"

Speechlessly she turned around and walked into the book-lined study.

"Please, sit down a moment."

She did as he asked, staring down at her hands as they kneaded and twisted the material of her skirt into ragged pleats.

"You knew I would come, didn't you." It was a statement, not a question.

She nodded hopelessly.

"You knew I would turn over heaven and earth to find you."

"I knew you would," she said dully, working intently on creating tiny, twisted knots.

"Why? Why did you run? How could you have done it? I have been in complete hell all this time." He plowed his fingers through his hair with sudden violence, cradling his forehead, covering his eyes. Then he lifted his face and looked at her, searching her. A slow smile spread across his mouth, a knowing, hungry gleam came to his eyes. "I have found you now."

"Yes," she answered, a prisoner on the witness stand who has given up all hope of a favorable verdict, ready to accept all consequences simply from sheer exhaustion, simply to be done with it already.

"Each day we have been away from each other, my love has grown, you know. . . ."

She looked up at him with horror. Was it a joke, a sick joke? But there was no humor in his face. It had that gleaming, all-encompassing passion that had once seemed so appealing to her. "After everything that has happened?" she said with disbelief.

"Nothing has happened," he replied calmly. "Small things have happened. My feelings have not changed. They grow like a lake fed by melting snow, overrunning the banks, rushing, turning white."

Could he be serious? She felt a strange glow of the old passion pass through her like a distant memory. "I have lost everything! My child, my husband, my family, my home . . ."

"My darling! I will make it all up to you. I swear. You will never be sorry. I am here in New York now. My father-in-law arranged work for me in the diamond district in Manhattan. I will rent a beautiful little place for you. You can work or not, whatever you choose. We can even have a child together, if that would make you happy. We will be together always." He reached out to touch her.

She moved away, but sadly, as if a bit reluctant but resigned. "And your wife and children, where are they?" Her tone was calm, almost indifferent.

He made a deprecating sweep of the air, as if brushing off an annoying insect.

"Did the Morals Patrol make you divorce her?"

"Well, actually . . . no. They just insisted I move away. Threatened to tell my father-in-law."

"So you are still with your family? You haven't lost your wife or children. You have a new home. While I . . ." Her voice grew soft with shock and incredulity.

"I can take you out of here now. I can take you with me. I have lawyers. . . ."

"You come here," she said thoughtfully, as if trying to understand, to make some sense of it, "after the way we parted from each other? You come here to tell me you love me?"

"What happened in the hotel . . . it meant nothing," he said with slow precision, a strange calm. "You don't know anything about me at all if you think I would let that change anything. You are mine. You will be mine forever. I want you more than ever. It's like a madness."

His words passed through her like white hot needles. He had lost nothing! Neither home nor wife nor child. He was alive and well and prosperous. He could come to her now, freely, with these propositions. The same crime, and yet those who claimed the righteousness to judge had meted out punishment with such appalling inequity. For the first time she gave thought to the possibility that Rabbi Kurzman with his white gloves might not be G-d's representative on earth after all.

Noach took her long silence for agreement. He reached into his pocket and took out a velvet jewel box. "Here, my darling, just the first of so many."

With almost trancelike tranquillity, she opened it. It was a bracelet of rubies and diamonds set so beautifully, it seemed as if only the air connected them. It sparkled and burned against the black velvet.

Noach smiled and took the bracelet out of the box, his smooth fingers locking the clasp securely around her childish wrist.

Dina watched his fingers working. She felt the touch of his warm hand and the cold grasp of the gold, like handcuffs, around her wrist. "And will you leave your wife, then, and marry me?" she asked in the same tone a wife would say to a husband: "Will you pick up the clothes from the cleaners? Will you buy the evening paper?" It was not so much a question as a description, a passionless discussion of practical events that would or would not take place.

He hesitated. "You are my wife, you know that. The other . . ." He shrugged. "Well, she takes care of my children. You wouldn't want me to leave them, would you?"

"And what of my child?" she said calmly. "What of Yossele?"

"We can have other children."

Only then did she fully understand him. He would set her up in an apartment in Manhattan, and he would continue living with his wife and children. He would visit her, pay her bills. And she would live here while her family, her child . . . She held her throbbing temples, wondering how she had not before grasped what kind of man he was, that he could think to propose such a shameful thing to her.

She wept. She wept for the life she had left behind—the real love, the respect, the care of a man she had never appreciated. She wept for the child she had abandoned, for the aging father she had hurt, the sisters she had shamed. She wept for the green dark hills and the milky, silver sky that gleamed over Jerusalem on a rainy day like precious beaten silver. But most of all she wept for herself and the G-d who had turned from a dearest friend into an enemy that allowed her to suffer so. That allowed a man like Noach to prosper.

"Darling . . ." He put his hand on her shoulder. "I—"

She tore the bracelet off her wrist and threw it on the floor, stamping on it with all her might.

"Dina!" He reached down to rescue it, and she pounded his skull with her fists and tore long welts in his cheek until she felt her arms pinned cruelly to her sides. As if in a dream, she saw his hands suddenly release her, reaching up to touch his cheeks, his eyes staring in disbelief at the dark blood that stained his fingertips. She heard his feet pound the floor. She heard the front door slam. Only then did she stop struggling.

Who can gauge the limits of a person's capacity for suffering? Who can predict when or why a soul that has ballooned to encompass pain or tragedy will suddenly burst? Her measure was suddenly filled. Some fragile membrane burst open, carrying her beyond grief to an unknown emotion too unfamiliar and vast to completely explore. She didn't fight it but let it fill her, the way light fills a glass bottle. For an instant, she felt with stunning tragic clarity that there was mercy and forgiveness in the world and that it was in a place she did not know how to reach.

She walked out into the street, her spirit beyond plans, beyond fear, beyond guilt, beyond doubts. Oddly, she was suddenly free. She walked slowly through the dark alleyways of Manhattan, through the festively lit main streets, the echoes of joyous childhood melodies coming back to her in all their sweet harmony. She found herself humming, and as she sang, her voice growing louder and more joyful, she heard the noise of passing trucks, of honking taxis, suddenly disappear. She listened to the silence for a moment. Even her own footsteps had faded. She was all alone, in this great, endless city. All alone, she thought, puzzled but not unhappy. She sang, swaying with blissful forgetfulness down the streets, through the strange silent crowds that suddenly appeared out of nowhere. Their faces stared at her oddly or turned away. Some opened their mouths, as soundless as fish.

She walked faster, her goal becoming clearer. And suddenly there were the quiet Sabbath streets, the cobblestones glistening from the sharp winter rains; the scent of spicy cholent bubbling up from the hot plate; the heavy women, their arms crossed over their chests, their faces comfortable and smiling as they greeted each other outside the crowded synagogue. And there were her brothers in their *payess*, their dark little suits and snowy white shirts.

She was home.

It was so good to be home! There was the Sabbath table with the challah and the wine. Her mother leaned over to pass the heavy platters, to smooth back her hair. And then the meal was over. She followed her sisters into the bedroom, listening to the homey clatter of dishes, her mother working in the kitchen. It was a comforting sound, and she was suddenly very, very tired. She took off her clothes in the quiet darkness, still smelling the waxy remains of the Sabbath candles, still tasting the sweet wine from her father's silver goblet. Above her in the darkness, the moon rose, a sliver of hopeful light.

She lay down and closed her eyes, dreaming. "*Ima*," she whispered as her mother stood suddenly before her, her eyes loving yet troubled. Like the unseen, untouched scent that clings to a flower, her mother's presence brought with it a sense of utter simplification. Everything was suddenly reduced to one straight line that led easily from the good to the good. But somehow, in her dream, her feet could not follow. She kept falling down, losing her way. She felt bruised and sick and lost. She called out to her mother, called her back, and there she was again, but this time her eyes were wide with questioning, with disapproval.

She couldn't bear it. She turned her back and ran, light swift steps, like the steps running down the stairs, knowing that he was waiting for her . . . Noach! The sense of waste and shame and deceit rose up like the jutting edge of a great overhang high above the sea. She found herself walking toward it, then running. Something good would be there. (Judah! She wanted so to see him, to explain.) Or Noach? Or perhaps they would both be there! And her father! And her mother! And the dark-coated men, the white-gloved stranger . . .

She felt herself running, and suddenly she wasn't Dina anymore, but someone grown gross and ugly, full of sores, shamefully undressed. She tried to cover herself, her breasts, her white thighs, but her hands were too small.

They were all there—everyone—she suddenly realized, waiting for her by the edge. They would see her like this, naked! . . . Horror filled her. She felt herself running faster, being chased. And all of a sudden she was at the edge. Far below she saw the sharp black rocks, the white, crashing waves. She had two choices: to stand before them all in her nakedness or to cover herself the only way left, by jumping down, down deep, laying deep beneath the water, where she would hear no accusing cries, see no disgusted stares, where all her shame would be invisible. The water would cover her, protect her. She would hear nothing, see nothing. She would be nothing.

She stood for one last moment, looking at the sky, the earth, all the faces of those she loved, and then she felt the earth disappear, the water cover her head with kindness, like a blanket tucked around a beloved child.

CHAPTER 44

Judah held his crying baby in his big, rough hands, his lips tasting the salty wetness of the child's flaming, agitated cheeks. "Sha, sha, Yossele," the father crooned. The child's misery, sudden and petty, was more than he could bear. He felt like a pot boiling over a high flame. The slightest addition of even the smallest drop of pain would send all his carefully controlled emotions flooding messily over the top. He walked through the dark rooms where only a few months before he had been so incredibly happy. It seemed like someone else's home now, uncherished, abandoned. He stroked the little warm back, the white, perfect toes, trying to still the tears—his own and the child's.

The incredible good-bye letter she had written him lay beneath his pillow, along with the other note he had found crumpled on the floor. Both were in her handwriting, yet how different they were! What to believe? What did it matter? he told himself in the mornings, when the light streamed into the house, illuminating all the dark corners, simplifying and straightening all the twisted, dark confusion that descended on him every night. What did it matter what had happened? She was gone. She'd left him of her own free will without even trying to explain. She had not trusted his love, the depth of his care. She had run like a spoiled, guilty, frivolous child. It had been an entire month, and no word at all had been heard from her.

It wasn't right to still love her, he told himself in the mornings. She didn't deserve his love, after everything she'd done. And sometimes the feeling of hard justice was potent enough to last the whole day, giving his shoulders strength to keep from rounding, giving his neck a reason to stay erect, to hold his chin up from his chest.

The pressure from Kurzman and his henchmen never let up. They were after him constantly, by phone, with notes, in person. Divorce her, they demanded. Now. It is only right, they insisted. You are a good man, why should you share in her sin? Acquit yourself. Do the right thing.

And sometimes, in the mornings, he felt himself agreeing with them. He had even set the date in the rabbinical court for the proceedings. Her presence wasn't even necessary. It would be delivered to her by proxy. She'd just open the envelope and find herself divorced, with no say in the matter, no property settlement, no visitation rights. Nothing. Sometimes that thought even pleased him.

The baby's sobs subsided into a sleepy whimper. He tiptoed into the nursery and laid the child on his stomach in the crib. He stood there a while, rubbing the little shoulders, the tiny spine, watching the child's chest heave spasmodically with a stubborn attempt to rekindle his fury. Yet already his little lashes swept his downy cheeks, his breathing growing steadily deeper and calmer. He watched his little son. He had her hair, her eyes. Every time he looked at Yossele his heart bled anew with a fresh agony of loss.

It was at dusk that all the hardness left him, the certainty. All he could think of was his beautiful little flower of a wife, his gentle, sweet Dina. The rest was a nightmare, too vile, too incredible, to have any truth. And sometimes, at night, he blamed himself. Why hadn't he put a stop to it? Why hadn't he had eyes to see and ears to hear, a nose to smell what was going on beneath it? He could have saved her, if only he had been paying attention, he chastised himself.

And then still another stage came upon him, when dusk turned to the pitch blackness of night: suddenly he couldn't think of anything. He would crawl into bed, his whole body a great shout of longing, of pain, all the shoulds and shouldn'ts of the morning draining away and leaving him with pure, mindless sensations. He felt deeply, strongly, honestly—unhampered by any rational thought. And it was at these times that he realized that even in the vacuum, in the great, raw hole that had been ripped out of his life, that old passion for her still burned with a hot and steady flame. He didn't understand it. And yet, still, it was true.

He sat down on the rocking chair and closed his eyes, and it all came back to him: the weight of her warm, womanly body on his lap, the fragrant scent of her clean skin as her head pressed against his shoulder. Then, slowly, painfully, he opened his eyes and stared across at the bare, uncurtained windows of the apartment across the way, torturing himself with an insistence on figuring out the details. How had he looked at her for the first time? Had she responded immediately, or had she resisted? How had it gone from looking to speaking? From speaking to meeting? He felt his whole body tense with the crescendo of anguish as these thoughts finally rose as high as they could go and then collapsed of their own weight.

The apartment across the way was vacant now, emptied hastily by burly movers who had unknowingly removed along with the furniture his last hope of getting any answers to his questions. The Saltzman family had just disappeared, almost overnight. No one even knew where they'd gone. Some said to Bnai Brak, while others claimed they were in the *haredi* stronghold of Borough Park, Brooklyn, in New York City.

Judah felt a muscle in his jaw flex with fury. He would have torn the other man apart with his bare hands. He should have done . . . something. Done something, he repeated to himself with a dull litany of regret and self-hatred. He rocked wearily, his body cold and separate and unbearably wretched with loss. How would he go on? Perhaps they were right. The divorce was necessary to put an end to the dreaming, to salvage something of his self-respect. He tried to imagine where she was and what she was doing. Perhaps she was with him, her lover, even now! Yet, somehow, that thought was almost more bearable than the idea that she was far away, alone, and unhappy.

He rocked back and forth, trying to lull his senses, to deaden them. If he had been a drinking man, he would have gotten roaring drunk. But the idea of involving alcohol, which religious Jews used to sanctify every joyous celebration, in such a joyless enterprise seemed to him almost a sacrilege. So he stayed sober, drunk only with pain.

Moishe adjusted his army beret over his head, tucked in his army dress uniform, and walked briskly toward the exit to the base. He passed his sergeant, stopped, saluted smartly but didn't look him in the eyes (with the situation on the borders what they were, there was no telling if and when all leaves would be instantly canceled), then heaved a sigh of relief when the man continued walking. He hurried.

At first he didn't think it was she. She seemed so tall, so thin. Her hair, gathered together in a velvet ribbon, fell down her back in a great exuberance of curls, the wisps escaping and twirling around her face. He slowed his steps. The guard at the gate, a kid just out of basic training, had been trying to be cute with her, he could tell. She had turned her back to him, and her posture was stiff and defensive. The dress was elegant yet absolutely modest. She would have fit in on any street in Bnai Brak, he thought a little anxiously. He had not seen her in six months.

"Chaya Leah!"

He saw her turn, startled. A deep, warm smile spread over her face. She bent down and lifted a shopping bag, tucking her purse smartly under her arm. She took a few steps toward him. Then they just stood together, not touching, not speaking, just drinking in each other's presence.

Her eyes roamed over his face, his body made unfamiliar by the khaki. His arms were so strong and tan, his bearded face weathered, toughened. He had also grown taller and slimmer. She blushed, feeling herself in the presence of an incredibly attractive stranger.

"Well, aren't you going to say anything?" He laughed, turning around to present her with a total view of Moishe: Tank Commander.

She looked into his eyes and smiled. "Anything."

"I've only got a few hours off, and then our unit is moving out. Let's not waste any time." He reached out and took her arm, steering her into the parking lot. She moved subtly but firmly away from him.

This, Moishe thought, was not good news.

They took the bus into Tiberias and walked down to the wharf, which was crowded by summer vacationers. The place was bustling with waiters carrying steaming platters of fried and grilled St. Peter's fish, large baskets of pita bread, and plates of humus. Pleasure boats blaring the latest Israeli hits carried families across the incredibly blue waters from the western to the eastern shore of the lake. Motor boats dragging water-skiers vied for space with fishing boats and small foot-propelled paddle boats. And all along the boardwalk, young couples linked their arms together and strolled, happily, timelessly, intoxicated by the heady first taste of love.

Moishe and Chaya Leah found themselves walking farther and farther apart. He kept his hands in his pockets, and she held on to her purse and shopping bag. Finally he looked up at her. "What is it?"

She shook her head. "Don't. Don't make me. It'll ruin it all."

"That bad?" He had no inkling what it could be.

"Worse."

"Come, let's sit down. I've got my pay. I can afford it."

They found a dockside table in the shade of a gay umbrella.

The waiter was rude but anxious to be finished with them, so the service was at least quick. She squeezed the lemon over the fish, then took a fork and just picked at it idly.

"Well, this is where it all began, isn't it?"

She looked confused.

"Fish," he said soberly.

"Gefilte fish," she said, suddenly smiling, her eyes bright with tears.

"Hey, love, what is it?"

"I can't see you anymore."

He sat back, eyeing her with stunned incomprehension. "What have I done?"

"Nothing." She shook her head miserably.

"Then?"

"It's my sister. She's left her husband. My father is sick about it. I can't even tell you. It's even worse than when my mother died. Oh, Moishe, he's so ashamed. He can't look anyone in the eye anymore. He says it was his fault, how he raised her. That he's failed. Oh, I hate her! How could she have done this!"

"But what has your sister running off got to do with us?"

"Don't you understand? She's put us into the spotlight now! All our walls are glass. People never stop looking, whispering. If anyone even suspected I was meeting you today . . . I think my father would just die, and I'd have killed him. Just like I . . . my mother . . ."

He reached out to her. "Hey, stop. Stop doing this to yourself . . . my love."

She was quiet. She wiped her face with the back of her hand. "He's all we've got left. The boys . . ."

"So we'll get married!"

"I can't marry you."

"Why not?"

"Because everyone would ask questions about how we met. Garfinkel would tell the whole world it wasn't through him."

Moishe gulped down his Coke. He took out a package of cigarettes and tapped one on the counter and lit it. Then he leaned back and stuck his thumb in his belt, curling his fingers around the cold metal of his army-issue revolver. Trapped. The street was always stronger. Its arms reached out and captured you no matter how far you fled.

He looked at the beautiful blue waters and the hills in the distance, where even as they spoke enemy mortars and PLO guerrillas armed to the teeth by the Saudis and Libyans and Syrians were now massing. The future seemed so unreal. The moment, that was the only truth he knew right now. He turned his attention to the lovely young woman who sat across from him, reaching out and squeezing her hand gently. She looked around nervously, then relaxed, returning the pressure.

"Come, let's not talk anymore. Let's just be together."

She nodded, surprised. She had expected him to be angry, to rage. She took his acquiescence as a sign of hopelessness. A dull anguish blunted her feelings so that she almost felt refreshed, renewed. Whatever was going to happen would happen, she told herself, slipping her arm through his. His muscles pressed back, young and healthy.

They walked for a long time, not speaking of anything, the silence winding around them, hovering over them like a canopy. Her heart ached with love for him, this handsome young man. She couldn't think of losing him, of pitting her need for him against her responsibility to her family. Yet there it was. When she was with him, her family didn't exist, and when she was with her father, her own needs didn't exist, or at least could be forgotten.

He held her in his arms, and all her fears dissolved, melting away all her resolutions and decisions. "Moishe, my love . . ." She held him close. His lips brushed her temple. His arms were strong and young and handsome.

"We'll think of a way, Chaya Leah," he murmured just above the sound of the water lapping against the rocks.

Despite everything, she felt a small kernel of hope begin to grow.

And then, incredibly, the hours passed and he had no choice but to get back to the base. They agreed to part at the central bus station. His bus came first. He held her close for a moment, then kissed her softly on the lips. She watched him walk away, jaunty, handsome, a young Israeli soldier going back to the business of defending his tiny country against the heartless old enemies who never grew tired of death and killing.

Then she remembered. She ran to the bus and tapped on the window. It was already moving. He opened it and leaned out recklessly. She threw the shopping bag into his arms. "It's a sweater," she told him, "a green sweater, with little fish on it."

"Fish is my favorite color," he yelled back at her as the bus swept him away.

She stood watching until even the tiny trail of smoke from the exhaust was no longer visible.

CHAPTER 45

THE YOUNG DOCTOR WOVE HIS WAY THROUGH THE CROWDED cafeteria, his eyes hunting through the lunchtime crowds, his face registering disappointment. Then all of a sudden he grinned and waved urgently. "Hey, Charlie, over here!"

A face in the crowd looked in his direction, puzzled, until his eyes focused. He grinned back and made his way in the direction of the voice.

"I've been looking all over for you for weeks. Where've you been, Charles?"

"Well, hello to you, too, Dennis. Wisconsin. There was a three-week course with Dr. Shelton on process conception in psychotherapy."

"I'm impressed. How'd you get the department to loosen its claws on you for that long?"

"I promised to work through August."

Dennis shook his head in disbelief. "August in Prince County nut ward. You're a braver man than I."

Charles raised his eyes and mouth in an impish smile that was full of good-natured self-mockery. He was in his late twenties, on the short side, with increasingly thin golden-brown hair that fell across his forehead and into his eyes with an annoying frequency he found helpless to prevent. He wore gold, wire-rimmed frames and lenses that grew thicker every year, hiding eyes that were a bright sky blue. They were eyes filled with a child's unfeigned curiosity and only a hint of the intelligence and perception that had made him both a top medical student and a top resident specializing in psychotherapy. In fact, his whole demeanor was so modest and unassuming that the nurses and even the orderlies regularly bossed him around.

"Well, Charles, learned colleague, have I got a case for you."

Intense interest immediately filled Charles's whole face.

"It's a girl, a woman, actually, but she seems like a little kid, she's so fragile and small."

Charles waited patiently. He could understand why Dennis was always getting reprimanded for long-windedness at staff meetings. He would no doubt be one of those who finished a grueling decade of medical training and then decided to write novels in a house in the country.

"Well, anyway," Dennis continued, "the cops brought her in eight days ago. They picked her off the street in midtown half-naked and totally nonresponsive. Thought she'd OD'd, but the blood work-up turned out cleaner than Perrier. Catatonic is as close as we've gotten to a diagnosis. Doesn't talk or respond. Minimal physical movements. Heck, she's lain in bed like a teddy bear for the entire time she's been here. Now listen to this. Yesterday this woman shows up, frantic, and says the girl is her Israeli maid and she wants to take her home. I explained to her that in this state she wasn't going to be much use in mopping the floors, unless she used her for the mop." Dennis stopped, waiting for some sign of appreciation of his wit.

Charles sighed. "Go on."

"Well, that's about it. . . . So I started thinking: Didn't you once tell me how your parents were super-Orthodox and sent you to this private boys' school to learn Talmud in Hebrew when you were a kid?"

"A yeshiva, Dennis." The other man grinned. "And it's true I know Hebrew, but not the kind they speak in Israel. The biblical kind."

"How is it any different?"

"Well, they didn't exactly have words for cars, or neckties, or CD players in biblical times."

"How would you say 'CD player' in Hebrew?"

"*See Dee*," Charles replied, grinning.

"No joke?"

"At least they did last summer when I was in Israel. But I guess I'm still way ahead of the rest of you guys no matter how much I know. When can I take a look at her?"

"After lunch?"

Charles took big bites out of an egg-salad sandwich, which swiftly disappeared. "Just so happens I've finished eating."

"But I was just about—"

Charles put a firm hand over the other man's shoulder, steering him through the crowd. "Dennis, do you know how many calories you're saving yourself, not to mention cholesterol and triglycerides . . ." He handed him a candy bar. "This should keep you."

They rode up the huge, crowded elevator, then walked purposefully down the endless gray corridors. The air was thick and foul with cigarette smoke and bathroom odors. But worse than that was the noise: television sets tuned to silly cartoons, phonographs blaring horrifying rock group noise, a woman out of control screaming obscenities. Fighting. Crying. People walking in hopeless, aimless circles. A woman clutching her knees, rocking back and forth, banging against a wall. The wretchedness. The aimless, mirthless laughter. And always the sense of danger, of pent-up violence just waiting to explode.

Charles tried to fight against the numbness that seeped into his soul each time he entered this place. No matter how much time he spent here, he would never grow used to it. So many failures, so few successes. Prince County was a short-term facility. Most cases admitted were simply emergencies who would remain only a few weeks at the most before being shipped off to some upstate facility that would make Prince County seem like the Plaza. They would enter an inexorable cycle that would rapidly erode all their basic human rights and pleasures, condemning them to a lifetime of ugliness; a lifetime where each day, every day they lived, would be spent smelling these smells, listening to these noises, and watching these scenes of bedlam. Day after day after day.

It was only the idea, the small hope, that he, through some personal skill or knowledge or plain, sheer luck, might succeed in plucking one out of the cycle for a different fate that gave Charles the determination to continue.

"Well, well, the natives are restless today," Dennis said cheerfully.

He had the right attitude, Charles thought with a touch of envy. Never let it get to you. It was a job, like welding pipes or laying bricks. What happened happened. That didn't necessarily make Dennis a bad doctor, only a successful one who would live to enjoy his success.

The two young men walked into the room. It smelled of urine and sour disinfectant. An older woman wandered dancing around the floor, another sat by the window, staring.

Dennis walked over to the foot of a bed in the corner. He pulled the sheet down a little. "Here she is. Must have been a pretty little thing, don't you think?"

Charles walked over to the bed. He crouched down

until his head was level with that of the woman in the bed, who lay facing the wall. He held the chart in his hand, reading. "G-d damn it, Dennis, nothing at all has been done for her! She's been pumped so full of drugs most of the time, she probably couldn't have moved if she'd wanted to!"

Dennis cleared his throat. "I did stop all that."

"But only after a week!"

"Well, we were just following standard procedure for suicides."

"Suicide?" He flipped through the chart. "I don't see any evidence of suicide, not in the admitting report."

"Don't you?" Dennis grabbed the chart, flipping it over with haste. "Well, I think, then, someone, maybe the cop who brought her in, must have just said he figured it was something like suicide."

"So they pumped her full of antidepressants. Great. Who the hell brought her in, anyway?"

"It's in here, it's all in here." He flipped the pages nervously. "Ah, there it is. Johnson, Alex . . . something, writing's not the clearest, but no matter, a cop from midtown."

"And do we have the address and phone number of the woman who claims to know her?"

"Uhm, wait a second. I think I wrote it down." He checked his pockets, looking over little pieces of paper.

Charles watched him, the muscle in his jaw flinching.

"Here it is! Joan Rosenshein. Good address." He handed it to Charles, who copied it over to the chart.

"Shalom," Charles whispered to the back of the golden-brown head. "*Korim le Chaim. Ani rofay. Bati la'azor lach.*"

"What was that you told her?"

But before Charles could reply that it meant "They call me Chaim. I'm a doctor. I've come to help you," the small head turned over and he found himself staring into the two most beautiful, most tragic eyes he had ever seen.

CHAPTER 46

From the personal notes of Dr. Charles E. Shulman:

Dina G., a white female aged nineteen, an immigrant domestic worker from Israel. Admitted through emergency. Response to visual, auditory, and tactile stimuli almost zero. Uncertain as to depth of psychological trauma. Could be true psychotic episode or simply deep depression. The discovery of a language barrier was the first step toward some initial progress. Addressed in her native language, Hebrew, she responded with a body movement in the direction of the speaker.

WEDNESDAY, AUGUST 1

Sat with patient for several hours. I spoke in a crude form of Hebrew, filled with expressions from the Bible and Talmud that I remember from my lost yeshiva days. She continued to watch me alertly, her eyes moving as I changed positions around the room. I asked her her name. No response. I asked her if she knew where she was. No response.

THURSDAY, AUGUST 2

Found patient with her eyes open, as if waiting for me. I spoke to her of memories from my own childhood, the holidays, Shabbat, the trip I just took to Israel. I showed her pictures of Israel and asked her some questions. There was no verbal response, but her face registered some strong emotional response, especially at the pictures of Jerusalem. Still, she hasn't said a word. But I'm encouraged by the movement of her face muscles, the change in her expression.

Phoned Joan Rosenshein, supposedly her employer. She seemed genuinely concerned, in fact, agitated, much more than what one would expect from an employer with a recent employee. Perhaps there is something more to all of this? Has agreed to meet with me this afternoon. Actually she was ready to come over immediately, but I want some more time to think this through. The meeting should be enlightening.

CHARLES EXPECTED TO SEE SOME AGGRESSIVELY THIN, HAIR-sprayed matron with color-coordinated eyelids. Joan expected an imposingly tall older man, with distinguished graying sideburns.

"Dr. Shulman?" she asked, looking over the short young man's unruly hair.

"Mrs. Rosenshein?" Charles responded, taking in her paint-stained fingers, curly hair, and jeans.

"You're not what I expected," they said together, then laughed.

"Can I get you something? Coffee?"

"You have no idea how horrible it's been!" Joan burst out, holding back tears. Her passion took Charles by surprise. "When I came home that night and saw she'd just vanished, I was just sick about it! I kept thinking I hadn't really told her about how dangerous New York is. You see, I'd kept trying to make the city sound like fun, like she could learn something from her time here. And I didn't want to scare her. I thought she'd been . . . Oh! The thoughts in my head! The idea of that poor kid out there by herself . . . I've been just sick about it! Simply sick! I went to every emergency ward, every police station. You have no idea how many there are! And then finally someone, an officer at midtown, called me back. He said they'd picked up a young girl fitting her description and brought her here. When can I see her? Is she all right?"

"Well, it's hard for us to tell. She hasn't been physically or sexually abused. . . ."

"Thank G-d!" Joan covered her face, shaking.

"But something serious has happened to her, and we're trying to find out what it is. Could it be something that happened while she was working for you?"

"Well, there was all this problem with food at first—she would only eat *glatt* kosher, Jewish milk. . . . But I finally found out where to get it for her, so we kept the kitchen stocked. And then there was the business with Saturdays. She seemed very depressed that we didn't take it more seriously. I mean, I once asked her if she wanted to go to the movies with us. It couldn't be that, could it?"

As she spoke, Charles found his hypothesis of cruelty, abuse, and exploitation quickly dissolve. There was sincere concern here. Genuine affection. Kindness. All the more impressive because the speaker was not conscious of it. If anything, she had an exaggerated sense of guilt and responsibility. He found himself wanting to comfort her. "It sounds like you were model employers."

She shook her head. "I blame myself. I should have

realized how desperately unhappy she was. I kept thinking that it would pass, that it was just normal homesickness. . . ."

Charles leaned back and tapped a pencil to his forehead. So if it wasn't something that happened in the last month, then it must predate her coming to the States. "Who would have some background information on her before she arrived here?"

"Well, I suppose Bertha, the agency person, might. It's really confidential information. At least, she didn't share it with me."

"Shall we call her now and see if she can join us?"

"She's also upset. I think she'll be happy to come."

Bertha arrived within twenty minutes. She played with her bag. She squeezed her fingers together. "Look, I only found out this information myself a little while ago. Most of the time my boss doesn't share this with me. But I told him the cops were already involved in this one, so he gave me what he had. Dina was running away from a bad marriage. He claims she was grateful to hide out in America. She has a little baby she left behind with the husband."

A baby! The fleeting memory of the dark cloud that had passed over Dina's face. "If you had any children . . ." "Why not relax and enjoy yourself?" And all this time, she's been thinking of her baby, aching for it! A flash of perception suddenly illuminated Joan's confusion. "Bertha, Dina didn't come here willingly, did she?"

"I . . . well . . ."

"Bertha"—Joan stared into the woman's frightened eyes—"she never would have left her child willingly. I don't believe it. . . ."

"There is some kind of dirty business going on. I don't know what it is, or what the truth is. We get these very religious girls who come over from time to time. Very few of them seem happy to be here. I don't know how the arrangements are made. Some very strange people are involved, that's all. Will she be all right, Doctor?" Bertha asked anxiously.

Charles shrugged. The statistics on recovery from mental illness were not overly encouraging. And there was so little to go on. No family members to question, no background, the language barrier. And she'd be shipped upstate if there wasn't some sign of improvement soon. "We can hope. Anyhow, thanks for coming."

"Send her my love." Bertha sighed, taking a silent, solemn vow to begin looking for another job.

"Please, when can I see her?" Joan pleaded.

He looked her over, considering. "What about right now?"

Joan took a deep breath when she got off the elevator and walked down the corridor. How could anyone stand it for minutes, let alone hours, days?

She saw the soft little head on the pillow, the sad, immobile features. She reached out and took Dina's hand.

"I'll get you out of here. I'll take you home," she whispered, caressing the childish hand.

The small fingers curled trustingly around hers. Joan looked down, choking back tears. Poor little kitten, with all those invisible bands around your neck. If we could just see them, just cut them loose . . .

Joan walked into her home and just stood still for a few moments, relishing the small blessings of her life, the things she always took for granted: the wonderful coolness of air-conditioning, the clean, sweet fragrance of a well-cared-for house and garden, the lovely quiet of a house with few inhabitants and many rooms. She felt as if she wanted to wash the hospital away like some filth accidentally stepped in. But she knew she couldn't. Not while Dina was still there.

The children were in the den. The TV was on. She sat down next to Steven on the couch and took Suzy onto her lap. They were watching some movie about a small boy, about Steven's age, who wished to be a grown-up and suddenly found his wish granted. Joan chuckled, enjoying the children's laughter as the small boy-man got a job, found an apartment . . . But then a woman started coming on to him. She went up to his apartment. . . . Joan felt the discomfort growing inside her. But it was a children's movie! Surely the writers, the directors, the producers . . . but no! There he was, and it was clear what was going to happen, all the sexual innuendos. . . .

She jumped up. "This is not appropriate for you!"

The yelling and screaming began. They were in the middle.

"You're disgusting," Steven screamed at her.

She looked at him, her eyes taking on a steely glimmer. "What did you say to me?"

"He said, 'You're disgusting,' " Suzy replied helpfully. "And you are, you are! You ruined our show!"

"Don't you ever speak to me that way again. Not if you want to live. Do you understand me?" she said calmly, but with a strange intensity that shut them both up immediately. "And now you can both go to your rooms. I'm going to take a look at some of the other videos you've been watching."

She put on *Batman*. It was all there. The parents being attacked and murdered. The burned corpse, the vat of acid. There was even a scene in a museum where works of art were vandalized to the accompaniment of music by Prince. And her son, her little boy, had seen this dozens of times. He thought it was funny.

She felt like weeping. Then she felt angry, betrayed. There was supposed to be someone out there who took care of these things! Something called a collective culture in which civilized people agreed to shield children in a civilized world from things that were bad for them. But that old agreement had broken down. It was each man for himself.

She went into the kitchen and took out a pair of pliers. Then she went into the den, unplugged the TV, and cut off the cord.

The idea struck Joan as soon as she opened her eyes the next morning. Friday, she thought, reaching for the phone.

"Dr. Shulman? Joan Rosenshein. I have an idea. . . ."

Joan returned in the late afternoon. She placed the candles by Dina's bedside in their exquisite little holders. She placed the wig by her side and draped the long silk dress over the foot rail. On Dina's bedside tray she arranged two little golden challah breads and a small bottle of wine. "Dina. It's Friday. Here are all the things you need. Please get up," Joan begged her. She touched her arm gently, shaking her. And then, with a strange, sure instinct: "Dina, *maideleh,* it's time to get up."

Charles took a step closer. He called to her softly: "*Zman lakoom, Dina. Od miat Shabbat. Heneh ha narot. Heneh hachalot. Bo-ee. Tasimi et ha pay ah.*" And then they waited, watching the back of her fragile, unmoving head. The minutes passed like hours. Nothing happened. Then, suddenly, she turned over. Tears were streaming down her cheeks. Her hands reached out for Joan, and she pressed her face into the older woman's soft shoulder, hugging her.

"It's all right, it's all right, darling. It's all right now. . . ." Joan patted her helplessly.

What happened next would remain with Joan as one of her happiest memories and with Charles Shulman as one of his supreme moments of professional satisfaction. In a clear, sweet voice, Dina Gutman said: "I must get dressed before I light." Then, turning to Charles, she said: "*Todah.*"

"*Bevakasha,*" he replied.

When she came out of the bathroom, she had changed into the clothes Joan had brought her, washed her face, combed her long blond wig. She looked like those fresh-faced Hasidic girls you saw all over Crown Heights or like the religious girls he had seen in Israel.

She lit the candles, closing her eyes, her lips murmuring softly. Her eyes were bright when she opened them. Alive, Joan thought with relief.

"Please, make kiddush for us over the wine," she asked Charles, putting her arm around Joan's waist and leaning against her shoulder.

Charles nodded, oddly apprehensive. He had not said a prayer for years, ever since his break with religion, the huge, bitter battle with his parents. . . .

"But you must cover your head first," she told him.

He looked around and found a napkin. He put it on his head, then lifted the wine. The Hebrew words came up painfully from his bowels, his chest. Yet there was an oddly pleasant nostalgia that accompanied them as well, like the smell of spicy cookies on a winter's night.

He poured some wine off into her bedside cup, and she drank it. Then she got up again and washed her hands, reciting the blessing over the twin loaves. "You must wash, too," she told them.

Joan watched her, her heart light. She had not only spoken, walked, eaten, and dressed, but, more important, she had related to those around her, assumed a connection between them that had even allowed her to boss them around. And she had done it all within the space of fifteen minutes!

"Now you get a double mitzvah. Not only for saying the blessings, but for getting me to say them. I haven't for years," Charles told Dina, smiling.

"For years?" She seemed amazed. "And hasn't G-d punished you?"

He thought about it and shrugged. "My life has been good."

"It could be better," she said sadly, her eyes going from Joan's face to his.

Joan hugged her, trying not to cry.
He nodded thoughtfully. "Perhaps."

AUGUST 14

The progress continues in therapy sessions with Dina. We have almost gotten past the first stage where she didn't seem to acknowledge herself at all. She refused to communicate any feelings, any personal meanings. She'd say things like "You must never lie. It's wrong to lie." Or "Bad people deserve to be punished."

This fixed life view, rigid and problemless, blocks her internal communication. She is afraid to look inside her own heart, to acknowledge the contradictions. Is it the average person's failures she denies, or is there something more? I am trying to convey total acceptance to her, to make her feel that whatever she says, or thinks, or does, she will not lose my friendship, my approval. This is the hardest part, to win her trust. Joan continues to visit. The two have formed a significant personal bond that is important to her therapy. Dina trusts her, depends on her.

AUGUST 18

Progress. She told me today that she loves her father, and that her mother has died. She said something shocking. That she was glad her mother was dead, because what had happened would have killed her. She didn't say what that event was. But I suspect it is pivotal. She continues to disown her feelings. "Why do you think you wound up here, in the hospital?" I asked her. Her response was: "I suppose it was the sins."

She didn't say: My sins. Or elaborate. It's still being kept at arm's length. She still cannot face it. I don't know how to get over this hump.

AUGUST 20

She is really down. The question was, If you could have anything, what would it be? Her answer: "I want to die." But then she immediately corrected herself. "I don't deserve to live."

I don't think she is suicidal—that quick correction shows something else. Someone or something has trampled on her ego so powerfully that she is actually convinced being alive is more than she deserves. Would explain her initial symptoms, the total paralysis, the affectation of lifelessness.

AUGUST 21

She spoke of her parents today. Genuine affection, tremendous guilt. Her feelings seem to be thawing. She has begun to use "I." "I" hated some of my teachers, she is willing to admit. "I envied the girls who went into the army." Still, she is far from revealing her deepest feelings. She has given me a long list of things she wanted to do when she was growing up which were denied her, mostly by her own inhibitions, her internalized policeman rather than any outside force. Yet she hasn't expressed any resentment toward the people or social conditions which circumscribed her life. "I wanted to, but I couldn't," is as far as she is willing to take it.

AUGUST 22

Tried an imaging technique. "I want you to think of the worst thing that has ever happened to you. I want you to imagine it, step by step. Go through all the motions, slowly," I asked her.

She wept. "I can't do it. Don't make me."

I told her to relax. To begin it again and to stop when it became too painful.

She refused. I didn't pressure her.

AUGUST 23

She began to tell me about a distant relation, an ancestor called Sruyele. Apparently, the woman broke her engagement and was not only ostracized but cast shame over the family for generations.

"Do you think this is what Sruyele deserved?" I asked. I could see the question shocked her.

"I never thought about it before. It always seemed as if what happened had to happen."

"Is it so terrible to change your mind? Is it so terrible to fall in love?"

"Yes." She shook her head vigorously. "It is a terrible thing, the worst thing in the world."

"Is that what you think?" I pressed her. I could see how hard it was for her to reply. "Not terrible in itself, but terrible because of how it hurts so many others."

"But why should it hurt anyone if a young girl changes her mind and decides to share her life with someone else? Aside, of course, from the man she was engaged to. But even then, the man might understand. Might forgive."

"I don't know."

"Could it be that choosing to feel hurt was their choice, their problem, and not Sruyele's?"

"I don't know," she said again, but this time slowly, thoughtfully.

AUGUST 24

A breakthrough!! Small but significant. She said, "The idea of needing to please people—of having to do it—that's always been a basic assumption (she used the Hebrew word) of my life. I don't know. I never questioned it before. It's as if I have no choice. I just have to."

This is the first time I've seen her questioning, giving a fresh description of the past, a personal conclusion. It gives me hope.

AUGUST 25

I've decided she needs to get out. She's very determined not to, but I've managed to get her to see it as medicine. I've suggested to Joan that she take her to the city—concerts, plays. Everything. The more the better.

At Lincoln Center, hearing Dvorak's New World Symphony for the first time in her life, Dina felt a strange sensation. It wasn't just her ears that were involved. The music seemed to enter through her chest, as if she were a string vibrating to some invisible bow. She closed her eyes and saw the calm majesty of vast new spaces to be explored. She heard the birds singing in snow-capped mountaintops and seemed to rise above them, looking down on a fresh, bright earth full of promise.

At the Metropolitan Museum, it was the same. She looked around at the paintings, the sculptures, the tapestries, the antique furniture and rare jewels. How much creativity there was in human beings! How could that be bad? To be like Him, the greatest innovator, the Creator of all things? It was part of all she had been taught. She watched the admiring eyes of the people around her pay homage to the timeless results of human inspiration. And suddenly she thought of all the *kollel* men, almost indistinguishable in their dark suits and beards. The society in which she was born and raised gave no value to innovation, to individual human expression! The opposite! Everyone had to dress the same, act the same, *feel* the same! Imagination, self-expression, was a threat, an evil to be throttled and repressed.

And then she thought of her husband in his work clothes, his body bent over the turning lathe, his skilled fingers carving beautiful small objects. She had never valued his talent, his remarkable creativity. She had wanted him to be like all the others. She had been ashamed of his uniqueness. But it wasn't my fault! she cried out silently, hot with shame. I didn't know. I didn't understand.

As she wandered through the halls, her face kept lighting up, almost incandescent. It was as if she were affected physically by the colors and shapes, her body growing lighter, almost weightless. It was the still lifes, especially the flowers, that touched her the most. They would never wither, never suffer from thirst or harsh winds, heat or cold. They were caught in their greatest moment of beauty. She remembered those moments in time she had felt made all of life worthwhile. The artist captured those moments so that you could wander through rooms and rooms of them, remembering why life was rich and beautiful and infinitely worthwhile.

Good, Charles said when she told him. Keep going.

She rode on the Staten Island ferry, saw the circus and the ballet. She sat in Carnegie Hall and listened to Daniel Barenboim. She saw *Les Misérables* and *The Sound of Music*. She wandered through little art galleries uptown and in SoHo.

This was the world she had been taught to shut out, the world that she had been taught would take the holiness from her life. Instead it was filling her with new joy, new meaning, new understanding. Like so many other things she had always accepted blindly, she saw the fear that had been bred into her was false. A lie. The fear was a fence erected to keep out temptation, evil. But instead of filtering and shading, it blocked out all light, all sun. It kept out so much that was good! And in the last analysis, it was ultimately useless: the evil in human beings was inside them.

Slowly the fear that had circumscribed her life began to dissolve.

She let the city enchant her. She could not get enough of its variety, it creativeness. Yet with all of this, she did not let it dazzle and blind her. The first time she saw a poor, homeless man lying on top of a subway vent to keep warm, she was appalled. "How can people sleep at night knowing this man is out here in the cold? Why doesn't anyone help him?"

Joan, who never ran out of places to take her or words to describe them, couldn't come up with a single, satisfying word of explanation. She found herself forced to focus on and explain a different side of the city she loved—its vast callousness, its wastefulness of both things and people, its frightening unpredictability. In a way it opened her eyes, too.

All along, Joan's idea of success had been not only to help restore Dina's hold on reality, but also to enlighten and guide her through all the wonders of Western culture: its freedom, its easy, nonjudgmental morals, its respect for individual choice and individual liberty. All the things Dina's own culture and society seemed to lack. Slowly Joan began to realize that each of the gifts also bore a curse. The freedom also meant the freedom to watch your neighbor starve or get mugged. Individual choice gave sanction to those who chose to live lives full of filthy books and movies, selfish and careless. Or lives that were an endless cycle of shopping trips followed by garage sales.

More and more Joan found in Dina's description of her childhood, her life, a society whose hands reached into the individual's life, constantly interfering yet also constantly helping. You were not poor alone, nor sick, nor heartbroken. If only there could be some balance, if the helping hand could be prevented from its excesses, from the murderously unfair blows that it had been allowed to give Dina Gutman, blows that had almost ended her young life.

"I'd like to take a course," Dina told her. "One of those you mentioned."

Joan was delighted. "Screen painting?"

"No. I'd like a course in weaving."

Joan looked at her curiously. "Do you feel up to it?"
She nodded. "I'm not afraid, Joan. Not anymore."

Her first tapestries were the dark place she had been—mainly grays, browns, dark greens, and black. Yet slowly she worked in the yellow. There was the sun coming in. At last. There were blue threads—they were the sky. And green, the color of soft, fragrant spring grass. And also a red-orange, like the sunset over the mountains. Dina lifted the threads, her fingers tingling with excitement. Could they be woven into her tapestry? Could she dare to claim such things again, the beautiful memories of her old life, so rich with quiet pleasures? She looked at her loom hesitantly, wondering, afraid.

AUGUST 28

A real breakthrough!! For the first time, she expressed anger, fury at some unknown person. "I would kill him if I could!!" Yet she will not tell me who this "him" is. In general, there seems to exist a certain traumatic event which is central to all this, which explains it.

She is being held back by some powerful, invisible force, like the angel with the sword of fire that stood in Balaam's way, visible only to Balaam's ass. I need to find Balaam's ass.

They want her released or sent upstate. I must speed things up!!

"I think they've done all they can for her, Maury. I think she'd be better off with us."

He folded the *New York Times* and looked up at his wife thoughtfully. "You would take that responsibility? You would bring a mentally unbalanced person into your home and care for her?"

"You make her sound like some kind of psychopath!

She was just depressed, unhappy. Believe me, she's a lot more normal than ninety-five percent of most New Yorkers. And a lot less dangerous. She needs me, Maury. She's all alone. I think I can help her."

He stared at her, touching her face. "Another kitten? And tell me, what sense does it make to give the maid's room over to a disturbed waif who won't be any help in the house at all?"

"Maury, please. I'll hire someone else to do the housework. I mean, what's the use of being rich if you can't indulge in something as foolish as this? It would be a mitzvah. Your *bubee* would be proud of you."

He laughed. She'd touched all the right buttons, and she knew it. "Go ahead. Take her out of there. And I'll tell you something else. That girl doesn't need a shrink. She needs a rabbi."

Joan looked at him, thunderstruck.

"It can't hurt," Charles agreed. "In fact, she might confess things to a rabbi she feels unable to face with me. After all, I can't give her absolution, can I? But I think it's a question of finding the right one. Do you have any ideas?"

Joan walked into the Orthodox synagogue for the first time in her life. She had always thought only old people went to Orthodox services. But everyone here looked so young. It was filled with young singles, "yuppies" in every respect except that the men wore skullcaps. She sat upstairs in the women's balcony. The prayers, chanted in Hebrew, were totally foreign to her. There was a lot of standing up and sitting down. Joan had no idea what was going on. Yet she felt the sincerity, the spontaneous warmth. The Hebrew gave the service an authenticity, an inexplicable meaning.

The rabbi too looked like a kid. Yet there was something very powerful about his speech that was geared to the university-trained skepticism of his audience.

Joan went up to him after the service and explained the situation.

"I don't think I could help," he said with startling frankness.

"Sorry I wasted your time, Rabbi," Joan said with a touch of anger.

"Please . . ." His voice interrupted her bitter thoughts. "Come into my office. Sit."

Joan sat. The room was lined with books. Idly she took a Bible off the shelf and leafed through it, the stories, the phrases, catching her eye. She felt a sudden longing to read it cover to cover. To understand.

"You were offended, insulted by my refusal, my friend," the young rabbi said affably, closing the door behind him.

"I have no right to be. After all, it's my problem."

"It's true that you have no right to be insulted, but not for that reason. All Israel is responsible for each other. I didn't say I didn't want to help, but that I couldn't. Your friend is from Jerusalem. She wears a wig. Do you think she would accept my word for anything?" He smiled, rubbing his clean-shaven young cheeks. "Get someone with a beard and *payess*, preferably someone going a bit gray. Only from such a person would she accept religious counseling."

Of course it was true. "You wouldn't happen to know anyone like that, would you?"

"As a matter of fact"—he smiled, looking through his Filofax—"I think I have just the one. A Koliver Hasid, who became religious late in life. He spent his youth on a hippie commune after getting both an M.D. and Ph.D. from Berkeley. Call me after the Sabbath for the phone number."

On Sunday Joan found herself down on Eastern Parkway, only houses away from the famous court of the

Koliver Hasidim, followers of Rav Mendel Mordechai Koliver.

She rang the bell, her body tensing. Hasidim made her nervous (actually, she found them sort of embarrassing) when she saw them across the street. Now she was walking right into the tepee.

The man who opened the door wore the long beard, *payess*, black coat, and hat she expected. But out of a face mostly hidden by the heavy dark growth of beard that was now turning gently gray, bright blue eyes sparkled with unexpected humor.

"Come in, come in," he said with sweeping openness. "The natives are friendly."

She laughed, feeling her nervousness fade. "I guess I *am* nervous. It seems like a different world down here. Like I've left America behind."

He shrugged. "Is that such a bad thing?"

"Well, not bad, exactly," she hedged, not wanting to insult him.

"Yes, you're thinking, bad exactly. Weird. Cultish. You're wondering what's a nice M.D. from Berkeley doing in a place like this all dressed up like someone out of a medieval Polish village?"

"Well"—she smiled, again relieved—"something like that."

"You know, back in the sixties I lived on a commune with about sixty other people. We were all at the university. All bright. All spiritually starving. We all basically traveled the same route: drugs and sex; travel to India and the Himalayas. Then, the ones who survived mostly packed away their tie-dyed T-shirts and joined banking firms and the staffs of large hospitals. I don't know if they're still starving. But I know I'm not. I can't tell you how I wound up this way—it would take all your time and credulity. But trust me when I say that it was a well-thought-out decision that fulfills all of my needs. Can you accept that?"

Joan nodded, unsure of her real feelings but relieved at the atmosphere of candor.

"Now how can I help you?"

The conversation was long and involved. Joan found herself forgetting about the strange outfit, the stranger credentials, admitting to herself that she was sitting across from an intelligent modern physician, open-minded and knowledgeable.

When the arrangements for the rabbi to visit Dina were completed, Joan held out her hand gratefully. "Thank you, Doctor . . . ? Rabbi . . . ?"

"Please . . ." The blue eyes sparkled as he tactfully avoided the hand. "Just plain Eli will do. And thanks are unnecessary. You're doing me a favor by allowing me to share in your good deed."

"Shalom," Rabbi Eliezer said to Dina.

She looked at him like a startled small animal caught and revealed by the searing, dangerous headlights of an oncoming car.

He sat down and unbuttoned his vest. He leaned forward, his hands cupping his knees in an attitude of expectation. "So, *maideleh*, how can I help you?"

"Can I ask how it went?" Joan asked him anxiously when he emerged about two hours later.

"Hard, very hard." He wiped his glistening forehead. "All the unanswerable questions. Evil and good, and death and suffering and punishment . . ."

"Were you able to help her find some answers?"

He shrugged. "Who says there are answers? But I will come back. She seems to want that."

CHAPTER 47

Dina was pacing the floor, running to the window anxiously to see if he had arrived. It was Rabbi Eliezer's fifth visit. She felt the mixture of dread and unbearable expectation of a woman at the end of her ninth month of pregnancy. Something was growing inside her. She needed to push out all the old anger, the shame, the guilt, the pain, to make room for it. Slowly she had begun to reach toward G-d again, forgiving him for her mother's death. She had looked at death as the ultimate evil, the ultimate punishment. But death was simply a point on a circle, Rabbi Eliezer had helped her realize. There was a continuation, a reckoning in which everything came full circle and justice was ultimately done.

She felt close to Rabbi Eliezer. He reminded her of

the wise, good men she had known in her old world—rabbis, teachers, relatives—but somehow without their harsh judgment. She felt she could tell him things too shameful to tell her own family. Also, it was easier and more rewarding to talk to him than Joan or Charles, who could never understand the severity of her crime, who would judge leniently and forgive easily, making their compassionate acquittal worthless.

She was happy when she heard his footsteps in the hall and then walking up the steps. It was late afternoon. The room was bathed in soft shadows. "Let's not put on the light, Rabbi Eliezer. I feel better this way," Dina said softly. What she had to say would be unbearable in the harsh glare of full illumination.

He nodded.

"When I was sick, it was always dark. I remember feeling that I could not escape it. That it was hopeless. That the only solution was just to sleep and not to let anyone wake me. Sometimes I'm sorry I did. Wake up, that is. I don't deserve to live after what I did."

"Dina, I want you to listen to me."

She sat up, startled. His voice was very firm, nothing like his usual gentlemanly, hesitant probing.

"A sin can never be altered. It is what it is. But the bad deeds never cancel out the good ones. They are completely separate. The most terrible deed in the world can never alter the existence of even the smallest good you've accomplished. Every kind thought, every helping hand, they all exist, too."

"But you're saying I can never undo the harm. That it will always exist!"

"I didn't say that. In fact, every human being has the G-d-given ability to transform the past, to transform himself, to direct his own destiny at any moment he decides. G-d wants you to get well. That's why you are alive. He wants you to be happy. He wants to forgive you."

"But how can he? I can't forgive myself."

"No? Well, you studied the Torah, didn't you? Here, open this and read it." It was the first chapter in Leviticus.

There was silence in the room as she slowly turned the pages. "But what does it mean? All those sacrifices in the Temple. We have no Temple."

"Dina, read it again."

Again the pages turning, rustling softly.

"If a person sins . . . If the high priest sins . . . If the whole congregation sins . . ." she read softly.

"You see? No one alive is blameless. Sin is part of life. But G-d throws no one out. He's made provision for our foolishness, our stubbornness. As it is written in *The Song of Songs Rabbah:* 'My sons, open for me an aperture of repentance as narrow as a needle's eye and I will open for you gates through which wagons and coaches can pass.' Of course, if you've hurt other people, you must ask them directly for forgiveness. G-d cannot forgive in their place." He paused. "You have a child, don't you? Now I ask you, what could your little boy do that would be so terrible you would never forgive him?"

"There is nothing in the world he could do!" she cried out in anguish. "Nothing so bad I wouldn't love him forever!"

"Of course. But if you were a good parent, you would want to see him become a better person. You would want to be sure he sincerely understood what he'd done wrong and that he regretted it. Deeply. So deeply that he'd changed into the kind of person who would never do such a thing again. It's this transformation that cuts a person off from the past, so that they're no longer the same person who did that wrong. In a very real sense, such a person is given a new heart by G-d which is blameless, released from the responsibility of all his former deeds. It is possible for anyone to make such a new beginning. Dina—look at me. No, not at the wall, look at my face. Who do you see?"

"I see a rabbi, a Hasid. A pious man."

"Fine. Now look at this photograph. No, don't avert your eyes. Study it. Fine, good. Who do you see?"

"I see a goy, a half-naked wild man, a man surrounded by immodest women. A man who cares for nothing. . . ."

"You see two different men. And yet both are me! What would you say if I told you I had never entered a synagogue until I was thirty years old? That I had never said a prayer, or put on tefillin? That I had eaten every forbidden food—pork . . . You shudder? Shellfish, rabbits, crabs . . . Yes, yes. And I knew women. Married and unmarried ones. . . . Nothing was sacred to me. Take your hands away from your face. Yes, yes, such Jews exist, such people exist. You never knew that, did you? So you magnify all your own sins.

"All these bad things I brought with me when I decided to change my life. I couldn't change the things that I'd done, the food I'd eaten, the women I'd known. But I was no longer the same person capable of doing such things. And so, the person I am now is not held responsible by his Father in heaven for the past. The slate is washed clean, Dina. The scarlet thread becomes as white as snow. This is the work of our compassionate Father. Now, I repeat, is there anything your little boy could do which you would never forgive?"

Her weeping was loud, almost hysterical.

"We are G-d's children," he said gently. "He loves us the same way we love our own. He is always there, waiting for us to come home. Come now, take your hands away from your face. Here, blow your nose. . . . What? Say it louder. You are not qualified to punish yourself. Of course you can be forgiven. Didn't G-d forgive the executioner of the great Rabbi Hananya Ben Teradyon, who all at once regretted and repented his whole life in one, supreme moment by jumping into the flames and dying with his victim? And so, Dinaleh, what have you done that was worse than the executioner of Rabbi Hananya?"

There was a pause as her labored breathing filled the

room. It was almost like being present at a birth, he thought. A hard labor. If she succeeded, she would give birth to herself, clean and new and ready for the rest of her life. But if she failed . . .

"I want to tell you." Her voice was a broken sob.

Something stung the rabbi's eyes. It was such a pitiful sound.

"I met a man who was not my husband. His name was Noach. At first, it was his words I wanted. My husband gave me everything else: love, tenderness, care. But he didn't give me enough words. And I felt that what I wanted was simply to listen, to be comforted by ideas. And more than that . . . I wanted to do something on my own. It seemed that all my life I had been pushed and shoved. What I learned, what I wore, how I spent every minute of every day . . . Even the man I wanted to marry was denied me. . . . I wasn't sure when I married my husband that he was the right one for me. There was something about him I thought I could love if I could just find it, explore it. Also, I felt—given my choices—he was the least objectionable. But that isn't a real choice, is it?" She wiped her eyes and took a deep breath. "I didn't touch Noach, not at the beginning. He didn't seem to want that so much. I told myself it was wrong, but if I didn't touch him, it might not be so wrong.

"But then, I realized, that for Noach, the words were not the important thing. He wanted my body. He made me think I wanted his. I was confused. It got worse and worse. I didn't know how to stop, or even if I wanted to. He asked me to meet him and stay with him overnight. And I wanted to. My feet flew down the steps."

She stopped, weeping with heartbroken abandon. It was the kind of sound the rabbi had heard only in places like the waiting rooms of intensive care units or in the halls of pediatric oncology.

"Go on, Dina," he said encouragingly. "Still the sin

has not reached that of Rabbi Hananya's executioner, remember?"

She took a deep breath. "I lied to my husband. I met this other man. . . . We went to the beach. I had never been to a beach where the men bathed with the women, but only to the separate women's beach in Tel Aviv, where the only man was the lifeguard. I saw the bodies of the men and women, so tan and free. No one seemed ashamed. I liked it. I liked it very much. Can you understand that? We sat together. We held hands. And then . . . we . . . went . . ."

There was a long, long silence. Then, firmly but not unkindly, he completed the sentence for her: "To the hotel room."

"I couldn't say the words, you see. Yes. To the room. It had a big double bed and dark red curtains. Even the light coming in seemed red. Like blood, like heat. Then he held me. I was still wearing the wet bathing suit underneath my skirt and blouse. I was even still wearing a wig. His hand felt damp, clammy, as it pressed against me. I didn't like the way it felt. He pushed me down on the bed. He didn't say a word to me. He seemed so different without his words. I didn't even remember who he was, or what I was doing there. . . ."

"Go on. Don't stop. This is the first step, remember," he urged her.

"He began to . . . take off my blouse. I saw his fingers on the buttons, and they were very different from my husband's fingers. . . . And, suddenly, I felt afraid, and so ashamed."

She stopped.

"And then?"

"Rabbi, this is . . . the thing I . . . I pushed his hand away and he slapped me. And a wonderful thing happened. I woke up. I saw how small he was, how petty and unremarkable. He was pinning me to the bed, but I somehow found the strength to push him away. He called me a whore. His whole face was full of hatred—he, who had been so loving! I ran out. I spent the night on the beach. And then I went home."

"And that was all?"

She nodded with strange relief. "You see? I do deserve to die. An adulteress deserves death."

"But, Dina, you aren't an adulteress!"

"We bathed together at the beach! I let him hold me and kiss me! I did it behind my husband's back. . . ."

"Dina, that was all wrong, all a sin. But not the sin of adultery. Your punishment is not death. And Judah doesn't have to divorce you. This is the law."

"He doesn't? But he should. I don't deserve him."

"You have to tell him the truth, then let him decide. You have to ask his forgiveness for all the things you did to hurt him. But not for all the things you didn't do."

"He came here, to see me. This man. This Noach," she said hopelessly.

"Here?" There was a sense of shock in the rabbi's tone.

Dina clasped her hands together tightly. A sudden painful relief coursed through her. To tell it all, now, everything. "He asked me to be his mistress. And you see, the worst part, the worst thing . . . He hasn't lost anything. He still has his wife, his children. How is it that I have been punished by losing everything . . . how is it that rabbis, scholars—Rabbi Kurzman and the others—forced me to write lies, to tell my husband I'd slept with Noach? . . . Forced me to leave my home? How could a rabbi make me lie like that? He seemed so righteous, so good, and yet . . ."

"You can't tell anything about a person by his outer shell, his appearance. Not every Hasid is a Hasid. Not every hippie is a hippie." His blue eyes lit up with mischief.

Dina let herself relax, wishing she could hug him as

she had hugged her father and mother. Those who had given her life.

"Dina, there's something else I want to tell you. A message for you to hold on to. You won't understand it now. You might even laugh. But one day it will be there for you like a great torch of light when all you see is blackness. It's . . . it's only one word."

She waited, almost breathless. "What is it?"

He hesitated. "Sift."

Dina bit her lip in disappointment. She had expected some astonishing revelation, some wisdom, some truth beyond anything she had known. "Sift? Like with flour?" Her tone was dazed.

"If I explain it to you, it will come to you from the outside in, through your ears only. But if you come to understand it yourself, it will come from inside you. It'll transform your life forever. Just think about it. Try to apply it to your life, everything you've seen, and learned; and experienced."

"That's all? I feel so empty, as if my whole life is finished."

"Dina, you're just at the beginning! You've taken the first step. You've faced your past. Now there is the next step. You must do it as soon as possible. I think you know what that is."

"I can't. I can't face them."

"You have to. You remember the cliff in your dream, the one you stood at the edge of? You must go back there, and this time instead of jumping, you must turn around and face them, your accusers and all those you love."

She wept for a long time. It was pathetic and heartsickening, almost unendurable to listen to. Rabbi Eliezer was about to get up and leave when Dina suddenly lifted her face up toward him. It was a mother's face after birth, when the hope of the moment suddenly pushes the pain back into dim memory.

"I'll go," she told him.

When he emerged from the room, he wiped the sweat from his forehead. "She's going to be all right," he told Joan, who had been listening outside the door, wringing her hands.

CHAPTER 48

DINA WAS ODDLY SUBDUED THE WEEK FOLLOWING HER SESSION with Rabbi Eliezer. Joan, braced for some dramatic announcement, felt strangely deflated when she said nothing. Yet she seemed more relaxed and peaceful than Joan had ever seen her, spending even more time at her loom.

She was working on a new tapestry. This one was all white, as before it had been mostly black. It had small splashes of color: splendid blues, turquoise green, a dash of red. Still, there was a restraint, a holding back, as if the full palette were somehow not yet available to her. She made up for it with an endless variety of shapes—fantastic, flowerlike objects, each one a separate vision.

The idea of each flower being different, and yet each achieving its own kind of beauty, she had explained to

Charles recently, was very significant. To bloom in your own way within the fenced-off garden. To be watered and allowed to grow toward the sun.

He had understood the metaphor perfectly. He too had felt something of that sense of strangulation in his yeshiva days. He had been a good student, but his interests had ranged far beyond his classmates. There had been no way to stay, to grow alongside them in the walled-off garden, a flower of a different shape and color. So he had left, carelessly, tearing out all roots, even the ones that had given him nourishment.

Joan watched her working, fascinated by the swift, sure movements of her delicate fingers.

"It's beautiful, Dina."

She looked at Joan and smiled.

"Dina, these are for you. Bertha brought them."

Dina looked at the letters apprehensively. The first mail she had gotten from home! She reached out and touched the envelopes, tracing the handwriting as if trying to feel the warmth of familiar hands.

She wandered slowly back to her room. Kneeling girlishly in her bed, she examined the envelopes. One was in Chaya Leah's messy, large hand, full of furious cross-outs and write-overs. The other was in her father's neat, almost miniature script, rivaling that of Rashi's. The third, beautiful and simple, was from Judah. And the fourth, in a thick cream-colored envelope, was addressed in a very masculine hand she did not recognize at all. Yet, instinctively, she knew exactly who it was from.

And when she had finished reading them, she knew the decision she had been avoiding was finally made.

At their last session together, Charles took Dina for a walk through Central Park. It was one of those crisp, shining fall days filled with blazing golden-red trees that somehow compensated for the loss of summer.

They were talking about Abraham Breitman.

"I saw him once, about a year and a half later. He looked well fed and miserable," she said. "His wife was short and dark with no ankles. She was very pregnant."

"And how did you feel about that?"

"I had fantasized so much about it. But when it actually happened, it was nothing. I felt as if I were seeing some former neighbor, someone I had only known briefly, superficially. But by then I was already seeing Noach."

Charles waited. Finally he said gently: "Do you want to talk about it?"

She shook her head. "Rabbi Eliezer has helped me over that. I can look at what I did honestly—not making it bigger or smaller. I can understand what drove me to it. I can even hope to make up for it one day. But I don't want to talk about it anymore."

She'd leapt over the barrier. It was behind her. He felt that odd mixture of satisfaction, pride, and regret that a high school teacher feels seeing his star pupil graduate and go off to college.

He automatically held out his hand to wish her a final farewell, then realized she would probably not touch him or any man again except her husband, father, brother, or son. He wondered what he thought of that, if he had done his job properly. He had not liberated her into a modern Western woman. He studied her face a moment, and his doubts faded. Her beliefs made her happy. They gave content to her life, a richness and depth he sometimes missed. They also provided a safety net that would catch her even if she fell again.

She didn't need him anymore. He would miss her.

"I'll always remember the sound of your voice coming into my grave," she told Joan with a small smile, pulling her coat closer to keep out the wild October winds at Kennedy Airport. "I wasn't very sure I wanted to hear. I felt so cold, so helpless. I didn't think I could move. But it reminded me somehow of my mother's voice waking me on those cold winter mornings, reminding me of my obligations. I wanted so much to see where the words were coming from. And then, I saw your eyes. They were like my mother's eyes, brown and kind."

"And yours were so green and sad." Joan couldn't help smiling, although her eyes remained somber and pensive.

"I was not sure I wanted to be alive. Being dead was so much safer. But it was also so . . . cold. All the time. A gray, dull, cold, even darkness that protected me. The first time I opened my eyes and saw you, I felt blinded and I wasn't sure if it was terror or happiness. I remember the story of Rabbi Shimon Bar Yochai, who hid in a cave from the Romans for twenty-four years. And when he came out and saw the state the world was in, he went back in. I didn't want to go back in. I am not brave enough. I love life too much, the sounds and the colors."

"Lincoln Center and the Met." Joan laughed.

"And Mama," she threw in.

"MOMA," Joan corrected her.

For an instant the two women looked at each other across the vast abyss of culture, of purpose, that separated them and that could have pitted them so mercilessly against each other. Instead, miraculously, they'd bridged it, crossing over to bring each other some comfort and understanding, enriching each other's lives. Instead, they were friends.

"How do you thank someone for your life? For making you want to live? For giving you back your eyes and ears and voice?" Dina said.

"You thank them by living and by being happy," Joan replied, her eyes swimming brightly. "Want to live, Dina. Don't be afraid to reach out to the world, to love, to hold on to the things that make you happy with every ounce of determination you've got." The idea of never seeing her again was very painful. "If you ever need . . . You could write, or come back," Joan hedged.

"My place is in my own home, with my husband and child. I don't know what will happen. I'm frightened sometimes. But this I do know: I want to go home. To take the steps I must to be forgiven."

Her eyes caressed Joan's with warmth: "Good-bye, my Joan. I hope, one day, I can be as good a person as you are."

Tears of deep emotion stung Joan's eyes at the unexpected words. "Good-bye, Dina. You *are* a good person. You deserve a good life."

They hugged each other, long and hard.

Then Joan watched her walk past the El Al security guards into the glowing terminal until the doors that had opened to accept her slid decisively shut.

CHAPTER 49

THIS WAS THE SECOND TIME IN HER LIFE SHE HAD EVER BEEN IN an airplane. The first, only a few months before, had been a completely different experience. She had been frozen. The dark night sky had seemed a chartless road full of painful accidents waiting to happen.

Now she leaned back and looked out at the regal elegance of the blue firmament stretching in all directions like a blue silk canopy over a wedding party. Unlike being in a car, where you felt you had some sort of control, where the dangers were visible and sometimes avoidable, a plane was totally out of your control. You were truly in G-d's hands. She felt her whole body relax with that knowledge. He could read her thoughts. He knew that her trip back was a step toward atonement. He would not let anything bad happen to her now.

She would not look at the letters now, she told herself as the stewardesses rolled the tinkling carts down the narrow aisles, offering little cans of soft drinks and bottles of wine. She would allow herself the few hours of contentment to build her strength before confronting their difficult messages again. If she read them now, she might lose all control and weep in front of everyone.

She calmed herself by remembering the last conversations with Charles and Joan, the admirable cool rationality she'd been able to achieve then. In fact, she'd been disappointed that they hadn't seen beyond her good show to her absolute terror of what lay ahead. It wouldn't have made any difference, though. She was absolutely determined to face the horrors that awaited her in Israel, because she knew she had no choice but to settle the past and push on toward the future. She tried not to think too much, to feel too much.

Yet even as she was resisting the urge, her hands went compulsively to her purse. She opened it and took out the letters.

The first was Chaya Leah's short, bitter note:

Dear Dina,

I was going to write "Dear Sister," but after what you've done to me, I disown you. Your selfishness is unbelievable!

You've ruined my life. Because of you, I will not be able to marry the man I love. I was the only one of the three of us with the guts to find a man on her own, to fall in love, instead of being matched off like a pair of old socks by garlic-breath Garfinkel. But because of the disgrace you've brought down on our heads with the divorce [the first time Dina had read the letter, her heart had stopped at the awful word. Was there going to be a divorce?!] *there is no way I can even hint to Aba I've done such a thing. IT IS SO UNFAIR!!!!! After all, I am a single girl. All I did was fall in love with a good man, even if he is a Hasid and he is in the army.*

None of this is the reason I'm writing. For myself, I don't care if I ever set eyes on you again. But you have to know this: Aba has been ill since you've left. His heart. The doctor says he needs rest, but I know what he really needs. To see you.

If you have a shred of decency left (which I doubt. What mother could abandon her baby?!), come home.

With no wishes at all,

Chaya Leah

Dina rubbed her palm over her suddenly parched lips. Then, slowly, she opened the next letter.

Dearest Daughter, my beautiful Dina, may she live long,

My child, I hope this finds you well. I don't know what strange and wondrous plans the Almighty has for you, but I have faith that His compassion is vast and everlasting. Whatever you have done—and I know my good child you cannot have done anything that came from a badness of heart, anything that was more than a momentary folly, unintentional and deeply regretted—please remember that repentance is always possible.

I blame myself. If I had been a better father to you all . . . If I had been home more, instead of looking for strangers in the street who needed my help. My heart is broken when I think of how I've failed you all. Your sins belong to me.

Your cruel separation from those who love you cannot have been easy for you. Yossele is well, growing, but he needs his mother. Judah, your wonderful husband, has suffered much. But I trust in his good heart and his good sense. Until the divorce is final, we may still hope.

How I pray that I might see you!

With a thousand blessings of good health and good mazel, I leave you. Your loving,

Aba

Like some Hindu penitent in India intent on whipping his own skin bloody, she doggedly took out Judah's letter. Inside was a simple notice from the Jerusalem Rabbinical Court informing her that divorce proceedings would take place on October 15. Just a few days away. In a small note attached to the notice with a paper clip, Judah had written three Hebrew words: "*Bevakasha tovo-e habayta*"—"Please come home."

"Please come home." She had gone over the words again and again, analyzing each one separately and all together. She tried to imagine the different ways he could have said them: Please! Come Home!—a heartrending plea. Or softly, whispered with compassion, gentleness, forgiveness: Please come home. She tried to comfort herself that he had added "please." After all, "come home" would have served the purpose if all he wanted was simply for her to be there to catch the bill of divorcement he intended tossing at her, throwing her out of his life.

It made no difference. Written, they gave her no clues. It was simply a polite request, neither more nor less. But if he had decided finally to do it, she reasoned, why would he have written anything at all? The notice would have been enough to inform her of his implacable intentions. That is, if they were implacable.

Still, as much as she tried to comfort herself, she could not help absorbing with cold horror the incontrovertible fact that he had actually gone to the judges of the rabbinical court and officially asked to be divorced from her. A cold sweat broke over the pinched skin of her forehead, furrowed in agonizing doubt. What would she do if he went through with it? If he insisted on having Yossele with him? Her baby would hardly know her now anyway. He would cling to his father, her mother-in-law. A few months in a baby's life was like years in an adult's.

The last letter was the worst. She had no strength to go on. Before she could confront it again, she needed medicine, the best medicine of all, better than anything even good Doctor Charles could offer her. Charles hadn't realized it, but it was this all along that had provided the megadose of courage she'd needed to get on a plane that would bear her back into the eye of the cyclone that might very well smash her to bits.

It was an ancient remedy, used by her people for thousands of years, through wretched, heartbreaking times so dark with hopelessness and death that words like "hope" and "future" had been simply discredited, like childish fairy tales. It was odd how just the silent mouthing of verses, poems written by another bruised and beleaguered distant relative, could fill her with so much vibrancy, so much confidence that "hope" and "future" were real, meaningful elements in her life again.

She took out King David's Psalms and began to read:

I have waited for the L-rd in the past, striving after Him, and He inclined to me and heard my cry.

He has raised me up from the pit of desolation, from the miry mud; He has set my feet upon a rock, and firmly established my steps.

He has put a new song into my mouth, a praise of G-d's mighty acts, so that many shall see, and fear, and at the same time learn to trust in the L-rd.

Happy is the man who has made G-d his trust, who has not turned for comfort to the arrogant, the faithless, the deceivers. . . . Thou, O L-rd, withhold not Thy compassion from me even now; let Thy mercy and Thy truth continually preserve me.

For uncountable evils have surrounded me, my sins have overtaken me once more so that I cannot see; they are more numerous than the hairs of my head, my heart has failed me.

Want, O G-d, to save me; Hurry, O L-rd, to deliver me.

Where was David when he had written those words? she wondered. Hiding in a cave from Absalom, his own faithless, patricidal son? Running from the jealous, murderous rage of King Saul? Or was it simply in the dark of the night as he sat in his palace, alone and friendless, remembering his desire for Bathsheva, another man's wife, and the great sin he had committed in consummating that desire? Her heart burned with hot compassion and pity for King David, for Chaya Leah, for her father, Judah, Yossele. Herself. Yet David had survived. He had been forgiven. And more than that: he had been blessed.

Her hands trembling, she opened the thick, cream-colored envelope and took out the last letter. She sat with it folded in her lap, not daring to open and read it again. Not daring. Just touching it made her sick with a kind of nauseous fear, the deepest kind of fear a person feels, when the enemy is oneself and those things one might be tempted to do despite all one believes and feels to be right. She had been weak once. Was her new strength real, her regret real, or simply a wrapping that, ripped away, would reveal all the old frailties and imperfections? She held the cream-colored stationery folded between her thumb and forefinger.

Strong winds buffeted the plane, making her body shake. But the plane, like the glinting, sharp blade of a sword, cut through all resistance, cleaving heaven itself as it thrust on toward its goal.

CHAPTER 50

First there were the clouds that fogged the windows, and then, as the plane sank and her stomach lurched, she saw the white coastline of Tel Aviv, the lapis blue waters, the clusters of dark rooftops, and the tiny hint of human beings.

The safety of heaven and then the unpredictability of earth. The transition seemed unbearably abrupt. People began to clap and sing "Jerusalem of Gold" and other cloying little tunes that had never appealed to her before. Yet now they brought tears to her eyes. Home.

She did not push her way out of the plane as the others did. She waited until the aisles were almost empty, then walked down slowly. The light of day seemed almost tangible. The sun was so much closer than in New York! It was close, intrusive, a hand on her chest, a soft palm on her cheek. Home. She wanted to weep.

She showed her passport and waited for her luggage. She had no idea where to go. Her father's? How could she, with Chaya Leah feeling about her the way she did? Judah? The thought filled her with horror and longing. No. He had sent her this divorce notice. She could not just move in on him. Dvorah? She thought about it. She had not heard anything from her eldest sister. Perhaps . . . ?

She went to the phone booth and dialed, dropping in all her phone tokens, hoping they would be enough.

"Dvorah?"

"Dina?"

Dvorah's familiar voice, the voice of nighttime confidences, whispered plans, encouragement, friendship. She felt a fist grab the back of her throat as she pressed back the tears.

"I'm at the airport. Can I come to you?"

"Dina! How could you . . . ?" Her voice was cold with fury, strange, unfamiliar.

"Please, Dvorah. I'm asking a *chesed!* Please, take me in for a little while. I have no place else to go."

"It's a disgrace. My neighbors . . . my husband . . . How could you put me into this position?"

"Dvorah, just for a little while. I'm begging you."

"It's not my decision to make," she began to hedge in a prissy way that sickened her sister. "I have to ask my husband. He'll be home around six."

"But what will I do until then? Where will I go?"

"You should have thought of that, shouldn't you?" Dvorah said cruelly.

She had held it in and held it in, all the pain, the uncertainty, the humiliation, the regret. Now her heart was finally going to break, Dina thought. "Dvorah, we're sisters. Please." Her voice was thick with humiliation, degraded yet somehow refusing to give up hope, to slink away quietly. She didn't understand herself why she was prolonging her agony, why she didn't just hang up in anger or shame or simple acceptance.

"You've ruined me, destroyed our good name. I have to be ashamed to walk down the street. You should see how they whisper!"

"What good is all your piety, your keeping all the laws, if you can treat your own sister so cruelly!" Dina shouted, her heart breaking, not so much with shame as disappointment. "You've learned nothing from the Torah, nothing from our parents, if you're capable of turning your back on me! I won't let you become one of them! One of those vile hypocrites that pretend piety, pretend goodness, and are nothing but dirt, dirt—black and common all the way through! I won't let you do that to *Ima*'s name! It's worse than anything I've done, do you hear, Dvorah! A million times worse!"

There was a moment's silence, and then the voice on the other end, surprised and heavy with emotion, shouted back, "Dina . . . come. Come now." And then the phone tokens ran out and the phone, knowing no compassion, having no curiosity, went dead.

She felt it the moment she stepped out of the taxi. The eyes, everywhere. They peered without mercy from behind gently pulled-back curtains; looked with insolent boldness from the faces of little girls; with sly, cruel enjoyment from young women who whispered behind outstretched fingers. But worst were the matrons who stood near the stoops: solid, unforgiving, ignorant. They stared with spiteful, unrelenting judgment, stares like cold knives, like rocks flung from a high tower.

She looked back at them, friends, acquaintances, suddenly turned malevolent strangers. She walked into the building, her head held high, her heart beating rapidly. Home. Or was it? Could it ever be, again? Then she went in to face her sister.

She knocked apprehensively, wondering where all the determination that had forced this meeting had now fled. She felt dry and empty, like a piece of yellowing newspaper, ready to crumple and disintegrate at the first harsh breath of wind.

The door opened widely. Her sister was standing there, trembling, her eyes red. She was holding a tiny infant in her arms and her stomach was already swollen with the next soul G-d intended to entrust to her care. On both sides of her, small children grappled with her skirt, using it to shyly hide their eyes.

"It's your auntie Dina, children," Dvorah said softly. "Go, Shlomie, Malka, kiss her, welcome her." The children dropped their mother's skirt uncertainly, taking tiny, hesitant steps forward toward the pretty, sad young woman they dimly remembered. Dina crouched down, holding her arms out to them, and they politely allowed themselves to have their small, tender cheeks crushed against her smooth, wet one, their little backs and waists encircled and hugged.

"She's crying, *Ima*," the little girl said curiously, surprised, smoothing away the wetness from her own cheeks.

"Mustn't. Mustn't say that!" the little boy reprimanded her in a loud whisper.

Dina looked up at Dvorah. Her elder sister held out the baby. "This is Nechama. Here, hold her."

Dina took the incredibly soft, delicate bundle, the weight agonizingly familiar on her arms, the feel of the baby skin almost killing her with longing. Yossele, Yossele. Little baby. Little boy.

"Here, you'll drown her. Give her back to me. She's wet enough!" Dvorah said, a glint of humor in her tear-filled eyes.

"That's because you're such a bad mother. You have no experience changing diapers." Dina smiled, embracing her sister and the baby, not moving, not speaking, for a long time. She felt her body tremble with love and despair;

then, quieted by Dvorah's responding warmth, the sisterly pats of love and acceptance, she felt calmer.

"It's all right. It's all right. You're home now."

"Am I? Can I ever be? You were right. The way they look at me. Everyone knows!" Her hands flew to her cheeks, which had gone from paleness to flaming rose in seconds as the truth dawned on her. All those months in New York where no one even knew his neighbor's name had made her forget what life was like in Meah Shearim.

"Of course. It's just the thing people love to discuss. But don't talk anymore. You look so tired. Come, sit down, eat."

The echoes flooded the room. It was their mother's voice, their mother's words. Dina looked at her sister. Her mother had had eight children, one after the other. This is what she must have looked like, been like, along the way. She was overworked, exhausted. Yet there was steel in her, as there had been in their mother, a strength born of acceptance and deep faith. But their mother had not had the disgrace of a close family member to deal with, to add to her burdens. What right had she to ask Dvorah for anything? She, who had done nothing to help but had only added an extra burden to her heavy load?

"I shouldn't have come to you. You have enough to do. I'm so ashamed, I could die!"

"No, Dina. I'm the one. I'm ashamed. What you said was true. I didn't want to take you in. It was easier for me to be on their side, to make believe you were a stranger. No, worse. I think I would have taken in a stranger who begged me for compassion. But you, my own sister. I hated you! Can you forgive me for that? What good is all my piety, all my struggling to lead a good life, if it's made me someone who could do a thing like that to her own sister?" She sat down. Her shoulders slumped, defeated.

"I want you to know, whatever they say, I didn't . . .

that is . . . I . . . am innocent of adultery. Innocent of that, at least. I did some foolish things, horribly wrong things, but I never—"

"Thank G-d!" Dvorah said, shuddering with relief. "For your sake! You have no idea what a wonderful man Judah is! Do you realize how much he loves you?"

Dina's eyes shot up and riveted themselves to her sister's face. "Still?"

"Listen, Dina. You've put him through hell. But he's a saint, nothing less. He comes here often. He brings Yossele to play with my children. He's constantly making toys and putting up bookshelves, and banging together closets and beds. . . . He is a man with a heart very nearly broken. But it's such a big heart! He's very, very angry. But I think partly it's at himself, too. He blames himself. He feels somehow that he never deserved you and so letting you go would be the right thing to do. This is just my guess. I suppose when he filed for divorce he came to some final decision."

Dina's face fell.

"But there's something else you should know. He's under tremendous pressure from Kurzman and his group to divorce you. They are at him day and night. Yet, if you ask me, he still loves you. It used to make me pity him how much! But he's lost all hope of your wanting him. Do you? Or perhaps you want it also, the divorce. . . ." She looked at Dina questioningly.

"No! I don't want that! But what can I do to stop it? I'm too ashamed to even face Judah after what I've done, afraid he won't even want to talk to me . . . that his eyes will be like those women standing there out in the street. I couldn't stand that. Not from Judah. I'd rather die than have him look at me that way!"

"Just talk to him. Tell him what you've told me, about the other . . ." She stopped, delicately. It was too awful to even talk about! And yet, sometimes, in the dark of the night, weary with breastfeeding, with folding endless diapers, lonely in the quiet dawn in front of the dark window . . . What if there had been someone who had looked back at her with equal longing? Someone who promised an attractive diversion, who'd made her feel like a desirable, spoiled girl again? Was it so hard to imagine the secret meetings, the delicious long talks . . . Was she really so different from her sister? Her eyes softened. "Dina, talk to him."

"I know, I must," she answered, twisting the fabric of her skirt. "To him, to *Aba*, to Chaya Leah . . . It's just . . . it's so hard. . . ."

"They have to forgive you, as I have."

"Have you?" Dina probed her sister's face for hints of the truth, reassurances.

"Dina, you're my *sister!* Bad luck!" She smiled ruefully.

"No, bad education." Dina smiled back. "Rebbetzin Morganbesser didn't do her job properly. I might tell her one day. . . ."

"And give her a heart attack. . . ." They giggled, then hugged each other gladly, forgetfully.

"What should I do next?"

"Go to *Aba* next. He hasn't been well." Dvorah made an effort not to sound judgmental.

"That's also my fault! I feel like I'm trying to dig a ditch and with each shovelful the earth keeps falling in on me again."

"It isn't so. You and I have spoken, right? We are all right again, aren't we?" She wiped her younger sister's face with the edge of a diaper she pulled off her shoulder.

"It smells like sour milk and vomit." Dina smiled.

"Be glad it's nothing worse, *fineshmecker*."

"Believe me, that's the wrong word to use. Do you know what I did in America? I cleaned toilets. I washed floors on my hands and knees."

"You were a maid? Why did you do that? How horrible!"

"I didn't. It was Reb Kurzman. The Morals Patrol. They arranged it all. They forced me to leave. . . ."

"You mean, it wasn't you who ran away? But we all thought . . . we thought . . . it was the man you were going to in New York."

Dina stared for a moment, the full significance of the idea exploding on her consciousness. "You mean Reb Kurzman didn't tell Judah it was he who arranged for me to leave? He didn't explain? He let everyone think that Noach and I . . . Oh, the miserable, rotten mamzer! . . ."

"*Ben Zonah!*" Dvorah joined in, shocked at her use of such unclean language, yet feeling no other words would do.

"Then all this time, that's what everyone's been thinking of me! It's so unfair!" she wept bitterly. Then she looked up, her eyes suddenly, strangely dry and clear. "It's evil, really, there's no other word for it. And to do such a thing in the name of G-d! It's a profanation. And all this time I thought they were the zealous ones, the ones so pure in motive, that I was less than they. It's all a show. They are ugly, base . . ." She could find no words, the shock of disillusion was too great. Clouds of dust as if from a tremendous explosion seemed to obscure her thoughts, her ability to reason. Only her feelings were clear: utter betrayal and the ultimate disillusion. "I must tell *Aba*, Judah." Her face was white.

"Soon. But now you must do only one thing: go to sleep. Come, there's a bed in the enclosed porch. It will be quiet there. Rest. Later I'll go with you. You won't be alone. I'll help you."

"Dvorah, I'm so sorry. And you're so good. . . ." She was babbling in total exhaustion. Then her head hit the pillow and the dense white confusion began to clear and lift. The sheets were cool and clean. The hand that tucked her in was a kind woman's hand. Her mother's hand, smoothing her brow, comforting her. There was still compassion. There was still affection and kindness. Home.

CHAPTER 51

To Dina's surprise, it was dark when she opened her eyes. At first she didn't know exactly where she was. A small, strangled cry of alarm rose in her throat. And then she heard the voices: Dvorah and her husband, Yaakov. They were talking softly in the living room. She lay back, almost scared to listen.

"Of course, you did the right thing, Dvorah dear. It's a great mitzvah. She's your sister. After all, the Torah tells us to judge every man leniently. Still, what you tell me about Reb Kurzman . . . he's a man so respected. I find it hard to believe . . ."

"Believe!" Dvorah responded harshly.

"This is upsetting you, dearest. And in your condition . . ."

"Oh, my permanent condition! I'm always going to be in this condition! Forever! So let's not talk about it anymore. I simply need your help."

"But what can I do?"

"I want you to go with me and my sister. To stand by our side." She was terrified to ask. Because even a tiny pause, the slightest hesitation in his response, would diminish him forever in her eyes, a man she had come to love and respect so deeply through time. Her own hesitation, her own initial anger at Dina, was forgotten. As every woman who ever loved a man, Dvorah wanted Yaakov to react the way she should have reacted. To be herself recreated flawlessly. She almost held her breath, waiting.

"Of course, dear."

And now, perversely, having gotten exactly what she wanted, Dvorah hedged. "It won't hurt your standing in the yeshiva? It won't cause them to talk behind your back?"

"What an idea!" He seemed genuinely shocked at such a suggestion. "Who do I know that indulges in gossip? Why, gossip is as great a sin as murder, our sages say. As for my honor, let a man honor G-d in his actions, and honor from his fellow men will surely follow. Please, darling. You've had a hard day. You are tired. I'll clean up. Just go to bed, will you?"

In the darkness of her little alcove, Dina felt the world of her childhood, of order and kindness and true piety, flood over her again. She closed her eyes to a dreamless, restful sleep.

She awoke refreshed to the morning light, gold-tinted with coppery orange streaming through the curtains. She pulled back the curtains and saw the quiet streets fill with men in their dark suits and white prayer shawls walking home from morning prayers; the Hasidim holding towels emerging cleansed and uplifted from their morning immersion in the mikveh. The trees moved gently in an easterly breeze that seemed to bring with it the smell of cakes and kugels baking in honor of the coming Sabbath, of laundry —men's white shirts and children's festive Sabbath dresses —flapping dry on outside lines. The houses were poor, full of patched-up asbestos and tin add-ons; cramped. But there was such a sense of order, of care, of gratefulness for every crumb of material blessing. Whatever one had was appreciated, recognized, enjoyed. This too was home.

She padded into the kitchen to wash her fingertips from the uncleanness of sleep, then recited her morning prayers, something she had not been able to do for a long time. Dvorah was still sleeping, as were the children. It was barely five o'clock in the morning. But Yaakov was up, getting ready to go to the synagogue and then the yeshiva. He had an open book in front of him and was studying.

"Welcome, Dina," he said kindly.

She nodded, feeling awkward and somehow stained in his presence. She had hurt him so much, his standing in the community, even his chances for receiving a really prestigious teaching post in one of the best yeshivas. Still, there was no anger, no recriminations. How could their small world produce men like Yaakov and men like Kurzman? The same Torah, the same strict adherence to law, and yet the results were so utterly opposite! Like the patriarch Isaac having twin sons: one Yaakov and one Esau. What did it mean? How could you make sense of such a world?

"Thank you so much for letting me stay."

"Please, Dina. I should thank you. You've given me the opportunity to do a good deed, no?" His eyes were merry.

"But I've hurt you. I'm sorry . . ." Her eyes fell in misery.

" 'The level on which a true penitent stands, not even saints can hope to reach,' " he quoted. "Please, I'm not the western wall, you don't have to weep to me. I'm just a simple human being, struggling every day. G-d will judge me by my sins, my good deeds. Only His good opinion matters. You should feel the same."

"But still, I ask your *mechila*, your forgiveness, for anything I may have done to hurt you."

"And I give it with all of my heart and wish you well," he said, trying and failing to button the last few buttons on his suit jacket. As usual, it was hopeless.

But Dina didn't see that. Somehow he looked wonderful to her. She couldn't imagine how they had ever thought otherwise.

When he was gone, she boiled some water and slowly drank a cup of coffee. The house was clean, if not orderly. There was a sense of life flowing through the small, cramped rooms—vivid and rich. She could hear the breathing of the small children, her sister's contented deep sighs.

It was hard. It was exhausting, her sister's life, her mother's life. But the struggle brought so many rich rewards she had never fully understood or appreciated before, having never had any basis for comparison. It brought the sense of fullness that comes in having many children and watching them grow, healthy and uncomplicated, rooted deeply in the same rich soil that had nourished thousands of generations before; the sense of a deep, satisfying relationship with G-d; the sense of loyal, close connection with a life partner who was flesh of your flesh, bone of your bone. It brought the feeling of basking in so much love, pouring down on you like sunlight as you grew rooted in your safe, protected niche in the walled garden, warmed by caring family, kind friends.

But what happened once you were ripped out of that spot, your roots torn, replanted hastily in a pot that had known burning sunlight and full shade, cold and sickening heat? Once you had seen the ugly flea beetles, the aphids, the snails and slugs, that lived all around you, laying secretly their ugly yellow eggs, spreading botrytis, viruses, fungus?

It was so complicated. It made her head ache, her heart sink. Perhaps one had to be very, very intelligent and clever to live a satisfying life. Perhaps she was just too stupid to figure it out as so many others she knew had. Or perhaps it was just a gift bestowed by good angels at birth, a second sense that told you just which roads to choose, how to navigate all the dangers successfully. That thought surprised her. It was so lazy and fatalistic. Good angels, good fairies. It would be so easy if one could only blame one's shortcomings on that.

She dreaded going to see her father. Talking to Chaya Leah. Even the idea of just being in the street in her old neighborhood filled her with a sickening anxiety. All those eyes, multiplied. All those young women she had grown up with, and their mothers, who had been her own mother's friends. It was not only a dread of ostracism and abuse, but also a dread of seeing so many people she had always liked and admired suddenly embrace falsehood over truth, filthy rumors over fair judgment. She felt as if she were an unwilling possessor of a magic lens that stripped the fresh veneer off everything, revealing the old, rotting wood beneath.

She was afraid, afraid. Of so many things.

Can I really do it? she wondered seriously. But what was the alternative? To go back to New York? To Noach? Her chest contracted in panic. Or just to disappear somewhere, far away. To live unconnected, uncaring, unnourished.

Was there an alternative she hadn't thought of?

A low knock on the door startled her out of her painful thoughts. She was inexplicably afraid to answer it, yet Dvorah was still sleeping, it wasn't fair to wake her.

"Yes?"

"It's me."

Her heart jumped, banging like an enemy against her ribs.

"*Aba?*" She opened the door and there he was, older,

shockingly grayer, but with the same serenity, the same kindness. As his eyes reached hers, she felt the somberness lift from his sagging old cheeks.

He had no right to be so forgiving, so understanding! It made it all so much worse! She backed away, looking at the floors, her eyes focusing on a simple, homemade baby toy, old socks filled and sewn together to make a caterpillar. She picked it up and held it against her breast, resting her lips against it, trying not to cry. So many tears. No, she didn't want to wring sympathy from him this way! She wanted him to hear her out, to judge, as G-d would no doubt judge. She wanted his absolution based on justice, not mercy.

"Can't you even look at me? I know I have failed you, but still, there must be some forgiveness in your heart still for your old, foolish father?"

She couldn't believe her ears! She forgive him?

"*Aba*, I . . ." She couldn't speak. *No!* she shouted to herself, *I don't want this!* But she couldn't stop crying. She cried and cried and cried like an infant who has no sense that love is in the world, that a warm breast is on its way, that a dry clean diaper and soothing cream exist. It was a hopeless, desperate crying. She felt his hand on her head, smoothing back her hair. Again and again, a wordless touch of comfort, of acceptance. "Sha, sha," she heard him whisper. He lifted her chin. He dabbed her flooded face with a clean handkerchief. His aging fingers, surprisingly agile, patted her cheek as if she were six and had just fallen off the swings. "Sha, enough."

And it was enough. All the tears were gone, used up, or simply irrelevant. "Come, child. Sit with me."

"*Aba*. I was planning to come to you. You haven't been well. Why did you have to trouble yourself? To travel, to walk up so many steps? . . ."

"I thought it would be easier this way. Besides, I couldn't wait to see you."

She hesitated. "You don't . . . hate me, *Aba*, do you?"

He didn't answer her, just smoothed her flaming cheek. "You have your mother's face. Exactly that. I miss her. I've missed you."

"I have to explain to you what happened. I don't know if you can ever understand. I myself . . . don't . . . really . . ."

"You don't need to come up with excuses!" he cut her off. "You're my daughter. You've come back. It's enough."

"*Aba*, it's not enough! I want you to understand the truth. To understand and to forgive. But first you must know the truth, otherwise it's not a real forgiveness. There wouldn't be any strength . . . any real meaning in it."

His eyes rested on hers. He nodded with sad agreement.

"About a year after I was married to Judah, another man began to . . . He was a neighbor, a married man. And he . . . he began to come to the wool shop. . . ."

"*Ima*'s store?"

She heard the pain in his voice, which stabbed her soul like a sharp, pointed sliver of broken glass. She nodded miserably. "I don't know how, or why, but I started to talk to him. Then I found I . . . wanted to be with him."

"But why did you need this other man? Why did you . . . ?" He was trying to understand, flailing hopelessly against his dark incomprehension, finally realizing it was too vast to ever overcome.

She shook her head gently, resting her forehead on her palm, afraid to raise her eyes. "*Ima* had just died. My heart was empty," she said with a brave effort, then faltered, her voice failing.

"And wasn't your husband enough to fill it?"

She shrugged. "*Aba*, who can understand what fills the emptiness in a person's heart? I don't know why Judah couldn't at that time, why I needed Noach. I can't explain it. . . ."

His mind wandered: *Let her go where her heart is.*

"But I never . . ." she tried to continue, and the growing agitation in her voice brought him back to the present with a jolt of pity.

How could she go on? To talk to her father, to *Aba*, about such intimate things! The words rose and backed up in her throat, choking her. "*Aba*, I never . . . I . . . transgressed the laws of *yichud* and *negiah*. Yes, I was alone with him and we touched . . . but nothing else, may *Hashem* forgive me. And I didn't run away—not to him, not to anyone. I didn't want to leave my husband and child, you and the rest of the family. Reb Kurzman and the others . . . the . . . Morals Patrol . . . they made me go . . . they arranged everything. They told me I had no choice. . . . They sent me to America to be a maid. The people I worked for were wonderful people, but they did not keep the law. They worked on the Sabbath. They had only one set of dishes. . . . But I was careful. I didn't work. . . . I ate only kosher food. . . . *Aba*, I got sick there. . . ." She felt it all rushing out, becoming incoherent. She stopped a moment to collect her thoughts. Only then did she notice the drastic change that had taken place in her father's face. He was utterly devastated.

"You mean they made you go, without telling anyone?" How could such a thing be? Such a transgression, such a violation? "And these men, this Morals Patrol, they are Jews?"

"*Aba*, of course they're Jews. They live right here, among us, right here in Jerusalem."

"Among us, here, in Jerusalem?" He shook his head in wonder and consternation and disbelief. "But they are not G-d-fearing, surely. They are *chilonim* or—"

"No, *Aba*. They are all *haredim*, just like us. They all have beards and wear dark suits. Like Noach."

"But why? Why would they separate a woman from her husband, her child, her family?"

"They thought I was an adulteress," she said, wondering when she would be struck by lightning for uttering such a word in her father's presence.

A deep shock settled into his eyes, the look that happily married people get when suddenly widowed; that parents get when they bury a child.

"But it wasn't true. I never did. You have to believe me!"

"But they had no proof! Two witnesses they needed before acting on such an accusation. Two. . . ." He shook his head in disbelief. "That is the *halacha!*"

She sat down urgently at his feet, holding his hands in hers. "*Aba*, I was wrong. I began a relationship with a man who wasn't my husband. I deceived Judah. But I'm innocent of anything worse. I wish there was a holy Temple, that I could drink the bitter waters in front of the whole town and they'd see I'm innocent."

"A *sotah*." He looked at her, stricken, his hands resting helplessly in his lap.

"But I've been through the ordeal, the public shame."

"And the *sotah* who is proven innocent, she is left alone. She goes back to her husband, her children. Will you go back to Judah?"

"If he'll have me. I don't know." She took a deep breath. "*Aba*, can you forgive?"

He hesitated.

She froze.

"How can I forgive?" He shook his head sorrowfully. "I would like to. I should. But how can I? It's too terrible. Too terrible."

The sharp sliver in her soul grew into a stake, embedding itself deeper and deeper. She felt the excruciating pain of her speared heart splitting. It was unendurable. "Please, I beg you!"

"But, child, how can I? Kurzman, those others who forced you to leave, who told us nothing. Worse, who let us believe the worst. How can I ever forgive them?"

She covered her face with both hands and laughed

into them, a hysterical laughter that was nevertheless not without some joy. Then she embraced him, hiding her eyes, her mouth, in his dark, warm coat.

"*Aba*, then you do forgive me?"

"Forgive you . . . you?! My dear child. . . . Do you have to ask . . . do you . . ." His veined palm brushed warmly against her cheek.

The stake melted like ice, leaving no scar.

"*Aba*, there's something else. It's Chaya Leah. She's so unhappy and she's afraid to talk to you about it. She doesn't want to hurt you. But, *Aba*, her heart is also empty. . . ."

Let her go where her heart is.

He stared at his daughter, his little Dina, his good child, and saw the face of his dear wife peering out at him with accusation. A flash of guilt forked lightning bright into the darkness of his incomprehension, bringing sudden, brief illumination. He shuddered. And then he understood why G-d, with true justice and not without mercy, had brought all this suffering upon him.

CHAPTER 52

Reb Garfinkel wasn't particularly happy to see Rabbi Reich standing on his doorstep immediately following a heavy lunch of gefilte fish, horseradish, boiled chicken, and borscht. Any reminder of a bad match, especially one doomed to end in a scandalous divorce, was disastrous for his delicate digestive system. Rightly or wrongly, such matters always pointed an accusing finger at the *shadchen*, as if he were somehow supposed to magically detect that beneath the demure, pious exteriors of these little brides beat the heart of a passionate wanton! But go try to sell that reasonable idea to the public! Ignorance, pure ignorance.

Still, Reich was not the type to complain. In fact, he recalled vaguely, there was another unmarried daughter—big, heavy, a good worker with a yarn store in a wonderful location near the *shuk*. He wiped the chicken grease off his lips and belched with satisfaction, ushering the good rabbi in with as much grace as he could muster.

"My dear Reb Chaim," Rabbi Reich began cordially.

"My dear Rabbi Reich," the other man answered with a suspicious smile.

There was a pause.

"A drink, perhaps, Rabbi?" the *shadchen* offered, safe in the knowledge that such courtesies were never accepted. To his surprise, Rabbi Reich nodded. In fact, to his amazement, no sooner did the rabbi swallow one plastic cup of schnapps than he poured himself another. Only then did Rabbi Reich begin to speak.

"My dear Reb Chaim, as you know, my good wife has passed on to her reward, and so it is now my responsibility to care for my children. I have, thank G-d, three beautiful daughters, may they live long! Two are married, as you know, you were the *shadchen*."

Garfinkel tensed. Was there a tone of accusation there? Undecided, he said nothing.

"Wonderful marriages. Two fine sons-in-law I have, thanks to you."

The *shadchen* allowed himself another small release of gas, mellowing. Boiled chicken, he comforted himself, was after all very easy to digest.

"So of course, who should I come to now that my Chaya Leah is ready to be married?"

Garfinkel took out a toothpick and began to mine his molars meditatively. A smile of pleasure spread across his face as he opened his little book and began to flip the pages.

"Let's see . . . there. Ah. Just the one. A family of rabbis. A fine, upstanding young scholar. So, a small limp, I see. But not in the family; a little accident. . . ." He looked at Rabbi Reich hopefully. "So, we start with someone else. Here, in Bnai Brak. Just in from Crown Heights. American income, a job in his father's travel agency, a serious part-time learner . . ." He looked up. Rabbi Reich looked uncomfortable.

"My dear Reb Chaim," Rabbi Reich began. "These sound like wonderful boys. I know that they will find their happiness through you and your blessed efforts. But . . . I have something else in mind."

"Something else?" What else? Garfinkel considered guiltily. A cripple and a yeshiva dropout. Maybe he was insulted. "I'm sorry. I don't know. I wasn't thinking. Of course, here"—he riffled rapidly through the incomprehensible handwritten pages—"here. I don't know where my wits were. Here, the perfect one. A *kollel* boy, a cohen with a father who owns a plumbing supply store. Maybe you could expand the yarn store, open up a section for plastic pipes. . . ." He looked at Rabbi Reich and began to sweat. Still, that uncomfortable look of dissatisfaction. He was growing annoyed. His stomach rumbled.

"Well, I must be honest with you. I have an idea of my own."

"I'm here to listen," Garfinkel said with forced amiability.

"Well, there is this boy I know. A fine learner. His father owns a fish store in Meah Shearim."

"What's the name?"

"Minskoff's Kosher Fish and Poultry."

A new light dawned in the *shadchen*'s shrewd eyes.

"Minskoff is a Belzer Hasid. And his son Moishe is in the army."

"Well, Hasidim are also Jews, pious Jews. And the country needs an army to defend us from the *goyim*," Rabbi Reich said mildly.

Garfinkel smiled amiably. "I don't deal with Hasidim. They have their own *shadchonim*. But, back to my list . . ."

"Yes, I know. But this is a special case. You see, I think this is what would be good for my daughter. My wife, before she died, she asked me about this boy. She wanted the match."

Garfinkel's hand slammed down on the table. "*He's a Hasid and he's in the army!* It's out of the question. I can't be involved in such a thing. It would ruin my reputation. Besides, the match seems to have been made by other means already." He stood up abruptly.

"Please, please, Reb Garfinkel. Sit a minute." He sighed. "It has been a terrible year. My wife, my dear wife, may she rest in peace, I lost her. A young woman. And so many small children still to raise. You understand? The responsibility. Now, all on me. I never knew . . . she worked so hard."

There was silence. Garfinkel sank back down onto his chair.

"Then all this business with Dina. You must have heard? . . . Ah, yes. Hard, very hard. But I want you to know she is a good girl. She is back home. And, G-d willing, soon back with her husband, a wonderful man. . . ."

No divorce, then. Garfinkel felt his anger ease. That was worth a lot.

"Still, I appreciate your problems. I know what it is to try to find a match for a girl whose family has been talked about. It's very, very hard." Garfinkel nodded, grateful for the sympathy and understanding, commodities in short supply among his customers. "This boy, Moishe, is a good boy. He will make a good husband for my daughter. Besides, it was my wife's dying wish that they be married."

"But a Belzer *Hasid* . . ." Garfinkel protested weakly. What could you say against a wife's dying wish?

"I want to tell you something, a thing I just found out recently. There are among us, Jews, in Jerusalem, who dress like *Bnai Torah*, have beards like *Bnai Torah*, but are simply Esau in Jacob's clothing. Hasid, Misnagid. Just words. If they keep the Torah and raise the children to be good Jews, can we ask for anything more? Besides, Reb Chaim, who can understand what fills the emptiness in a person's heart?"

Garfinkel looked at his fingertips, which needed clipping badly, and sighed. "Your wife's dying wish," he muttered. "What else can I say?"

"And please consider, my dear, good Reb Chaim. This will be an easy match, with no negotiations. Yet the fee, the fee will remain the same. I wouldn't dream of anything else."

Garfinkel's tragic face broke into that rarest of expressions, something he had experienced maybe twice or three times in his life: glee sanctioned not only by profit, but also by a mitzvah. "My dear Rabbi Reich, may you live to see many grandchildren, and may they all decide to be Misnagdim!"

"Amen."

CHAPTER 53

"You don't have much time. You're due in court this afternoon for the divorce hearings. Let Yaakov and me go with you to Judah. Let us help you expl—"

"No!" Dina cut her off. Then, contritely: "Thank you. But I have to do it myself. Just me and Judah, together. It's the only way I've ever envisioned it in my dreams and nightmares. So many times, just that way. It can't be any other way, don't you see?"

Dvorah nodded slowly, with inexpressible sorrow. Dina still looked as she had as a child, too soft and breakable to withstand deliberate unkindness. How many times had she accepted blame simply to bring peace? To avoid even confronting her accusers or putting the true culprits in a bad light? Would she be able to do it now? "Tell him the truth, no matter how much it hurts. He has a right to know."

"It is what I plan . . . I want to . . . I . . . have to. . . ." She sighed, as if already at the end of one of those long, exhausting days of housework that come just before Passover. Days spent cleaning up a whole year's dirt in neglected dark crevices, closets, and drawers, knowing that no matter how hard you work, you'll never get it all.

How could she ever make it all come clean and right again with Judah? It seemed impossible. There were too many dark corners to lighten, too many foul stains that had been left untreated too long. . . . And so she had reduced her hopes to something more feasible. All she wanted, all she could think about, was seeing the baby. That and perhaps some kind of postponement of the inevitable. Despite everything that Dvorah had told her, she still felt Judah probably hated her. She was ashamed to look him in the face. After all, only she knew how badly she had treated him and how little he had deserved it. Her heart felt cold.

"Take a coat with you," Dvorah fussed for lack of anything better to do. "It's cold, although it might warm up if the clouds clear and the sun comes out."

"I'll only take a sweater, then. I want to be ready when the clouds clear and the sun comes out," she said with a sad smile.

Outside, the eyes were there again, singeing her with the heat of their condemnation. Or were they? she suddenly wondered. Perhaps it was not the eyes of others at all, but some inner eye, the eye of her younger self, that stared with such unflagging condemnation. She felt exposed, indecent.

She almost ran to the bus stop.

She stood there, trembling, when two men in black approached her. At first she thought they were simply going to ask directions, but then she noticed the narrowed, intensely hostile eyes. And, of course, she remembered, such men would never ask a strange woman anything, even the time of day.

"Dina Gutman?"

Without knowing why, her heart began to pound. "Yes?"

"Rabbi Kurzman wants you to know you've made a serious mistake coming back from America. His patience is not as everlasting as the Almighty's. If you go straight to the Beit Din this afternoon and finish with the divorce, no harm will come to you. But if you try to talk to your husband, to talk him out of it . . . we pity you."

Why aren't I more afraid? she wondered. "Why shouldn't I try to talk to my husband?" she said boldly, amazing herself.

They seemed flustered. "Because men are vulnerable. We cannot allow you to take advantage of his weakness. Our law forbids it."

Her skin prickled. "And if I . . . I don't listen to you?"

"That would be disastrous. Most of all for your husband. He makes holy objects. We will see he never sells another one. He will be ostracized. Thrown out of the community."

She stared at them, looking beyond their clothes and beards, the showily long *payess* that grazed their shoulders, until she could actually envision the petty smallness of their minds and the enormity of their egos. Her fear was gone.

Then she looked down at the ground modestly and, before they could figure out what she was doing, deftly maneuvered her way back into the thickest part of a crowd of religious women who stood nearby. The men stood watching her, helpless, frustrated. There was no way they could pursue her decently without breaking all their own rules. Before they could decide on their next step, she quickly hailed a cab, jumped in, and locked the door.

"Where to?"

She hesitated. Then, summoning up all the courage and faith she possessed, she answered: "The Street of Carpenters."

She got out just in front of the shop. Standing silently at the threshold, she studied Judah's dark head bent in total concentration over his work. His face was thinner, older than she'd remembered it, the dark thick waves of hair casting shadows on the hollows of his cheeks. A strange tenderness awoke in her. She wanted to smooth away the lines of concentration on his forehead, to make it carefree and young again.

She wanted to twine her fingers through his.

She waited patiently for a lull in the noise of the machine, then took one small step over the threshold.

"Hello, Judah."

He looked at her intently, then lowered his eyes, turning his back and walking deliberately to the other side of the shop. He took the newly formed wood and sanded it, stopping every few minutes to rub his hand over the surface to test its smoothness. With maddening slowness, he took out a can of varnish, pried open the lid, and dipped in a paintbrush.

Her whole body began to burn slowly with shame and rejection. *Well, what did you expect? For him to throw out his arms and welcome you back?* a small voice inside her jeered. But this coldness, this . . . indifference. He was a stranger. She stared at him dully, despairing, not knowing where to begin. "Judah, will you at least listen to me? Let me explain? . . ."

Judah put down the brush and sank heavily onto an old stool. "So you've come back, then, have you? All these months, not a word . . . and now you want to tell the big fool some more stories?" She had never seen him angry before. His fury was palpable.

A sharp pain cleaved her heart. "Judah, please . . . let me just speak to you. I know I don't deserve it, that you can throw me out, and you'd be right. But at least let me try to beg your forgiveness. I want so much to come home."

"Home?" His tone was dull, expressionless. "You came because of the letter . . . from the court?"

"No. I came because this is my home, my life. Because I never wanted to leave. It was never my idea."

"You ran away! You left me, you left your own child!"

"No!" she shouted. "No, Judah, as G-d is my witness, I was forced to leave! Rabbi Kurzman and the others . . . they arranged everything. . . . They told me I had no choice because of what I'd . . . what they said I'd . . . But I never did. Judah! Please, you have to believe me!"

His face registered total confusion.

"I know I've lied to you in the past. I went behind your back. I want to tell you the whole truth now." This was so hard! She wanted to stop and run away. It was the hardest, hardest thing she had ever had to do. The truth was so ugly, so hurtful, and he was so angry and hurt to begin with. She felt her throat knot, her eyes drown. She wasn't going to cry. No! She didn't want to manipulate him.

He looked at her, his face frozen.

Where should I begin? she wondered suddenly. With Noach? Her mother's death? Or long, long before when she was a frightened little girl docilely accepting blame, locking her trunk of passions, burying her needs?

"Judah, all my life I've been treated like a good little girl. All my life I've acted like one. I was a good student, which meant I accepted passively everything that my teachers, my parents, taught me. I buried my questions, buried my doubts. I wanted to do what was expected of me. But so many times I found that the world was not the place that I'd been taught it should be. And each time it happened, there was this other whole person inside of me that kept shouting at me that I'd been tricked, that kept getting angrier and angrier."

He took up the wood and began the slow process of burning a design into it. She watched as the fire of the soldering iron seared the surface of the wood, her own face burning with shame. "I didn't want to listen. I wanted the other voice to go away. It frightened me. I kept trying to smother it, to kill it. But I couldn't. It was so angry, all the time! Angry that money seemed to decide even who we could marry, even though all the people around us mouthed pieties about how only character, only spirit, had value. It was angry that the university was a closed door, that the army was a closed door. And when my mother died, I stopped fighting the voice. I too became angry.

"I was angry at the hard white ground for yielding so easily to accept my mother's body so long before her time; at G-d for putting her there; at you . . ."

He looked up at her, pain, confusion, fury, contorting his features: "Me? You were angry at me? For what?"

"Yes, at you," she repeated, "for not seeing inside my heart, for not chastising me for my doubts, for not comforting me, for not giving me long, long speeches about G-d's justice and compassion, speeches that would make everything come all right again. And most of all, I was angry that all my life every single personal choice seemed to be stolen from me, even the choice of who to marry."

His face was stricken.

How could she have blurted that out? She looked down at Judah's shoes, her sudden burst of courage leaving her. "But that doesn't mean . . . ! I *did* want to marry you, Judah! I really did! There was something about you I felt I could love, something inside that I knew was there, that I hoped you would show me once we were married. There had to be if you could see the loveliness around you and carve it into wood the way you did.

"Except that after we were married, you were so quiet, so terribly, terribly quiet. Not that you weren't good to me.

You were too good. You made things too easy for me. I wasn't used to it. I was used to love meaning criticism, demands. And you asked for so little! I felt guilty and then ashamed. That I wasn't supporting you, that you weren't a *kollel* man, that . . ." She looked down at her hands, her face reddening with shame. No. She would not hide anything or make herself nicer than she'd been. "That . . . that your fingers were stained instead of clean and white. I'm so ashamed to admit that! And I don't feel that way anymore! But then I was young, narrow-minded, and ignorant! I was like everyone else in our world. I couldn't appreciate what you were, your specialness.

"When my mother died, my heart was breaking for someone to talk to. And Noach looked at me through the window, he came to the store, he took me out in the car. And for hours and hours and hours, we simply talked. He kept telling me about so many things that were fun to do —going bathing, seeing movies. And I was so angry, I wanted to punish G-d, to tell him I too could break the contract! I too could change the rules! And you didn't want to hear of it. 'What would I need with fun?' you told me. I was angry you wouldn't be my partner. And Noach . . . well, he was there.

"It was all words at first. Only later . . . did we begin . . . touching. I didn't need that. You were always so kind and loving! I always loved you to touch me, to feel you against me. But he . . . it was the price for his words. And then, he wanted more. He demanded it. That I . . . that I spend the night with him in Tel Aviv. I didn't want to! And then . . . then . . . I thought . . . perhaps . . . I did." She stopped, wiping her eyes. The shop was suddenly filled with the acrid smell of burning as Judah allowed the soldering iron to consume the beautiful wood.

"Judah, no! Please, your beautiful work!"

He placed the soldering iron down carefully on the table. "I knew you couldn't love me when you married me," he said softly, his anger gone. "I'm so big and clumsy and awkward. But I was so in love with you! You were everything beautiful and pure and decent to me. I wanted to spoil you! For you to have everything! I thought, if I tried very, very hard, you might come to love me. I was afraid to intrude, to push my way into your life, to tell you my thoughts, to insist on hearing yours. I'm always being pushed and lectured at, and I hate it! So, I kept waiting, waiting for you to come to me, to show me, to tell me that you were ready to let me in, to tell me what you needed, to listen to my needs. If you had only come to me, told me. I would have given you everything."

"I didn't want to be given anything! I wanted you to talk to me. I wanted words. And most of all, I wanted to choose—my own engagement watch, my own furniture, my own ideas . . ."

He was listening, motionless, soundless. His silence, more frightening and threatening than any screamed obscenities, was unendurable. There was no clue to his reaction. So she plunged back in desperately, swimming on. It was either that or slip again into deep, cold grayness. She had promised Joan not to do that. She had promised herself.

"The sand on the beach was warm and lovely. The men and women seemed so carefree, so young. It made me happy to try something new. I didn't really want to leave the cool water, to go into the hotel room. But I did. I went, willingly. Only when I got there and he got into the bed, I knew it wasn't him I wanted. It was you. Your face, your hands, your body. I knew he was forcing himself on me and somehow that other voice, that wild, rude, passionate one, finally got through to me. I didn't want this! I pushed him away. And Noach, he slapped me. He called me a whore. And I knew that all along I'd been fooling myself; that all along that's what he'd thought of me. And that it was true.

"I ran down to the sand and rested my face against it. I think I was hoping a great wind would come and bury me in it. I was cold and wet and heartbroken. I only wanted to come home to you, to tell you everything, to make you understand. To start again.

"But Kurzman was there at the door. And suddenly everything I'd thought was between me and G-d, me and you, was public! I was so frightened that I did everything he asked, horrible things that made no sense. I even wrote you a letter telling you I'd slept with Noach! Kurzman was so sure, I even thought he might know more about that than I did, too! That somehow it had happened without my knowing about it! It was as if I didn't trust my own mind anymore, as if I had no right to even think. He said if I left immediately, he wouldn't make it public, he wouldn't disgrace you and my family. And I was so grateful to him for his compassion, I almost kissed his feet."

She wiped the sweat from her forehead, remembering giving birth, the wave after wave of horrible pain, and then the astonishing moment when it was all over, and she was so happy. She tried to focus on that, on it being over. "I was a maid for a wealthy family in New York City. I scrubbed toilet bowls and polished silver. The lives around me were so strange, so full of contradictions. Jewish children who yelled at their parents! Jews who desecrated the Sabbath with work, who ate pig and shellfish. And for a while I began to feel a little better, as if what I'd done was not so terrible compared to the lives these people lived.

"But then I got to know them. The woman, Joan, was such a good person! She was kind to me, generous. She was a caring wife, a loving mother. While I had abandoned you all!

"I didn't know what to believe anymore. Nothing was simple, straightforward. Only this: I wanted to be with you, with the baby. I was tortured by it, every single day. I worked and worked and worked, washing floors and windows, dusting, scrubbing. I wanted G-d to finish punishing me so I could go home again. And then, Noach came to see me."

The shadows deepened in the shop. She could just

make out Judah's hands suddenly tightening around the black, ruined wood. "I hadn't known he was in New York. He—" And for the first time since beginning, she felt her throat clamp closed, choking her. "He asked me to be his mistress. And then he slipped a ruby-and-diamond bracelet around my wrist, as if I were some . . . G-d! I wanted to kill him!" Her fist slammed down on the tabletop, and she saw Judah cradle his head in his hands. "I had his blood on my hands. I guess I'd scratched him. Nothing worse. But seeing my hands with blood, it must have . . . something must have . . . My mind . . ." She shrugged. "I started walking home. That doesn't make any sense, does it? Maybe a little part of me was thinking it was silly, that I couldn't actually get home by walking, but then I saw all of you! And I was in my own home, my own bed. I could hear *Ima* working in the kitchen, I could even taste the Sabbath wine. . . . I was so relieved, so happy, I didn't care how I'd gotten there, but only that I was home! And then, suddenly, it all changed. Everyone I loved, you, Judah, my father and mother . . . you all stood around me, pointing and accusing . . . everyone I loved! I felt myself dying. I was dead."

She heard his labored, uneven breathing, as if he were carrying a heavy weight up a steep hill. She stared at the shadows moving across the wall, trying to see in them some reflection of his face. But it was dark and meaningless. "I woke up in a mental ward. The horrible noise, the smells! But then I saw your candlesticks, you know, those little ones you carved me for my birthday? And I felt if I could light just those two little candles, maybe the darkness would start to go away. It was the beginning.

"So many people helped me, strangers. Joan and Dr. Shulman, and Rabbi Eliezer. They convinced me that it's all right to be angry, to be confused, to doubt, to fail. They taught me that there is real compassion, real forgiveness, in the world. They helped me see how much I love you, Judah, you and the baby, my family, G-d, Jerusalem. I found out that to be like Him, to be holy, doesn't mean we all have to be the same. It doesn't mean keeping out the world with high fences, lead screens. It means listening to your mind and heart, not shutting out the voices that question, that seek answers. And it doesn't matter if everyone else around you accepts the answers they're given and are satisfied. I have a right to my own answers." She took a deep breath. "I need you to help me find them. To love me like a woman, to talk to me, to listen to me. To help me go my own way toward G-d again."

All this time she had been looking down at her dress, twisting it into knots. She had no idea of the expression on his face. Was it full of anger still, or horror? Or, worst of all, did it look like the faces of the women on the stoop or the men who followed Kurzman? Just the thought paralyzed her. And then suddenly, she had to know. She ran to Judah and sank down on the floor in front of him, looking up fiercely, helplessly, into his face, his stubbornly averted eyes.

"Judah," she said finally, with desperation, "do whatever you want to me! I deserve it! But before you throw me out of your life, please, please forgive me! I can't change the past. I can only tell you that person, the one who hurt you, doesn't exist anymore." Then, softly, "I've suffered so much. Please, at least don't stop me from seeing the baby. You won't try to take him away from me, will you?"

His eyes looked down on her steadily for what seemed an eternity. "You're his mother. He needs you," he said in a voice hoarse with emotion. Then, softly, so softly she could not be sure it wasn't simply a strange, happy dream: "I need you."

She looked up at him, not daring to believe, taking both his large hands into her small ones, kissing them a hundred times, her tears washing off the honest white dust on his battered, stained fingertips. She felt him smooth back the hair from her forehead, trace the clear line of her flushed cheek, her neck.

He crouched beside her, holding her in his arms. "I didn't do anything right! I could have saved you from all this suffering, if only . . . if only . . ."

"No," she protested, "I didn't really give you a chance, did I? Judah . . . can we try again to make each other happy? I do love you."

He restrained the urge to crush her to him, to smother her in the encompassing warmth of his grateful, forgiving arms. Instead he hugged her gently, so that they remained two separate people, each supporting the other. They sat there in the dusty, dark shop, in the pale shadows of the big machines, clinging to each other like sole survivors of a great natural disaster.

She looked into his deep, forgiving eyes, and then she remembered the narrow, violent eyes of the other men; the superior, contemptuous eyes of the women. The irony of it struck her. He, who had been so unfairly treated, so unbearably misused, would forgive her. Yet Kurzman and his cronies, the women and girls who looked at her with such unrelenting malice at every street corner, people she had never harmed in any way, they would never forgive or forget. They might look and dress the part of those who belonged to the tradition she'd been brought up in, but they were not part of it. They were bugs, hiding in and befouling life-giving flour.

"Sift . . ." She suddenly understood.

All her life she had accepted the world of her parents as a whole, organic and indivisible: charity to strangers and Mrs. Morganbesser's rules on how long to wear your sleeves. The smell of citron and willow branches on the Feast of Tabernacles and throwing rocks at cars that passed through the neighborhood on the Sabbath. But it wasn't a whole! she realized. Just as Joan's world was neither the fearsome, despicable entity her teachers had portrayed it nor utopia. It too had good and bad.

She did not want to live her mother's good life or her sister's, but a good life of her own choosing filled with the rich bounty of all that she loved and respected in both worlds.

And then, with a revelation just as sure, she understood that she would not be able to do it here.

She took Judah's hands into hers, enfolding them. This was her first choice, the foundation of her new life.

"Judah, I can't live here anymore," she whispered.

"But why? Is it Kurzman? Is it? Because if it is, I'm not afraid . . . my word is stronger than his among the people I respect. . . ."

"No," she answered him with sudden understanding. "It's not him. I have this . . . letter. From Noach. It's a description of everything that happened between us, how he wants me back. It proves what I've said is true. I thought to use it, to fight Kurzman, to prove my innocence. But I can see now that it really doesn't matter. I'm not afraid. It's just . . . I just . . . can't . . . live here anymore. Among all these eyes who'll be watching me, making sure I keep all the rules they've set down. I'm not talking about *halacha*. I know you can't pick and choose among G-d's laws. I'm talking about rules that have nothing to do with G-d, all those narrow-minded mistaken decrees our world has invented to somehow seal us off, to keep us all the same. I'd suffocate. There are so many good things outside our world, Judah. Music, art, wonderful movies and plays and books. I need to be able to choose what I let in. It makes me happy. And I think it will help to make me a better person, too. Can you at least try to understand that?"

She saw his eyes moisten as he glanced around the old shop at his little refrigerator, the boxes filled with prayer books in the back. From the street came the high whine of the Austrian's drill, the heavy pounding of Lazarovich's hammer. He couldn't imagine being anywhere else.

Then he looked at her. He didn't understand her, not yet, not completely. But he did understand himself.

"You are my home." He shrugged. "Wherever you are,

that's where I want to be. We'll talk about it. We'll decide. Together."

And then she saw it, that quality in him she had always known was there, buried within his human form, hidden within his skin and bones, his blood, his muscles, his fleshy human organs. What would you call it? she wondered. Depth, courage, unselfishness? And yet that wasn't it. Not exactly. It was stronger and more beautiful. Whatever words she thought of only seemed to squeeze it down, turning it into something pettier and more familiar.

She, who had always loved and needed words, who had respected them so much, suddenly realized their weakness, their limitations. Whatever it was, words couldn't contain its breadth and strangeness and shining exuberant beauty, which spilled over, a mighty river overflowing its man-made banks. They could do no more than hint at the magnificence of his soul in all its simple goodness and steadfast love.

Slowly she brushed the tear from the corner of his eyelid, wetting her thumb, her fingers spreading out like a delicate web across his forehead, reaching back to caress the softly quivering warmth of his pulse, which throbbed, exposed and vulnerable. She traced the small, growing smile where his lips curved up into his cheeks, transforming his face.

Her love for him was just beginning.

EPILOGUE

Ten Years Later

The little rental car strained up the steep climb from the Sea of Galilee to the hills of Safad. "Fantastic!" Maury exclaimed. "Why didn't we do this years ago! I know! Don't say it. 'Because years ago, you were too rich and successful and important to risk enjoying your life,' unquote. Isn't that what you were going to say?"

Joan said nothing, her eyes resting on the hills that undulated with liquid grace, rising up green and fertile toward the sky. Below them, the blue haze of the ancient harp-shaped lake shimmered in the vivid sunlight.

They'd be leaving in a few days. It had been almost like a dream: the blossoming orange orchards of Tel Aviv, the dark green pine forests of the Carmel, the barren majesty of the desert. But it was Jerusalem that had enchanted them both most of all. Yet Joan had felt a strange, sad longing as they'd walked the cobblestoned streets among the dark-coated Hasidim.

She had looked up Dina's old address from years ago and had even located the apartment building. But there had been no one of her name living there. Faced with a group of youngsters who eyed her sleeveless dress with passive hostility and who pretended they didn't understand a word she said, she'd embraced defeat with as much grace as she could muster.

It wasn't important, she told herself. She had merely wanted to say hello. Nothing special. A small hug, perhaps, and then to exchange like gifts some moments from their last ten years. Perhaps in a way, she thought honestly, it was better not to have found her. Time was often cruel. Did she really want to risk facing her now, transformed by a decade of experiences she had no way of gauging?

They parked beneath a flowering acacia whose extravagant red-orange bouquet seemed straight out of the palette of Gauguin or van Gogh. Maury took her hand. "I think the artists' homes are this way. I think there are some old synagogues, too."

"Safad is the home of mystics. Did you know that?" Joan asked suddenly.

"Mystics?"

"The Kabala was written here. It's supposed to contain all the hidden meaning of the universe. Didn't you ever hear that Rabbi Loew of Prague created a human being, a golem, using the magic in the Kabala?"

"My, those classes you've been taking have certainly given you some strange expertise," he teased her.

She'd started right after Dina left. Classes in Hebrew, Bible, and biblical archaeology. Classes in Jewish law and history. In a way she was glad she'd never been to Israel before. If she'd have come years ago, it would have meant little to her. But now everything—the hills, the city names, the ancient pottery—all tugged at her unceasingly with a thousand different meanings. It slapped her into a new consciousness. Birthplace, homeland. The words clanged inside her sonorously, demanding attention.

They walked slowly up the steep winding road past quaint, flowering courtyards where artists' signs welcomed visitors from eight to one, four to seven. It was just after two. Everything was closed.

"Well, we can get a drink and just wait for them to reopen," he suggested.

"No, let's keep walking, if you're not too tired," she said with a strange eagerness.

It reminds me of somewhere, Joan thought. The rolling hills, the little courtyards. Even the people. . . . She saw men in Hasidic dress and pious women in wigs and head scarves weaving their baby carriages through the narrow old streets. Yet they seemed to live side by side in perfect harmony with the bohemians sitting with easels and messy tubes of paint at every street corner.

"Here's one that's open," Maury called down to her. "Look, Joan, tapestries! Look at the colors!"

She caught up with him and looked into the shop window. Wall hangings ranging in size from one square foot to eight-by-eight feet covered the walls.

"And look at these wooden objects—*mezuzahs* and spice boxes and sculptures of gardens with houses . . ."

She walked into the store with a sense of excitement so strong it bordered on dread. There was a child behind the counter of no more than eight or nine. A little girl with blond hair and green-blue eyes. Her heart seemed to jolt as she looked at her.

"Cute," Maury said. "So are you the one in charge here, young lady?"

The child nodded soberly. "My aunt Chaya Leah soon comes. Can I . . . fix you?" she asked politely.

"I think you mean help, not fix, but it's okay, kid." He

chuckled. "Joan, practice your Hebrew on this child. Ask her how much things cost, and who makes them."

Joan stood staring at a collection of photographs that covered one of the walls.

"Those are pictures of the family. My father says if we add any more, we will have to rent another shop," the little girl said in fluent Hebrew, giggling.

Joan turned to her, understanding only every other word. But somehow it didn't matter. Her face spread into a slow smile of recognition. "Come, tell me who all these people are."

"Well, the first is a picture taken at my aunt Chaya Leah's wedding to my uncle Moishe. He's an officer in the army," she said proudly. "And that's them with their little boys—Avremie and Shukie. They live"—she pointed out the door—"just down the block. My aunt Chaya Leah helps my mother with this store and the other store in Jerusalem."

"And what about this photo?"

"Oh, that's my aunt Dvorah and my uncle Yaakov—who is a very important *rosh yeshiva*, the head of Misifte Moshe Yeshiva in Meah Shearim. It was taken last year, when they had ten children. Now they have eleven. They live in Jerusalem and so does my grandfather, who is very old and a very great tzadik," she said with authority. "And we go to visit them all the time and they come here. And these are wedding pictures of my uncles Ezra, Asher, and Shimon Levi. Uncle Benyamin just got engaged to a girl from Bnai Brak, and my mother says I can have a new dress for the wedding. And this is Uncle Duvid. He's still in yeshiva."

Joan listened to her with only part of her attention, all the while concentrating on the picture in front of her.

"That's my *ima* and my *aba* with me and Yossele. That was before the twins were born."

"What is she saying, Joan? Did she tell you who the artists are?" Maury asked impatiently. "Ask her."

"I already know," Joan answered softly, restraining a desire to touch the child's smooth, rosy cheek, her shining soft gold hair. "And what's your name?"

"Faigie. Like my grandmother, may she rest in peace."

"And where is your *ima* now?" Joan almost whispered.

"Why, she's in the house, at her loom," the child said with surprise, as if it were impossible not to know such a basic thing.

"Maury, would you excuse me for a moment? I'll be right . . ."

She stepped out into the sunlit courtyard that ran along the back of the store. The main house was close by, down a small footpath leading to the edge of the hill. Next door there was a carpenter's workshop that sounded with the noise of the turning lathe. She walked down the path to the house. It was a wonderful old place. Old dark stones covered the facade, and boxes of geraniums, petunias, and phlox rioted in uncountable window boxes.

From the companionably open door, the rhythmic click of the working loom wafted gently into the courtyard like the calm, even beat of a satisfied heart.

Joan stood by the open door, looking in.

Behind a loom placed before a large picture window with a breathtaking view of the hills sat Dina Reich Gutman. Sunlight was pouring in gently, gilding the room and the tiny wisps of hair that escaped from beneath her blue silk head scarf. There was a small satisfied curve to her arms, a straightness and assurance in her small, firm back. She looked as young as a girl with remarkably unlined skin. At her feet two infants crawled, making delighted sounds of discovery, tumbling over each other. And then Joan looked at the loom.

The shapes were fluid, dreamlike, like plants growing without pruning. In it she found the colors of peaches ripening in the sun, the soft black of night, the redeeming gold of morning. It made her think of sadness known and spring envisioned, a child's eyes after crying, a young girl's hopeful lips, the sky at daybreak, the sea lying under a cloudless sky, the earth, the moon, the color of laughter and music, the color of bright joy and dark regret. There didn't seem to be any color missing.

She stood watching for several minutes, hesitating. Then she stepped away soundlessly, turning and going back into the shop. She was part of Dina's past, a dark and tragic part that she found no evidence still haunted her. It would be a great *chesed*, she thought, not to remind her. Besides, she had found out what she wanted to know.

She slipped her hand through her husband's.

A tall, auburn-haired woman was behind the counter holding a plump, frisky redheaded toddler. She was very helpful, and they bought many gifts for everyone they could think of.

One, however, they kept. It was a small, colorful tapestry. Joan hung it in her office, and every evening she took a few moments to commune with it. It had some magic healing power that never failed to cheer her.

NAOMI RAGEN is an American writer who has lived in Jerusalem for twenty years. *Sotah* continues the intimate exploration of observant Jewish life and love she began in her best-selling first novel, *Jephte's Daughter*.